Eli

VALLEY OF CHAYA
Book 2

TRACEY HOFFMANN

Eli

Cover design by Dawn Esmond

ISBN-13: 978-1503137189 Createspace
ISBN-10: 150313718X Createspace
Eli ISBN978-0-9871824-4-9 (pbk) Edition 1.1
Published by Dawn Esmond Publishing, Australia

National Library of Australia Cataloguing-in-Publication entry
Author: Hoffmann, Tracey
Title: Eli / Tracey Hoffmann
ISBN: 9780987182449 (pbk.)
Dewey Number: A823.4

I dedicate this book to all individuals and organizations actively working to see an end to human trafficking, and the tireless efforts of those assisting victims.

Special thanks to all my readers who were impacted by Valley of Chaya and their encouragement for me to continue the story.

Chapter 1

Eli sees their faces. Nameless women staring at him, with empty haunted eyes. Girls stretching out their hands, begging him to save them. The moment before their fingers would touch his, he drops his hand, steps back, and turns away.

The dream was unrelenting. Eli thrashed against the bed, pushing the blankets off as heat scorched his body. He woke panting and grabbed at his throat.

He swung his legs to the side of the bed, and leaned heavily on his knees.

"I'm sorry," he whispered, cupping his head. "Forgive me."

He'd promised he would go back for them. Too many girls were still in captivity, he had to do something.

Restlessly he pushed his hair off his forehead.

Eli picked up his discarded T-shirt, pulled it over his head, and then pushed his legs into his jeans.

The cold floor sent a chill up his bare feet as he crept down the dimly lit hallway to Ashok's door. That the eleven-year-old boy was now officially his adopted son gave his life meaning.

Entering Ashok's room, Eli stood watching him. He looked so peaceful in sleep, yet there were many nights when Ashok cried out for his sister, Shanti.

Eli's mouth tightened, and tension gripped his neck muscles. That he'd been too late to save Shanti's life, was his greatest regret. The look on Ashok's face as he watched his sister die, was something Eli would never forget.

Gathering the blanket, he placed it over Ashok's chest, and stared down at the boy's soft brown face. As Eli listened to the rhythmic sound of Ashok breathing he wanted to hold his son close and tell him nothing bad would ever happen to him again.

"Lord Jesus," Eli whispered, "bless my son and look after him. Let him be a boy who laughs and is happy." Eli's eyes watered as he turned from the bed.

He tiptoed from the room, crossed the hall to the kitchen, and turned on the light. He waited for his eyes to adjust to the sudden brightness, then filled the electric jug with water and stood staring at the steam curling from its spout as it boiled. He grabbed his favorite cup and poured a heaped teaspoon of instant coffee into its depth. Then he added milk and hot water.

Taking the steaming mug, he trudged into the living room and picked up his Bible. He placed his drink on the small coffee table and sat down.

He'd spoken to Phillip about his nightmares, and his friend had told him it was normal to have flashbacks after such a traumatic time.

Eli rubbed his forehead. He didn't believe he was suffering from post-traumatic stress. Yes, he had the same nightmare over and over again, and there were times he felt uneasy when he was out and about; as if someone was watching him. But considering what they were doing at *Shanti's Rest*, he couldn't be too careful.

He liked his life.

Young Ashok kept him on his toes, and his love for Gargi was growing stronger by the day.

If only he could stop thinking about the multitude of girls he'd left behind in the brothels when he'd searched for Charlotte and Shanti.

He took a sip of coffee, but the hot liquid didn't soothe him.

He'd always been a person who made plans and liked order in his life. His mother said he'd inherited that trait from his father, and Eli had to agree. His dad liked to prepare for any contingency.

The thing was, he wanted to marry Gargi.

When he'd first met her, she was fragile like a newborn baby. Slowly she'd gained confidence, and now Gargi was a force to reckon with. Her eyes sparkled with life, and when she laughed it warmed a place in him he hadn't known existed.

He could picture the three of them as a family and wanted

to settle down and build a life with her.

Leaning his head against the chair's headrest, he sighed. Gargi wanted the same things he did, he was sure of it. He'd watched her face as they'd talked of helping Charlie build more transition homes like Shanti's Rest for girls rescued from sex trafficking. Homes where they could be restored to freedom and taught of God's love.

Surely that was a good cause?

Why was he feeling so unsettled? Didn't he have the right to get on with his life and build a future with the woman he loved?

His eyes itched from lack of sleep and he scratched the lids. Glancing at his watch, he sighed. There was no point in going back to bed now.

Sweat broke out on his forehead; he dreaded sleep and what followed.

If only he could be released from their faces.

~

Padma linked her hands together and watched Charlotte carefully. Her Australian friend was a mystery to her. Charlotte had welcomed her into Shanti's Rest with open arms and celebrated her arrival as if she were of utmost importance.

Charlotte was known as Charlie to all her friends and Padma was honored that she too was encouraged to use the word Charlie.

Never before had she lived in such a warm place. It wasn't just the heating in the old building that chased away the cold. Somehow the walls themselves beckoned her to call this place home.

Charlie had told her she wanted the place to feel cozy, so she'd picked soft, warm colors to grace the walls. The room Padma waited in reminded her of sunshine. The mild scent of vanilla incense wrapped around a bamboo stick made her want to close her eyes and rest.

The young girl Charlie was talking to had recently arrived at Shanti's Rest and kept glancing nervously at her feet.

Padma recognized the shadow of pain that darkened the girl's face.

Some were so young, just like Shanti had been. Sadness clogged Padma's throat and she blinked several times to stop her tears spilling over.

If she'd helped Charlie rescue Shanti sooner, maybe the child would still be alive. Padma knew she'd taken the easy road, been too afraid to get involved. Even now fear pulsed through her heart as she waited for Charlie to realize she was there.

Padma twisted her hands together to stop them from trembling. She hated the way her emotions were triggered so easily by her troubled thoughts. The hard shell she'd established within the brothel was crumbling down more each day, and she felt so vulnerable.

Hearing laughter, Padma sighed. Every day more girls needed refuge than there was space for, and Charlie wouldn't turn anyone away. There was talk of finding another house to provide for the growing need.

She wanted to talk to Charlie, tell her what she'd heard in the market. A shiver raced down her spine. Her back straightened as she crossed the room to stand in front of her friend.

"Charlie, may I have a word with you?"

Charlie smiled and nodded. She placed her hand on the shoulder of the young girl she'd been talking with. "Keep up the good work. I'm proud of you."

The young girl responded with a cautious smile, turned and walked away.

Stepping back, Padma allowed Charlie to lead the way to the office.

"Padma, what a day. Would you like a cool drink?" Charlie poured herself a glass of water from a jug on the desk.

The last thing Padma wanted to do was drink water. She felt she'd choke on any substance she tried to swallow right now. "No, thank you. Charlie, I've been visiting the markets regularly to keep up with news from the street."

"Why? I've told you, you're safe now." Charlie clutched Padma's arm. "You don't have to live in fear."

Padma shook her head and sighed loudly. Her friend was foolish to think evil would simply disappear and leave them alone. "There is talk of a syndicate rising up. They are not happy with what you have set up here."

"Of course they're not. But that's just too bad." Charlie sat across from her and frowned. "Before I was abducted, I was aware of poverty in the general sense, but the personal stories of bondage are so real and so heart wrenching."

"Charlie, please, you need to focus on the matter at hand," Padma urged.

"But don't you see, it's all connected. More than thirty million people are in some form of slavery worldwide. Thirty million!" Drumming her fingers on the desk, Charlie gave a weak smile. "I cannot stand by and do nothing. India has my heart and sadly it is one of the worst countries for human trafficking. You and I can attest to that."

Padma sucked in a deep breath. Her stomach churned, and she pushed at the nerves causing a storm within her. "You are mistaken to think you can make a difference to these girls. Once they leave this place, what then? They will be back on the streets—homeless, hungry, and desperate for the security they once had in the brothels."

"I don't agree. If only one girl sees her value and lives a life of freedom, then we have achieved something. Remember how you felt when Saul forced you to do things that were unspeakable? You were dead inside, my friend." Charlie's eyes welled up. "What is it that has weakened your faith and your resolve to be here?"

Charlie was right. There had been times when Padma started to relax and feel safe. She'd begun to hope for freedom from the voices in her head. But guilt had become alive like a dog following her around. It taunted her, told her she was no good, and that it was her selfishness that had led to the abuse of many. That she was no better than a festering sore.

How could she explain to Charlie that her actions had helped keep the girls captive and that she'd chosen to allow them to suffer so it would be easier on herself?

Nothing could cover the things she'd done.

Charlie placed her glass on the small tray by the jug of water. "We must focus on the here and now," she said firmly. "The programs are working. Girls are learning to value themselves. Many are making decisions to believe in Jesus. I believe in the work we're doing." Charlie leaned forward and grasped Padma's hands. She looked deeply into Padma's eyes as though seeing into her soul. "When will you surrender, accept that God loves you, and that you are safe?"

Shivers raced down Padma's arms. She pulled her hands free. The thought of Charlie knowing everything she'd been involved in, made her feel ill. She was not worthy of Charlie's love and trust.

Padma raised her chin. "I love you, Charlie. I thank you for all you are doing for me, but you are mistaken to think that your God can want me. I must make restitution for the things I have done."

"Stop beating yourself up," Charlie challenged gently. "There's nothing you can do to change the past. Accept this and trust in God for your future."

Padma stood and paced the small room. "Enough of your preaching. I came to tell you that there are whispers on the streets about Shanti's Rest, and when I approach the local vendors to talk to them, they turn their backs on me."

"You're reading too much into this. Next week they will be beckoning you over to spend money in their stalls."

"No, something has frightened them. I want you to stay off the streets." Padma gripped Charlie's hand and glared into her eyes. If she could take care of this well-meaning but foolhardy woman, then maybe she'd be forgiven for the murders—and worse—she'd been involved in. "Give me time to investigate what's going on," she begged.

Charlie's hand cupped her face. "Padma, I will not live in fear. I'm careful when I go out. It's okay, please relax."

Tap, tap.

Padma leaned against the desk, frustrated at the interruption.

Charlie opened the office door and smiled at the young woman holding a large bunch of flowers.

"My gosh, aren't they beautiful?" Charlie took the flowers and closed the door. "There are two cards, Padma." Charlie carefully removed the cards and smiled. "One's for me, and the other ones for Eli." Placing Eli's card on the desk, she opened the card addressed to her. The smile left her face.

Padma's eyes narrowed. Moving across the room, she took the card from Charlie and read the large, black words scratched across the smooth surface.

Looking forward to seeing you again. Saul.

Charlie grabbed the flowers then stormed over to the waste bin and angrily pushed them headfirst into the circular tube. "How dare he threaten me with flowers?"

Padma sat heavily in a chair and let the card fall from her hand. Her heart raced and she frantically tried to stop herself from fainting.

"Are you all right, Padma?" Charlie raced to her side.

Padma gestured to give her a minute. Her skin felt clammy. She sucked air into her lungs.

Saul. Her husband. Of course, that wasn't his real name. Saul was what Charlie had called him. Padma knew him as Scarface, but his real name was Khlaid Mallick. He used to laugh at her and tell her he was immortal. Part of her still believed this.

She jutted out her chin. He would not do this to her again. She would not cower in a corner and give him power over her life. She would rather die.

Padma's face burned with hatred for the man who had destroyed her life, and she steeled herself to remain quiet as she watched her friend pick up the phone.

"Eli, phone me back. I just received flowers from—from Saul." Charlie quietly placed the phone back in its cradle and turned to Padma. "I knew the police hadn't been able to find him, but I'd presumed he would be long gone from the district." Charlie massaged her temples.

Emotion flicked across her friend's face as she glanced at the rubbish bin.

"He will want revenge." Padma heard the tremor in her voice and wanted to curse.

Chapter 2

Standing outside Gargi's apartment with flowers in his hand, Eli felt nervous yet excited. He glanced at the bright array of color and hoped Gargi would be pleased to see him.

He couldn't wait any longer to share his dreams for their future together. His heart pounded as he waited for her to answer his knock. Sweat formed on his forehead, and when the door finally opened, he felt like a teenager about to ask a girl out on their first date.

"Eli, hello." Gargi glanced at the flowers. A small crease appeared between her eyes.

Extending his hand, Eli offered her the bouquet. "I thought these might brighten up your day."

"Thank you, they are beautiful." Taking the flowers, she lifted them to her nose.

"May I come in and talk with you?" Eli asked softly.

"Yes, of course. I think we do need to have a talk." Gargi

opened the door wider for him to enter.

"Please wait in the living room while I put these in water."

He wanted to follow her into the kitchen, but it was more important to respect her request.

"Please be seated." Gargi waved to a chair as she entered the room. "I have something I want to tell you." She cleared her throat. "I have decided to return to my home village."

"What?" His chest tightened. "Are you k-kidding me?"

"I believe God wants me to go and take the Gospel to my people. I want my parents to know I forgive them."

"Write them a letter! There is no way I'm going to let you go off on a tangent and put yourself in danger."

"I'm sorry you feel that way, but you have no say in what I do," she stated calmly as she loosely clasped her hands in front of her.

Eli rushed across the room and took her hands. He rubbed his thumbs across the soft skin. "Gargi, I love you. I want to spend the rest of my life showing you just how much. I want you to marry me—let me take care of you."

Pulling free, Gargi stepped back. "I love you too, but not in the way you want. You are like a brother to me. We can never be more than friends."

The catch in Gargi's voice tugged at his heart. She blinked several times and wouldn't look at him.

His stomach twisted and locked as fear pushed at his insides. He loved her so much and couldn't fathom the idea that she'd turn him down.

"I don't believe you. I've seen the way you look at me, why are you trying to convince yourself otherwise?"

"I will never marry. My future is to tell others about God's great restoring love. I believe someone has to start telling the girls in the rural villages that they are at risk. I have done much research into this, and it is education that will make the difference."

"You can still do that if you're married to me. I'm not going to try and control you, you will be free to do as you please."

"Really?" She widened her eyes. "Already you are telling me not to return to my village."

"Be reasonable, Gargi. Your parents sold you into slavery. I'm not saying don't forgive them, but to place yourself in danger again is just plain crazy." He hadn't meant to call her crazy, but this conversation wasn't going at all like he'd planned.

"You are my friend, Eli. I am sorry—really sorry if I've misled you to believe that we could have a future together. I cannot ever marry you. I do not love you like you want me to."

Tears filled her eyes, and Eli wanted to take her in his arms and reassure her that he would give her time. He raised her chin with his finger.

"Sweetheart, please don't cry. We can work this out. I love you."

She slapped his hand away. "There is nothing to work out. There is no *we*. I do not want to marry you, I do not love you in that way, and if you cannot remain my friend only, then I do not want to see you."

"You expect me to switch off how I feel? That's impossible. I will not stop loving you because you're too scared to admit you have feelings for me."

"You are right. I do have feelings for you. You are my best friend's brother and I love you. But I am not *in* love with you. I will not allow myself to fall in love—ever. I cannot be a wife." Her chin rose. "You of all people should understand why I feel this way."

Eli wanted to scream at her and make her understand. He pushed his hand through his hair in frustration.

"So you're just going to roll over and let the past define your future? Is that it? I thought you were braver than that." Anger laced his voice, and he wanted to shake some sense into her beautiful, befuddled head.

"You do not know me at all if you think that is what I am doing. I have made my decision. It is best that you go now." She stubbornly folded her arms.

"I'm not giving up on you, on us. Have you talked to Charlie about this?"

"Yes, but I refuse to discuss this any further with you. Eli, I want you to go—please," she faltered.

His dreams were crashing down around him. He couldn't believe she meant what she had said. If he stayed now, he might say things he'd later lived to regret. Stiffening his back, he nodded and headed for the door.

~

Eli drove his fist into the punching bag at the gym and wanted to scream at his inability to make Gargi see reason. Sweat streamed down his back, and he tightened his mouth. He couldn't believe he was losing her.

He punched a solid right followed by two heavy short left punches. The bag swung away from him, and his anger deflated, leaving emptiness in its place.

Grabbing the bag with both hands, he leaned his head against the rough vinyl and took deep breaths. His eyes closed; he pictured her face as she told him of her decision to return to her village and seek out her parents.

Like a fool, he'd bared his heart trying to convince her to stay, telling her they had a future together.

He flung the bag away, then wiped his hands down his track pants.

That she could forgive her parents for selling her was one thing, but to return to make peace with them was another. What sort of danger would she be putting herself in?

His sister had warned him that Gargi might never be ready for an intimate relationship. He'd felt sure he could convince her of his love and that time would bring her around.

Now she was packing up to leave on a quest she believed God was calling her to. Where did that leave him?

Alone.

Breathing heavily, he staggered across the gym and slumped onto a bench seat.

Sweat pooled on his forehead. He yanked off his T-shirt and roughly wiped his face with it. The last three months had gone by so quickly, and his life had seemed so full of purpose.

Would that sense of purpose change if his hope to marry Gargi were taken from him? What of his son? His heart twisted as he thought of the pain Ashok would feel when he found out Gargi was leaving.

Gargi loved Ashok; he saw it in the way she freely touched his hair and often sought him out. How could she walk away from him when he could be the son she longed for?

The noise around him made it difficult to think. He glanced over at a guy on the bench press who'd obviously racked the bar with more weights than he could lift. The words coming out of his mouth made Eli cringe. The consistent *thup*, *thup*, *thup* of someone skipping vibrated through Eli's head.

He sprung to his feet and headed for the showers. Maybe Charlie could convince Gargi to stay.

Chapter 3

The compassion on his sister's face irritated him. "Don't look at me like that! I don't need your pity, I need your help." He'd entered her office unannounced and had been ranting and raving for the last two minutes. He took a step away from Charlie's desk and sat on the two-seater couch by the small window.

"I'm sorry, Eli. I can't help you." Charlie set aside a stack of invoices she'd been entering into her computer.

Eli was proud of the way Charlie was meticulous in keeping up with the accounts for Shanti's Rest. He took a moment to survey her office as she finished what she was doing.

She'd made this small room into a haven from the busyness of the women's activities outside the door. The photo wall behind the desk, the live potted plant in the corner by the door and the soft teddy sitting on the couch next to him made the room feel soft and inviting.

Charlie sat back in her chair. “This is between you and Gargi. I did warn you she might never be ready for the type of relationship you want.”

“Surely you can talk to her, explain to her that God has set her free and challenge her not to live in fear.”

“Eli, you’re seeing this from only your perspective. Gargi doesn’t think she’s living in fear—she just doesn’t want to marry. She wants to be like Paul in the Bible and dedicate her life to the mission she feels God has called her to.”

“You agree with her, don’t you? You’re my sister, you know I love her, yet you’re not prepared to help me.” He heard the cutting tone in his voice.

Her soft smile annoyed him. He felt like a small child being reprimanded by his mother.

Charlie darted across the room and joined him on the couch. “I love you. And if I could make this happen for you, I would. The more you try and pressure her to do your will, the further you’ll drive her away.”

“Are you telling me if I love her then I should let her go? What of the danger she could be stepping into?”

“Didn’t you just say she shouldn’t live in fear?” She pushed her hand into his shoulder and gave him a slight shove. “Danger surrounds us, yet we walk in the presence of our Savior, that’s the difference.”

There had been a time when Charlie would come to him for advice, but now she had a look of peace on her face that spoke of maturity well beyond her years. Having lived through such a nightmare had changed her; she was no longer just his little sister but an adult in every sense of the word.

He still had no answers to what had happened to her, or how it could have happened. Every time he thought of the innocent women and children being abducted and forced into the sex trade, his blood boiled.

Charlie took his hand in hers and relaxed back onto the couch beside him. "My life has been so different to Gargi's," she explained. "I have loving parents and had a safe, innocent childhood. Gargi has known of God's love only a short time. This is the first time in her life she's felt loved and accepted unconditionally. She's drenching herself in the word of God, and her love affair with Jesus has no room for another right now. Would you stand in the way of Jesus, Eli?"

Heat scorched his face. There *was* room for both Jesus and him. "I understand what you're saying, but I can't help but think Gargi feels she's not good enough for me. That it's not just about her relationship with Jesus."

"Maybe. She knows she can't give you children, and that could be in her mind. I don't know."

"I've told her it doesn't matter. I have Ashok, and she loves him as much as I do." His eyes watered as he felt hope slipping from his grasp. "I watch you and Phillip, I see you getting closer and closer. Why can't Gargi see that you two believe love is possible after such a—traumatic time?"

Charlie's face flamed and Eli's mouth curved. She was so beautiful and somehow still so innocent in many ways. It was hard to believe she'd been imprisoned in a brothel for months.

"I think the difference between Gargi and me is that I am open to falling in love with Phillip. I was already attracted to him before I got abducted."

"Charlie, what if Gargi never—I mean, she's saying she will never marry. Where does this leave me?"

"Right where God wants you. He has to come first, Eli."

His eyes welled up and he struggled to hold back his despair at her words. He had to let Gargi go even though everything in him rebelled against losing her.

Charlie's arms encircled him and he allowed his tears to flow. Pulling her close to his chest, he rested his chin on top of her head. He couldn't help but wish Gargi would let him hold her even as innocently as this.

He lightly kissed Charlie's cheek and stood up. "I'm okay. Thanks, Sis."

"I know you'll work this out. You're an amazing man and I don't know where I would be now if you'd given up on finding me. I love you so much, Eli."

"I love you too, bud." He rubbed his hand over his face to remove any signs of moisture. It was hard to think; it felt like all his plans for the future had been ripped from him.

Eli noticed tension around Charlie's mouth and wondered what had caused it. She shifted in her seat and pulled something from her pocket.

"We have a slight problem, Eli." She gave a shaky laugh. "I received a bunch of flowers today and two cards." Charlie spoke calmly but a shadow passed over her face and then it was gone.

Maybe he'd imagined it.

"Phillip must be getting serious to be spending his hard-earned cash on flowers. Where are they?" He glanced around the room and raised his eyebrows.

"They weren't from Phillip." She held one card out to him.

Scanning the words, Eli looked at Charlie and shrugged. "Who's Saul? Have I missed something here?"

He watched Charlie's grip on the other card tighten.

"He is the man from the brothel. The one everyone called Scarface. Padma's husband."

His eyes narrowed. "Are you kidding me? No way!"

"Yes way," she answered.

"Have you notified the police? How dare he threaten you in this way." Eli's voice sounded too loud. This was the man who'd beaten Charlie and Gargi, hurt Ashok, and abducted little Shanti. And he still had the power to create fear.

His breath tightened in his chest and he longed for his punching bag. If it were the last thing he did, he would find this man called Saul and put an end to the threat over his family.

"Eli, the other envelope is addressed to you. I haven't opened it." Charlie held it out to him.

He took it from her and ripped it open.

A dirty piece of paper smeared in blood and burnt on one corner had words written across the middle of the page.

First I'm going to kill you, and then I'm going to take your sister and make her life a living hell.

~

Ashok loved holding Gargi's hand. As they walked together toward the entrance of the Hanging Gardens, he started to get excited.

This was their place. She'd brought him here three times now, and each time he'd seen more. His favorite was the hedge in the shape of an elephant. He wished he could ride an elephant.

Gargi told him one day he could ride an elephant if he wanted to badly enough. She told him he could do anything he put his mind to, that he was a smart boy, and that she was proud of the way he was learning at school.

He glanced at the flowerbeds and wanted to pick a flower for her, but he wasn't allowed. Gargi had explained to him it was good to enjoy the flowers here, that way others could come after them and take pleasure in them too.

He loved Gargi.

Hope bubbled in his heart at the thought of his *baap* marrying Gargi, and then she would become his *mam*.

It was his dream.

"Can I run up there, Gargi?" He pointed up the terrace to the shrub he'd discovered last time. Butterflies fluttered around it, and he wished Shanti were here to see it.

"Of course, you go and I'll wait there." Gargi pointed to a bench.

As he ran off, he wondered at the look he'd seen flash across Gargi's face. She'd looked sad. He hated sad. Maybe he was mistaken.

At the shrub he stopped and held out his hand, hoping a butterfly would land on him. One landed on his shoulder and he carefully angled his head to see it.

It was like a splash of yellow paint had covered the center. He smiled, imagining God carefully painting oval red tips on some of the wings. It was beautiful and he wished he could take it home.

Butterflies didn't live long, he'd learnt, and it was important not to touch them or bruise their wings. He stood completely still and breathed in softly.

It felt like Shanti was standing beside him, and his smile grew.

The butterfly lifted off his shoulder and flew to the bush. He glanced back at Gargi to see if she'd seen what happened. Her head was bowed.

Was she praying? He'd seen her praying often, but today for some reason his heart twisted in fear at the picture she made.

Slowly he walked back toward her. His feet dragged along the ground as if they knew there was something bad going to happen. He glanced around him, expecting to see danger lurking in the shadows.

He'd had this feeling of dread before, many times, and he'd grown to trust it. Straightening his shoulders, he tried to make himself taller and forced his feet to walk faster.

He sat beside her and twisted on the bench to look at her. He decided not to speak until she told him what was wrong.

She rested her hand on his arm. "Ashok, you know I love you, don't you?"

His skin burned under her fingers and a coil tightened through his body. She was going to leave him—he just knew it.

He bit his bottom lip and nodded slowly.

"I have news for you. I'm going on a trip to find my family." She circled his shoulders with her arm.

He pulled back and looked up at her. "You're leaving me?"

"I have to do this. I need to find my parents and tell them I forgive them. I have to go back and show them God's love. It's what I must do."

"When will you be back?" He could cope with her going for a while as long as he had an idea when she'd be back.

"I'm not planning on coming back," she said softly and tears flooded her eyes.

He shook his head. "No, you must not go. My baap loves you and so do I. Please, I want us to be a family." He grabbed her hands and held on tight.

Her thumbs rubbed across his skin, and she leaned down and kissed his cheek. "I wish I could stay. But I must follow my heart. Follow where God leads me. I will write you, I promise."

He pushed her away and jumped to his feet. "You don't love me. If you did, you would not leave me," he sobbed and took off.

He had to put as much distance between them as he could before he embarrassed himself and begged her to stay.

Everyone he loved left.

First Shanti, now Gargi.

Did that mean Baap would leave him too? Tears streamed down his face and he wished he'd never loved her.

Love brought only pain.

Dropping to the ground, he hugged his knees and wept.

Did God see his pain? He wanted Jesus to take away his sadness.

His heart pounded. Gulping deep breaths, he tried to unlock the tight knot under his ribs.

He had a piece of paper saying he was Eli Turner's adopted son and Baap had given him his name.

He was now Ashok Turner, but that was just a name on a piece of paper. Did they think he was just a child who didn't understand the way things worked? Paper could be burnt and discarded when it wasn't wanted any more.

Chapter 4

The room seemed to close in around Eli, and he pressed his hand over his eyes. He relived in his mind the nightmarish phone call from Charlie. He'd been in Australia, she in India. He'd heard her scream as someone broke down her hotel door.

Never in his life had he felt so helpless. He couldn't save her then, but he could get her out of harm's way now.

He grabbed her arms. "Charlie, you have to go back to Australia until this guy's caught."

She shook her head and shrugged out of his arms. "No way! That's what he wants. I'm not going to cower like a frightened mouse and scamper off every time something comes up to threaten the work we're doing here."

Sweat broke out on Eli's forehead. Could she sense the fear pulsing through him? Was he destined to have in his life only women that wouldn't listen to reason? It was not safe for

Charlie to stay here, and he had to make her understand that.

"I'm not giving you a choice. It would be completely selfish of you to put Mum and Dad through this again. You will go until this guy's locked up or dead." His voice rose with the strength of his convictions.

Charlie folded her arms. "I'm sorry, Eli. But you cannot tell me what to do." Her chin rose. "And don't you dare try to manipulate me by bringing Mum and Dad into it."

The corner of his mouth rose at the picture she made. Standing there glaring at him as if he were the enemy. She'd come a long way from the young girl who'd hated to upset anyone, to the point where she'd continually let others have their way to keep the peace.

"Exercising wisdom isn't showing weakness," he stated calmly. "Surely you can see the threat. Saul is taunting you, letting you know he could grab you at any moment. How often are you alone or surrounded only by women who would be too afraid to stand up to such a powerful man?"

"What do you suggest, that I lock myself up and continually look over my shoulder?"

"What harm would it do to visit home for a few weeks?" He changed tack and settled back into a chair as if he suddenly were relaxed. "You could take Ashok and make a holiday of it. You know that Mum and Dad, not to mention Nan, would love to have some time with you. Ashok would love to see kangaroos, and I was telling him about blue-tongued lizards the other day—he'd love it."

Charlie rubbed her neck. "I need to think about it," she said wearily. "I know you, Eli. You'll go after him."

"What other option is there? He's out there and a threat."

"You are not the police," she proclaimed. "There are right ways to do things—and hunting him down could get you killed. This is not just about us, it's about every girl who's at risk of being trafficked."

"You think I don't know that? Their faces and voices haunt my dreams." Standing, Eli moved to the window. Charlie's room was in the back left corner of Shanti's Rest and the view from her window was of a busy street. A rickshaw stuffed with people was stopped at an intersection and boxed between two buses. People of every imaginable age squatted around the footpaths of the old neighborhood.

"They're out there, Charlie. In captivity—where I left them. I can't live with that anymore. I have to go back and get them. No matter the cost."

When she touched his arm, he jumped. He hadn't heard her approach.

"What of Ashok?" she countered. "You would leave him, abandon him after promising him security and a father to rely on?"

His gaze fixated on the pulse moving in her neck. That she knew firsthand what it was like to be forced to submit to violence had just about destroyed him. And he'd made promises to Ashok and intended to keep them.

He put his hands on her shoulders and looked into her eyes. "Rosebud, do you know how much I love you?"

Charlie wiped her eyes. "Yes, but I love you more."

Eli hugged her. "Here we are trying to protect each other. Me trying to bundle you off to Australia and you trying to tell me to leave things alone."

"There is sense in both things. I'll pray about going to Australia for a few weeks with Ashok." Her face softened. "Maybe we should all go."

"If we both leave, then Shanti's Rest will be too exposed." There was no way he was walking away from this.

He picked up the card and read the mocking words once more.

This was his fight. Saul had thrown down the gauntlet and he was accepting the challenge.

~

Standing at the gate to Shanti's Rest, Charlotte looked down the street. Could Saul be watching her now? A chill raced through her body. She rubbed her hands up and down her arms trying to alleviate the feeling of being on display.

Saul's face clouded her vision. She'd called him Saul because she'd prayed for him to change. To become a man who sought after God, who would seek forgiveness for what he'd done.

She'd stopped praying for him after Shanti died, and tried to push him from her mind.

If she closed her eyes, she could see his bleak stare and the scar snaking down his face. She could smell his stale breath as if he were hovering beside her.

She gagged and clutched at her stomach.

Would she ever fully recover from the hands of strangers forcing her to bend to their will?

Moving across the dusty compound, she stood gazing up at the structure that housed Shanti's Rest. It had taken a lot of money to transform the twenty-four-year-old, three-storey building into what it was today. Its facelift included cream paint and colorful curtains at every window. The potted plants around the entrance were a trial as they often went missing. Flowers were the option she went with now and the girls took pride in tending them.

The building was a beacon of light in the old neighborhood.

So many people had turned up to help paint and bring life to what had once been a deserted, run-down building. Money still dribbled in from different sources; mainly from Australia, where her parents actively sought funding to help run Shanti's Rest.

She thought of Jennifer, who'd arrived one day saying she was here to help teach the girls. Jennifer had heard of Shanti's Rest through someone who knew Phillip and had decided to self-fund for a year.

People really were compassionate if they knew the need and had a way of helping. That Jennifer was an experienced English teacher was such an answer to prayer. Charlotte loved the way she encouraged and had fun with the girls.

Charlotte bent to pick up a dirty plastic bag that had blown in from the street. So much rubbish remained in broken lives.

Each time she saw hope in a girl's eyes and the tears of

healing begin to flow, she knew she was in the right place. She didn't want to leave.

Why would Saul tell them he was here? Surely by alerting them to his plans, he was giving them time to prepare?

She couldn't let Saul play mind games with her. "Lord, help me to take captive every thought and make it obedient to Christ," she murmured. "You did not give me a spirit of fear, Jesus, but one of power. I have a sound mind and I will not bend to the enemy who wants me to run and hide." She straightened her shoulders and raised her chin.

She glanced back at the iron gate. They always left it open. Charlotte started to make a mental list of things they could easily do to make the place more secure.

She didn't want to close the gate. Screwing up her face, she felt annoyed. The whole idea was that anyone could walk in off the street and get help. She'd been in a locked compound, and the loss of freedom to leave whenever she wanted was something she never wanted to put on anyone else.

What was the answer?

"Charlie, phone," Padma called from an open window.

Trotting toward the door, Charlotte felt overwhelmed with the decisions she had to make.

Taking the phone from Padma, she mouthed the words *thank you.*

"Hello, Charlotte speaking."

"Eli phoned me and I think he's right," Phillip stated. "You need to leave for a while."

"He didn't waste time getting reinforcements," she growled. "I've made a decision, Phillip, and I hope you'll support me in it. I'm staying."

The silence felt heavy. She waited. She wouldn't try and make this right for him; he was a big boy, and she had enough to worry about without trying to fix things for everyone else.

"Okay. If that's your decision, then we need to beef up security. Let's call a meeting and get some support. I'll call Pastor Tanvir and see if I can get someone from the police to attend. You can call Eli and whoever else you want. I know a guy who runs a security company, so I'll see if I can get him to come."

"You knew I wouldn't go, didn't you?" For some reason she felt soft inside.

"I thought it highly unlikely you'd leave your girls unprotected," he informed her. "I have to be honest with you, Charlie. Part of me wants to bundle you up and put you somewhere safe. But there's bound to be ongoing opposition to what you've started here, and we should be here to stand up to it."

Chapter 5

As he trudged home from school, Ashok kicked a stone ahead of him. He didn't feel like going to an empty apartment, and he knew something was up because he could see the strain on his baap's face.

Why wasn't anyone telling him what was happening?

He'd go and visit his friend Bashaar. Baap wouldn't even know he hadn't gone straight home.

He walked back down the street and turned left to enter the alley that would take him to where Bashaar usually worked.

As he sprinted down the familiar dust-covered street, his hand longed to hold Shanti's. She had been his shadow, always skipping along beside him, chattering nonstop about silly, girly things.

Tears flooded his eyes. He stopped and pushed his hands against his eye sockets to stop the tears from falling. His chin trembled, and his chest felt like he had a gaping big hole in it.

Did you ever stop missing someone?

Sometimes it was just too hard. He tried to remember a Bible verse to help him feel better; but nothing came to mind—and he didn't want to feel better, he wanted to feel Shanti's hand.

He wanted his sister back.

Maybe it wasn't such a good idea to visit Bashaar after all. His friend thought he was the luckiest boy alive, being adopted by a rich white man.

Ashok sighed. He loved Baap, but he hated secrets and was frightened by the things that weren't being said.

His shoulders slumped, and he felt sick in his stomach. He had to talk to his baap. If he was going to leave him like Gargi had, then he wanted to know. He still couldn't believe she'd gone without saying good-bye… again.

She'd left him a picture she had drawn of Shanti, and a short letter saying she loved him and would write as soon as she could. She was just learning how to write English and had crossed out some of the words in his letter. If she'd stayed, he would have helped her.

He loved the pencil picture of his sister's face.

Ashok sat on the road and took the picture out of his pocket. The eyes weren't quite right, but he liked the way Shanti's lips looked. She had always smiled a lot, seemingly unaware of their empty stomachs and the cold nights.

Aunty Charlie had loved his Shanti, and she had shown him in the Bible where it talked about Shanti being with Jesus in heaven. He closed his eyes and tried to imagine Shanti holding the hand of Jesus.

Flexing his fingers, he nodded. "I suppose it's okay that she holds your hand now, Jesus," he whispered into the cooling air. "It's just that no one loves me like she did, and I miss her too much."

~

Glancing at his watch for the third time in five minutes, Eli felt worried. If Ashok didn't show up in the next few minutes, he'd go looking for him.

He opened the front door and peered down the street.

The boy had better have a good reason for being two hours late. When Eli had entered the empty apartment, he'd tried to come up with logical places Ashok could have gone; but as time slipped by, his heart rate accelerated and worry filled his mind with all the things that could go wrong.

He'd decided to come home early to explain to Ashok why he was sending him to his grandparents in Australia.

The fading light cast long shadows and he took another step toward the street. The sight of his son's slouched form in the distance made Eli sigh in relief.

It was his job to make sure Ashok was safe, that he didn't get hurt.

The one thing that mattered to Ashok the most had been his sister, and Eli had failed Ashok in the worst possible way. His gut twisted as he acknowledged how he'd let the boy down.

While his focus and energy had been on Gargi, he'd managed to push aside the agonizing thought that he could have saved Shanti if he'd arrived sooner.

Every girl he saw unaccompanied on the street took on Shanti's features. He hated the internal battle that waged war within his spirit.

At night he would lie in bed and imagine he'd arrived in time to save Shanti. He'd pick her up and cradle her to his heart. Then he'd carry her out of that hellhole and stand her beside Ashok and watch them embrace.

His jaw tightened as he stepped back and allowed Ashok to enter the apartment. The look on the boy's face stilled the angry words Eli was about to say.

He waited until Ashok had dropped his school bag, and then Eli laid a hand on his son's shoulder. "I was worried when you weren't here. Where have you been?"

Ashok shrugged. "Just walking around. I didn't want to come here to be on my own for hours." He shrugged again and stomped into the kitchen.

"Ashok, don't walk away from me when I'm talking to you." Eli didn't want to reprimand the boy, but knew he couldn't let Ashok be disrespectful.

Turning, Ashok glared at him. "Before I was your son I was your friend. You treated me better then. I don't think I like being your son, you don't talk to me anymore." Tears welled up in Ashok's eyes and he spun around and headed for the door.

Eli caught him and pulled him to his chest. Why hadn't he

noticed Ashok's swollen eyes?

Ashok struggled against him, but Eli patted his back. "Hush, son. I'm sorry. I love you."

When Ashok's head burrowed into Eli's shoulder, he let out a deep breath.

"Come and sit down and we'll talk. I have things to tell you." He kept his arm around Ashok's shoulders and pulled him into the large armchair. He wasn't ready to let him go.

He wanted to protect his son from what was happening but realized Ashok was right. He wasn't an ordinary eleven-year-old. He'd lived through things most adults knew nothing about.

"Please, Baap. Tell me what worries you?" Ashok rubbed his fingers across Eli's forearm in a childlike caress.

"I will tell you, Ashok. But you need to know I wanted to protect you from what's happening."

"No, no. You cannot do that. I know there is something bad happening, I can see it on your face." Ashok wriggled off the chair and plopped down on the floor in front of Eli. He rested his hand on Eli's knee. "I know you are sad because Gargi has left us. This too pulls at my heart. I cry because she can leave without a thought to my pain."

"That's not true. She loves you, I know she does. She was very sad to leave us. Sometimes what you want to do doesn't line up with what you have to do. Does that make sense?"

"I suppose so, Baap. Is this what makes you sad, that Gargi has left us?"

To say Gargi's leaving was the only reason he was worried was tempting, but Ashok deserved the truth. "I love Gargi.

But it's not that simple. She doesn't love me the way a woman loves her husband. She loves me like a brother. I can't change her mind, and because she is not my wife, I cannot stop her from going to a place that could be dangerous for her."

"You want to protect her, yes?"

"Yes." Eli wearily rubbed his eyes.

"You are not God. God will look after her." Ashok gnawed the side of his lip. "And if something bad happens to Gargi, then she will be with my Shanti and Jesus. This is true, yes?"

Catching his breath at the truth in Ashok's words, Eli mumbled another yes.

"I try to trust Jesus more and more, Baap. But today I miss my sister too much. I look at the picture Gargi drew for me, but it cannot laugh and play with me. I sometimes wonder how long I will have to live before I can be with Shanti again."

"Years and years if I have my way. Shanti loves you, but she doesn't need you right now, not like I do. So get used to it. You're here for the long haul with me and that's that!"

Ashok gave a small chuckle and stretched. "What's to eat?" He rubbed his stomach and jumped up.

His son had been through so much, yet his childlike faith was so strong. Eli remembered Nan saying after Pa died that she had a choice to make. Either sit in a corner and slowly die, or get up and live. God gave people the ability to bounce back after difficult times, she'd told him.

"We're going out to grab something. What do you feel

like?"

"Shanti's favorite, *vada pav* and *kulfi* after," Ashok said with undisguised excitement.

"Always ice cream to follow. You're sure you wouldn't prefer fruit?"

Ashok hugged him and ran to the door. Eli felt better but still had to tell his son about his pending trip to Australia.

If only he could be sure Ashok would go willingly and not make his life more difficult by arguing.

Eli locked the door and then followed Ashok down the steps. He stopped and surveyed the street.

His forehead tightened and tension screwed with his shoulders. He felt like a deer caught in the headlights of a car.

Exposed. Vulnerable.

Hunted.

"Ashok, come back. We're going to take the car."

Chapter 6

Khlaid scowled at his reflection in the mirror. He tried to straighten his back and stand taller, but the pain in his legs made it difficult for him to bear his own weight.

Charlotte would pay for what she'd done to him.

He rubbed the muscles in his thighs. His doctor could find nothing wrong, yet still he struggled to place one leg in front of the other.

She'd cursed him, he was sure of it.

He'd crawled out of the compound that night with the aid of one of the girls and spent months trying to get movement back into his legs. It was degrading; and now that he needed assistance bathing, he would make sure it was Charlotte who helped him.

Before he took her, he would play with her mind and teach her he was in control over more than just her life.

But first he needed to focus on the problem at hand. The pressure to provide more girls was mounting. He hobbled back to his desk with the aid of his sticks and glared down at the sheets of paper in front of him.

In a way the brothel being raided was a good thing. With the boss arrested, he'd gone up the ranks from enforcer to supplier.

An easier job with more prestige on the streets. He deserved his new position. His lips curved in a self-satisfied smile.

He'd been involved in snatching girls before, but not the ordering and transfer. He had much more power now.

Scanning the first list of requirements, he tapped his finger on the page. His predecessor had not lasted because he didn't think of the big picture.

Khlaid knew he had to have an ongoing supply of young girls available, and he knew how to jump on top of others' success.

He'd send a team of people to Nepal to increase his numbers. Rural Nepal continued to have poor crop yields, and hungry people became desperate when they couldn't pay off their debts or feed their bellies.

A knock on the door drew his attention away from the information in front of him.

"Come," he called.

"Boss, the property you requested be purchased has been secured and is now ready. I have arranged for it to be fitted as you ordered."

"Good." He clasped his hands together. A sense of

achievement filled him every time he heard someone call him boss.

He felt powerful. Not only would the new property house the girls waiting transfer, but he could also keep one or two to start his own collection.

Why not offer some fresh blood to the locals? As long as he didn't encroach on someone else's turf, he'd slip in unnoticed. Once he had a clientele of his own, he could push his competition out of business.

"Frank, I want two men ready by the end of the week to do some picking." He sucked his tongue noisily.

His father had sold him into forced labor when he was twelve years old. He could still picture his father's ugly face as he'd explained that as the eldest child in their family it was Khlaid's responsibility to help the rest of the family survive.

His father was the first man he'd killed, and he had no regrets. Now he was the one convincing parents to part with their children as if they were nothing but livestock to be sold off at the markets.

Often all it took were false promises and the hope of work to lure the stupid girls out of the villages.

He'd already charged into the international market; and the fact that the young girls were usually dead before they turned twenty only increased the need for more merchandise.

Higher demand, more money.

If his father were here now, Khlaid would take great pleasure spitting in the face of the man who had sired him. His father had hurt him—badly. Rejected him over his siblings. He clenched his fists. Burning anger rose within his chest, merging into a knot of pain above his heart.

His eyes clouded over, and he snarled. His father had deserved to die—yet Khlaid longed to see him.

He glanced at Frank, who was waiting patiently for further instructions.

Dropping his gaze, Khlaid tried to pull his thoughts back to the matter at hand. There was no point in looking back, he'd come so far, and the feeling of success was addictive. He wanted recognition of his power. He wanted everything money could buy. He wanted to be seen as a man of influence among the very people he hated.

"Help me up, Frank," he ordered and leaned heavily on Frank's arm.

Frank had come highly recommended and would help him infiltrate the circles he wanted to breach. He hated depending on anyone, but needed a right-hand man who could teach him the way to act if he were to carry out his plan.

He had to stop seeing himself as Scarface.

Moving across to the mirror, Khlaid leaned close to the glass and ran a finger down the familiar scar. It would seem strange looking at his reflection and seeing a different face.

~

Phillip glanced at the growing line of children waiting for his attention. The next patient was a small girl, and he lifted her up onto the collapsible table he used as a hospital bed.

It was impossible to see all the children that showed up each day.

Phillip wanted time off so he could court Charlie, but every hour he took off meant sick children had to wait for treatment.

He couldn't tell these little ones to go away and come back in a month when there would be more help available.

Charlie understood what drove him to spend so many hours working. She had such a soft, caring heart, and he loved it when she surprised him by turning up to spend time talking to the children waiting for treatment.

If only she could be his assistant.

He loved her. It was that simple. He wanted to spend the rest of his life showing her just how much she meant to him.

His gaze dropped to the child's large brown eyes staring trustingly at him. He winked. When he touched her arm and she didn't cry, the inner strength of so many of his tiny patients struck him anew.

She didn't speak English so he didn't waste his breath trying to explain that she needed to be more careful where she slept.

The rats seemed to be getting more aggressive, and he was seeing more children with rat bites and infections. The problem wasn't going to go away anytime soon with millions of vermin roaming the streets of Mumbai.

He knew there were rat killers employed to go out at night and kill rats, but sadly the odds weren't in their favor.

The girl coughed and the sound of congestion rattled in her

chest, making Phillip shake his head. He hoped the medicine he had given her would kick in fast.

"There you go, sweetheart. Good as new." He gestured toward her arm and helped her off the table. "Off you go." He pointed to the door.

She bowed in front of him, and her toothless grin made him smile. As she left, the smile faded. He'd been working this clinic for five years, and sometimes it felt like he'd never make a difference.

He closed his eyes briefly as the lie galloped through his mind.

Angrily he snapped open his eyes and rubbed his forehead. Of course he was making a difference. Even to one little girl who'd had a rat bite treated and been given a dose of antibiotics. That made a difference to her.

He was bone weary. When he'd first volunteered his time with Hope Mumbai, it had been for a six-month stint before he joined a medical practice back home.

But India had become home.

And then he'd met Charlie. He knew his work was valuable, but he wanted more.

He wanted Charlie. He wanted children of his own and he wanted to help the women and children that were abused because they were so vulnerable.

The door creaked. Phillip turned to see who had joined him.

Ashok waited by the door with his hands behind his back. "Dr Phillip, can I speak with you?"

"Of course." Phillip beckoned him in. "I was just going to

have a short break and some water. Do you want a drink?" He wondered why the boy wasn't in school.

"Please, *saab*." Ashok entered the small room and picked up a bandage and fiddled with the edge of the fraying cloth.

Handing him a bottle of water, Phillip waited.

The boy unscrewed the top of the bottle and took a long swig then wiped his mouth with the back of his hand.

"I did not want to go to school today. I know of what is happening with Aunty Charlie and Baap. I think Baap wants to send me away, he wants to talk to me tonight about some plans he has made." Clearing his throat, Ashok continued, "Dr Phillip, can I stay with you? I don't want to be sent away as if I don't matter."

Resting his hand on Ashok's shoulder, Phillip leaned forward, and his gaze locked with Ashok's.

"I think I'd have to fight Eli to get you to stay with me. Lad, you're worrying for nothing. Eli has your best interests in mind and loves you. You are his son, and you have to trust him."

"I want to trust him, but I am scared too. Before Baap there was a doctor and his wife who helped Shanti and me—but they left us. They didn't want us when it came down to making a commitment to take care of us." Ashok straightened his shoulders and folded his arms. "I am not a boy to be put aside while adults try and fix things that are wrong. If I am not with Baap, then I would rather be with you or back on the streets."

"Don't talk like that," Phillip commanded. "You need to talk to Eli about how you feel. He would not thank me for encouraging you to place yourself back in danger."

Tears flooded Ashok's eyes, and Phillip felt his own eyes water in response to the boy's confusion and pain. Ashok had been through so much, and in a normal world he would be more concerned about playing football and having fun.

A part of him wanted to bundle Ashok up, and take him on a day trip to the zoo, but the noise from outside was calling for his attention, and he had to get back to work.

Phillip had seen many children like Ashok who would rather go it alone than be hurt by rejection. The boy was no mere child and deserved to be treated like a man.

Rubbing his hand over his eyes, Phillip yawned. "I sure am tired. I could use some help around here today. Any chance you have some free time to give me a hand?"

"You want my help? How?" Ashok whispered in a sad voice.

"It would be a great help if you chat to the children while I work on them. Help by handing me things. In fact if you want to make some pocket money, you could come here after school each day and give me a hand until Eli gets home. Talk to your dad about it and let me know."

"Yes, yes," Ashok said, his eyes brightening. "I could be a big help to you."

Chapter 7

Macy's gaze fixed on the calendar page. Today it was a year since Charlotte had gone to India. She screwed up her face. Why did it have to be that both her children lived in India?

Surely it wasn't selfish to want her children closer. Close enough to hold. Close enough that she could be involved in their everyday life.

She felt lethargic and knew she could easily climb back into bed and stay there all day. It would be simple to give into the depression that was scratching at the door to be let in.

Maybe she should have gone for a walk with Bill. He'd wanted her to, but the thought of lifting each leg to match his stride had seemed too much this morning.

She was proud of the way Bill was so disciplined with his health. He would pat his chest and say he was off to work his heart muscle.

Since the heart attack, he'd changed so much. He seemed

to cope so well with his dietary changes. No more pancakes dripping in syrup, or rich butter on his potatoes. He was annoyingly self-controlled, and now she felt she had to sneak the odd treat, whereas before he would have shared them with her.

She wondered what time it was in India. Even the time worked against her; she couldn't just pick up the phone on a whim and call her daughter.

Crossing to the window, she looked at the bleak day and sighed. It was June and winter was fast approaching—maybe that was why her mood was heavy. She didn't like the colder weather. Rubbing her hands up and down her arms made her shiver more. She slumped away from the window.

Why had God given her children if he was going to take them from her? Her head bowed and she closed her eyes.

Lord, surely you see my pain?

Her hand rested on her chest and she let the tears fall. She knew the work Charlotte and Eli did was important and life changing. But surely she mattered too?

What about her needs as a mother? She'd never visualized herself alone with just Bill. She wanted a full house of laughter and children's voices.

At her women's Bible study, all her friends were becoming grandparents, and she longed for the day when she could hold a grandchild in her arms.

Her stomach twisted. She pressed her tummy and trudged to the kitchen to get a glass of water.

She knew Eli loved Gargi. It had been a surprise when Charlotte told her Gargi had gone off on some mission of her own with no return date planned.

Did that mean Eli would eventually meet someone else, and fall in love again? Have children and give Ashok a sibling?

Heat charged up her neck at the thought. She loved Gargi and she needed to be praying for the young woman who had captured her son's heart. Not hoping that Gargi be replaced with a better model, a childbearing type.

Macy felt haunted by the longing to have more.

The thing was, she'd loved being a daughter and having a mother who was active in her life.

Her mother was her best friend and had been such a support when the children were young. She wanted to be that person to Eli and Charlotte, not some distant person on the end of a phone.

Removing the photo of Ashok from behind the fridge magnet, she gazed at the young boy. Her eyes watered. She held the photo over her heart.

He was precious to her, but how could she be his grandmother if she never saw him?

How on earth had Mary the mother of Jesus coped with Jesus going off to save the world? Surely she'd missed him and longed to hold him in her arms.

Did Mary want to see Jesus happily married with children? Or did knowing he was the Son of God release her from natural desires for her son?

Sitting heavily in a dining room chair, Macy cupped her head in her hands and glanced at her white leather Bible on the table. Jesus had said, "Who is my mother, and who are my brothers?" The verse weighed on her heart.

He'd then pointed to his disciples and said, "Here are my mother and my brothers. For whoever does the will of my Father in heaven is my brother and sister and mother."

The words just made Macy's mood heavier. How would Mary have felt hearing those words? Even though Mary had known Jesus was destined for great things, surely she would have been hurt; how did Mary manage to keep her eyes on the bigger picture?

Macy had read of another mother who had lost her son to the call of God. Flipping through the pages of her Bible, she searched through 1 Samuel until she found the story of Hannah.

Hannah was barren in a time when people believed a large family was a blessing from God. Not only was she barren, but her husband also had another wife that had borne their husband children, who taunted Hannah mercilessly.

Macy remembered her earlier thoughts about it being easier if she'd never had children than to lose them like this.

Her chest constricted and she caught her breath. "Forgive me, Lord. Thank you that I was able to have my children without any trouble or heartache." Poor Hannah. What a terrible time it must have been for her. Macy couldn't imagine having to share Bill with another wife, let alone watching the other woman boast of her fertility.

Hannah had prayed. Not just once but many times. She had faith and believed God had the power to help her. She never doubted God's abilities.

Taking a small sip from her glass, Macy wondered at such

faith.

Hannah's strength was in her continual prayer, even though God was silent toward her request for a child for many years. Did Hannah also mingle prayers and tears as she took her desire to have a child to the mercy seat of God? Did her prayers ease her soul enough for her to get on with life?

What of Hannah's weakness? Was she so obsessed with having a child that it drowned out all the good in her life? Was she so influenced by other women conceiving and having children that her self-esteem was affected by what others thought of her?

Macy acknowledged that she did feel different from the other women she knew. They had their children close and grandbabies either on the way or in their arms. It was a given that this season in life brought an increase in your family.

Yet her children were off doing other things.

She was proud of Eli and Charlotte—wasn't she? Or did she harbor resentment because they didn't seem to consider what she wanted?

What would her prayer be if she could ask God for one thing? Hannah hadn't given up praying. Macy knew she should pray without ceasing, yet she hated going over and over old ground.

She had to focus and not give in to this feeling of melancholy. If she did give in, she was sure she'd never get out of the dark hole that beckoned her.

Patting her hair into place, Macy knew she had to deal with this and somehow get it clear in her head.

Was God asking her to let go of Charlotte and Eli and the

dreams she had for them?

Tears blinded her. She shook her head in denial. She couldn't do it.

~

There was no use putting off his conversation with Ashok any longer. The sooner he told his son that he was sending him to Australia for a while, the sooner Ashok could adjust to the idea.

Phillip had phoned and told him he'd drop Ashok home but that he needed to go back out and wouldn't be there for dinner. His friend's willingness to share his small apartment was a great blessing. Once his boy was safely with his parents, Eli thought he'd give Phillip some space and take up Ted's offer of a suite at the hotel.

He decided not to address the issue of wagging school. It was the least of his problems.

The sound of a door banging alerted Eli to Ashok's arrival.

Eli moved into the lounge and dropped into a seat to wait for his son to join him. As the minutes ticked by, Eli started to feel his nerves bristle.

Wearily, he pushed to his feet and took a moment to ready himself before heading to Ashok's room.

That his son had gone straight to his bedroom and stayed there was sending out a clear message—he didn't want to hear what Eli had to say.

Eli knocked, then opened the door. Ashok was sprawled across the bed, staring at the ceiling, and didn't look at him as he entered the room.

Sitting on the edge of the bed, Eli tried to hide his smile. Sometimes Ashok seemed too old for his years; yet other times, like now, he was just a little boy like any other, trying to get his own way.

"Son, it's time we talked."

"I don't want to. I've been busy helping Dr Phillip and I'm tired."

"Sit up, Ashok. We *are* going to talk," Eli said firmly.

This fathering sometimes wasn't fun. No one had warned him that you often had to play hardball.

He wanted to be his son's friend and was tempted to give Ashok everything he wanted. When Ashok was happy and smiling, Eli felt content.

A pillow sailed past Eli as Ashok made a big deal of swinging his legs over the side of the bed.

Eli thought of his own father's patience. While a much younger Eli hadn't understood at the time, now he realized his dad had modeled how a good parent often said no. His father's words and wisdom came back to him now and reassured him.

"*I can't always be your friend, son. Sometimes I have to be your father and the adult here.*"

Eli's mouth twitched and he relaxed.

His dad was his hero. When Charlie had wanted to go to India on her own, their father forbade her to go. His dad hadn't tried to make things pleasant for his sister but had stood his ground.

The realization hit him between the eyes like a blast of cold air. If Charlie had obeyed their father, she never would have been abducted.

He stretched back and eased himself further onto the bed.

If Charlie hadn't come to India, he wouldn't be sitting here with his son. The very idea of not loving this young boy was too painful to comprehend.

Tears welled up in his eyes, and he secured Ashok in a bear hug and kissed the top of his head.

Ashok stiffened and Eli let him go. Seeing the stony look on his face, Eli gave in to the urge to tease the boy and reached across the gap between them and ruffled Ashok's hair.

Leaning back on his elbows, Eli relaxed. "Son, I've been honest with you about the threat on Aunty Charlotte's life and mine. I'm respecting you enough to tell you the truth and not treating you like a little child. I expect you to hear me out before you jump to conclusions, okay?"

The closed look on Ashok's face spoke volumes. He wasn't going to make this easy.

"First," Eli continued. "You are my son and always will be." He tenderly touched Ashok's face. "I love you."

"I am unsure of this love." Ashok dropped his head dejectedly. "You are angry with me. You speak in whispers on the phone and hide things from me. Things have changed between us."

"You're right, things have changed. I take being your father seriously. I want to protect you, give you a good life. I want you to have a good education—and a childhood." Eli placed his hands on Ashok's shoulders.

"I can't lose you," he said solemnly. "I have to make sure you're safe. Until we capture this lunatic, I want you to spend time with my parents."

"No, no," Ashok cried and pushed out of Eli's arms. "I want to stay with you."

"I'm sorry, son, but I'm not giving you a choice. You *are* going to visit your grandparents until this is over."

Ashok jumped to his feet and placed his hands on his hips. "You *are* sending me away! I knew it!" he screamed and spun around toward the door.

As Ashok shot past him, Eli grabbed his arm to stop him from escaping. "We have not finished talking," he stated firmly. "You will hear me out. Sit."

When Ashok's sad eyes turned toward him, Eli just about changed his mind about sending him to Australia.

"Your grandparents long to see you," he said gruffly. "Mum's been begging me to send you for a holiday, but I've been selfish and wanted to keep you with me. I know you don't want to go, but once you're there, I know you'll have a great time. There is so much for you to see—and for once in your life you can be a boy."

"I don't want to see Australia without you showing it to me," Ashok mumbled.

"I wish I could come with you, I do. But I need to finish this."

"But you will be in danger. You may die like my Shanti."

Ashok burst into tears.

"I won't die," Eli reassured him. Even as he spoke the promise, he wondered if it was his to make. Ashok was no fool and understood that even the best intentions didn't always work out the way you planned.

"I do not want to go to Australia. Please, Baap, let me stay," Ashok begged.

"As much as I want you with me, you have to go. Please help me out here. If you're safe in Australia, then I won't have to worry about you being hurt. I couldn't stand it if you got hurt." Tears flooded Eli's eyes and he rubbed his forehead, trying to get a grip on his emotions.

"You think I won't get hurt in your Australia? I know no one there. Even your parents are like strangers to me," Ashok countered. "I don't want to go, please don't make me."

"You are going." Eli deliberately slowed his breathing. The desperate look on Ashok's face had just about been his undoing. "I've arranged for an escort to fly with you. You leave tomorrow."

~

Ashok knew he could slip out of the apartment without Baap hearing him, yet something stopped him. He blinked into the soft darkness and wiped away a stray tear that dripped down the side of his face.

He couldn't sleep. Turning onto his side, he drew his hands together under his head. His gaze rested on the night-light Baap had pushed into the power socket to make the room feel cozy. He still had bad dreams, but the light did help if he woke.

There were lots of little things his baap did for him that spoke of a great love. Simple things like checking to see if his toenails needed cutting, or reminding him to clean his teeth.

He ran his tongue over his front teeth, liking the smooth feeling. He hadn't known about toothbrushes before, and Baap had even shown him how you could brush your tongue.

The most special thing his baap did was sneak into his room at night to check on him. Sometimes Ashok pretended to be asleep and listened to his baap stand over him and pray. The whispered prayers made him feel—closer to God, protected somehow.

But it was the soft kiss on his cheek that he liked the best. Swallowing past the lump in his throat, he sighed.

God had given Baap to him, he was sure of it. The feelings that pounded through Ashok's heart told him Baap was his real father and he was Baap's real son.

He didn't want to leave. What if something happened to his baap while he was in Australia?

Ashok hugged his knees. Did Baap want him safe in Australia so that if anything did happen to him, then he would have grandparents to love him?

The thought made Ashok tremble.

"Jesus," he whispered. "If I go, can you look after my baap for me?"

Chapter 8

"Are you kidding me?" Charlotte asked, her voice rising.

Eli smiled at her and did that thing with his eyebrows that he knew annoyed her. She wanted to slap the condescending look off his face. Crossing her arms angrily, she turned to face Phillip. "Don't you stand there looking at me like that, Phillip Mangan. I can't believe you'd go along with this."

"It's all arranged, Charlie," Phillip replied. "It's only for two weeks and it's time you had a break. It's time *I* had a break. I'm looking forward to getting to know your parents better, and Ashok needs escorting to Australia."

"I won't go. Now is the worst time to leave the girls, especially with the added threat. You go, Phillip."

"Come on, bud," Eli coaxed. "I need your help. As Phil said, it's only for two weeks. Get Ashok settled with Mum and Dad for me, then you can come back."

"A lot can happen in two weeks and you know it," she said

stubbornly.

Eli opened his mouth, but Phillip held up his hand to halt him.

Charlotte narrowed her eyes as Phillip stepped toward her and placed his hands on her shoulders.

She wanted to shrug him off, but the look on his face stopped her.

"Charlie, I've been trying to get some time alone with you for months. I need this break. I'm tired and Ashok needs family. You promised Shanti you'd look out for him. He needs his aunt with him to help him through this transition."

"I don't like that you're using Ashok to try and convince me," she grumbled. "It's not fair."

"I agree, it's not." Phillip shrugged. "But look at it from my perspective. There's never going to be a good time for me to take a break from the clinic. The missions employed a locum to take my place for a month. I'm no good to anyone if I don't look after myself."

Charlotte stared closely at Phillip. He did look tired, and the dark rings under his eyes worried her. She touched his face.

As her fingers came into contact with his skin, they spread out in a fan across his cheek. Her eyes widened as she looked at him. She loved so much about him. She loved his eyes and how the color changed when he was upset. Right now they beckoned her to agree with his plan.

Heat spread up her neck into her face and her mouth dropped open.

She loved him. So much.

Charlotte stumbled and dropped heavily onto the couch.

"Are you okay?" Eli squatted beside her. "You've gone quite pale."

Right now she felt incapable of speaking. Inhaling a long breath, she nodded. She loved Phillip. What would that mean?

There was no turning back from the emotion that was pumping blood into her face.

Eli looked worried.

These two men meant so much to her, and they were both so sweet.

"I'll go—not because you've railroaded me into it, but because I see the sense of it."

Phillip pushed Eli aside, took her hand, and gently pulled her to her feet.

"Thank you, sweetheart." He leaned down and brushed his lips across her cheek.

Ducking her head, Charlotte hid her face for a moment. She'd never felt so flustered before and was sure everyone in the room could hear the pounding of her heart.

She stepped back to give herself room. "Does Mum know I'm coming?"

"No, I thought you'd like to give her a call on the way to the airport."

"All right. But you two need to fill me in on what security you've set up to keep my girls safe. And I need to speak to Padma before I go. What time is the flight?"

As they discussed the plans, Charlotte's heart refused to slow down.

Could she embrace love? Or would her past stop her from entering an intimate relationship with Phillip?

She wished these things weren't so, that she didn't have to consider the physical side of a marriage relationship. But she'd be foolish not to consider the difficulties she might have being intimate with Phillip.

~

Padma glanced around the small office and shook her head. How could Charlie leave her in charge of such an important job? She knew it was only two weeks, but the burden of not letting Charlie down lay heavily on her.

She nervously smoothed the creases on her sari as she edged behind Charlie's desk. That she had been in charge of the girls at the brothel and shown no compassion to their misery, brought shame to her now. She'd become a hard woman; it was the only way she could survive her hopelessness.

Khlaid had seen to that. She refused to call him Scarface anymore. She had to make him seem more human—he was just a man.

How could she have believed his lies in the beginning? That she was still his wife made her feel like a filthy rag.

He'd never loved her. Right from the moment she'd signed her name on the marriage certificate, he'd changed and continuously abused her.

Then she'd abused others by her uncaring attitude and hard words. Some of the girls at Shanti's Rest didn't trust her. She could feel their animosity like an electric current running through her skin. That this was her own fault tore at her heart.

She had to show them she was sorry, and if it took the rest of her life to bring restitution, then so be it.

Knowing Khlaid was out there somewhere—waiting, watching—made her want to curl into a ball and hide.

She'd always hidden from anything unpleasant. Pretending you didn't care was hiding. Acting tough was hiding. Shutting down and allowing your mind to go blank, not thinking of the things going on around you, was hiding.

She glanced at the list of jobs Charlie had left her. Her friend must have been up all night writing out instructions and trying to make things easier for her.

Padma scrolled down the list of phone numbers and her gaze locked on a name.

Pastor Tanvir Gupta.

Her mouth felt dry and she licked her lips. She knew Charlie attended the church with the red door. She'd heard her friend talk freely about how much she was growing to love the people who attended.

Some of the volunteers at Shanti's Rest were from this church; they came regularly to help with maintenance and cooking.

Padma couldn't count the number of times Charlie had invited her to go to church with her, but Padma was adamant it wasn't for her.

If she'd gone, she would have known sooner that Tanvir

was there.

Would he recognize her after all these years? Tears flooded her eyes and she coughed at the sudden emotion rising from her chest.

Her brother, lost to her for what seemed a thousand years.

How could she go to him with all the stain on her soul? Surely he would see the filth she tried so hard to cover up.

How had he become a Christian minister?

What of their parents, were they still alive?

She raised her head and gasped at the thought of a second chance with her family. A small flame lit inside her and a spark of courage grew. Maybe Tanvir had a family of his own. She could be an aunt to little children. A tentative smile touched her lips and she shifted in her seat.

Tanvir had warned her she'd live to regret her worldly ways. She shuddered as she remembered their last conversation. He'd screamed at her and told her she was a disgrace to their family.

Bowing her head, she could still hear the anger and hurt in his voice. She'd shared with him that she was in love with a man from America. He'd somehow got it out of her that she'd slept with the American.

Funny how the face and name of the American was long forgotten, yet the mingling of anger and sadness on her brother's face was etched like a painting in her mind.

They had been so close growing up. Inseparable. She'd followed him around and he'd always had time for her. Why hadn't she listened to him? He'd warned her that she couldn't date so many men the way she was, without being seen as an easy target.

Her vision clouded and she thought of Shanti. The child hadn't stopped believing that Ashok would find her.

Had Tanvir looked for his sister? She'd left after their fight and not looked back. She'd convinced herself that she didn't care about him or her parents.

What a fool she had been.

Her shame was so deep that the thought of seeing him again twisted her stomach. But she had no choice; she had to know if her parents still lived.

She had to know if Tanvir still loved her.

Chapter 9

Ashok twisted his hands as he worried about who'd be escorting him on the plane. Dragging his feet, he followed Baap to the car and handed over his small suitcase.

"Right, let's go. Are you ready for an adventure, Ashok?" Baap's voice sounded much too chirpy to Ashok.

He wouldn't answer. He could not pretend to be happy about leaving. Folding his arms tightly around his stomach, he looked out the side window.

Ashok dipped his head as moisture spiked his eyelashes and blurred his vision. As much as he wanted to visit his grandparents, he still felt sad. Opening and shutting his eyelids, he concentrated on not crying.

He'd prayed last night, asking Jesus to take the fear from his heart. Every time he closed his eyes he saw Baap lying in a pool of blood in an empty alley. He shivered as the picture pushed into his head.

"You are going to be all right," Baap informed him and reached over to squeeze his shoulder.

"I don't like strangers, yet you have me starting my journey with someone I don't know," Ashok muttered.

Baap started the car and pulled out into traffic. "I would never do anything to hurt you, son. As I said, I can just about guarantee you will have a great time. In fact, I'm jealous I'm not getting on that plane with you."

"Please, Baap, come with me. This would make me so happy."

"Happiness is a choice, Ashok. Often situations change in a millisecond—you have to decide for yourself that your joy stays even when your situation changes."

Cars whizzed past. Ashok knew the drive to the airport wasn't far. He didn't want his last conversation with his baap to be an argument.

"I love you, Baap. I will have a good time, I promise. Will you phone me?"

"Every chance I get." Baap grinned broadly. "We're here."

Ashok saw Aunty Charlie and Dr Phillip standing by the departure line. His eyes widened and he reached over and pulled on Baap's shirt.

"Have they come to say good-bye to me?" he asked, pointing.

Baap's hand rubbed his shoulder, and they strolled across the floor to stand next to Aunty Charlie.

"Hey, Ashok. Isn't this exciting?" Aunty Charlie squatted beside him. "I'm so looking forward to our flight. I love flying."

"Are—are you coming with me?" he spluttered.

"Yes, and Phillip," she said and drew Ashok close for a hug.

Ashok looked over her shoulder at Baap and his eyes watered.

"Was this a good surprise, son?" Baap asked.

Nodding his head, Ashok tried to hold back his tears.

The flight was called and Baap turned to him with open arms.

Ashok buried his head in his baap's stomach and gave way to his tears. He couldn't stop. Too much love pumped through his heart for his baap.

No one had ever loved Ashok like this before, not even Shanti. Shanti had been his sister, and it had been his job to look after her. His bottom lip quivered and he grabbed it with his teeth.

"Okay, that's enough, you two," Aunty Charlie interrupted. "We need to board. Give me a hug, big brother, and make sure you take care of yourself."

Standing to the side, Ashok watched Aunty Charlie and Baap hug and then Dr Phillip and Baap.

Aunty Charlie dabbed at her eyes and grabbed his hand.

"Let's go." She brushed her lips over Baap's cheek and then led the way toward the departure gate.

Looking back over his shoulder, Ashok watched Baap and let his tears run down his cheeks.

"Wait," Baap yelled and sprinted toward them. "I almost forgot to give you this." Baap yanked his ring off his finger and handed it to him along with a thin piece of leather.

"I love you, son. Take care of this for me. I'll get it back off you when you come home." Closing Ashok's hand over the ring, Baap turned and walked away.

As Ashok followed his aunty toward the exit, he remembered Baap telling him that the ring was a symbol of love. The gold felt warm from where it had been on Baap's finger. That Baap had given him the ring to look after once again meant so much to him.

He clenched his hand tight and felt the metal dig into his skin. He didn't care; nothing could steal the happiness he was feeling right now. He wanted to jump up and down and yell.

His feet skipped, and it felt like he could fly.

Laughing, Aunty Charlie joined him, and they charged ahead of Phillip toward the last departure gate.

~

Leaning against the bonnet of his car, Eli watched as a plane flew overhead and wondered if it was Ashok's plane. He felt in no hurry to leave the busy car park. Somehow he found comfort in all the noise.

Everything around him seemed to hone in on this time and place. The sounds of rushing traffic, car horns blasting, people talking, and suitcases being dragged across the rough pavement all seemed to merge together.

The scene from *The Matrix* where Keanu Reeves stood and turned slowly, as he watched a crowd of people rushing around him, could have been written to show how Eli felt. Disconnected and alone, even in a crowd.

He blew out a deep breath.

Already he could feel his emotions shutting down as he started to harden himself for what lay ahead.

Tilting his head, he stared at the cloud-covered sky. He needed this moment to focus on God. To remind himself that he wasn't alone.

Lord, lead me. Help me not to lose sight of goodness and hope, as I go after the Enemy.

The screeching of tires and a loud bang startled Eli and he jumped.

He rushed around his car and saw what had happened. A man had driven straight into a raised pedestrian barrier.

There were a number of people helping him out of his mangled car, so Eli decided against joining the crowd of spectators.

Eli was about to look away when he noticed the mobile phone in the man's hand, and their gazes met across the distance. An eerie chill crept up the back of Eli's neck.

He spun around and got in his car. If he started thinking everyone was watching him or out to get him, he'd go nuts. It was only a coincidence that the man had looked his way.

He gripped the steering wheel hard as he maneuvered the car out of the parking lot and headed southeast toward Western Express Highway. The ten-lane road made the trip fast and he had to concentrate not to miss the right turn onto Ram

Mandir Road.

Jutting out his chin, he tried to release the tightness locked in his jaw. With Charlie and Ashok out of the country it was time to get to work.

His frown deepened and he wished Gargi were safely deposited with his parents in Australia as well.

Eli had done everything he could to ensure her safety, but she hadn't reached out to him since she'd left. He couldn't force her to make contact with him if she didn't want to.

He wished he'd been able to give Gargi more money. He hated that she was out there somewhere and may need more cash to take care of herself.

Gritting his teeth, Eli realized his lack of wisdom in not keeping a buffer in his bank account.

Pouring all his cash into the setting up of Shanti's Rest had been the right decision at the time, he was sure of it. But now he was strapped. It had been over a year since he'd pulled a wage and it'd been humbling e-mailing his father requesting backing for the next couple of months, but he'd had no choice.

It wasn't as though he'd ignored his financial responsibilities as a father; he'd budgeted starting a casual contract with Ted at the hotel complex next week to tide him over until he found full-time employment. For now he'd have to rely on his father's help once again until things were settled.

Visions of the life he'd hoped for with Gargi were quickly fading away. He wasn't even sure he wanted to stay in India anymore.

Charlie didn't need his daily input as much, and he knew

Phillip loved her. His friend's face went all soft and mushy when he was with Charlie.

Eli knew he had to take a step back and allow his friend to become the man Charlie turned to.

He felt displaced and lonely.

What of the girls you left behind?

Too many. Eli allowed his thoughts to travel to the brothel where he'd left the American girl. He still remembered the look of death on her face.

He'd wanted to know her name but she'd refused to tell him. When he found out she knew nothing of his sister, he'd given her money and promised to go back for her.

Would she still be there?

Sharp guilt stabbed through him, making him wince.

Had the girl's sister given up on ever seeing her sibling again?

He was responsible for leaving her there. He'd judged her life as less important than Charlie's.

Charlie had challenged him before she left, and her words echoed through his mind. "*Do you think by going back and rescuing the girls you left behind, you will be able to stop the dreams from coming?*"

Slamming his hand on the steering wheel, he didn't know if the dreams would stop, but he had to do something to try to end them.

~

The smiley face balloons bounced in her hand as she waited at the arrival gate. Macy's heart pounded and she took Bill's hand and twined her fingers through his.

Tears welled in her eyes as she watched other families greet their loved ones, and anticipation swelled within her.

Her precious daughter—and Ashok. She couldn't believe they'd be here at any moment.

She felt all jumpy inside and couldn't keep still. She edged away from Bill and peered around the people gathering at the gate. She sighed and turned back to him.

He waggled his eyebrows and grinned.

How could he appear so calm? She knew he was excited and was looking forward to getting to know Ashok. He'd spent hours in the garage doing something that he'd said was top secret until Ashok arrived.

Their grandson.

She marveled to think that finally she'd be able to pour her love into the boy. Her hands itched to hug him. She glanced at the sign indicating the plane had landed and she wanted to scream for the pilot to hurry up.

People started to file out of the closed-off customs area, and she stood on tiptoes trying to see the next person coming through the door.

Bill came and stood beside her. "Not long now, sweetheart."

"If they aren't out soon, I'm sure I'm going to burst," she laughed.

"There." Bill pointed.

Phillip, Charlie and Ashok moved toward them.

"Charlie," Macy screamed. She waved frantically, causing the balloons to jerk through the air.

Charlie dropped her bag and charged toward her.

As she hugged her daughter, Macy felt her shoulders relax. Tears streamed down her face and she laughed.

"Oh, Mum," Charlie whispered, trying to catch her breath. "I've missed you."

Macy kissed her face and hugged her tight.

"What about me? Doesn't your father warrant a hug?" Bill asked with a chuckle.

Laughing, Charlie threw herself at Bill, and Macy dabbed her eyes with a tissue.

She turned and looked over at Ashok.

The boy stood like a statue beside Phillip, and she stepped toward him and opened her arms. "Come to Grandma," she called softly. "I've waited too long to have you back in my arms."

He stepped forward and his grin was like honey to her soul. His little face lit up and she loved him. How could she have doubted that this little man would fill her heart with love?

She showered kisses all over his face and he giggled.

"Mum, stop, you're smothering him," Charlie laughed.

"That's too bad," Macy replied, stepping back. "You'll have to get used to it, Ashok, because I'm going to kiss you every chance I get. It's so good to have you here."

"Mrs Grandma. I am so happy to see you."

"Just call me Grandma, sweetheart. Come and have a hug with your grandpa." Charlie stood beside Phillip. They looked so good together. Phillip's gaze rested on Charlie's face and Macy had to hide her contented smile.

"Grandma, can I hold that thing please?" Ashok asked, his eyes wide in anticipation.

The balloons. She'd forgotten she held them.

"We got them for you," she explained and handed them over.

Chapter 10

Over the last year Eli had spent a lot of time forming good, but fragile relationships with the men who were responsible for law enforcement and investigation in Mumbai.

His forehead creased as he spoke the words of the police motto aloud in the silent car. "To protect the good and to destroy the evil."

He needed to become their biggest advocate and put aside his thoughts on how inefficient they'd been helping him find Charlie.

His father had taught him there was an order to doing things—and he knew he needed to respect the police. They were doing the best they could with the resources they had available.

When Charlie had hosted a fundraising dinner on behalf of Shanti's Rest, he'd invited the police inspectors from the twelve zones that made up the Mumbai police. He'd also invited the Joint Commissioner of Police, who headed up the Missing Person's Bureau.

Eli's mouth twitched. Isak was a comic and acted the fool, yet he meant business and was committed to doing whatever he could to eradicate trafficking in his city.

Eli chuckled at the way his friend liked to quote Yoda from the Star Wars movies.

"Ready are you? What know you of ready?" Eli mimicked the voice of Yoda and laughed. His rendition couldn't hold a candle to Isak's; who squinted his eyes for emphasis as he delivered the words in his heavy Indian accent.

The quote seemed appropriate somehow. He had no idea what hornet's nest he was about to open—but open it he would.

Isak had agreed to meet him for coffee, stating he would of course be drinking tea, as he was a stickler for tradition.

Parking his car, Eli turned off the engine and climbed out. He began to stroll toward the coffeehouse. He was early so he stopped to buy a copy of the *Mumbai Mirror* and folded the newspaper under his arm.

He spotted a table in the sun, sat down, and opened the newspaper. Isak was never late so he knew he had exactly ten minutes to spare. Skimming the headlines, he looked for something that would grab his interest.

His mood darkened as he read about the collapse of a building causing seventy-two deaths. The building had been made of substandard materials with shoddy methods in order to offer rock-bottom rents to low-paid workers.

He closed the paper in disgust and pushed it away. Poverty

caused more than just empty bellies.

As he looked up, he saw Isak approaching.

"Eli, my friend, good morning."

Eli stood, extended his hand and grasped Isak's fingers firmly. "Thank you for meeting me. Take a seat and I'll order your tea." Dodging between tables, Eli went to place their order and then returned to join Isak.

"Did your family get away on time?" Isak asked as he pulled his chair closer to the table.

"Yes. I've come straight from the airport." Eli knew Isak wouldn't want to make small talk, so he pushed the card across the table.

"What's this?" Isak's eyebrows rose as he opened the card and began reading. His mouth tightened. "When did you get this?"

"Earlier this week. I wanted to get Charlie and Ashok safely away before we took action."

"There is no *we* in this matter. This is police business."

"This man is threatening my sister and stating he's going to kill me—and you expect me to sit back and wait for the police to catch him? I don't think so."

Isak nodded several times. Then he shrugged. "At least I can say I told you. Death threats don't quite fit within my portfolio, but how can I help?"

"Obviously this man wants us to know he's around. That alone is interesting. He wants to intimidate and frighten Charlie. It would be easier to kill me if I were unaware of the threat. By sending the card, he deliberately ensured we would put up our guard."

"Yes, yes. But what game is he playing?"

"I'd say… revenge. He wants the satisfaction of drawing out the kill. I can't wait around for him to act. I refuse to be on the back foot."

Isak placed both hands on the table. "What do you need?"

"I need a partner. Someone to watch my back and someone prepared to step into the dark side with me. You up for it?"

Isak picked up his cup and absentmindedly swirled the dark liquid around.

Eli smelt the spicy aroma of cinnamon rising from Isak's chai tea and screwed up his nose. He refused to think about how the scent reminded him of Gargi. He had to focus.

Clanking the cup onto the saucer, Isak sat back. He folded his arms. "Fear is the path to the dark side. Fear leads to anger. Anger leads to hate. Hate leads to suffering. Yoda said that and it makes sense. Are you fearful, Eli?"

"No. Are you?"

"Maybe a little. These men are evil and put no value on human life. But fear will only make us vulnerable."

"Is that a yes?"

"Yes—but we stay within the law."

"Deal," Eli agreed, knowing Isak's history of making things happen when they needed to.

"What's first? Have you a plan?" Isak asked as he pushed his empty cup away and glanced at his watch.

"I'm going to see Pastor Tanvir and arrange a prayer covering. I believe it's crucial."

"I'll leave that to you, my friend. Then what?"

"We begin our search. There are a few places I want to visit." Relief surged through Eli at Isak's commitment to help.

~

The quiet woke Ashok. Everything was so still, and the lack of noise was strange to him. He wiggled out of bed and stood. Tilting his head, he listened.

He could hear birds singing and the sound of a dog barking, but apart from that the house slept. There was no traffic noise.

Tiptoeing down the stairs, he crept into the living room and climbed into one of the big, soft armchairs.

This was the home his baap had grown up in.

He glanced around the tidy room, and his fingers itched to touch things. He captured his hands beneath his legs, then he shuffled back in the seat.

The gurgling sound of his stomach grumbling made him tighten his mouth.

Even though he felt hunger, he knew he wasn't hungry. Whenever he wanted to eat, there was always food available for him to choose from. He freed his hands to examine his clean nails.

It seemed like only yesterday that he'd dug through the rubbish looking for some small scrap of food for his sister to eat. The many nights they'd gone hungry, because he'd been unable to provide food for them, still made him sad.

He rubbed his stomach and wished Shanti were here to see how well fed he looked. His eyes watered as he tried to picture her face. Would he ever stop missing her?

Angling his head, he saw a group of photos displayed on a wooden cabinet and got up to look. One photo in particular grabbed his attention.

He gulped as tears flooded his eyes and spilled down his cheeks. He picked up the photo and pressed it to his chest.

Sitting cross-legged on the floor, he rocked back and forth, sobbing. Pain locked in his throat and he couldn't breathe.

"Ashok, honey, what's wrong?" Macy raced across the room and squatted beside him.

His chin shook as he gulped back his tears. He passed her the photo.

Macy looked at the picture of Eli and Charlotte, and she frowned. "I don't understand. Can you tell me why this photo has upset you?" She rested her hand on his shoulder.

Ashok bowed his head and mumbled, "I—I'm sorry I took the photo off the cabinet."

"Honey, it's okay. Can you tell me?" she prodded gently.

Ashok licked his lips. "In the photo Baap and Aunty Charlie are the same age as—as Shanti and me. When I saw Baap's arm around Aunty Charlie's shoulders—and the big smile on her face—I wanted to hold Shanti just like that." He gave in to a fresh batch of tears.

Macy pulled Ashok into her arms and rubbed his back. "I'm so sorry."

"Grandma," Ashok whispered, pushing back. "I miss her and when I looked at the photo I felt sad. I don't have a photo of Shanti. What if—um—what if I forget what she looks like?"

"You won't forget. She's locked in your heart," Macy stated firmly, dabbing at her eyes. She stood up and took his hand.

Ashok raised his other hand to wipe his nose.

"You can use my tissues, sweetheart." She placed two clean ones in his hand.

After Ashok had blown his nose, he pushed the dirty tissues into his pocket. "If I close my eyes, I can't see her. I want a photo too." He let go of her hand and placed both his palms over his eyes and pressed, hoping to see Shanti's image in his mind.

He looked at his grandma. "Is it wrong for me to be sad? I know she is with my Jesus, but—" He stiffened his back. "I want her here."

"Of course you do. I'm sad and I never got to meet your sister. It's what we humans do, we grieve, and it's natural to feel sad."

"I am sorry, Grandma. I was jealous of the photo," he confessed as he inched closer to her.

When she kissed his face and hugged him, he felt warm.

"You told me Gargi drew you a picture of Shanti. Have you got it with you?" Grandma asked.

"Yes, it's in my bag."

"Do you want to put it in a photo frame so you can have it by your bed?"

For a moment Ashok considered the idea. He liked the drawing, but it didn't really display the beauty of his sister. She looked sad in the drawing, and it hurt his heart to think that Gargi knew Shanti only in that bad place.

He made his lips smile. "It is good, but not quite my Shanti. I am glad for it, but I do not want to look at it always."

"You are a wise boy. When my father died, I was so sad for a long time." Grandma stared down at her hands. "I would have given anything to have some more time with him. Do you know what I did to make it a little easier on myself?"

Looking into his kind grandma's green eyes, he noticed her tears; and somehow this made him feel better, as if she really understood. "What made it easier, Grandma?" He loved saying the word *grandma.* Last night as he lay in bed, he kept saying *grandma* and *grandpa* over and over.

"Well," she said, leading him toward the kitchen. "I would pretend I was saying hello to Dad again and say something like 'Hey, Dad, I'm missing you a lot today.' Then I'd imagine him replying to me in his deep voice, saying something like 'It's okay to miss me, but do you remember the day we went fishing and you fell out of the boat?' Macy laughed and sat down at the kitchen table and patted the chair next to her.

"When I remembered good times with Dad, it made him seem closer, still here." She touched her heart. "That day when I fell out of the boat, my dad tried to pull me back into the boat, and he ended up in the water too. It was so much fun."

The picture Grandma painted made Ashok smile. "Yes, yes! This is a very good idea. Shanti loved to laugh and dance. She would remind me of the time we danced on the street with my friend Baashar. We pretended we could hear the sound of music, but the only music was Shanti humming."

Macy laughed. "What did her voice sound like? Did she like to sing?"

"Her singing voice was not like an angel's." Ashok giggled and grabbed his stomach. "She had a scratchy voice which went up and down at the wrong times. She used to laugh at herself. Shanti was always laughing. Her laugh made me happy."

"Can you hear her laugh in your mind? Imagine it and see her face."

He closed his eyes. He could see Shanti in his mind.

Her large brown eyes were surrounded by thick, black lashes and twinkled when she was happy. She had the softest round face and brown, almost black hair fell messily around her neck. Her full lips were smiling at him.

"I can, I can! Thank you, Grandma." He jumped up and wound his arms around her neck.

Chapter 11

Gargi lovingly caressed the steering wheel of her little red car as she drove. She felt humbled by the gift from Eli and would have refused the car if he'd given it to her directly. Charlie had told her it was God's provision and not to be prideful.

A stray tear slipped down her cheek and she swiped it away. Not only had he brought her a car and a mobile phone, but also he'd put the phone on a plan and was taking care of monthly payments.

Eli was the man of her dreams—but he was foolish to think she was the woman for him. He needed a whole woman, and although he'd tried to convince her she was whole in every way that mattered, she knew she wasn't. She loved him too much to let him settle for less than perfection.

Her fingers tightened on the shiny vinyl wheel. She couldn't believe she was driving on her own. The one-hour driving lesson she'd taken had not prepared her for traffic and long-distance travel. She jerked the steering wheel hard to the left to pull the car back into her lane. She needed to concentrate.

A small smile tugged at the corner of her mouth. Even though Eli wasn't here, he was trying to take care of her. It was just like a man to consider petrol consumption when buying a car. Her hand reached over and picked up the envelope poking out of the small shelf on the dash. She glanced at her name written in Eli's bold strokes and lifted it to her lips as if kissing his hand.

Shaking her head at her foolishness, she put the envelope down. She needed to keep two hands on the steering wheel.

His note had been practical and straight to the point. He'd told her that the Muruit Suzuki 800 was estimated to do around 16.1 kilometers per litre of fuel. What that meant Gargi, had no idea.

The picture of Eli sitting down to work out how many kilometers she had to drive to get to her destination and estimating the approximate cost of petrol, then leaving that amount of money in the envelope, took her breath away.

She'd never had someone want to take care of her before and found the concept difficult to comprehend. Her skin heated and she fanned her face.

Touching the base of her neck, she pulled at the material of her shirt as if it were choking her.

She was sure she was doing what God wanted her to do—wasn't she? Her stomach fluttered and she worried her lip. What if she'd made a horrible mistake by leaving Eli? She'd been brutal in her words and tried so hard to push him away;

she'd lied about not loving him in the way he wanted.

The interior of the car seemed to close in around her.

She'd lied. Did God allow such lies? She'd thought that by pushing Eli away, she was protecting his heart from the hurt of loving her.

The truth will set you free.

Gargi steered the car over to the side of the road and turned off the engine. She remembered reading that verse about truth.

Closing her eyes, she acknowledged that there was never any excuse for lying. She'd told herself she was protecting Eli, but really she was frightened by her feelings for him. She was okay being alone, it was something she was used to. But the thought of letting her heart soften even more toward Eli terrified her.

"What should I do, Lord? I've lied to Eli. I do love him, but I don't know if I can allow myself to believe he will continue to love me once he really knows me."

The truth will set you free.

The words came alive around her, challenging her to right her wrong. Her fingers shook as she picked up her mobile phone and touched the speed dial Eli had set up with his phone number.

She didn't know what she'd say to him, how she'd explain her lie, but she had to tell him the truth.

She loved him.

~

Standing across the street from the brothel, where he'd abandoned the American girl in order to rescue Charlie, Eli stood frozen like a statue. That he'd waited six months to return for her shamed him. The hot, dank air was a stifling assault. He wiped his forehead. He remembered how the sound of his feet crunching on the loose gravel near the door had alerted the two guards to his approach.

He glanced at the filth on the street and hated all that it portrayed. Here was a place where depraved men could use women to satisfy their sickening lusts.

This wasn't how God had made men. Man's job was to protect women and children. To make sure they could feel safe and loved—without abusing their independence.

He pulled further back into the shadows as he watched two young men approach the door, they were directed up the few steps into the building. It was like their eyes were blinded to where they were going.

His father's words rang clear in his mind.

Keep a vigilant watch over your heart; that's where life starts—watch your steps, son, and the road will stretch out smooth before you. Leave evil in the dust.

Didn't they realize or care that they were about to wound their very hearts?

A vibration in his pocket alerted him to his mobile phone ringing. He instinctively went to pull it out and check the caller ID.

He dropped his hand. Whoever it was could wait. His current task could not afford distractions.

Walking around the block, he approached the brothel from the other direction. If all went to plan, he could slip out the back entrance and cut through the alley to where he'd parked his car. There were no vehicles on the street; it seemed like everyone who travelled this road came by foot.

Eli walked in the middle of the road, uncaring that he was visible from all directions. It felt like he'd stepped out of his body and become this other person. His hat was shoved down over his hair; he wore a black leather jacket, black jeans and dark black-rimmed sunglasses concealed his eyes. If they recognized him, he'd be surprised.

He stopped in front of the two men blocking the doorway and grinned.

"How much for half an hour?"

One man grunted and stated an amount.

Handing over the money, Eli entered the building.

After the door closed behind him, he removed his glasses. He blinked several times to help his eyes adjust to the dim lighting. The sound of depravity slithered through him until it tasted like gravel in his mouth. The stench of sin made him want to cry out. No matter how much he tried, he could not harden his heart to what went on in places like this.

"What you want?" an ageing woman demanded.

"Last time I was here you gave me an American girl. I want her again."

The woman led him down the hallway and pointed to a

curtain. She huffed and walked away, her job finished.

Slowly Eli pushed the curtain aside. He'd already decided that whoever was behind there was coming with him. He hoped it was her, but either way this girl was being rescued.

The partition was the same as he remembered it. Steel rails suspended from the walls and clipped together like tent poles. Thick canvas sheets thrown roughly over each pole to separate each cubicle.

Noises he longed to forget came at him from either sides of the sheets and he clapped his hands over his ears.

He'd never felt claustrophobic before but his sensitivity to every sound made the walls pulse.

His skin crawled.

Eli's gaze moved to the woman and he gasped for air.

She was like a skeleton and her flesh was all but rotting on her.

Holding his hand over his mouth, Eli tried to stop from gagging.

The woman shifted her head as he moved closer to her, but she didn't open her eyes.

He squatted beside her and cringed at the state of the mattress she lay on. Her hair was matted and the stench coming off her body was like musty urine.

The scant clothing she wore hung in shreds. She made no effort to acknowledge his presence.

His eyes flooded and a thick swell formed in his throat.

He remembered her.

Brushing her hair out of her face, Eli leaned forward to speak. "Can you hear me?"

As he lifted her into his arms, her eyes opened and she stared at him. Although she looked straight at him, it was like she didn't see him. Her eyes appeared distant and unfocused.

His heart slammed against his chest. He'd seen girls do this before. Totally disconnect from what's going on around them to survive.

Tears streamed down his face. "It's okay. I've got you, you're safe now."

He hoisted her closer to his body and approached the curtain.

Eli dipped his head close to the filthy fabric and listened to see if there was anyone in the hallway.

Inching the material back, he slipped out from the makeshift room and hurried down the hall, deeper into the building, looking for the back entrance.

Eli stopped before the only door at the end of the hall. He planted his feet in a wide stance. Whatever was behind that door was not going to stop him.

He barged in as if he owned the place.

A man sat hunched over a table eating and jerked his head in surprise as Eli marched toward him.

The man's gaze flitted from Eli to the girl cradled in his arms. Harsh curses spewed from his mouth, and he jumped up, knocking his chair to the ground.

Eli swiped everything off the table and placed the girl on the square top.

He spun and lunged across the room, grabbing the front of the man's shirt and hissed into his face.

"It's not worth dying over," he snarled, shoving him toward the door.

The man stumbled backwards, his arms waving frantically as he tried to stay on his feet.

Eli took advantage of the guy's lack of balance and flung his fist hard into the man's chin, sending him rocking to the floor. The man's head snapped back and his eyelids slid shut.

Eli slipped his arms under the girl's armpits and around her back and hoisted her over his shoulders in a fireman's carry.

Glancing at the prone man, he listened. All was quiet save the sound of the three of them breathing, and he muttered a prayer asking for help to get away safely.

Eli shifted the woman's body on his shoulders. He opened the back door and stepped into the alley. A sense of urgency hit him and his heart rate accelerated. He had to hurry before the alert was given.

Tightening his hold, he jogged down the alley to his car.

His fingers fumbled with the car keys. He made himself slow down. He inserted and turned the key to unlock the doors, then opened the back door and laid his precious cargo across the backseat.

A clamor erupted behind him and he glanced over his shoulder. Two men were running toward him, shouting.

Slamming the door, Eli grabbed the keys and climbed into the driver's seat. His fingers felt twice their usual size as he flicked the lock to secure the doors.

His breath came fast. He turned the key and started the car.

A loud *boom* made Eli duck. The back window cracked and chunks of glass pelted the back of his head as they sprayed into the car.

He floored his foot and zoomed around the corner, away from the advancing men.

The explosion of another bullet entering the car made Eli jerk the steering wheel and he cursed.

The woman groaned.

He looked back at her and saw blood oozing through her dress. "Hang on!" Eli demanded.

He swerved the car past a slow-moving van and cursed as traffic congested his escape route.

His knuckles turned white as the pressure inside him mounted. He had to get her to the hospital.

The short drive seemed to take forever and Eli kept glancing at the still form behind him.

"Don't you die," he yelled over the noise of traffic coming through the smashed window.

Screeching to a halt, Eli parked crookedly in front of the hospital entrance and scrambled out of the car.

He flexed his hands briefly to stop them from shaking. He yanked open the back door, leaned in, and brushed off the fragments of glass that blanketed her still form. He gaped at the amount of blood soaking through her clothing.

Eli slid his hands underneath her and lifted her close to his chest.

Faces turned toward him as he barged into the emergency room and everything seemed to go into slow motion.

"Help me, please!" His voice sounded weak to his own ears.

"Quick, bring her in here." A slight man beckoned.

Eli placed the girl on the gurney and stepped back.

Sweat formed on Eli's forehead as a team of people swarmed into the room. He watched helplessly as they ripped off the remains of the girl's filthy rags.

Track marks ran along the veins on her arms and her bruised skin was covered in scabs.

Tears flooded his eyes at what she'd been made to endure, and he steeled himself from looking away.

The doctor started firing out instructions. "Two IV lines. Get some saline running. Central Venous Pressure line into the side of her neck as well. Alert theatre to stand by."

The nurses worked together like a well oiled machine, each person seemed to know their specific role to help stabilize their patient.

Eli felt woozy and he sucked in a deep breath. One of the nurses took his arm and led him out of the room and insisted he sit down.

"The doctor will speak with you once the patient is on the way to surgery." She turned and hurried back to the room.

Time seemed to slow down, but in reality Eli knew it was only minutes before the doors swung open. He stood and watched as two orderlies pushed the hospital bed out of the room and down the corridor.

Part of him wanted to run after her, but he felt frozen. His arm's hung at his sides and he looked at the floor. Blood covered his clothing and he didn't know what to do.

The squishing sound of rubber shoes on shiny tiles alerted him to the doctor's presence.

Eli searched the man's face for any sign of encouragement. “Will she be all right?”

“We’ve done all we can and I wont lie to you, it’s not looking good. The damage to the lung is extensive—but there’s always hope.” The doctor pointed to the reception desk. “I need you to fill out forms. The police have also been notified, because of the nature of her wound.”

Eli rubbed the base of his neck. “May I talk with her once she’s out of surgery?”

~

He waited two hours before they let him into the room where they’d placed her.

The nurses had wiped the grime off her face, and Eli’s hands clenched as he saw her fading beauty.

Who was she? Had any of the men who’d abused her even taken the time to look into her eyes? His shoulders drooped, and he rubbed his eyes trying to clear his vision.

Pulling a chair close to the bed, he sat on the edge of the hard plastic surface and picked up her emaciated hand. He stroked her dry skin with his thumb. How fragile her fingers felt.

“Lord, help this girl. Don’t let her die—please, Jesus.”

The fingers he held shifted, and he glanced down at her face.

Her gaze locked on him and her lips moved.

Eli tried to capture her words.

"My name's Suzi Wells," she said in a voice below a whisper. "Tell my sister I love her."

"Suzi, I'm Eli. I told you I'd come back for you—you can tell your sister yourself." He brushed her hair back from her forehead. "You're going to be all right. You're safe now."

The tip of her tongue slid across her cracked lips and she closed her eyes.

Eli raised his shoulders and tried to release some of the tension that was locking his muscles. He needed sleep, but he couldn't leave her; he had to sit with her and be her family.

Her hand trembled in his and his chest felt weighted down with pain.

Her eyes opened and it seemed they looked right into his soul.

"Eli." Her breath seemed to catch in her throat.

"Hush, Suzi. We can talk later. Save your strength," he ordered softly. He wanted to pick her up and cradle her. He wanted to right all the wrongs that had been carried out against her.

Tears spilled from the corners of her eyes and ran down her temples into her hair. "Why didn't you come sooner?" Her eyes closed, and all the air in her lungs seemed to gush out through her mouth.

Her words slammed into Eli's brain. "I'm sorry—I'm so sorry," he whispered. His throat felt thick and he struggled to swallow.

Suzi's fingers went limp in his hand and he reached out to touch her still, still face. A moment later, the jagged line tracing her heartbeat flattened, and the monitor emitted a piercing squeal.

He wanted to deny what his heart knew.

Someone came in behind him and pushed him away from the bed.

The sounds around him condensed and blurred to muffled murmurs as he watched the doctor try and resuscitate her, but it was too late.

He was too late.

Chapter 12

Her grandson's delight as they entered the animal park made Macy smile. Never again would she take such places for granted. Bill leaned over the open pen, and she watched as Ashok's hand hesitated above a wombat.

Macy saw Ashok look up for reassurance from Bill before he stroked the short, pudgy marsupial.

Ashok giggled just as Macy snapped another photo.

Featherdale Wildlife Park was another world to the small boy, and Macy tapped Ashok's shoulder to point out the kangaroos wandering around.

"You're allowed to touch them. They'll just hop away if they've had enough."

A large kangaroo sprawled out on the ground in front of them, her huge feet stirring up a cloud of dust.

Bill laughed and squatted beside it. He ran his hand over

the coarse hair down its back.

"Come touch her, Ashok. She won't hurt you."

"Grandpa, I have never seen such an animal. Its tail is so long and thick, like a tree trunk."

Macy pointed to the two hind legs. "They hop on their back legs and use their tail to balance. Their front legs are small and mainly used for grazing."

"Grandma, look!" Ashok pointed at the small head poking out of the kangaroo's pouch. "A baby."

The kangaroo gracefully got to her feet and hopped away; Ashok hopped up and down, following it along the path.

She slipped her hand into Bill's. They didn't need words to express the emotion that passed between them.

This boy was changing their lives.

~

It was late but Eli couldn't face the thought of going back to his room at Ted's hotel. He rubbed his forehead as he trudged toward his car. The frown seemed to be imbedded between his brows, and his eyes felt gritty.

Isak had come through for him and was making all the arrangements to take care of Suzi. He had no doubt his friend would be able to track down Suzi's family.

Placing both hands on the roof of the car, he extended his arms and lowered his chin to his chest. He leaned heavily on the car and gazed unseeingly at his feet.

He hadn't saved her.

The weak state of her body hadn't been able to fight the trauma of a gunshot wound.

If he'd left her at the brothel, she'd still be alive.

Eli pushed away from the car and angrily stuffed the car keys into his pocket. He walked into the night not caring where he headed.

The sound of his footsteps echoed around him and screamed of his loneliness.

Eli's shoulders drooped, and he curled and uncurled his fingers.

He could still feel Suzi's hand in his and longed to change what had happened. He wanted to deny his part in her death.

How long had she suffered?

What is the question?

Halting, he spun around.

Heart pounding, he panted as he caught his breath. Everything in him wanted to flee from the voice that spoke to him.

Uncontrollable tears streamed down his face as he collapsed to his knees.

"You could have saved her!"

He swiped the moisture off his face. "I don't understand."

What was the point in his rescuing Suzi if she was only going to die?

Someone laughed, and the air around him seemed to thicken and come alive. Scrambling to his feet, he charged down the road back to his car. He yanked open the door and collapsed into the front seat. Closing his eyes, he leaned his forehead on the steering wheel.

"What's the question?" His voice sounded loud in the empty car. "What I need to know is—why? Why don't you do something?"

Heaviness pulled at his chest, and fresh tears flowed down his cheeks as more questions came to mind.

What was the point of trying if God didn't help? Was God just going to stand by and let innocent people die?

"It's too much, Jesus. I feel—kicked around, and uncertainty rises within me. I cannot carry on without your help."

His breathing became labored and loud. He had to get a grip. He had to focus on the truth.

God would never leave him.

"What do you want from me, Lord?" The hair on the back of his neck rose as he acknowledged God's presence.

"I just don't understand."

You don't have to.

He let the need to have answers slide from him. His love for Jesus wasn't conditional on having his own way.

He believed, which meant he had to trust in the overall plan God had.

As he repositioned himself on the seat he remembered he'd turned off his phone. He switched it back on and glanced down at the screen. He'd had several missed calls, and his gaze scanned the list of numbers.

Gargi had called, but left no message.

Eli pressed the redial on his phone. He waited impatiently for her to pick up and absently tapped the dangling keys, setting them in motion.

The phone rang through to her message bank and his mouth tightened. She hadn't bothered to leave him a message, and he squirmed at his childish desire to hang up.

He rubbed his eyes and forehead. "Gargi, sorry I missed your call. Is everything all right? Call me back—please."

Chapter 13

The room was just as Charlotte had left it, yet it didn't feel like home anymore. She rubbed her finger over the fine fur of one of her *Sylvanian Family* bears. She'd collected the tiny figurines for years and had loved to arrange them on top of her bookcase. She used to imagine the little creatures living in the idyllic world of Sylvania and playing happy families.

But now they no longer held such importance to her.

Drifting over to the wall mirror, she stared at her reflection. She'd showered and was ready for church an hour early. That she could no longer sleep in didn't bother her; she'd always been an early riser; but now it seemed each new day beckoned her to get up and get going.

What would her friends see when they looked at her?

Tears stung her eyes as she took in her image. Would they see the Charlotte who knew firsthand what it was like to be trafficked—the forced prostitute? Or would they see a strong

Christian woman who headed up a transition house for survivors just like herself?

When she realized she'd buttoned her blouse right up to her neck, her mouth tightened. She unfastened the top button and fluffed the collar.

"Lord, I'm not the same girl they knew. What do I say to them?"

Tap, tap.

Charlotte waited for her mother to enter. Each morning she came up with a glass of freshly squeezed orange juice and they would talk for a while.

Her mother had changed too. She was softer somehow.

The door opened. "Morning, Charlotte. How did you sleep?"

Macy greeted Charlotte with a warm smile as she moved across the room to place the glass on the bedside table.

Charlotte joined her mother by the bed.

"Not bad. I didn't realize how tired I was. I didn't dream, so that was good."

"You look pretty." Her mother reached out and touched her collar. "How are you feeling about going to church this morning?"

Lifting the glass, Charlotte took a small sip. She licked her lips and placed the glass down.

"I'd be lying if I said I wasn't nervous."

"You don't have to be, they all love you." Her mother patted her hand.

"I know that. But I'm not the same person and I don't want to be. I've changed in so many ways. I don't want their sympathy." Going back to the mirror, Charlotte peered at her face. "Everything that happened to me has made me who I am today. It affected every part of me—and I know it sounds crazy, but I'm glad."

"Honey, I—" Charlotte held up her hand to stop her mother talking.

"No, let me try and explain it to you so that I can get it straight in my head. I hate what happened to me, what continues to happen to the innocent, yet for me it forced me closer to God. I had to choose, really decide, what I believed." Spinning around, she grabbed her mother's hands and leaned closer. "Bad things happen every day. Life is not always easy, yet God is always faithful, always present."

She blinked several times. She'd put on mascara and already her eyes were tearing up.

Her mother clasped her fingers. "Can I say something, Charlie?"

Charlotte dabbed at her eyes with a tissue. "Yes."

"As much as you don't want sympathy from your church family, these people have not stopped praying for you. They love you. When your father had a heart attack and was so sick, I got casseroles and flowers. Love poured in from all directions." Her mother sighed. "You are the answer to their prayers. I know it's going to be difficult for you, but can you try and see it from their perspective, and let them tell you how happy they are to see you?"

"What if they avoid eye contact? What if they see me as damaged?" She groaned as the words slipped from her mouth. Did she see herself as damaged, not whole?

Sitting heavily on the bed, Charlotte slapped her hands against her legs. When would this end?

Her mother grabbed her hand. "Charlie, you have been through a terrible time. If you see yourself as damaged, then that just breaks my heart. You are my baby girl and I don't look at you and see you as broken!"

"But you have to say that."

"What rubbish. I feel so angry right now. What happened to you is a crime! You are not to blame, and yes you got hurt, but it's over. Don't let your thoughts attack you. You—are—not—damaged! You're beautiful in every way."

As much as she understood what her mother was trying to say, Charlotte didn't totally agree with her. She was no longer a virgin. Her body was not the same and she had scars to prove it. She'd been tortured in ways she would never talk about. But for her mother's sake she would smile. A rush of love for her sweet, determined mother lifted her despair. "Oh, Mum, I love you. I've had a similar conversation with my counselor. I know these things in my head, but I suppose it may take a lifetime to believe it when the lie jumps out to make me remember."

"How can I help?" Macy opened her arms.

Charlotte snuggled into the comfort her mother offered. She smelt the floral scent of her mother's perfume and was reminded of happier times.

She raised her head. "Just being you is helping. It was easier staying in India than facing all these people. Yet you're right, they just want to love me. I can't believe I so easily slipped back into being a victim." Shaking her fist in the air,

Charlotte stood. “I’m no victim. I’ve been made clean by the blood of the Lamb. It happened, but it has made me stronger, more determined than ever to make a stand.”

A gurgling sound drew her eyes back toward her mother. Their gazes locked and they both burst out laughing.

Smudgy eyes and laughter brought relief to Charlotte. She would let her friends have today to offer their condolences. After that she wouldn’t let them focus on what had been, but on what was and what could be.

“Your father invited Phillip over for breakfast.” Her mother’s mouth gave a happy grin. “I like him, Charlie.”

“Me too.”

“Do you want to talk about how you feel toward him?” her mother asked.

She couldn’t talk about her feelings for Phillip right now. She had to hold it all together just to get through this morning. “Maybe, but not now.”

“Right, then.” Macy stood. “I’m going to freshen up and meet you downstairs in ten minutes.” Her mum pulled her close and hugged her as only her mother could. “I love you so much. I’m so proud of you. God’s not going to leave you alone today, remember that.”

Chapter 14

The last time Gargi travelled this road she'd been tied up in the back of a truck.

She was surprised at how smooth the road was, except for the occasional pothole. She'd read that the Korean government had helped with the construction of the concrete road fifteen years ago.

She'd been driving eight hours straight. The knots in her shoulders, from holding the steering wheel too tight, were making her cringe in pain. She'd crashed through a number of potholes, jarring her neck, and now her head ached from the stress of driving.

She'd thought the closer she got to Nepal the hillier it would become, but she was driving through a plain. The straight road went on and on.

She was hungry and tired of driving. Her clothes felt rumpled from being slept in and she longed for a wash. She decided she'd never sleep in the back of a car again but stop driving in daylight hours so she could find accommodation.

Gargi knew she didn't have long to go before she reached her destination. Her insides churned with nerves.

Up ahead she saw a good place to pull off the road. She steered the car across the dirt verge and parked under a tree.

The road had grown quiet over the last hour and she liked the solitude. Glancing up at the tree, she angled her head to see the sun sparkling through its branches. Trees had it simple. All they needed was good soil and a source of water. They didn't have to question the actions of their parents or suffer from painful memories. One day to a tree was pretty much the same as the next as long as it had its roots down deep, securing it to a solid foundation.

She leaned her head back and closed her eyes. She needed to process what she was about to see.

Would her parents still be there? Could her mother have survived her father's beatings? What of her brother?

Rubbing her eyes, she sat up and stretched her neck to the right then circled it to the left in an attempt to release some tension from her muscles.

She grabbed her bag, then climbed out of the car. Gargi spread a towel on the grass and sat cross-legged with her bag on her knee.

As she placed the small bowl of rice beside her, she remembered her phone had rung while she'd been driving. She listened to Eli's voice message and wondered at his tone of voice. Was he still angry with her? She couldn't help that; she'd done what she needed to do.

Before she could lose her nerve she phoned him.

"Hello," he answered on the first ring.

"Eli, hello. How are you?"

"I've been better, you?"

Her nails cut into the palm of her hand and she frowned. If she felt this nervous just talking to him on the phone, then how would she have been in person?

"I am just about at my village. I called you last night. I wanted to talk to you about something." Her heart raced so fast, it was like fear had gripped her chest, making it hard to talk.

"I'm listening."

"You don't sound very interested. If now isn't a good time to talk, I can call back later," she stammered.

"Of course I'm interested. You're the one who didn't want anything to do with me, remember? I was surprised to see you'd called."

Gargi chewed her bottom lip. She couldn't blame him. She had pushed him away.

"Um, the car is such a blessing to me. Thank you for arranging every detail of my trip. I cannot repay you."

"Is that why you called? I don't expect anything from you in return. Not everyone is out to get something from you. There are still good people in the world and I had hoped you would have seen me as one of them."

"I do! Oh my goodness, I am not able to say things that I feel to you. I am missing you, Eli. I—I wanted to tell you that, I—um—I love you."

The silence stretched. Gargi's heart skipped madly as she

waited for his response.

"What did you say?"

"I said I love you." Her voice gained strength and she laughed.

"You love me? You tell me this when you are thousands of miles away and I can't see you."

"Is that all you can say? I tell you I love you and you growl at me."

Her insides were bubbling and she felt suspended in time. She could hardly breathe, waiting for him to say something.

"Where are you? Can you come back here? I'll pay for the flight."

"I am waiting for you to tell me that you love me back."

"I've told you once, and I'm not saying it again until I can look into your eyes. Forgive me if I'm having trouble believing you. I think your words were 'I love you like a brother'."

"I lied. I am sorry. I thought I was saving you—from me." Now that she'd admitted it, she felt so foolish.

"That's just plain dumb," Eli blurted. "Don't ever lie to me again. You either love me or you don't. So are you telling me you love me as a woman loves a man she wants to spend the rest of her life with?"

Her lips parted in a smile. "Yes. The forever, romantic kind of love," she declared.

"Gargi, will you come home? I need to hold you close to my heart right now."

Eli's voice warmed her. He did love her; he wanted her back with him. Yet she needed to finish what she'd started.

"Give me a couple of months, then I'll join you. I have to

see this through."

"I'd rather have you here where I can keep an eye on you."

"Don't think because I've told you of my love that you'll become the boss of me. Eli Turner, I want my husband to be an equal partner, not another man telling me what to do," she stated angrily.

"What ever happened to the quiet, meek woman I first met? And I don't recall asking you to be my wife." The sound of his laughter sent heat scorching up Gargi's face, and she cupped her eyes with her hand.

"I will not be your woman unless you marry me. I will hang up now."

"No! Don't hang up. I'm sorry. I shouldn't be teasing you. But let me propose when the time's right, okay?"

Tears sprung to her eyes. He would not say the words… but the promise was there. "Give me two months to see my family and feel my way through my past. Then I will come back to you."

Eli gave a soft groan. "I won't stop you, but sometimes the past is best left behind. What do you hope to achieve?"

His question was reasonable, yet she felt challenged. She'd been so sure that going back would bring closure and that the Lord would somehow use her to make a difference in Nepal.

"Eli, I do not know how to explain. I just believe that I must do this."

"How can I help?"

"You already have. The car, the money for petrol, this phone, the little gun. I'm so grateful. Could I phone you each day?" Already she wasn't feeling so lonely, and hearing the worried tone in his voice made her smile. To have someone care about her in such a way was like unwrapping a gift.

"Yes, and if I don't hear from you, I'll call."

"Thank you for being patient with me. I promise we will be together soon. Good-bye for now."

"Gargi, wait. I love you. Keep safe."

He'd said the words. Tears pooled in her eyes as she set the phone down.

He loved her. Gargi couldn't stop smiling. Her heart felt light.

She picked up the small container of rice and spooned it into her mouth with her fingers. The spicy taste made her lips tingle, and she licked the corner of her mouth.

How easy it would be to turn the car around and head back to Mumbai, where she knew she had people who loved her.

Ashok. Her arms longed to hold the boy close. He would be her son. The realization brought a sense of possessiveness over her. If anyone did anything further to hurt her boy, that person would have to deal with her.

She hadn't even asked Eli how Ashok was. Shaking her head at her neglect, she brushed her hands together then packed away the bowl.

The sound of another vehicle approaching made her glance down the road. She was exposed sitting here alone beside her car. Gargi gathered her things then raced back to the car. Once she was inside, she locked the door.

An old, heavy-looking truck thundered past her and she shivered. It was just a truck, yet something dark had crossed her spirit as it passed.

The closer she got to the Nepal border, the more rural the countryside became. She leaned forward as she drove and slowly read the words indicating Immigration. She'd already found out that she had nothing to do here and could drive straight through.

Gargi slowed the car as she approached the checkpoint and wound down her window. A man in an official uniform frowned at her then ran his hand over the car bonnet.

She hated confrontation of any sort, but she'd prepared for this stage of her journey. "Good morning, saab. Please let me pass. I am returning to Nepal to visit my family." Her words came out quickly. She prayed he'd let her pass without a sce-ne.

"You have a Nepali license? Show me!"

Gargi raised her chin. This man would not intimidate her. She knew the law and she had taken great care to be ready to pass through the border.

She smiled and handed over her papers.

A frown creased his forehead, and his gaze snapped from the papers to her face. "Are you returning for good or is this just a visit?"

"Visit, maybe two months." She held out her hand for him to return the papers.

"It will be easier for you if I stamp your papers. You understand this will cost you eight hundred rupees. It will go well for you, yes?"

"Four hundred." Taking the prepared money out of her bag, she then held it out to him.

He shrugged, stamped her papers, and pocketed the cash.

With a wave of his hand he sauntered back toward the building he'd come from.

She released a long breath. Driving through the gate, Gargi accelerated the car. As the distance from the border increased, she started to relax and think about what she'd learned about Nepal prior to setting off on her journey.

Going to school had never been an option for her, and now that she'd started to learn things, she was hungry for information. When life was all about surviving, she'd had no desire to learn anything. All she'd wanted was to live through another day—now she had an insatiable appetite for knowledge.

Would the streets and the countryside seem familiar to her? Would she remember faces? Nepal was home to the world's highest mountain, yet she couldn't remember ever seeing Mt. Everest.

She liked the countryside and wanted to take in as much as she could. She dropped her speed back and glanced out the side window as she drove.

Nepal was landlocked by India on three sides and Tibet to the North. The country's stunning, stark beauty made her chest ache… but not as much as the statistics she'd read about Nepal's darkest secret.

The number of girls being taken from rural Nepal shocked her. Her eyes misted over and she blinked to clear her vision. She'd never thought about the other girls stolen from her village.

When she'd lived in the brothel her main emotion had been anger. She'd given herself permission to feel indifferent to those around her. But now all she felt was sadness for the sickness of humanity. Her shoulders drooped as she thought of Shanti's sweet face.

The article she'd read said that around twenty thousand girls a year were lured by the false promises of traffickers.

She hated the word *traffickers*. She hated that she'd been trafficked—not lured, but sold by her parents to men who saw her only as a way to make money.

She wanted to go into the villages where girls were most at risk and warn them of the dangers. Would they listen to her? Persuading parents to keep their daughters in school, when they could be a source of income, seemed almost impossible. Yet she had to try.

The road all but disappeared, and she slowed the car down to a crawl. A film of dust coated the window, making it hard to navigate; yet the thought of leaving the car did not sit well with Gargi. The car bumped over loose gravel and finally she pulled to the side of the road and climbed out of the car.

Gargi stared at the young girl gazing at her. The red rhododendron pushed into her hair seemed bigger than her face and Gargi smiled. Her clothes were simple and she wore a pair of scuffed leather shoes that seemed too big for her feet.

"Who are you?" The girl asked in Nepali.

"Hello, I'm Gargi. What's your name?"

The girl stepped closer to the car and squinted. "I'm Amita. Are you lost?"

"I hope not. I'm going to Murma village. Am I close?"

Amita nodded, then reached out and touched the car. "I like your car. It's better than the truck that came by before."

The sound of the child's softly spoken words in her native language made Gargi catch her breath. Amita looked so small, so young. Yet her age was close to how old Gargi had been when she'd been taken.

"Amita, can you speak slowly for me? It's been a long time since I've spoken Nepali."

Gargi pointed ahead of her. "Is there another road, do you know? This road doesn't seem passable by car."

"Would you like me to show you?" Amita stepped forward. "I would be most pleased to ride in your car with you." Amita grabbed Gargi's hand. "I will help you," she said proudly and raised her chin.

"You must not get into vehicles with strangers, it could be dangerous."

"What is vehicle, Gargi?"

Gargi couldn't resist the girl. She wanted to hug her but instead she touched the flower. "This is very pretty and you are very beautiful. A vehicle is anything with wheels." She pointed to the tires. "You said you saw a truck. Did you also offer to help the people in the truck?"

Shaking her head, Amita frowned. "No. Two men were driving the truck so I hid. They carried on down by the rice fields."

"Wise girl. I'd be very grateful for your directions."

Once Gargi had backed up the car so she could go in the other direction, she followed Amita's instructions to the road she'd missed on the right.

"Have you always lived here, Amita?"

"Yes. When I'm older I am going to travel into the city to

work. My mother says I can earn good money for the family as a domestic worker."

"Do many girls in the village leave to work in the city?"

"Yes. I think this is why the men in the truck come every year or so."

Gargi stared in horror at what Amita had said. "You mean this truck you saw has been here before, taking young girls to the city for work?"

Amita nodded, then ran her hand over the dashboard in wonder. "Many girls went last year. They have not come back for holidays, and people grumble that they do not send money back to help their families. I will not be like this. I want to help my parents. My mother is not always well."

Biting down on her bottom lip, Gargi tasted blood. The possibility of these men being here to steal young girls from this village was too real.

Amita shuffled in her seat. "Who is it you are here to see, Gargi?"

Gargi's neck felt stiff with tension and she made her fingers relax on the steering wheel. She shouldn't jump to conclusions. The village loomed ahead of her and she parked the car on a grass verge out of the way of other vehicles.

She remembered this place. It was like looking at a faded photo, hoping to see some color or life.

The feel of cool fingers touching her arm shocked her. She'd forgotten she wasn't alone.

"Did you want me to help you find where you want to go?" The child's eyes locked on hers and Gargi nodded.

"I used to live here a long time ago, and I want to see if I still have any family in the village." She gave the name of her parents and watched as her little friend's eyes widened.

"I live not far from your mother, so I would be glad to walk with you."

"Thank you. I'll just get my bag and lock the car."

Chapter 15

Charlotte felt crowded. Arriving a half-hour early for church had been her mother's idea. It had made sense at the time, something about jumping in feet first and saying hello to people before the service started.

Phillip came up behind Charlotte and touched her arm, making her jump.

"How are you holding out?"

Turning, she gazed into his concerned blue eyes. "I'm okay, but this is exhausting. Mum was right, though, they deserve to know I'm okay."

"Of course. It's not about you; it's about making everyone else feel okay. Good on you, Charlie." He rolled his eyes and crossed his arms.

"Stop it, Phillip. I know what you're trying to do and it won't work. Just because I agree to do something does not mean I'm being submissive. I'm choosing to honor these people for caring and praying for me."

"Of course you are. It doesn't matter that it's making you go pale each time someone touches your arm and says she's so sorry you had to experience the abuse in the brothel. Really, what was I thinking?"

Gasping, Charlotte closed her eyes and swayed. He was right. The service hadn't even started and she was shattered. Why had she allowed herself to be set up like this? She should have been firmer with her mother and arrived five minutes before the service began. What was it that had triggered her into being compliant again?

Charlotte opened her eyes then blinked back tears. She didn't want to disappoint her mother, yet this was too much.

"Wait right here." Phillip headed across the crowded foyer.

Her breathing felt jerky as she watched him talk to her father, who looked her way and nodded.

Phillip strode over to her, took her hand, and led her out of the building.

She stopped walking. "What are you doing?"

"I told your dad we would come to the evening service—unless you've changed your mind and want to go back in?"

"No. I think I'd like to take a walk."

"Good. Let's go to Manly Beach and walk around the shore, then have lunch."

It felt like a hand reached out and embraced her heart. He teased her, challenged her, cared for her. She wanted to touch him. She looked at him through her eyelashes and suddenly felt so young. Her heart raced at the thoughts galloping through her mind. “Thank you, Phillip.”

“You’re very welcome.” He swung his arm across his stomach and bowed low like a knight before a princess, and Charlotte giggled.

“I want to go home and change into my jeans.”

“Your wish is my command, Princess Charlotte.”

“Anything?” she asked and batted her eyelashes. She couldn’t believe she was flirting with Phillip.

“Anything in my power,” he stated. She knew he meant it. He’d proved himself time and time again.

~

The reflection of the sun sparkling on the water was like a million diamonds merging together to create a dance of light. Charlotte pushed her fringe out of her eyes and reached for her sunglasses. She loved the beach, and this place in particular brought back many happy memories for her.

She smiled. “Eli used to race me to the back of that shark net.” She pointed to the bobbing plastic buoys creating a safe place to swim. “He’d try and put me off from entering the water by telling me stories of people seeing sharks peering at them from the other side.”

“Nice brother.”

“He was such fun. He always had time for me. Gosh, I miss him.” Watching the people in the water, Charlotte tried to focus on happier times. She hated that Eli was alone in India.

Phillip waved his hand in front of her eyes. "Relax. I can sense you tensing up just talking about Eli. He's a big boy and can look after himself."

"I just wish things had worked out for him and Gargi." Charlotte slanted her face to capture the sun's rays. Warm waves of heat caressed her skin, and she ran her tongue over her lips. "I'm trying to relax, but as much as I love seeing Mum and Dad, I'm ready to go home."

Phillip picked up her hand and watched her intently. She slowly allowed her fingers to grip his. Holding his hand was new to her, and as much as she wanted to, she had to stop herself from thinking about the message she was sending him.

He leaned forward and dipped his head toward hers.

Charlotte jolted back before his lips met hers.

Straightening, Phillip stepped back. "It's okay, Charlie. I can feel the tension in your hand. I'm not going to rush you. Trust me."

She swung around and glared at him. "I do trust you. It's just that you want to hold my hand and kiss me, and I think of all that follows after you hold my hand."

"Well, don't."

"It's not that easy."

"Yes it is, just don't." He let go of her hand and walked toward the water's edge.

Charlotte looked down and kicked the sand, causing small grains to slip inside her sneakers.

She'd ruined the moment. Sighing, she joined him.

He didn't look at her as she reached his side but continued to stare out at the small boats anchored close to the shore.

Charlotte hated that the simplicity of holding the hand of the man she loved had become complicated by her body's reaction.

Lord, help me out here.

Phillip turned, and then his gaze dropped to her lips then rose to her eyes. "How about we make a deal to be completely honest with each other?"

Nodding several times, Charlotte swallowed and tried to think of something to say. Of course she wanted to be honest with him, but most of the time her reactions seemed out of her control.

"Good. I'll start." He coughed into his hand. "I love you. There, I've said it. I want to marry you." He held up his hand as she opened her mouth to speak. "Don't say anything, please. I'm not asking you to marry me at this moment—because it's too soon. I just want to be up front with you."

Charlotte's lips trembled and she wanted to cry. This should be the happiest moment of her life, yet her insides were shaking.

He gently tilted her chin with his finger. "Sweetheart, it's all right."

"No, it's not!" she snapped, her mood changing from despair to anger in an instant. "I want to hold the hand of the man I love without feeling queasy inside."

"Queasy? Great," Phillip mumbled, and a frown deepened the crease in his forehead.

Without thinking, she rubbed her thumb across his skin to smooth away the line. "You just told me you love me. I should be swooning at your feet wanting you to kiss me!"

"I can wait. When you're ready, just let me know."

"Oh, sure. I'll just say, 'Phillip how about a kiss, I'm over feeling sick to my stomach when we touch'. How romantic is that?" She screwed up her face and stamped her foot at the unfairness of it all. She wanted to freely love him. "I don't understand why this is happening. That old part of my life is over. I feel free most of the time. It not you, Phillip—it's me."

"It is not you, it's *us*. Let's not overcomplicate this. You react when I touch you, but mainly when you're overthinking it. You didn't even realize you just touched my forehead, did you?"

"Did I?" She felt her face flush.

"Yep, and I liked it." He placed his hand on the spot that she'd touched. "It may take us time to work this out, but we will get there. I'm committed—are you?"

This was a moment of truth. A small part of her acknowledged that it would be easier not to state her intent to work through this with him. To live her life alone so she didn't have to address the sexual aspect of a marriage relationship.

Phillip's face was so dear to her. She gazed into the question in his eyes. "My counselor said body reactions are normal, that I have to remind myself that I'm no longer in captivity and have choices. I can't stop the memory sneaking up on me, but I have to stand up against the lie that your touch will hurt me."

She took a step closer to him. This was Phillip, not some stranger who didn't care about her.

This was Phillip. She whispered his name.

He didn't move; it was like everything around them stood still. She curled her toes in her sneakers and felt the sand prick her skin. She breathed in deeply and smelt the sea air; she heard the sounds of gulls above her.

This was Manly Beach, Sydney, Australia—not a brothel in India.

She inhaled through her nose and counted to five. This was now; her present—and it belonged to her.

And this was Phillip.

Standing on tiptoes, she placed her hands on his chest. Her face felt on fire and she was terrified yet determined. "Let's try that kiss again, shall we?"

Chapter 16

Gargi walked beside Amita. She remembered this place. The smells assaulted her and took her back to long, hard days working beside her mother in all types of weather conditions.

She stopped walking, stared at the terraced paddies and wondered if her brother still worked there. Two oxen pulled a plough through the mud, digging a channel through the dirty knee-deep water.

Women were bent in half with their hands submerged in the swampy water planting rice. Gargi's hand went to her back in sympathy. Her mother had always grumbled about her back aching.

She remembered having a mud fight with the other children who worked the field alongside her. Someone had started it by throwing a handful of stinky mud at a friend, and before long all the children were chasing each other. Laughter had broken out and some of the older boys had lifted the girls and completely submerged them in the dank water.

It had been fun, but her laughter had dried up when she got home and suffered her father's lash because of the state of her clothes. Never mind that her brother had participated and was as dirty as she. It was always Gargi who felt the sting of his words and the cut of his belt on her skin.

She shivered as if expecting her father to walk toward her with a scowl on his face. This was her last chance to change her mind. She could go back to her car, drive away and not look back.

She couldn't put it off any longer. Raising her chin, she thanked Amita for walking with her then headed in the direction of her family's dwelling.

It was smaller, shabbier than she remembered it. The door was the only feature in the front of the house and the latch seemed to be broken. The walls of the old house had once been painted a sandy white but now the cracked paint had a yellowish tinge.

The path was overgrown with weeds, making Gargi want to pull them out.

Standing outside the door, she hesitated. Would her mother recognize her? What if she didn't acknowledge her or invite her in? Her palms felt sweaty. Gargi fanned her fingers, trying to create a small draught.

Raising her hand, she knocked.

She could hear hesitant footsteps as someone came to answer the door. Her heart hammered and she smoothed down her clothes with shaking hands.

The door slowly opened, as if the heavy timber were difficult to budge. After a moment it swung inward far enough to reveal an old woman who was bent at the waist and whose greying hair and wrinkled skin spoke of an ageing, arthritic body.

Gargi's eyes stung to see how time had ravaged her mother.

Angling her head to the side, the woman squinted and licked her lips.

Gargi saw the flicker of recognition flash through her mother's eyes and smiled. "Mam, it's me, Gargi," she stated softly and extended her hand toward her mother.

"I know it's you, girl. What do you want?" she snapped in a gravelly voice.

Gargi's mouth fell open but she could form no words. She'd expected more. The tightness in her throat made it difficult to swallow. It was as if time stopped and she shuddered.

Gargi made herself stop shaking. "May I come in?"

Shrugging, her mother turned and shuffled into the dirty room. She lowered herself carefully into an old chair and joined her scaly hands together and waited.

Gargi placed her bag by the door then looked around the small room and felt displaced.

"Don't look down that nose of yours at my home. Just because you are a fine city girl doesn't mean you can forget your humble beginnings."

Images of her father grabbing her arm and dragging her across the room flashed through her mind. She'd begged him to let her stay, promised him she'd work harder and not cause him any problems.

He hadn't even bothered answering her. Two men had waited at the door and her father had taken their money and pushed her into their arms.

"I haven't forgotten." The trembling inside her chest made her want to throw up.

Her mother's eyes watered. "Why are you here?"

"I wanted to see you."

"Well, I don't want to see you. Not once have you contacted me or sent money. You stopped being my daughter the day you abandoned your duty."

"What are you talking about? You sold me into prostitution! I had no choice in the matter," Gargi stammered, bewildered by her mother's attitude.

"So what? We sold you, but you were meant to send us money regularly. That was the deal."

Gargi wanted to scream. She shook her head vigorously. "Was that all I was to you, a source of money?"

Her mother huffed and chewed her tobacco noisily.

Gargi surveyed the room. Her father's cane was not against the wall where he always left it. She shuddered as she remembered the feel of the wood on her back. "Where is my father?"

"Dead, good riddance."

Gargi felt lightheaded. All the things she'd wanted to say to him flooded her mind. Would she have been able to forgive him completely if she'd seen him? She would never know.

"You here to stay?" Her mother's voice sounded distant

and indifferent.

"Um, yes, for now. Is that all right?"

"You work, bring us money," she ordered. "No work, no food."

"Mam, what happened to you? When did you stop caring about yourself and your children?"

"I don't want to talk about the past. It's over with, girl."

Clutching her hands together, Gargi refused to be intimidated by the harsh tone of her mother's voice.

"No, you have to answer my question. I deserve an answer. I was a prisoner in a brothel for most of my life. I stopped counting the number of men who hurt me, and I closed my mind to the possibility of being free, being loved. I had died in every way except physically."

Her mother shifted in the chair, and her eyes darted back and forth across the room.

Gargi had dreamed of her mother opening her arms to embrace her. Welcoming her home with love and begging her only daughter for forgiveness. Gargi's throat thickened and she had difficulty talking. It seemed so unfair. It was a mother's role to protect her children, not the other way round. She was here to offer her mother the one gift she had that meant anything. "Mam, I came back to tell you, that—that I forgive you."

"*Barr ha*, I don't need you doing that. I have no need of your forgiveness. What is—is."

Gargi clutched her stomach as if the pain she felt was physical. "Are you saying you don't care that your only daughter was subjected to continual abuse? Sometimes thirty men a night."

Her mother's eyes widened. She shifted on her seat and scratched her chin. "Get over yourself. Girls are for sex, that's what my father told me. That's what happened to me. You think I chose to marry your father? I hated him!"

"I am your child!" Her arms felt heavy, weighted down with rejection. "Do you feel nothing?"

"Always fuss, fuss," her mother mumbled.

Gargi was sure she saw a glimmer of a tear in her mother's eyes. She leaned closer and touched her hand.

"Mam, I had to come and see you. I had to tell you that I've met Jesus and my life has been saved."

"Geeut rescue you from the brothel?"

"Jesus. Jesus is God's son, Mam. I came back to tell you that God loves you."

The door burst open and slammed against the wall. A young man with a weather-beaten face came in and stood looking at her.

Gargi's heart raced as she stood. "Nandi?" she asked as her lips curved.

"Who are—Gargi?" his eyes darkened.

"Hello, Brother."

"I gave you up for dead. What are you doing back here?"

"I came to see Mam and you. It's been a long time. How are you?"

"Like you care. You're wasting your time here. We have nothing to give you."

"I don't want anything, I just want to see you."

"Big city girl now! Think you can come back here and

slum off us. I want you out!"

"You can't tell me what to do. I will leave when I'm ready to leave." Gargi sucked in a deep, calming breath and glared at him. What a fool she'd been to think her brother would be pleased to know she'd survived.

"Boy, go home to your woman. Gargi is welcome here."

Gargi spun around and stared at her mother, wizened but fierce in her chair. She couldn't believe her mam had stuck up for her.

"Don't forget who looks after you, old woman," he snarled. "I'll leave now, but mark my word, she's nothing but trouble."

Gargi squatted beside her mother and touched her arm. "Thank you."

"Make some tea, girl," her mother ordered gruffly.

~

His grandma cooked nice food, but Ashok missed the spicy tastes he was used to. He felt restless and wanted to talk to his baap. Lately when he lay in bed at night, he could not stop the tears from coming. He felt more alone in this big house with his special grandparents than he did on the streets of India.

In the quiet of night, he felt sad.

"Jesus," he whispered. "I am the most ungrateful boy. I

want to go home now." He burrowed his head into the pillow and sniffed. He couldn't smell Eli in this room. If his baap were here with him, then maybe he'd feel happy. Ashok rubbed his forehead and turned over onto his back.

The hardest part about his sister being dead was that he couldn't look at her. Having Shanti always beside him had given him purpose apart from himself. He was never lonely because she was constantly with him.

His little shadow.

Maybe if he asked his grandpa, he'd let him phone his baap. Slipping his legs out of the blanket, he pushed his feet into the fluffy slippers and wiggled his toes around. He liked the soft woolly texture.

Ashok opened the bedroom door and then stepped into the hall. As he crept down the stairs, he hoped his grandparents wouldn't mind that he'd gotten up.

The television was on and some program blared away. Every time he tried to watch the television, he thought of his sister and how they had first watched the box together. She had loved it, and it hurt him now to sit and watch it without her. He could still hear her excited voice calling him to come and watch.

Tears welled and spilled down his face. He stood behind the living room door so he could wipe his face before anyone saw him. It was like his eyes had become a broken tap, unable to be turned off.

"What did Eli say when he phoned?" Grandma asked.

Ashok stiffened at the sound of his baap's name. Had he phoned and not wanted to speak to him? His chest tightened and he sucked in a quick breath.

"It seems the man named Scarface disappeared without a trace after the raid."

"Bill, I don't want Ashok to go back to India. What if something happens to him? Surely he's safer here until all this is sorted out?"

"No!" Ashok shouted as he burst into the room. "I want to go home."

Grandma raced across the room toward him and reached out her hand.

Ashok pulled back, shaking his head. He did not want her to touch him. "You cannot lie to me. I know my baap needs me."

"It's okay, honey. Come sit down and we'll—"

"I heard you. You plan to keep me here. I—don't—want—to—stay—here," he hollered.

"We're not saying you have to," Grandpa explained. "We need to talk to you about the options, that's all."

His grandpa's soft face made fresh tears spring to Ashok's eyes. He wanted to keep a safe distance from these people who said they loved him. His face warmed, and he narrowed his eyes.

Having only Shanti to love had somehow been easier than all these people who now cared for him—and made decisions for him.

Before, all he had to do was focus on keeping her safe, and he was the boss of the two of them.

He wanted to trust his grandparents, yet if he let them tell him what to do, he'd have no control over his life. "I have come here for a holiday. It is time for me to go home now."

Grandpa reached over and switched off the television. "Eli called and we have things we want to tell you. If you don't want to come sit down, then that's just too bad. It's up to you, lad."

Jutting out his chin, Ashok tried to look taller. He wanted to know what was going on, and he felt stupid for making a scene. "I wish to hear, Grandpa."

"Come and sit down, then. Macy, how about you make us all a hot chocolate and then we'll talk and see if we can get Eli back on the phone."

"Yes, yes! Please, Grandpa. I want to talk to my baap!" Ashok sprung across the room and threw his arms around his grandpa's waist. He could feel his tears soaking the material his face rested on, and for some reason he couldn't stop crying.

The pat on his back soothed him. As much as he wanted to snuggle further into the warmth of his grandpa's solid stomach, he inched away.

He fingered the ring on the thin leather strap around his neck. If his baap got into trouble and there was an ocean between them, how could he help his baap?

The tissue in his hand was soggy, he scrunched it up and rolled it into a ball. His hand trembled too much to pick up the cup of hot chocolate, so he watched the steam circle above it and waited for Grandma to sit down.

"Right, let's talk," Grandpa stated.

Ashok twisted in his seat and stared at his baap's parents. The look on their faces made him feel all gooey inside and he leaned forward. Something clicked in his mind. If Baap were here with him, he'd be happy to stay longer.

All his words dried up and he didn't know what to say. Living on the streets of Mumbai had been simple because all he had to do was find a place to sleep and food for each day.

Now he had all these feelings bubbling up on the inside of him, and he didn't know how to express them or cope with the way he felt.

Grandpa placed his cup on the saucer and wiped his mouth. "Your planned holiday was for two weeks. Eli wants to talk to you about spending a school term here," Grandpa informed him.

Ashok wondered how long a school term was. He glanced across at Grandma and she smiled.

Grandpa's bushy eyebrows touched and his face was so serious. "We're not saying you have to stay, we want you to because we love you. We want you to be safe and not alone. Eli is going to be away quite a lot and working with the police to try and catch the people who are threatening Charlotte and him."

Ashok gripped his stomach and wanted to bend in half to ease the pain he felt. "I don't want my baap to be in danger. Why does he have to do this? Why can't he come here and stay safe with me?"

"That's a very good question," Grandma agreed. "I wish he would do just that. But as much as I want him to be safe because he's my son, I have to trust that God will look after him."

"Bad things happen," Ashok whispered and dipped his

head.

"Yes, they do." Grandma gathered him close. "Honey, even though bad things do happen, God is still with us." She brushed his hair off his face.

"Grandma, my Shanti died," he sobbed. "What if I lose my baap?"

The arms around him tightened. "Then you would have us."

Grandpa coughed into his hand and Ashok turned his head to look at him. Tears glistened in his grandpa's eyes and he gave Ashok a watery smile. "Have you ever had a birthday party, Ashok?"

"No, Grandpa. I don't know the day I was born." He felt all hot. Why had his grandpa brought this up? Other children celebrated their birthdays, but he had no idea how old he was or how Shanti and he had survived the baby years on there own.

Grandpa stood. "How about we set a date for your future birthdays. If it's okay with your dad, we could make it in a weeks' time. We could have a party, balloons, food, games, gifts and some of your friends from your new school could come. Do you want to talk to him about it when you call him?"

Looking up, Ashok frowned. His grandpa wanted to make a date to celebrate his life.

A birth date.

He grasped his hands together, cocked his head, and stood very straight. "I would very much like that. Sometimes when I have seen other children celebrate their birthdays I have wondered why my parents didn't want Shanti and me. But I am not sad; I have you now as my grandparents. I thank my Jesus that you want to give me a party." He felt lighter, almost as if he could dance.

He would stay in Australia if his baap wanted him to.

"Can I phone Baap now?"

Chapter 17

The skin stretched smoothly across Khlaid's face, and he liked the tightness he saw in the mirror as he smiled. He'd been reassured the skin around his eyes would loosen up over time.

He looked completely different; even Padma would not recognize him.

"Boss, I have sent the letter as you requested." Frank stood waiting for further instructions.

"Good." Khlaid cleared his throat. "What do you think of my new voice?" He turned to face Frank. "I think it's quite interesting that I spend all this money to remove scarring from my face and then pay to have my vocal cords scarred. So what do you think? Do I sound like a different person?"

"Yes, sir." Frank stared directly into his gaze.

Khlaid squinted before he remembered his brows would not move. He wasn't sure he could read his right-hand man yet. There were times when it felt like Frank was the one in control.

He snapped his shiny new teeth together and disliked the full feeling in his mouth. That he'd had a complete makeover was of little importance to him. He had liked the way his old appearance had frightened those around him. He'd lived hard, and his new soft look didn't sit with who he was. His employers had given him little choice concerning the change. Change or leave.

"Have you a copy of the letter?" Khlaid growled.

"Yes, would you like to see it?" Frank replied smoothly.

"No. Tell me what you wrote."

"Just as you requested, sir. I addressed the correspondence to Ted Calston. He runs the hotel chain that has been responsible for doing most of the fund-raising for Shanti's Rest. He is also a close friend to Charlotte Turner's brother."

"Yes, yes, I know this," Khlaid said impatiently.

"The body of the letter requested a meeting to introduce my client—you—to the founder of Shanti's Rest. I hinted you were impressed with the work they are doing and want to become a serious benefactor."

Khlaid's jaw jutted out. Girls were nothing but tools to make money. He would teach Charlotte for thinking she could set up camp in his domain. His left eyelid twitched, and he pressed his finger against it to stop the movement.

There was something about Charlotte that drew him.

He had to have her.

"Go, leave me," he snarled. "Tell me when she is back in the country."

As the door snapped closed, Khlaid relaxed his shoulders. What was it about this blonde girl that challenged him so much? Wisdom told him to walk away from Charlotte and focus on his growing business, yet revenge and a yearning to make Charlotte his, clouded his vision.

He was a new man. Unrecognizable.

That Charlotte had never weakened, never lost sight of her so-called faith, infuriated him. In the end he had been the one made to look the fool.

Her god had smote him powerless. He'd been stuck on the floor, unable to walk, and Charlotte had been rescued.

She'd called him Saul. This name had hounded him, and he'd researched it to find it was a biblical name. The man Saul had been a king who had lost his kingdom. Had she been mocking him all along?

He punched the wall, liking the pain that shot up his arm. He missed the opportunity to inflict pain on the slaves, yet good business practice kept the merchandise in good condition.

He glanced at his watch. There had been no news from the pickers in Nepal. He grew impatient for action.

Picking up the phone, he buzzed his secretary.

"Boss?" she answered. That he had a secretary brought a smirk to his face.

"Has the container been fitted?"

"Just about. The oxygen cylinders are the last to be installed."

"When?"

"Two days. Then once the merchandise is loaded, the supplies will be delivered and it will be good to go."

"And customs?"

"All taken care of."

"The ship?"

"We have people on board who will take care of things prior to docking."

He hung up the phone and scratched his leg. Why did the itching continue? It was like some bug had gotten under his skin and refused to let up. The skin specialist had said it was in his mind, that there was nothing physically causing the inflammation except his continual scratching.

That he was now a man of means, meant nothing to him. He wanted power—and the contract with the Middle East was just the door he needed to increase his reputation for prime stock.

~

As she walked, Gargi took in the freshness of the morning. There were things she loved about this village, but poverty was not one of them.

The elderly sat around outside their houses. She waved in greeting.

No one smiled at her or called out to say hello.

Strolling away from the houses, she headed for the paddy fields. She wanted to see the children, and as there was no village school, most of them would either be working or playing around their parents' feet.

Amita skipped toward her and smiled shyly.

"Hello, princess," Gargi welcomed her.

Amita dipped her head and giggled. "Do you want to walk with me, Gargi?"

"Where are you going?"

"There is a meeting at the lower terrace. The men from the truck are offering money and jobs to us. My father said I was to go and see what they are paying."

A chill raced up Gargi's back and her hands went clammy. Were the strangers offering work to young girls when in fact they wanted them for prostitutes?

She grabbed both of Amita's hands. "I don't like the sound of this. Can you take me to this meeting?"

Amita pulled her hands free then stuck out her chin. "My father said these are good men, that they come each year and offer us good money. Come with me, I will show you."

The feeling of unease got tighter across Gargi's chest as she approached the group of people listening to the men talk.

"There is much work in the city." The man stood on a box and was a head taller than the people around him. He was dressed in pressed brown pants and a milky white shirt. His hair was swept back off his forehead with grease and his hands beckoned people in close. "The rich business people flock into Mumbai and want domestic servants to clean for them. They offer a bed, food, and also money to secure good employees. Your daughters will be able to send you money to help feed your other children. They will be able to save to better their futures."

Pushing to the front of the crowd, Gargi folded her arms. "I don't believe you. I was sent to the city and became a slave in prostitution. The only answer to bettering yourself is education." She faced the crowd. "You need to protect your daughters. These men cannot be trusted. I have come here to help you and tell you my story. I am one of you, a daughter of our people."

Harsh words erupted behind her. "Can you feed these families when winter sets in? Who are you, woman? You have money in your pockets like us to offer to these poor people? You can pay their debts that are strangling them?" He flung a handful of coins to the ground at her feet.

Children scrambled to pick them up and Gargi had to step out of their way as a fight broke out amongst two boys.

"Please—don't listen to them," she begged. "If they are honest men, they will tell you where the jobs are and you can go and check them out for yourself. You have to protect the women and children."

Nandi pushed to the front of the crowd. "Gargi, you think you can come back here and tell us what to do?" her brother demanded. "You don't belong here. We weather the storms that our mountain sends. We do life our way, so shut your mouth, girl!"

Her brother's glare did not intimidate Gargi. "I was sold to men like these who promised to feed my family. Did you see any of the money, Nandi? I was thrown in a truck like this"—she gestured—"and taken from here. Did any of you think of me once I was gone?" She could hear the high pitch of her voice and inhaled deeply to calm herself.

Amita screamed and the sound sent a chill down Gargi's back. She spun around and saw her friend being yanked toward the truck. Gargi sprinted toward them. "Let her go!"

Pulling out the small pistol Eli had given her, she clenched her fingers around the handle.

The man released Amita's arm and held up his hands. "Easy now, this girl's father told us that she was to come with us."

"Amita, get behind me," Gargi commanded. "You are not taking her. Get in your truck and leave this place before I shoot one of you."

The thick-chested man approached her from the other side and snarled.

Gargi shuffled to watch him. She swung the gun around and tried to cover both men as they approached her.

"Stop!" Nandi ordered. "I think everyone should go home and talk to your families. You men come back tomorrow and we will discuss this again." Nandi glared at her. His eyes looked cold and hard. "Gargi, come with me."

Walking backwards, Gargi followed her brother and whipped out her hand to grab Amita as they passed her.

Once they were a distance from the truck, she stopped and pushed the gun into her pocket. "Thank you, Nandi," she called to his stiff back.

He stopped walking and came back to stand in front of her. "I did not know you were sold to be—used like that. Our father said you ran away to work in the city." He bowed his head and shrugged.

"It's okay, it wasn't your fault," she said and gestured with her hand to Amita. "We can't let these men steal these girls. Help me make the villagers understand."

"I have a daughter," he said in a resigned voice.

"You do?" she stammered. "What's her name? I can't wait to meet her. How old is she?"

"She's two." He pressed his lips together. Rubbing the back of his neck, he frowned. "Our father told me that girls are of no importance, to be used to strengthen the family's position. Yet when I look at my little one—I question him."

"He was wrong, believe me." She grabbed his arm. "I am your sister and I matter to God. Your daughter matters to God. Amita's life matters. She is only a child—and if they take her, terrible things will happen to her."

He shook off her hand. "Is it better to watch your children starve and hear them cry out because they are hungry?"

"God will provide. Let me tell you about Jesus Christ and how he came to save us."

"No! Get out of my way, sister. I will make my own decisions without you trying to brainwash me." He pushed her away and she stumbled backwards and fell to the ground.

Amita squatted beside her. "Are you all right?" she whispered. Then she burst into tears.

Gathering her close, Gargi rocked the child. Was she mistaken to get involved? Her instinct told her that these men were predators. She ran her hand over Amita's hair and wondered how old she was. She looked a little older than Shanti.

Her heart rate galloped and she raised a hand to the spot where it felt like her heart was going to explode from her chest.

She could not let them take Amita.

Gargi stood and pulled the young girl up with her. “Amita, listen to me. Do not let your father sell you to those men. They will hurt you. If he tells you to go with them, run and hide. When it’s safe, go to my car. Unlock the door and hide in the backseat and make sure you lock the door so no one can get in.”

“My father would be very angry if I disobeyed him.” Amita’s eyes widened and she shook her head.

Gargi gently cupped her face. “Sweet child, you have another Father in heaven who does not want you to get hurt. I will talk to your father tomorrow. But if he does not listen, I want you to be safe.”

Stepping away from Gargi, Amita shook her head again. “I must go. My mother will be wanting wood for the fire.”

“Do you remember the log we sat on when you showed me the way to the village?”

“Yes.”

“I will put the spare key to my car under the edge of the log, right by where we sat.”

Amita shrugged, spun around and took off toward the village.

Slowly Gargi walked toward the fallen tree. She sat in the same place and slipped the key into the hiding place. She pulled out her mobile phone and pressed Eli’s number.

There was no connection.

She looked to the spot where he’d explained about the signal bars.

The screen was blank. She had no reception.

~

The idea of setting a date for Ashok's birthday had never entered Eli's mind. His frown deepened. He was glad the boy had agreed to stay with his parents for now; it was one less thing he had to worry about.

His father had reassured him that he was doing the right thing leaving Ashok in Australia, yet his arms longed to hold his young son. It still amazed him how much he loved the boy.

Placing his laptop on the table, he powered it up. Isak had told him he'd be here by 10:00 a.m. Eli glanced at his watch and saw he had half an hour before his partner would arrive.

Getting Ashok to safety after the threat from Scarface had been his immediate priority, and now he somehow had to lay down a plan. Busting into brothels and pulling out one or two girls at a time was not going to make much of a difference in a city where thousands upon thousands of women and children lived in hopelessness and torment. They needed to find the people at the top of the trafficking syndicate and expose them.

But how to do that? And would that lead them any closer to finding Khlaid?

He opened his mind map program and typed *Khlaid Mal-*

lick in the middle of the page.

That Padma had been married to this animal was unbelievable. She'd explained to him that she had believed Khlaid loved her. One month after their marriage, Khlaid had forced her to prostitute herself.

He'd used his own wife to work the streets to make money. It sounded like he had planned to do this from the beginning and only married her to force the point.

How had Khlaid and Padma become involved with the man who'd run the brothel where Charlie and Shanti had been held captive?

One note after another branched off Khlaid's name. Finally he felt like he was getting somewhere. He had direction.

His fingers tapped across the keyboard and he stopped to read the words he'd highlighted in bold.

To expose those who violate the freedom of others.

He removed the bolding from the text. He didn't want to reinvent the wheel. There already were a lot of good organizations bringing awareness of human trafficking and trying to educate the world to stand up against slavery.

So what did God want him to do? Scratching his chin, he stood and went to gaze out the window.

The low blanket of cloud made the view before him bleak. He squinted and rubbed his eyes. Right now he wanted to find Khlaid, yet Khlaid was just one of many.

If he did find Khlaid, what then?

They needed evidence to hold him—and Charlie, along with others, would have to press charges against him. Did he want to put her through a court case? Could they trust the justice system of Mumbai?

His sister was adamant she'd stand up in court and give evidence against Khlaid and the man the police had already charged with the murder of Shanti. They needed to send out a clear message to those who thought they were above the law.

Slavery would not be tolerated.

His blood boiled when he remembered what had happened to Shanti. Ashok's sister had been tortured in such a way that Eli had wanted to kill the man responsible.

But Charlie had shown him what it was like to forgive, and if she could live out her life showing such grace, who was he to hold a grudge and have murder in his heart?

"Lord, your Word says in the book of Isaiah, 'The Spirit of the Sovereign Lord is on me, because the Lord has anointed me to proclaim good news to the poor—freedom for the captives'. Instead of shame, Lord God, give the girls rescued a double portion, instead of disgrace let them rejoice in your inheritance!"

As he paced around the room, words burst from his mouth. "You, oh Lord, love justice. You hate wrongdoing. I commit myself to walk in your ways and with your help expose Khlaid and others like him."

The air in the room smelt different. Sweeter. Eli dropped to his knees. He spread his arms across the carpet and lay facedown.

Never before had he felt the presence of God so strongly.

Son, I am with you always, to the very end of the age.

Tears flooded his eyes and he twisted to sit with his legs outstretched. "Jesus, I love you," he whispered. "I need your strength, your peace."

A niggling thought tried to push through his mind. He was asking for God's strength yet he knew he had his own agenda. He wanted justice, yes—but he also wanted to remove any risk of harm to his family, and Khlaid was a risk.

Standing, he crossed the room and dropped into a chair. If the moment came and he had Khlaid before him, what would he do?

Kill him. Eli knew the thought wasn't from God.

He wanted to slam his fists into the man's face and make him unrecognizable. Every time he saw his sister, he saw the scars Khlaid's brutality had carved on her face.

Was it wrong to want revenge? Eli's head dipped in shame.

How did Charlie do it? How did she manage to remain sweet amongst such evil?

You will seek me and find me when you search for me with all your heart.

He picked up his Bible and fanned the pages. Then his gaze slid across the open page. "Jesus stopped and called over, 'What do you want from me?'

"They said, 'Master, we want our eyes opened. We want to see!'"

Eli's eyes smarted. "That's it, Lord! I want to see. I know these guys were physically blind, but so am I."

His chest tightened and his mind ran over the implications of asking such a prayer. If he were to see, really see the truth as God would have him see it, how would he respond? What would be expected of him?

The banging at the door sounded like someone was slamming a log into it. Wiping the moisture off his face, Eli hastened to open the door.

His lips curled at the welcome sight before him.

Isak had raised his booted foot and was about to kick at the door. In each hand he held a Styrofoam cup with liquid slopping across the lids. Eli couldn't help but laugh.

"Thought you were never going to answer," Isak complained. "Coffee, just as you like it." He held out the cup as he walked through the door.

"Thanks." Eli took a sip.

"You don't look so good, my friend." Isak raised one eyebrow.

Eli took another drink and enjoyed the strong flavor of brewed coffee. What could he say, that he'd just had an encounter with God and felt undone by the fact that God was his friend?

"If there is any sadness that I can eliminate for you," Isak asked waving his hands, "you tell me, yes?"

"I'm all good, mate. Come and sit down." Crossing the small room, Eli lowered himself into the seat by his laptop.

Isak lifted his cup. "Such nice tea. So refreshing, not like your dull coffee."

"I think we've had this conversation before, Isak. You waste your time trying to convert me to your feminine ways." Eli laughed and slapped Isak on the back just as he went to take a sip of tea.

Brushing the spilt liquid off his shirt, Isak scowled. "If I thought you did that on purpose, I might have to lock you up."

Eli raised his eyebrows and then cocked his head. "Have you any news?"

"Yes. I had a friendly talk with a vendor on Apollo Pier Road." He slapped his head. "I will never get used to the change of street names. It is hard enough remembering what the streets were once called—now I have to remember the old names before I can know the new names. I meant to say Chhatrapati Shivaji Marg Street! Such a problem for a man like me who has an ageing brain."

"You were talking to a vendor?" Eli reminded him.

"Yes, yes. There has been discontent on the streets about a change in management."

"What do you mean?"

"We see crime happening, but there is order to crime. To step outside the rules on the street can cause death and a change in hierarchy."

"Do you think these things are connected to Khlaid? To the brothels?"

"I can only guess, but yes, maybe."

"Did your vendor give you a name? Place?" Eli sat forward in his chair.

"No name, but he was frightened. Seems this new man is to be feared. I got information on where to find a street guard who may lead us to him."

"You've lost me. Street guard? Is this some sort of street jargon?" Eli gripped the table. This could lead to something.

"Street guards patrol the women outside the brothels. People can buy time with women and take them back to their motels—or use them wherever. Just another name for a pimp and the money goes to them."

Eli sucked in a deep breath. He'd seen furtive couples in dark alleyways and walked away, closing his mind to the fact that the woman may not have wanted to be there.

"Are you still with me, Eli?" Isak squinted. "These guards are employees, pawns in the play of things. Let us finish up here and take a little drive, shall we?"

Swallowing the remaining coffee, Eli scrunched up his cup. Finally they had something to go on.

Chapter 18

Pulling her scarf tighter around her face, Padma strolled down the street. She'd walked this road before but never noticed the house with the red door.

As she crossed the road, she glanced nervously around to see if there was anyone watching her. She'd come early, hoping to find her brother alone in the small house church.

Taking quick breaths, she stood in front of the door and raised her hand to knock. Her knuckles stopped inches from the door.

What if Tanvir didn't believe she'd changed? She took a step back.

She'd lived years without her brother; what made her think he'd be interested in getting to know her now? He was the pastor of this small church and she was a no-body, a woman who'd played a part in the murder and torture of innocent children.

She couldn't do it. The thought of his rejection tormented her. Dipping her head, she turned from the door. Her shoulders hunched, and she started to retrace her steps. Her gaze locked on the ground, and her feet felt like lead as she shuffled along the street.

She wouldn't matter to him. No one had ever cared about her, apart from Charlie. Yes, Charlie had told her she was important and that the past could be forgiven, but she didn't really believe her. The thought of seeing the disgust in her brother's eyes was enough to send her running.

Her body felt numb. As much as she wanted to be brave enough to face him, she just couldn't. Tears welled in her eyes and she blinked to stop them spilling. She stumbled and slammed into something hard.

Tilting her head back, she glanced up into the softest eyes she'd ever seen.

"Are you all right? I am most sorry. I saw you heading my way but got lost in my thoughts and bumped right into you."

Padma's eyes widened and she gasped. The tears she'd tried to capture spilled down her face.

"Please let me help you," he offered. "Are you hurt?" He bent down and gazed into her eyes.

"I—I am fine. It wasn't your fault. I wasn't watching where I was going."

He placed a finger under her chin and raised her face gently. "Padma?" Tanvir's eyes widened and the finger under her chin shook. "Is that you?"

Clearing her throat, she tried to speak. "I—yes," she sobbed.

He pulled her close. "My little sister, I've waited so long to hold you." His voice caught and she glanced up.

Tears flowed freely down his face and he smiled.

Her heart pounded. "Tanvir, I came to see you, but I—I don't know what to say to you," she stammered.

"You do not have to say anything. All I care about is that you are here. Come with me across the street, we can talk."

"I have done terrible things," she blurted out. "You must know that I am a bad person—before you let me into your heart."

"We are all bad, my sister. The Bible says all have sinned and fall short of the glory of God, and all are justified freely by his grace through the redemption that came by Christ Jesus."

She shook her head. "Grace is foreign to me. I have seen the love of your God through my friend Charlie, but she is a good person…"

"Charlotte Turner? Is this who you are speaking of?"

"Yes. I live at Shanti's Rest and help Charlotte—Charlie."

"Have you—" he gulped a deep breath and placed his hand over his heart, "were you in the brothel with Charlie?"

Heat flamed up her neck and she pulled away from his gentle hands. What could she tell him? Yes, she had been there… but had she really been a prisoner?

Avoiding eye contact, she shrugged. "I was there because of the choices I made. It is not as it was for Charlie."

"Never mind that now. Come and meet my wife and child." Tanvir laughed and picked up her hand. "They will be so delighted to meet you. I have told them of my little sister, and at times they have thought you are a figment of my imagination."

"Maybe another time," she murmured. "I need to be going." Her lips quivered and she inched away from him.

"What are you afraid of, that we will not love you? Do not allow your fear to steal our love for you. Come," he ordered.

The fight left her and she followed him meekly. But what he said could not be true. They would not love her and be her family. Not once they learned the truth of what she had done. He would realize that soon enough.

~

Raising her arms above her head, Gargi stretched to release the kink from her back. She looked across the small room and watched her mother drop heavily to the ground and shuffle her bottom on the hard wooden plank.

Gargi screwed up her face; she'd gotten used to sitting on a chair and having a table to prepare food on. She absently wound her hair into a bun and her heart warmed at the picture of her mam.

Grimy wrinkles added to the color of her chocolate skin, giving evidence of her mother's dislike of washing in the chilly river.

"Mam, can I help you with that?" Gargi hunched down beside her mother and reached to take the heavy pot.

The slap on her hand surprised Gargi and she pulled back.

"Dirty hands! Go fetch fuel." Her mother pointed to the wicker basket by the door.

The basket had seen better days and the strap that was meant to sit over her forehead was badly frayed. Gargi remembered the basket well, and she caressed the old strap as she recalled her childhood and how free she'd felt while out collecting wood.

"Who usually gets your wood?" She could hear the strain in her voice.

Her mother grunted and continued peeling an onion.

Clicking the door shut quietly behind her, Gargi swung the basket over her shoulder. Disappointment gnawed at her mind like a chisel shaping a piece of wood. When she was a child her mother had hardly spoken to her, yet now Gargi wanted it to be different. She wanted a mother-daughter relationship like she saw Charlie share with Mrs Turner. She wanted to love her mother, but the way her mother responded to her with little respect or interest—hurt.

Jesus, you tell me to honor my mother, but how do I do this when I don't even like her?

She dipped her head as she walked past several people standing in front of a shrine to some Hindu goddess. She'd grown up here and knew of the superstition and witchcraft that went on. Her mother believed in ghosts, and Gargi remembered her praying to spirits when sickness was in the house.

Shivering, she hurried her steps toward the bush where she could gather some wood. As she roamed farther from the village, darkness descended upon her like a cloak of fog.

She glanced nervously down the path she'd taken and slowed her steps. All her adult life she'd felt frightened and believed she was not her own. First her parents used her and then she'd been sold to wicked men.

When she'd been a prisoner in the brothel, she'd dreamed of the day she could make her own decisions and be free. She released a deep sigh as she realized she could be free no matter what her circumstances.

Charlie had shown her Jesus while in captivity and demonstrated that no one could own her thoughts or actions. Yes they could hurt her physically, but they couldn't take away her dignity unless she let them.

Her freedom had come at a price to her Lord, and she never wanted to minimize the cost.

"Lord, you've set me free from sin and death," she whispered into the chilling air. "I always longed for freedom, but I didn't realize what it really was."

A rustle of leaves to her left startled her. Stopping, Gargi listened. She peered into the shadows, expecting to see someone watching her, but no one seemed to be nearby. She had to get a grip on her thoughts. Her hand tightened on the strap and she bent to pick up some twigs and snapped them to fit in the basket.

This was a place where evil lurked. Witches were encouraged to cast spells, and payments were made to support their work with the spirits.

The waning light made the shadows seem more sinister, and her feet itched to retrace her steps. Stumbling forward, she tripped over something on the path and glanced down.

The small shoe was scuffed but in good condition. Gargi knew the value placed on such things here. She was sure it was the same type of shoe that Amita had worn. Hugging the shoe to her chest as if it were the child itself, Gargi looked for any other sign of a child.

"Hello," she called.

The ground looked disturbed, as if there had been a scuffle, and the undergrowth was torn. Her muscles tensed and she was ready to fight.

If the men from the truck had decided to steal children now would be the perfect time as families were preparing the evening meal. Stuffing the shoe into the basket, she raced back toward the village.

Her mind whirled as she navigated the tight path. Who could help her? The only person she knew of any significance was her brother, and she wasn't sure where he lived. Would he go against all their father had taught him and stand with her?

Throwing open the door to her mother's house, she jumped as it smacked against the inner wall, startling her mother.

"Mam, where does Nandi live?" she asked breathlessly. She was desperate to see if the truck was still by the paddies.

"Tomorrow you visit. Where is wood?"

Gargi's eyes widened. Didn't her mother see how distressed she was?

"No!" she yelled. "I need his help, tell me." She charged across the distance between them, then grabbed her mother's arm and yanked her to her feet.

Her mother's unblinking steely eyes met hers. "You want him, go look. I don't answer to you. Get out of my house!"

"Mam, please. I think a child has been snatched from the village. I need to help her."

Her mother placed her hands on her hips. "You can't change what is."

Gargi started to turn toward the door then spun back to face her mother. "You're wrong. Things change if people care. I care!" she screamed.

Striding from the house, she tried to prepare herself. What could she do if she found the truck full of children and the men present? It would be foolhardy to try and stop them on her own. If she followed them, she could see where they were going, then get help.

She retraced her steps to the house. She silently entered and pushed the few things she'd taken out of her bag into the front pocket.

Her mother stood watching her.

Gargi noticed a deep groove dug into her mother's forehead; her arms hung loosely at her sides.

"Mam, I'm leaving. I—I love you. You are my mother." She spoke urgently, as if this were her last opportunity to share her heart with the cold woman before her. "Do you want me to come back?"

Holding her breath, Gargi waited for an answer. She searched for any sign of softening, any indication that there was hope for them.

Her mother turned and went back to her cooking.

Tears sprung to Gargi's eyes and spilled over. She sucked in a breath through her teeth and wanted to shriek abuse at the woman who'd given her birth. Was she not worthy of an answer?

Everything in her screamed to leave and never return.

Not seven times, but seventy seven times.

Gasping, Gargi longed to ignore the verse that dropped into her mind. *No, Lord, I can't forgive her. She has no feelings for me.*

Her body felt frozen, and to take another step would crack her heart in two. It was easier to reject her mother and tell herself that she didn't care. Why give her mother power to hurt her? She didn't want to! Surely she had a right to—hate.

Gargi's mouth dropped open in shock. She wanted to hate her mother. She wanted to hit back in—revenge. The shaking inside her intensified and she gnawed on her lower lip.

Jesus. Help me. Her pulse thumped wildly in her neck and she cupped it with her hand. She needed to go. A few moments could make all the difference.

Turning her back on her mother, she dashed to the door. Her fingers locked on the handle but stiffened.

The opposite of hate is love, she knew this. Her head dipped in submission.

In my strength, daughter.

Retracing her steps, she crossed the room and hunched beside her mother. She cupped her mother's face with both her hands.

"I love you, Mam." She brushed her lips across the leathery skin and gently hugged her frail body. "I will be back."

Chapter 19

"Ashok, can you come with me into the garage?" Grandpa grinned. "I have an early birthday present for you, something I've made."

"You made me something?" Ashok had asked before if he could go into the garage and see what his grandpa did in there, but he hadn't been allowed.

"Macy," Bill called. "Ashok and I will be in the garage." He placed his arm across Ashok's shoulders and led him out of the house.

Excitement bubbled up inside Ashok. He'd been so curious to see what was behind the locked door. It was like a cave that his grandpa entered each day, and when he came out, he was smiling and often whistling.

Ashok's lips twitched and he hadn't even entered the garage yet.

As the key was pushed into the lock, Ashok held his breath

and peered around his grandfather into the large shed. His mouth dropped open at the big machines and he gazed around in amazement.

"Come into my workshop. These machines are called lathes. I use them to make wooden toys and other wooden things."

"Toys?" Had his grandpa made him a toy? He'd never owned a toy until his baap had given him a ball.

"I like to make trucks and cars and donate them to places where children are in need of toys. But I've something more special for you. Do you want to see?"

More special than a truck? Ashok wanted a truck; he could see a red one on the bench in the corner and wanted to go get it.

Bill laughed. "You can have any of the toys you see, son. But first I want to give you something I hope you will treasure."

"What is it?" Ashok turned away from the trucks. He watched as his grandpa went to a cabinet and opened a drawer. Leaning forward, he tried to see what was in his grandpa's hand, but it was wrapped in a cloth. It wasn't very big and Ashok thought even he could probably hold it in one hand.

A wide grin opened his mouth and he bounced from foot to foot. He couldn't imagine what was under the cloth.

Grandpa stretched out his hands with the small gift.

Ashok reached out and pulled off the cloth. He'd never seen anything so amazing. The color of the wood was golden brown and it shone and reflected light. "It's a bird," he said.

"Not just any bird, it's an eagle."

Ashok ran his finger over the smoothly carved wood and touched the sharp beak. He liked the way the wings were stretched out in flight. It looked strong.

Looking up, he smiled. "Thank you, Grandpa. I like it very much."

"Eagles have large wings which allow them to soar high above the earth. They have keen, powerful eyes and can see much better than people." Bill rubbed Ashok's shoulder. "Come and sit over here, I want to read you something from the Bible about eagles."

Ashok held the eagle carefully. It was of great value to him. He followed his grandpa across the room and sat on a stool.

Ruffling through the pages, Bill stopped and pointed at the words on the page. "But those who hope in the Lord will renew their strength. They will soar on wings like eagles; they will run and not grow weary, they will walk and not be faint."

"I want to be like an eagle." Ashok stretched out his arms.

"Me too," Bill agreed. "I think we can soar above pain and bad thoughts. God will help both you and me to fly high above the world. He will help us know the truth, what do you think?"

Ashok cupped the eagle in his palms. The wooden carving reminded him that God was strong and he could be strong with God's help. He glanced up and nodded.

"Can you teach me this verse, Grandpa?"

~

The day had dawned bright and the richness of the sunshine lifted Charlotte's spirits. Pushing her hand through her mother's arm, Charlotte enjoyed the smells of summer as they strolled along the gravel path toward the café.

She had fond memories of special times as a family and her mother had often been heard to say, "'Let's create a memory." She'd had a fun childhood and it was the simple things she treasured. Memories of playing hide-and-seek in the house and running from room to room, trying to find Eli. Planting bulbs in the garden and watching for them to poke through the soil.

The garden center café was one of her mother's favorite places and Charlotte wanted to create a memory of today for her.

Charlotte's gaze hungrily soaked up her mother's soft complexion; she was trying to memorize every detail.

Shaking away the thought, she stopped to touch an artificial butterfly that was poked into a colorful potted plant. The fake wings flittered in the slight breeze and Charlotte drew a deep breath. *Shanti.*

Would she always associate butterflies with Shanti? Charlotte recalled the story she'd told Shanti about the caterpillar breaking free from the cocoon and rising up to be a beautiful, new creature.

It was times like this that she missed Shanti so much.

Shanti would have loved walking around these plants and seeing the bright, summer flowers.

"Why don't we buy a few of these butterflies," Macy suggested. "You could take them back to Shanti's Rest to add some color to the place."

"What a great idea," Charlotte agreed.

"I'm paying. I'll ask them to pack them up for us so we can collect them on our way out. Do you want to go and get us a table?"

"Okay." Charlotte moved through the plants. She wondered what it would be like to buy potted plants for a house. Her chest tightened at the thought of setting up a home with Phillip and all it implied.

The sounds of people talking in the café seemed to amplify and join together. Her skin became clammy, and the idea of relaxing amongst all these people didn't seem like a good idea. She glanced around, trying to find a table that was a little separate.

A touch on her arm startled her, and she spun around defensively.

"There's a table over there, Charlie." Her mother patted her arm and smiled.

Charlotte wove her way through the tables to a lovely outside verandah.

Settling into her chair, Charlotte closed her eyes for a moment. Coming home to Australia was a new dose of culture shock. It seemed unbelievable that the things she once took for granted triggered sensations of sharp awareness.

A scraping sound caused her to open her eyes, and she

watched her mother lift the wrought-iron chair and pull it closer to the table.

"I hope you're hungry. I've ordered up a storm." Macy bent over and placed her handbag on the ground. Relaxing into her chair, she glanced across at Charlotte.

Charlotte knew the moment her mother realized something was wrong.

"I'm okay, Mum," she reassured her. "I just need a minute to adjust to being in a café. Silly, I know."

"Do you want to go?"

"No. I want to be here with you. In fact, I've been looking forward to having you to myself."

"The time's gone so fast. Are you sure you're ready to go back? You could stay another week." Her mother's voice was warm and inviting.

"Part of me wants to, yet—India is home for me now. Let's not talk about my going just yet."

As the food was placed before them, Charlotte laughed. "Who is going to eat all this?"

"We are. We're in no hurry and can just nibble our way through it."

Looking down at the table, Charlotte felt her mouth go dry.

Her poor mother. "I'm sorry, Mum," she said. "I know it must be hard for you having both Eli and me in India." Reaching out, she touched her mother's hand.

Macy intertwined their fingers. "Charlie, it's okay. I'd be lying if I said I didn't have moments when I felt hard done by, but who said life was easy?"

"You could always move to Mumbai." Charlotte clutched her mother's hand. "Dad's working less these days and you could be the mum at Shanti's Rest."

Macy shook her head. "This is home for us. I can't picture us living in Mumbai—but I do foresee many visits."

Picking up her mug of steaming tea, Charlotte breathed in the berry essences. As she took a careful sip of the hot liquid her gaze rested on the couple at the next table. Her heart flipped when the young man leaned across the table and kissed the woman on the cheek. The woman's laugh sounded happy and free.

Dropping her gaze, she stared into the darkness of her tea. She wanted to laugh like that.

"Mum, Phillip loves me. We kissed."

"Oh, sweetheart, that's wonderful."

"At first I pulled back—instinctively. I couldn't help myself. He was so patient with me. Told me he'd wait. But the thing is…" She turned her head to watch a small sparrow, which was perching close to them on a thin rail.

Are not two sparrows sold for a penny? Yet not one of them will fall to the ground outside your Father's care.

A small smile tugged her lips. *Yes I know you are faithful, Lord. Thank you.*

"Charlie?"

"Oh, sorry. What was I saying?"

"About Phillip."

"Mmm. I feel robbed of being able to be spontaneous with him. I had to tell myself over and over again that I was with Phillip and that he wouldn't hurt me. I don't understand why my mind and heart know one thing, yet my body responds differently."

"Have you spoken to your counselor about this?"

Charlotte nodded. "She tells me I have to keep telling myself the truth—and I agree with her, but I want an instant freedom from this."

Macy picked up her knife and cut a savory scone in half. She placed a piece on each plate and then shifted her piece around with her fork.

Charlotte yanked the material of her top away from her neck and then made herself relax back in her seat. "I'm sorry, Mum. Have I ruined your appetite? Maybe we should talk about this another time."

"No, now's a good time. Don't worry if we don't eat all this. I thought we could take some back home for your father." Macy placed her fork down. "I'm no counselor, but I do love you and I believe you can work through this." Leaning forward, she glanced around to see if anyone was listening. No one was. She smiled conspiratorially. "Sex is really special in a marriage, there's no arguing that. A gift from God to be treasured between two people. Can I be honest with you, Charlie?"

"You need to ask?" Charlotte inched forward on her seat and rested her elbows on the table.

"As I've gotten older, I've come to realize that sex is such a small part of a marriage. Yes, it's good—but if you did a graph on how much time you spend doing it and compare it to the other important parts of marriage, it would be a tiny fraction."

Laughter spilled out of Charlotte's mouth. She couldn't help it. Hearing her mother speak like this was so alien to her.

"Now you listen to your mother. Holding hands is just as important, rubbing your man's neck if he's been working hard, preparing a good meal even if it's his turn to cook." Macy gestured to the other women in the café. "If we were to ask them what was the most romantic thing their husbands ever did for them, I can just about guarantee none of them would say good sex."

"I want it to be good," Charlotte mumbled.

"And it will be. You deserve this man. It's so evident he loves you. He cares about how you feel. You are more than a body to him, and you need to believe him when he says he'll wait until you're ready."

"What if I'm never ready? What if I have to pretend I like it and live a lie?" Tears welled up in her eyes and she pushed her plate away.

Macy pulled her chair closer to Charlotte's. "I wish I could make this easier for you, but I can't. You don't have to marry him, you could remain single."

"But I love him."

"Then start acting like it," Macy commanded. "Did you hear me? Act like it until it becomes your reality. Look into his eyes and see the man *he* is, not the men who used you. Show him you love him by thinking about him, doing special little things to make him see your affection."

"Like what?" Charlotte pushed her hand through her hair. Surely it should be easier than this.

"I don't know, anything. Often the woman is the romantic

one and instigates things in a marriage. Like I tell your father I want to go on a picnic, make all the food, work out where to go—and he drives the car. I get to enjoy his company, hold his hand, sit outdoors in a lovely setting, and it's romantic."

"I could do a picnic."

"Another thing, men respond to affirmation. What things do you like about Phillip?"

Charlotte stared into space for a moment then looked up and smiled. "I love the way he loves children and interacts with them. He treats them with respect and care. He's passionate about his job and doesn't count the cost. He could be in a medical practice somewhere making lots of money but chooses to work with the poor."

"What else?" Macy relaxed back in her chair with a sigh.

"He's funny. When he and Eli get going, they make me laugh." Charlotte chuckled. This was working. "He found me, Mum. If it hadn't been for Phillip, Gargi could have died. He trusted my judgment in the brothel, and as hard as it was at the time, he took Gargi to safety and left me there."

"That must have been a terrible time for him, leaving the woman he loved behind and taking another woman away who may not even live," Macy agreed.

"So how do I show him I admire him?"

"You have to work that out, honey. Try to relax and enjoy yourself."

"I did enjoy going to Manly beach with him. Maybe I can spend another day showing him more of Sydney. I think he'd like to see the Blue Mountains, and it's a nice drive. Can I borrow your car again?"

~

"There." Isak pointed.

Eli looked through the car window and watched the man pace back and forth on the corner of the street. He stopped and lit a cigarette then threw away the match.

Glancing back at Isak, Eli lifted his eyebrows. "What now?"

"We need to see him interact with a girl, then we have a little leverage to persuade him to talk."

"So we wait." Why was it so hard to wait? Patience develops character; his father had drummed it into him. He could even quote the Bible verse that confirmed this—yet he wanted action.

Isak rested his hands on the steering wheel. "Have you heard from Gargi?"

"Not since the last time I told you. We agreed to phone each day yet I haven't been able to get through to her."

"Poor reception, I'm sure."

"I've never experienced this helplessness before. Since coming to India to look for Charlie, time and time again I've had to adjust to long periods of waiting. I have to tell you, Isak, it doesn't sit well with me."

"She will need to drive to where reception is better. Maybe she will think of this."

"One can hope." Eli shrugged.

Last night had dragged and he'd lain awake, thoughts reeling, because once again he'd found himself in the middle of a manhunt. He rubbed his forehead and scrunched up his eyes, trying to keep himself alert.

"We have action," Isak announced.

Sliding out of the car, Eli ambled across the street behind Isak, who seemed in no hurry to approach the man.

"Hello, my friend," Isak said cheerfully. "What do we have here?" He gestured to the young woman with money extended in her hand. "Doing a little business, are we?"

The man flinched and jerked back.

Flashing his police badge, Isak grabbed the man's arm and pulled him toward the car.

The woman couldn't be more than seventeen, and the haunted, frightened look on her face spoke volumes. Eli swallowed.

"Do you speak English?" He motioned to his mouth.

"A little. You want me?" she murmured drunkenly and pawed at his arm.

Grabbing her hand, he pushed a business card into it. "If you go to this place, you'll be safe and not have to do this work."

She glanced at the words. "I no read. I no go, I belong to him," she pointed to the man being interrogated by Isak.

"No, you don't belong to him. My friend is a policeman and we will help you get to safety. Shanti's Rest is a safe house for girls like you who have been forced into prostitution. Please wait here, then we will take you there."

"How I know you not worse than him?" She held her hands up like a shield between them.

"You have to trust me." Sweat broke out on his forehead.

"I trust no one." With gawky movements, she took off.

Eli wanted to charge after her, but knew it was hopeless. The girl would only be more frightened if he pursued her. He strode over to join his friend.

The pimp looked nervous. His eyes bulged out of their sockets and his breath came quickly. His chin trembled.

"Please, they are watching us! You are causing my death, saab," he muttered.

Eli pretended to ignore him. "Has he given you any information, Isak?"

Shaking his head, Isak shrugged. "Seems he's lost his memory."

Eli grabbed the man's shoulders and clawed his fingers into his flesh. "Give me a name," he snarled, "or so help me—"

"You can't hurt me, you are police." The man spat a gob of saliva on Eli's shoe.

Eli jumped back instinctively then regretted showing weakness. "You animal." He scrapped the spittle off with the sole of his other shoe.

Slinging his arm over the man's shoulders, Eli sneered. "My friend here is a police officer, but not me."

Forcibly helping the man into the backseat of the car, Eli motioned for Isak to join them. "Let's take a little ride, shall we?"

Eli made eye contact with Isak over the top of the car. He had no idea what he was doing, or how he was going to extract any information from the weasel in the backseat.

The man had said they were being watched. Eli's gaze

swept the street. Had it been this quiet when they'd arrived? Not even a car moved, and the silence felt foreign to this part of the city. It was like a switch had been turned off and everyone was in hiding.

Was it possible that news of what they were doing would get back to Khlaid? Or were they making a new enemy? Apprehension spiraled through his veins, and he tensed and straightened his shoulders.

Isak slammed his door.

Eli couldn't forget the hopelessness etched onto the young woman's face. He turned his back on the car and addressed the street.

"He will guard the feet of his faithful servants, but the wicked will be silenced in the place of darkness. It is not by strength that one prevails; those who oppose the Lord will be broken!" he yelled. "The Most High will thunder from heaven; the Lord will judge the ends of the earth."

Isak leaned out the car window and beckoned with his arm. "Eli, get in the car!"

Returning to the car, Eli buckled his safety belt. He tried to calm his breathing.

"What the heck was all that about?" Isak pushed the key into the car's ignition.

Eli shrugged. He didn't know where the words had come from, but he'd felt a righteous anger at the way evil could cause such destruction.

The words were from the Bible, that much he knew. He'd read them somewhere and they'd popped back into his mind to be spoken to the evil lurking on the street. Eli felt exuberant.

Twisting in his seat, he smiled at the stranger. "Mate, I'm sorry to put you in this predicament. You may not understand this, but I'm in the army of El Eloah's and he is more powerful than any person you will ever know."

The man slid farther away from him, and Eli laughed.

"You have been misled," Eli informed him. "Let me lead you to the one who can save you from yourself."

"Let me out of the car," the man screamed. "You are a crazy man!"

"I'm not disagreeing with you," Isak stated. "But I'd listen to him if you want to get out of this alive."

"I'll offer you a deal," Eli said. "You tell me who you work for—where to find him and everything you know connected to the prostituting of young women—and I'll help you make a fresh start."

"Why would you help me?" the man muttered.

"Let's just say I'm a generous man."

"And if I don't help you?"

"Then I can't be held responsible for your death. The choice is yours. You have until we get to the police station to decide."

"Wait, don't take me to the police station. You don't understand, there are—um, people who know me there, who would kill me and hurt my family if it leaked out that I spoke with you." He held his hands together as if in prayer. His face paled and he closed his eyes. "Have mercy on me, I beg you."

"Whom do you work for? A name!" Isak pulled the car to the curb outside the station.

"Hassy. That's the name of the woman who collects the money. I am left with little to live on and my family struggles to survive. I have no choice, please believe me."

"You always have a choice, my friend." Eli wanted to shake some sense into the man. The path he was walking would destroy him. "Where would we find this person called Hassy?"

"This I do not know. She comes to me on a Wednesday by platform three, Bandra Station."

"She'll expect you tomorrow. What time and what does she look like?"

"Yes, tomorrow. If news of my being picked up hasn't already reached her. The call girl may have returned to the base."

"Base? Tell us about this place."

Eli watched as Isak scribbled notes with his pencil in his small notebook.

The scratching sound of graphite on paper made him frown. His senses seemed to have stepped up a notch, and it felt like his vision and hearing was sharper, clearer, if that were possible.

He narrowed his eyes and looked through his slitted lids. It was like seeing for the first time. Really seeing.

He visualized the man stepping off secure ground and falling headlong into an abyss, screaming, "Help me, why didn't you tell me?"

Eli tried to shake the thought that it was his responsibility to tell the guy about Jesus.

Lord, I have things to do here. What do you want me to do, stop every time I meet a bad man and tell him about you?

"Eli, tell him," Isak ordered.

"What? What did you say?" Eli snapped.

"You weren't listening, were you?" Isak threw his arms in the air. "Can you please pay attention? Tell him how he can make a fresh start—you told him you'd help him. Although it is not our responsibility to fix the mess he's got himself in."

"A fresh start? I—I see," Eli nodded and licked his lips. "Get out of the car and I will show you."

Moving to lean on the bonnet of the car, Eli waited for the man to join him. He had no idea what he'd say but had to trust that the words would come out right.

Isak stood behind the man and Eli could see the question on his friend's face.

The man crossed his arms and looked jittery.

Eli's heart raced. "El Eloah is one of the names of my God. It means strong, all-powerful. But God has other names as well, one being Yahweh-Rapha, the God who heals. God loves you. He sent his only son, Jesus Christ, to the world to save you—and if you believe in him, you will not die but have eternal life."

"You are mad! Is this what you offer me as a fresh start? I don't believe this." He slapped his hand against his head.

"The Lord sees a man's heart and now is the time for you to repent," Eli said firmly. "You are a liar and a thief. You say you have a family to support, yet you live alone. God has seen all you do—you cannot hide from him."

Shuffling his feet, the man avoided Eli's gaze.

"How do you know I have no family?" He wrung his

hands together. "If I believe what you say, and ay, repent, will this stop me from going to prison? Being arrested?"

"No. You will be forgiven by God and have a hope for the future, but you will still have to pay the penalty of your crimes here. And if that means you get prosecuted for pimping, so be it."

"Then you offer me nothing!" he yelled.

"I offer you everything," Eli calmly countered.

The man screwed up his face and swore. "Take me away from this fool."

Isak shrugged and grabbed the man's arm. "Eli, I'll call you." Isak threw the car keys over the bonnet. "You may as well go. Take my car and drop it back later."

Regret pressed down on Eli's chest. He wanted to stop the man from walking willingly into his own destruction.

How must Jesus feel when people reject him?

Eli didn't want to care about a pimp, but he did.

Charlie had tried to explain to him that praying for Khlaid had helped her forgive him. She'd wanted Khlaid to turn to God and be saved.

Eli watched the man hurry alongside Isak toward the police station as if trying to put as much distance between himself and the crazy man as possible.

"Wait!" Eli called out.

The man turned and spat on the ground.

Opening his mouth, Eli went to call him to come back, but the words froze on his tongue.

To love a stranger—an enemy—was too new to him.

Chapter 20

Slinging the backpack on her shoulders, Gargi sprinted toward the truck. As she negotiated the path, images of how nasty she'd been to the other girls imprisoned with her in the brothel bombarded her mind. She'd only ever thought of herself. It was a matter of survival. Each day had dragged into the next; she'd hated her life and at times wanted to die. Now she longed to save even one girl from the abuse she'd experienced.

Sweat formed on her forehead and trickled down her face as she ran. She wasn't used to running, and the bag on her back seemed to get heavier with each step.

Would Nandi have helped her if she'd known where to find him? He was a stranger to her, yet she remembered loving him. Her feet slipped on the uneven path and she staggered to regain her balance. Stopping, she heaved in a breath and tried to work out where she was.

If she was in the right place, she should be able to break through the undergrowth and be at the field where the truck had been parked.

The sound of some animal whimpering sent shivers through Gargi. The noise changed, became human and she craned her head in the direction of the crying. Had she imagined it? Fear gripped her chest as she changed direction.

Her foot snapped on a twig and she paused, waiting to see if there was any response to the noise she'd made.

There was a shuffling to her left and she spun around.

"Who's there?" Gargi whispered, peering into the darkness.

Inching forward, Gargi reached into the undergrowth and pushed aside some dead branches.

Amita was huddled in a fetal position, sobbing.

"It's okay, Amita. You're safe now. Can you help me get you out of there?" Gargi reached into the small hole that the girl had squashed into.

Burying her head in Gargi's shoulder, Amita shivered. "My father—he—he—" She hiccupped and tears streamed down her face.

"Did he order you to go to the truck?"

"He sold me. Mam was crying and told me it was my duty to go and be a good girl. I argued with Baap, and—and he hit me," she cried, rubbing her swollen face. "I ran away before they could get me. I wanted to go to your car, but my—my legs have frozen up like my—broken heart," she cried dramatically. Her shoulders shook and she curled into a ball.

"Amita, I need to check the truck. There might be others

we can help. Will you come with me or do you want to go to my car?"

"I can't go on my own, they might find me," Amita whispered.

"Come with me, then, but we have to go now." Turning, Gargi headed out of the woods. She couldn't wait for Amita to catch up, she felt the urgency in her heart and she needed to hurry.

Amita joined her and they sprinted across the open stretch of grass and loped around the edge of the steeply sloped paddy to remain hidden.

Slipping her backpack to the ground in the eerie quiet, Gargi squatted in the muddy trench and motioned for Amita to get down. It was hard to see; darkness had pressed down around them.

"Wait here," she whispered. "I have to get closer."

Creeping along the edge of the raised mound, she was thankful that this section wasn't flat like the rest of the field. The smell was suffocating. The field had been recently ploughed and smothered over with cow dung fertilizer. Grass tickled her ankles as she crawled away from the paddy and closer to the truck.

She could see the silhouette of two men and froze to listen to what they were saying.

"That will have to do," a gruff voice stated. "Let's get going."

"The boss wanted twenty! He'll be cursing us for so few."

"We'll blame it on the woman. Eight is better than none. Maybe we can pick another couple on the way."

"Are they secured, silenced?"

"Yes." He laughed harshly, and the sound sent shivers down Gargi's back. "I don't expect any trouble. I helped myself to the youngest and made the others watch. I threatened I'd be back for more if there was a sound from them."

Tears spilled down Gargi's cheeks and she shoved them away. Now was not the time to cry. She had to stop these men from doing any more damage to the girls than they already had. Ordering her feet to move, she slipped behind the truck and reached up to feel for the chain that was bolted to the door. The padlock mocked her and she had to still her hand from frantically yanking it. There was nothing she could do.

She sprinted away from the truck. She'd follow them, find out where they were going, and get help.

"Quick, Amita, we need to run to my car." She grabbed her backpack, slung it over her shoulder and then took Amita's hand.

The sound of the truck engine being fired made her pace quicken. She knew the road they'd have to take to leave the village, and she reassured herself she had time to follow them without being seen.

Fumbling in her bag, she located her key and opened the car door. The young girl stood before her, uncertain.

"Come with me, Amita. I'll take care of you."

"My mam?"

"I know you're only young, but if you go back to your parents, there will be another day like this one and your father will once again sell you." Gargi pulled the child close to her chest. "I'm sorry. I want you to be safe, but it has to be your decision. One day we can come back and you can see your mam again."

The girl nodded. Tears flowed unchecked down her face.

Gargi wanted to say something that would stop Amita's tears, but there were no words to change what had happened.

It was like reliving her worse nightmare. She remembered the fear in the back of truck. The stale air and not knowing what was happening. No one had talked for fear of repercussions.

She helped Amita into the car and clicked the safety belt over the girl's shoulder.

Swinging around the car, Gargi took her seat and slammed the door shut.

Eight girls. Her hands tightened on the steering wheel and she took a steadying breath. How dare they do this? Were they the same people who had taken her?

She glanced at Amita. The girl had lifted her feet to the seat and circled her arms around her knees. Her forehead rested on top of her knees and her long hair, which cascaded down her legs, hid her face.

"Honey, your parents think you're in the truck. They don't expect to see you again. When it's safe, I'll bring you back to see your mam, I promise." Reaching over, Gargi swept the hair from the child's face.

Amita's lips trembled. "No. They—they don't want me. I thought Mam loved me."

"I love you, Amita," Gargi said.

The child hugged her stomach. "No, you don't. You're just

saying that to make me feel better. If my parents don't love me, then nobody can." She turned her head and gazed out the window.

What could she say to make the child understand that it wasn't her fault that her parents were ignorant and selfish?

Rubbing her hand wearily over her eyes, Gargi decided words would never be enough to convince Amita that she loved her. She'd have to show her.

She followed the road away from the village, hoping to see the tail lights of the truck ahead of her.

It amazed her that she had the capacity to love a stranger the way she did. She wanted to wrap Amita up and protect her from further harm. She understood what it was like to be abandoned by your parents, yet she'd come back seeking—seeking what from her own mother?

Love? Did she expect to build a relationship with the nasty old woman who had birthed her?

Her shoulders ached with tension and she shifted in her seat. She turned the steering wheel and the headlights sent beams ahead of her through the darkness, following the sweeping corner. As she pulled out of the corner, twin lights twinkled in the distances.

She sat forward in the seat. It had to be the truck.

~

Walking through the entrance of the hotel, Khlaid straightened his shoulders and tried to walk without a limp. His cane clanked on the highly polished white tile floor. The sound made him want to curse.

The made-to-measure suit sat perfectly on his shoulders, and his fingers itched to stroke the expensive fabric. Lifting his chin, he acknowledged Frank as he strode toward him.

He felt impregnable, powerful. This was his time and nothing would stop him from rising to the top.

"Mr Singh, your bags have been taken to your suite and everything is in place," Frank informed him.

K. L. Singh. His new name sounded alien coming off Frank's lips. Shrugging the thought away, Khlaid glanced around his new surroundings. This place was to be his home for the next month or two and he fully intended to enjoy it.

"Good. And the meeting with Ted Calston?"

"Tomorrow morning at eleven o'clock. I took the liberty of suggesting you meet by the pool. I explained to Mr Calston that you like fresh air. He is looking forward to meeting you, boss."

Khlaid allowed himself the luxury of smiling. Money was rolling in and he'd already received part payment for the shipment of merchandise to the Middle East. He liked his new position; and if things continued to go the way he planned, then by the end of the year he would be set.

He swept his tongue over his top teeth and growled softly. He had to stop moving his tongue around his mouth looking for a gap to poke his tongue through. Shrugging, he decided old habits die hard and relaxed his shoulders.

His new appearance had cost a small fortune, but the people he worked for hadn't blinked an eye at the cost.

When he thought of what could happen to him if he let his employers down, his gut churned. There would be no questions asked. He too was disposable.

Failure was not an option.

His gaze swept over the electrical fittings that glittered in the soft lighting, and his breath hissed through his fake teeth. He'd never been in such a place before today; if he'd tried to enter this hotel a year ago, they'd have laughed at him and led him to the door.

He hated all they stood for and was determined to use these people and bend them to do his will.

Power was best exercised over others when they didn't realize they were pawns. His fingers stiffened and he flexed them. The twitching in his left eyelid was a sure sign of pressure building.

He needed release. Needed to feel his hands spanning someone's throat before the tension inside him burst and destroyed his chances of a fresh start.

Laughter drew his gaze to the reception desk. The blond man leaning against the counter talking to a woman caught his attention. His forehead puckered and he glanced at Frank. The man's resemblance to Charlotte was unmistakable.

"Eli Turner, boss. He calls in here at least once a week to catch up with Ted Calston."

"I see. Perhaps now is a good time for an introduction."

"I would leave it until you've officially met Calston. There would be no explanation as to how you know who Eli Turner is."

Khlaid turned away. The elevator doors opened and he stepped into the box ahead of Frank. Once the doors closed on the lobby, he snarled.

Her brother. Had not his card with his carefully worded threat frightened him? The way he was leaning casually on the counter and laughing maddened Khlaid.

Impatience boiled inside him and he longed to get his hands on Charlotte and make her submit to his lordship. His lips tightened as he thought of all the things he wanted to do to her.

Flicking a glance at Frank, he stiffened his jaw. He had to keep his obsession with Charlotte a secret. He needed to be on his guard, he could not sabotage his future.

He knew Frank was stationed here to help him, to do whatever was requested of him. Yet Khlaid was not stupid. Frank was an influential man in his own right; they'd placed him here to keep an eye on him. Any mistakes would be reported and Khlaid would be strongly reprimanded.

So far Frank had not questioned his interest in Shanti's Rest. He agreed it was a good cover in his plan to appear interested in supporting those who opposed them.

His lips curled at the thought of beating them at their own game. He'd rise above the men who now owned him and nothing was going to stop him having his way.

How sweet Charlotte's fear would taste when he finally broke her.

Chapter 21

The boy looking back at him from the mirror was a stranger. Ashok pulled the hat farther down to hide his forehead. The school uniform felt stiff and uncomfortable. He glanced down at his sandals and stiffened his toes.

He tried smiling into the mirror then poked his tongue out and screwed up his face. Who was he trying to fool? He looked like a dressed-up brown mouse.

He flung the hat from his head onto the bed.

Grandma wanted him to try on his school uniform so she could take a photo and email it to his baap. Somehow going to school here seemed so final. He sat on the bed and slipped off his sandals.

He didn't want to leave his bedroom. The softness of the bed challenged his sadness. He should be happy to be in such a good place.

Maybe if Shanti… He curled on his side and laid his hand

under his head. He had to stop thinking about what could have been if Shanti had lived. Closing his eyes tight, he tried to visualize her face. It wasn't her features he saw but her laughter and her sparkly, trusting eyes.

Sitting up quickly, he crossed his legs. "Jesus, is Shanti still laughing?"

Warmth flowed up his neck and his arms felt all tingly. He could hear her and his mouth dropped open. The giggle that burst from his mouth surprised him, and he jumped up and down on the bed.

"Shanti, look at me," he laughed. "She can see me, can't she, Jesus?"

Ashok felt so happy. She could see him! He had to show her he was okay. "I miss you, little sister, but I'm going to be okay."

Was it silly to talk to her like this?

It was like Shanti was in another room; he couldn't see her but he knew she was there, waiting for him. He realized it was the same as Baap being in India. He couldn't see him, but Ashok knew he was there.

"I'll be a while in coming, Shanti. But until then…" He cleared his throat. "Until then I know you're with me, just like Jesus is, but in a different way." He placed his hand on his heart and moistened his lips. "Aunty Charlie and Dr Phillip leave tomorrow, and I'm wondering if I will ever see India again."

The soft tap on the door made him drop to the floor, and he watched as the door opened.

"Ashok, can I come in?" Aunty Charlie poked her head

around the door.

Ashok gave a little nod. He grasped his hands together as he waited for her to enter.

"Wow, look at you. You look smart in that uniform." Aunty Charlie walked around him and touched the uniform. She picked up the hat and pushed it onto his head.

Looking up at her smiling face, he felt sad all over again and flung his arms around her waist.

She sat on the bed and pulled him close. "I love you, Ashok."

Had she held Shanti like this? She flicked off his hat and smoothed his hair with her fingers. She kissed his forehead and he sighed.

She was his family. "I love you, Aunty Charlie," he whispered.

Her hands cupped his face and she peered into his eyes. "I'm so proud of you. You are a very brave, strong boy. I know it must be scary being in a new country and going to a new school, but I want you to remember that there is nothing you can't handle, because Jesus is with you."

"Jesus is with me. Yes, I believe this," he agreed.

The touch of her lips on his cheek made him close his eyes for a moment. His hand automatically went to the spot on his face to capture the feeling. Grandma kissed him too. At first it had seemed strange to him, but now he liked it.

"Aunty Charlie, will I see you again?"

"Of course, sweetheart! We're family. Eli's your father. Don't for a minute think that he doesn't want you. He's missing you so much but wants you safe. He will come for you as soon as we have put the danger behind us."

"Bad things happen." His eyes flooded.

"Yes, they do. But prayer is powerful and I know you'll be praying for us. You can't give up on hope."

"I hope," Ashok stated. "I believe—I do." He glanced down at his hands then lifted his gaze to her eyes. "I have more now than I have ever had before. People who love me, a bed, food, toys—school. I used to wish for such things when we were working the rubbish dump. Yet I don't have Shanti."

"I miss her too. It's okay to miss her, we loved her."

"I still love her, is it wrong to—to hold on to her?"

"No, of course not. Just because she's not here with us doesn't mean she's no longer your sister."

"If Shanti had not been, um, taken—I wouldn't have a father and grandparents. I wouldn't have you and Doctor Phillip in my life. Sometimes I feel guilty for having so much."

"You deserve it. God has a plan, always. We have to believe this. What's the verse, Ashok? I know you know it, because I've heard you saying it."

"Yes, yes. I do." He raised his arms high above his head. "The verse says, 'For I know the plans I have for you, declares the Lord. Plans to prosper you and not to harm you, plans to give you a hope and a future'," Ashok said. He dropped his arms to his sides and dipped his head.

"What is it?" Aunty Charlie leaned closer to him.

Ashok shrugged. "When I first read this verse, I got angry. Plans to prosper you and not harm you—I thought God lied. My Shanti was hurt bad and I didn't understand."

"Ashok, for me it's like this. Imagine you and I are taking

a trip; say to Disneyland. You have heard of Disneyland, haven't you?"

"Yes." Though he couldn't imagine such a place could exist—and when he saw the commercials on TV for it, he always felt a little relieved he wouldn't have to go on the big machines that made children scream with terror.

"Good. Imagine we get in our car and head off on our trip. On the way to the airport, there is a lot of traffic and we get stressed, thinking we are going to miss our plane. We phone Phillip and he's already boarding the plane.

"The plane leaves without us. We are so disappointed and have to wait hours for another flight that has room for us. Finally we are in the air and excited to arrive in America and meet up with Phillip." Aunty Charlie sighed. "The journey to America was difficult but we got there and it was wonderful."

Ashok remembered all the people at the airport sitting around waiting for their planes. He knew he would be very disappointed to have missed the flight to America.

"I don't understand." He rubbed his forehead.

"What I'm trying to say is that God's plans are bigger than ours. I don't know that we can really understand them, but he is God. Our life here is the journey to the destination. The destination is heaven, eternal life. Shanti's there. She just got there early. Like Phillip got to America before us in the story. Yes, she suffered here on earth, but earth isn't our home. Our home is in heaven with Jesus."

"Shanti saw Jesus, I know she did. She asked me if I saw him. He is with her," Ashok murmured.

"Yes, he is."

"He's with me too."

"Yep, me too," Aunty Charlie confirmed.

"He has a plan. I wish I knew what it was," Ashok grumbled.

"What fun would that be? Life's an adventure."

A chill sped down Ashok's back. He remembered the dark hallways of the brothel where they'd found Aunty Charlie and Shanti. It had been a horrible, dark place. "Aunty Charlie, how did you survive the bad things they did to you?"

Grabbing his hand, she rubbed his fingers.

Ashok had rubbed Shanti's fingers in a similar way when it was cold and they were huddled together for warmth. His skin tingled from Aunty Charlie's touch and warmth spread up his arm.

Aunty Charlie's eyes welled up. "There were times when I didn't think I would survive, but I knew Jesus was with me. You know something, honey? It's not until you need the strength to fight that you find it."

His lips curved. "One day when Baap was in trouble, I dragged his big body a long distance to hide him. He was very heavy, but I did it. I prayed for the strength of an elephant and Jesus helped me."

"I didn't know that." Aunty Charlie squeezed his arm. "It must have been a difficult time for you both, looking for us and not knowing whether you would find us. But you did."

Standing, Ashok brushed his hands down the side of his pants. "I think I am ready for Grandma to take that photo now."

"Good. I know you'll like school. I went there and made

so many friends. I hope you enjoy it as much as I did."

Ashok couldn't imagine having so many friends. His only real friend back home was Bashaar, and they never had much time together. School in India had been good because he had concentrated on learning.

"Aunty Charlie, do you think the children at school will like me?"

~

The blinking light on the car's dashboard caught Gargi's attention. She needed petrol. She glanced at Amita and hoped the child wouldn't wake when she stopped the car. The petrol station was about two kilometers away; she remembered passing it on the way to the village.

The lights of the truck veered into the station.

Gargi drove the car over to the side of the road and turned off the engine. She hoped the men in the truck wouldn't look back in her direction.

Slipping out of the car, she merged with the darkness and crept closer to the station.

Her hand shook as she pulled out her mobile phone and dialed Eli.

"Hello." His voice made her feel less alone.

"Eli, thank God you answered. I couldn't get through to you," she murmured quickly.

"Gargi, where are you? I've been calling and calling."

"I'm parked on the road verge about 200 meters from a petrol station. So much has happened..."

"Are you on your way here?" he interrupted.

Gargi squatted behind a shrub. "Eli, two men have taken children from my village. I've followed their truck. We need to rescue them before they get hurt." Tears gathered in her eyes as she thought of the little girl the man had already abused.

"What? Where's the truck?"

"It's filling up with petrol."

"Stay away from them, Gargi. I'll call the police."

"Yes, yes, thank you."

"Can you see the license plate number of the truck from where you are?"

"No, but I will get it for you. Wait a moment."

"Gargi, no..."

One of the men by the truck clicked the petrol gun back into the pump and banged the flap on the truck closed.

Gargi's heart skipped a beat and she took a steadying breath. She sprinted across the road then stopped in the shadow of the building and edged closer to the truck.

She whispered the letters and numbers to Eli then repeated them to make sure she had it right. "Did you get that?"

"Yes. What sort of truck?"

"It's an old truck. There is a tarp tied over the roof. Give me a minute and I'll try and get the model for you."

"Where are the men? Can you see them?"

"One went in to pay, I suppose the other one's in the

truck." She snuck farther up the road to get a better look at the front of the truck. "It's a Swaraj Mazda truck."

"Gargi, I want you to go back to your car and lock the door. Don't follow them anymore. I'll get the police to find them."

"No. We could lose them. I can continue following from a safe distance."

"It's too dangerous, these men aren't playing games. You are not to follow them!" he ordered.

A scream sent shivers down her spine. She turned in the direction of her car.

Amita struggled against her captor.

"No," she said, her voice rising. "One of the men is pulling Amita from my car." She raced to the shop window and banged the glass. "Help me," she begged at the man behind the counter.

The stranger shook his head and turned his back on her. Her mouth dropped open as he disappeared from view.

Twisting toward the car, Gargi froze. Fear gripped her chest as the man walked directly toward her. One large hand covered Amita's mouth and he easily carried her under his other arm.

Her small friend kicked madly at his legs and he laughed.

Something in Gargi snapped and she charged him. She grabbed his arm and dug in her nails. "Let her go." She yanked hard on his arm.

"Hello, girly." He laughed hoarsely.

Gargi kicked at his shin and bit into his hand.

He swore—and loosened his hold on Amita.

Gargi grabbed the girl and spun around, banging straight into the other man.

"Enough. Grab her," he ordered.

"Run, Amita," Gargi pushed the girl behind her.

Her skin went clammy as she realized they were trapped.

This was her fault, she hadn't locked the car.

"We can do this one of two ways," the man closest to her snarled. "The easy way, where you both just get in the truck. Or the fun way, where I break the girl's arm and you get in the truck anyway. What's it to be?" He took a step toward Gargi.

A chill touched the base of her spine and she knew without looking that they had Amita.

Raising her chin, she glared at him, then turned toward Amita. The stark terror reflected in the child's eyes made Gargi want to weep.

Chapter 22

Eli slammed his fist into the wall.

"Noooooo." The sound of his cry echoed around the empty room.

This couldn't be happening again.

His knuckles throbbed, and he started to turn then spun back. He didn't even know where she was; how could he have been so stupid not to get her location first?

His heart pounded and spots flew before his eyes. He tried to regain control of his mind. He needed to act, not give in to the weakness he felt in his stomach.

The truck's registration number—he needed to call Isak.

His finger felt numb as he punched the number into his phone. It was as if he had shut down a part of his mind to enable him to focus on Gargi alone. He had to take action, get to her as quickly as possible.

He grabbed his car keys, picked up his jacket, and ran out

the door as he waited for Isak to pick up.

"Isak, Gargi's been taken. I'm going to text you the details of the truck."

"Slow down, Eli. What do you mean, taken?"

"What do you think I mean?" Eli snapped. "Shut up and listen. I'm going to presume the truck will be heading toward Mumbai, and I'm going to take the same route Gargi took."

"I will come with you, you must not do this alone. Wait for me."

"There's no time. Just track the truck and phone me." Eli ended the call and ran down the street to where he'd parked his car.

He slammed the car into gear then swerved into the street. He peered out the windscreen and blinked away the wetness in his eyes. His stomach churned and bile rose in his throat. He never should have let her go. He tried to push the danger she was in out of his mind. She'd mentioned another name. Amita?

He could feel the tension building in his chest and pushed his foot down on the accelerator. He had to find her! The thought of her being hurt again stabbed at his heart. Tears welled again and he rubbed them away.

He had to focus. He was driving blind and didn't have time to get lost. He hated the streets of India and became confused every time he got behind the wheel. He tried to visualize the map he'd made for Gargi with the route outlined.

"Jesus," he muttered. "Lead me to her, please."

The car droned on and he shifted in his seat. Clicking the screen on his phone, he glanced down to see the time: 11:45

p.m. He'd been driving three hours and still no sign of the truck. He drove off the road and parked.

If they were coming this way, they would have to pass him. He welcomed the cool night air as he stepped out of the car. Shoving the door closed, with a bang, he stalked down the road.

He'd not seen a vehicle for an hour. Glancing at his watch, he saw that only fifteen minutes had passed since he'd last looked.

A soft shrilling sound made him race back to the car and grab for his phone.

"We have traced the truck, my friend. It is registered in Maharashtra, district fifteen, Kolhapur."

"Owner? Do you have a name and address?"

"Yes. And we have a team on the way there as we speak. Relax, we are fortunate that you had this information."

"I will relax when I have Gargi in my arms. Can you guarantee this?"

Seconds ticked by, and Eli leaned heavily on the car. "I'm sorry, Isak. This is not your fault. It's just that I feel so helpless."

"If you do not see the truck in the next hour, I suggest you head back here."

Closing his eyes at the thought of not finding her, Eli dipped his head.

"Eli, you could not have stopped this from happening. You tell me that your God is with you always, does this not also apply to your friend?"

"It applies," he said stiltedly. "I'll see you soon." Agitated,

Eli paced up and down the road for five minutes. Clenching his jaw, he knew there was nothing he could do; even if the truck came this way, all he could do was follow it.

He stared at the stars. "Lord, you're with her, give her strength."

~

The darkness in the back of truck was as potent as a nightmare. Gargi held Amita's hand and used the fingers of her other hand as a guide along the corrugated walls. Her hand came in contact with a warm arm and she stopped then squatted on the floor. She'd seen the girls huddled in the back left corner as she and Amita had been pushed into the truck.

Amita's hand trembled in hers and she pressed it gently.

"Hello," Gargi whispered. "I'm Gargi and my friend is Amita. Do you know her?"

"Yes," cried a small voice.

Amita crept along the floor of the truck to join her friend.

"We will be all right," Gargi whispered. She searched the shadows and drew closer to the little group. She could see the shape of a girl lying on her side away from the others.

Tears streamed down Gargi's face. The poor child. Gargi picked up the little one and gathered her close.

The child was so small and hung like a rag doll in Gargi's arms. It was like all the life had been sucked from her.

"Sweetheart, what's your name?"

The girl turned her head away and tried to get free.

"I'll let you go if you want me to, but I was hurt like you when I was a little girl. I want to hold you so that you know you're not alone."

The child sobbed and stopped struggling.

Gargi cupped her head and drew her close to her heart.

"Her name is Isha, she's only four," one of the girls cried. "Will they—hurt all of us?"

"We must pray for help," Gargi replied, not answering the girl's question.

The feel of Isha's slight form twisting closer made Gargi want to jump up with superhuman strength and break down the truck's door.

As she caressed the child's face she could feel the sticky texture of blood on her skin.

She smoothed her hand over the child's head and closed her eyes. She knew what damage would have been done to one so young.

Lord, I don't think I can survive going through this again. Gargi tried to swallow past the tightness in her throat. If Eli didn't find her in time, she'd rather die than be subjected to…

The shaking started in her chest and Gargi was sure Isha must feel her trembling. She breathed in deeply through her nose and tried to control her quivering. She wanted to shrink from what was in store for them if they weren't rescued.

"Gargi," Isha whispered.

Dipping her head, Gargi brushed her lips across the child's face. "Yes, Isha?"

"Am I dying?"

"No, child." Her voice caught. "Try and get some sleep."

Gargi leaned back against the wall and tried to get comfortable but the bumping of the truck kept jerking her head. The muscles in her arms locked and cramped from holding Isha.

Shuffling away from the wall, Gargi tried to sit unaided, but it was too difficult.

Lord, I'm new at praying. Charlie told me I needed to learn verses so that I could pray them over myself. I know you are with me because your Word says you will never leave me. Lord Jesus, I'm so tired. Gargi rubbed her eyes to try and stop them from stinging. *Jesus, my body is exhausted and my mind is in turmoil—I need rest for my soul.*

A child cried across from her and she wanted to hold all the girls in her arms at once. She wanted to comfort them. Softly she hummed. The words about the deer panting for a stream of water flowed into her mind. Sliding down, she repositioned herself on the floor. She visualized the Lord's hand reaching out to her, beckoning her closer. As the child lay in her arms, she visualized herself being held by God.

Warmth covered her and she felt safe. Charlie had shown her true faith. No matter what happens to the body, there was nothing that could separate her from God.

"Gargi," Amita asked.

Turning her head to the sound of Amita's voice, Gargi smiled. "I'm here, Amita."

"Can I—can you hold me too?"

Chapter 23

Macy ran the iron over Charlotte's top and felt tears blur her vision. She had to be strong for her daughter. She folded the fabric arms across the front of the T-shirt and added it to the pile.

The time had gone too quickly; she wasn't ready to say good-bye tomorrow. But what could she do? Her daughter's life was her own and she had to release her to live it.

Only a mother of an adult child could understand how difficult it was letting your children leave home. It seemed one minute you were taking care of everything for them, deciding what they ate, what school they went to, how late they could stay out at night, and then you had to stand back and let them make their own decisions.

Days went by when you didn't know what they were doing or where they were, and that was just the way it was.

Sighing, Macy turned off the iron and wound up the cord.

It would be so easy to slip into a pity party, but she refused to allow herself the luxury of doing that.

More than anything, she wanted to be an example for Charlotte. She wanted her daughter to see her as a strong Christian woman. To know that her mother was a woman she could come to for advice, not someone who fell apart every time things didn't go her way.

The door to the room opened. "Mum, you don't have to iron my clothes," Charlotte said.

Macy smiled. "I know I don't have to, but I wanted to." Picking up the ironed clothes, she stood in front of Charlotte. "All done now, do you want to put them straight into your suitcase?"

"Thanks, yes." Charlotte took the clothes and placed them back on the ironing board.

Lifting her eyebrows, Macy watched as Charlotte turned to face her.

"Thank you so much, Mum. I can't tell you how much being home with you and Dad has revitalized me. Having you as a sounding board where Phillip is concerned has helped me—I don't know, move forward." Charlotte grabbed Macy's hands.

"I think I can do it." Charlotte moved about the room, seeming unable to stay still. "I'm taking captive every thought that wants to steal my love for Phillip from me, and I'm telling myself the truth—just like you said. I do deserve Phillip. Gosh, I survived. God did not abandon me, I'm free, and I love Phillip."

"Of course you can do it. I'm so proud of you, Charlie."

Macy widened her eyes in an attempt to stop the tears that threatened to spill.

Running her fingers over the top of the pile of ironing, Charlotte frowned. “Do you think it’s okay for me to ask Phillip to marry me?”

Macy’s mouth dropped open. “No, absolutely not! Let him propose. Enjoy every minute of it.”

“But I’m ready.” Charlotte crossed her arms. “I want to be engaged now.”

Macy giggled and hugged Charlotte tight. “You are such fun, Charlie. Maybe you could hint to Phillip that he can propose anytime he likes, and sooner would be better than later.”

Banging through the door, Ashok screamed to a stop. “Aunty Charlie, I have drawn a picture for Baap. Can you give it to him for me?”

Macy crossed the room and took the picture from Ashok. “Oh my gosh! This is fantastic.” Holding the picture up, Macy twisted to show Charlotte.

“Are you sure you want to give this to Eli, Ashok?” Charlotte took it from Macy. “I love it.”

Ashok shuffled his feet and swung his arms.

Macy patted his shoulder. “Charlie, you will have to wait for Ashok to do another one for you. This one is for his father.”

“Yes, yes. I will draw another one for you, Aunty Charlie. This one is of an eagle for Baap. I copied the wooden eagle that grandpa made me.”

“What will you draw for me?” Charlotte smiled as she handed him back the picture.

Ashok grinned. "A kangaroo with a very long tail!"

"A kangaroo would be good or maybe a butterfly. Shanti and I used to paint butterflies in our minds. We played a game where we had to describe the butterfly and say what color the silky wings were. Can you draw me a butterfly, please?"

"Um, I don't think I can draw a butterfly." Ashok turned to leave the room.

Macy placed her hand on his arm. "Ashok, if Shanti loved butterflies as much as Charlotte does, then I think it's a great idea to draw one."

"No! I don't want to," Ashok folded his arms.

"Why not?" Charlotte squatted down to Ashok's level and then smoothed his hair off his forehead. "Do you think drawing something that reminds you of Shanti will make you sad?"

"I don't want to talk about it. I just wanted to give you my picture for Baap."

"Well, young man," Charlotte said. "I think it's time you started remembering things that Shanti enjoyed and let yourself enjoy them too. I think she would love you to draw me a butterfly. So when you get up enough courage to draw me one, I'm going to frame it and put it on the wall at Shanti's Rest."

Spinning around, Ashok charged out of the room.

"Charlie, maybe that was too much," Macy said.

"Mum, he has to let himself remember the good things. Shanti was a brave wee thing and so is he. I don't want him to be held back in any way. If Eli hadn't adopted him, I would have. I love him so much, you must know that."

"I know, sweetheart. But he is only a child and—"

"If we don't help him, who will?" Charlotte picked up the picture and gazed at it. "Do you think you could get a canister for this? I would hate it to get ruined in my suitcase. He really does have a gift. This is very good."

"I'll pop out and get one from the post shop." Macy wanted to disagree with Charlotte, but refrained. This was Charlotte's last night and she didn't want anything to spoil it. Once Charlotte was gone, she'd make it up to Ashok. The boy needed tender care right now, not being put on the spot.

~

"What do you mean, there's no one in the truck?" Eli demanded. He'd driven all night and had only just parked his car outside the police station. This was not what he wanted to hear.

"It appears the truck's been parked up all night. There is no evidence of it having had anyone in the back of it. There is no blue tarp over the top, and I have to question whether Miss Gargi got the plate number right."

"She did!" Eli affirmed. "It can't be the same truck. Could they have switched registration plates and somehow got them back to the truck you checked—or something?"

"It is possible. Miss Gargi's car has been located. The car

is unlocked and the keys were found across the road from the petrol pump. It would appear that someone must have thrown them there."

Eli couldn't fault the detective work. "What about the staff at the petrol station? Did anyone see anything?"

"Perhaps, but no one is talking. I hate to say this, Eli, but you know how this works. If we cannot locate the truck in the next few hours, it is unlikely we will."

Eli thumped his hand down on the roof of his car.

Isak touched his arm and Eli shrugged him off. "Don't touch me right now. I'm wired to break something."

Isak stepped back. "I am sorry, my friend. Do not give up hope that we will find her."

"I love her." Eli's eyes flooded. "I have to find her."

"We must continue the work we started. This is our only option, and God willing, we will stumble across Miss Gargi."

"Why is this happening to me?" Eli shouted. "God, where are you?"

~

Staring out the plane's window, Charlotte smiled at the beauty displayed. Luminous clouds, rich and pure, stretched out before her. From time to time sunbeams poured through narrow openings and painted the fringes in orange-yellow tones.

Even the threat from Saul couldn't dampen her mood.

She was heading home with the man she loved. Angling her head, she allowed herself the luxury of gazing at Phillip's face. She was no longer afraid to look at him and allow him to see her affection.

"Are you tired?" She touched his hand.

"No, not at all. You?"

She smiled. "I'm too excited to sleep." Her fingers caressed his arm.

"Charlie, I get the feeling that something's changed for you."

"Oh? What makes you think that?" She grinned.

Taking hold of her hand, he lifted it to his lips and kissed her fingers. "I don't know, maybe it's the way you're touching me all the time." He turned over her hand and kissed the palm.

She felt the blush rise up her neck and giggled. That she could feel shy like this was amazing to her. She'd experienced such sexual depravity, yet here she was blushing like an innocent young girl.

Phillip released her hand. "I spoke to your father." He wiggled his eyebrows up and down.

"What about?" She placed a finger on his brow to stop it moving.

"I asked for his permission."

"Permission? What do you need Dad's permission for?"

"Really, Charlie. Can't you guess?" He leaned back in his seat and closed his eyes.

She searched his face. He looked so relaxed, and when she

poked him, he refused to open his eyes.

"Phillip, what did he say?" Charlotte shook his arm.

"What did he say about what?" Phillip turned his head toward her.

"About the question you asked him. Come on, tell me."

Sitting forward, Phillip cupped her face. "He said I didn't need his permission to—um—to tell Eli to phone home more."

"That's not true," Charlotte laughed. "That is so not the question you asked. What—did—he—say?" She jabbed him in the stomach.

"Okay, okay! He said he would be honored to have me as a son and that I had his blessing to marry his daughter."

"Oh, Phillip." Charlotte clapped her hand over her mouth. "I don't know what to say."

Slipping out of his seat, Phillip knelt in the aisle.

Charlotte hid her face behind her hands. Tears welled in her eyes, and she couldn't help peering through her fingers to see if anyone was watching.

Everyone was watching.

"Charlotte Rose, my love." Phillip gently pried her hands away from her face. "You are the most amazing person I know. I love you and want to spend the rest of my life showing you just how much. Marry me?"

"Yes," she shrieked as she scrambled from her seat. She threw her arms around his neck and laughed as a loud cheer broke out around them.

As his lips met hers she relaxed and kissed him back. Her hand rested on his neck and she could feel his pulse under her thumb.

Tilting her head back, she smiled. "I love you. I love you so much."

"Give me your hand, sweetheart."

Her eyes widened and her fingers trembled as she placed her hand in his. The ring slipped easily on her finger and she lifted her hand to see the diamond more clearly. The gold claws circling the solitaire diamond seemed to embrace it.

"Phillip! I love it. Thank you."

~

Gargi gathered the children around her and wanted to protect them like a mother hen did her chicks. She glanced around the stark room. There was no furniture and the walls were painted white. A large rectangle mirror stretched across one wall.

She'd been in a room like this before. It was a viewing room.

She shuddered to think of people standing behind the two-way mirror and knew it was pointless to try and open the door.

"What's happening?" Amita pulled on Gargi's shirt.

Gargi's heart wrenched. Amita stood beside her, and all the other children tried to hide behind her. Isha cowered at her feet and clung to her leg.

Moisture filled her eyes and she blinked. She had to tell them. Prepare them for the worst.

"Girls, we are in a room where bad men look at us. I'm so sorry, but you need to know. If we are not rescued it will not go well for us," she said sadly.

"I want to go home," someone cried.

"Listen to me." Gargi squatted down. "A good friend once told me that even though bad men can hurt your body, they cannot destroy you. We must be strong, stand together, and love each other."

"What will they do to us? Will they—rape us—like they did to Isha?" a shaky voice asked.

"Yes," Gargi answered and swiped a tear off her cheek. "Isha, sweetheart, let go of my leg. Can you look at me?"

The deep brown eyes lifted and Gargi placed her hand on the girl's cheek. "I know you hurt inside. It was so wrong what happened to you, but I believe you're strong and will rise up to be a mighty woman of God."

Tears streamed down Isha's face and she shook her head. "I dead, like my mam."

"No, you are not! You are alive and just like me." Gargi made eye contact with each of the girls. "Just like me you will survive and be strong."

The girl on Gargi's left sobbed. "I don't want to be strong, ah—ah—I want to plant rice and play in the fields with my sisters. Why am I here?" She clawed at Gargi's top.

Gargi pulled her close. "You are here and you need to accept it. You will be strong, you will survive, you will look to each other and to God for strength."

Smoothing Isha's hair, Gargi's hand trembled. "We will focus on the good things. On memories of sunshine and laughter. We will win if we don't let them destroy our hope."

As the child relaxed in her arms, Gargi remembered.

Her skin turned clammy and her sight clouded. She'd been little for her age. More like the size of a ten-year-old than twelve. They'd stripped her and made her stand alone in a room with mirrors. Her hands had hovered over her private parts, trying desperately to hide her embarrassment.

When the door opened and two men came in, she'd hunched low on the floor trying to disappear.

They had pulled her roughly up and started mauling her. Squeezing her chest and laughing at the tininess of her young breasts.

She winced and had difficulty breathing. She could still feel their fingers on her body as they'd introduced her to the horror of abuse.

Gargi couldn't stop the shaking. Her hold on Isha tightened. All her attention went to the door.

~

Khlaid hissed out a breath as he peered through the mirrored glass. There was something familiar about the woman who squatted in the middle of the children. Her back was to him and he cursed.

Nine girls and a woman of about twenty. He'd expected more. Needed more. If he didn't deliver the number paid for, then he'd fry.

He glared at Frank. "The men said this woman was the cause of a disruption at one of the villages?"

"Yes, sir. She tried to convince the villagers that they were making a mistake giving their daughters away. Then she followed the truck."

"Women are stupid," Khlaid stated. "Now I have her, and the child that was with her." Shaking his head in disgust, he folded his arms and turned to Frank. "Have the teams gone out? I don't care where they get them from, but if they don't return with fifteen girls, there will be heads rolling."

"They know we need a total of twenty. They will be successful," Frank stated dully. He leaned closer to the glass pane. "The woman is young and very beautiful. She will fetch a high price." He licked his lips and laughed lewdly. "I would pay a high price for her."

Turning back to the window, Khlaid watched as the woman stepped away from the children and stared directly into the mirror. It was as if her eyes locked on his and searched into his soul.

He squinted and the action pulled at the tightened skin around his brow. Raising his hand, he absently massaged the frown that wanted to form. Then he recognized her.

Gargi! He'd thought her dead.

Anger boiled in the pit of his stomach. He'd been played the fool one time too many. He tried to recall the night she'd been discarded from the brothel.

She'd gotten pregnant and they'd botched the abortion. The doctor had told him that Gargi would die.

Charlotte had been in the room.

Stepping closer to the glass, he took in her clear complexion. The way she held herself spoke of confidence and—and what? There was a similarity to Charlotte! He wanted to slam his fist through the pane of glass and wipe the calm look off her face.

"Frank, I know this woman," he snarled. "I want you to find out everything you can about Dr Phillip Mangan."

"Phillip Mangan went to Australia with Charlotte Turner," Frank stated dryly.

"What?"

"This woman was at Shanti's Rest two weeks ago."

"Yet you didn't think to mention this to me?" He twisted to look at the man beside him.

"Boss, you told me to keep an eye on Shanti's Rest and that's what I've been doing. I did not know that this woman"—he pointed at window—"had history with you."

Dropping his gaze to his shoes, Khlaid sucked air into his lungs in an attempt to calm down.

"Separate her from the children. I will talk with her and gauge her connection with Charlotte Turner."

"Good idea, boss. See if she recognizes you."

Chapter 24

As Padma followed her brother into the house, all her words dried up inside her. He had become a man of God and she'd become a whore. Her face burned and she raised her hand to cover the evidence of her shame.

Tanvir's hand came out and he took hold of her elbow as he ushered her into the room.

The room was sparsely furnished with a few cushions in the place of chairs. A pretty young woman with long black hair falling down her shoulders reclined in the corner with a baby on her knee. She looked at them and smiled.

Tanvir released Padma's elbow. "Padma, my sister, I want you to meet my wife and daughter. Oni—" He glanced at Padma. Tears sprung to his eyes and his smile melted Padma's heart.

Clearing his throat, Tanvir tried again. "Oni, this is my sister, Padma."

Padma took a small step toward the woman and then stopped. Her hands trembled and everything in her wanted to run away. Would the woman judge her and not want her to be close to her family? Stiffening her back, she readied herself for rejection.

Oni stood. “Padma?” She was small, not quite up to Tanvir’s shoulder.

Padma raised her chin. Her stomach twisted as the need to distance herself started to seep back into her heart. This holy woman wouldn’t accept her.

Oni rushed across the room and shoved the baby into Tanvir’s arms then stepped close to Padma. She reached up and gently touched Padma’s face.

“I have prayed for you, my sister. I have longed to meet you. That you stand here in front of me is an answer to my prayers.” She raised her hand to her chest. “Your brother’s heart has been broken and today God has restored his sister to him.” Oni threw her arms around Padma and kissed her face.

Padma’s stomach heaved and she pushed Oni away. Bending over, Padma sucked in deep breaths. Everything in her had wanted to embrace the girl, but she’d stiffened her arms to control them from returning the hug. She couldn’t allow herself to hope. She was done living a lie.

When she looked at the baby in Tanvir’s arms, her heart ached. The child needed protecting from the likes of her. She took a step back then raised her chin defiantly. She wanted to claim these people as her family, but she didn’t deserve them. They needed to hear the truth.

“I am not your sister. You don’t know me—and if you did,

you would not want me in your house," she stated gravely.

"No, you are wrong. You are my sister, and I love you." Oni grabbed her hand.

Shaking her head, Gargi stared down at the soft fingers holding hers.

Tanvir laughed and kissed the child's cheek. "Padma, come sit. You are here, I am your brother, and nothing will let me lose you again."

"I'm a whore!" she yelled and then she crossed her arms protectively in front of her.

The baby stiffened in Tanvir's arms then let out a high-pitched scream.

The child squirmed and Tanvir patted her back until she calmed. "Our little one is not used to raised voices." He looked over the baby's head at Padma. "You are not a whore. Oni, my poor sister was locked up in the brothel with Charlotte Turner. Praise God she is now free."

"Stop!" Padma demanded. If she didn't tell them now, she'd be tempted to hide the truth and that would slowly kill her. She slouched across the room and dropped to the cushions on the floor.

Looking at her brother, she shrugged, then turned to stare at his pretty wife. "I was in the brothel with Charlie—but—I"—she shifted one of the cushions—"I am married to one of the men who ran the brothel. Yes, many men abused me, but I played a part in keeping the girls prisoners. I could have helped Charlie escape, but instead I chose to betray her."

She was filth. Pain clawed at her heart and twisted.

"Has Charlotte forgiven you?" Tanvir asked softly.

"She says she has. But that doesn't change the things I have done. Little Shanti died, and there were others. I could have done something." She dropped her gaze to her hands.

Oni hurried across the room and slid onto the cushion next to her. "You cannot change the past, Padma. I am sorry you have lived through such a horrible time. I promise I will not judge you, but you must forgive yourself. Jesus Christ loves you, and if you trust in him, he will help you work through the shame you feel."

"I judge myself. I do not want to hurt you or the baby." Her gaze locked longingly on the child's face. The little cheeks were rounded and chubby. She had the cutest little nose and full lips. The shape of the baby's forehead and eyes reminded Padma of—herself.

"Husband, give your sister her niece to hold." Oni's mouth opened in a wide grin.

Padma tried to deny the desire building in her heart.

Tanvir deposited the child onto her lap and she had no choice but to support its head with her hand.

The baby stared at her and curled its hand around her finger. Padma's heart pounded as the child's lips formed a soft, gummy smile.

Tears overflowed from her eyes and she couldn't wipe them away because she was holding the child. Sniffing, she looked up.

Tanvir and Oni laughed, and the looks on their faces reflected their love.

Oni touched Tanvir's hand. "Do you want to tell Padma our daughter's name or shall I?"

Tanvir knelt in front of Padma. He cupped both his hands around her face and wiped away her tears with his thumbs.

"Her name is Padma."

~

Walking hesitantly into the classroom, Ashok smiled at the faces peering at him. When no one smiled back his heart pounded and he glanced anxiously at the teacher. Her lips lifted in a small smile, which faded quickly as she spoke.

"Class, this is Ashok Turner. Ashok is going to be in our class for the rest of the term. Please make him feel welcome and show him around." She turned back to Ashok and pointed to a seat.

Moving down the rows of desks, Ashok took a seat between two boys. He nodded to them and slipped into the seat. Maybe these boys would become his friends.

"We don't want no curry munchers here," one boy whispered.

Ashok widened his eyes. "Are you talking about me?"

"Don't see any other darkies here, do you?" the boy mocked.

The teacher clapped her hands. "No talking. Open your books to page ten."

Ashok's hand shook as he opened the book. The words blurred before his eyes and he wanted to run from the room.

Why would they say such horrible things to him when they didn't even know him?

Confused he slipped further down his seat in an attempt to hide. He tried to listen to the teacher, but her words seemed to blend together, and the speed at which she spoke made it difficult to understand her.

He glanced at the wall clock and gripped the side of his chair. If he didn't make a friend today, he was not coming back tomorrow.

The shrilling bell made him jump and the children behind him laughed. He watched as they left the classroom and slowly got to his feet. At school in India the children all went to have rice at lunchtime. His grandma had packed him a lunch, but he didn't know where to go to eat it.

"You can come with me if you like." A girl standing at the door smiled at him. "I'm Chelsea. Don't pay any attention to those boys. They're just stupid."

"Thank you, yes please," Ashok answered hurriedly. He grabbed his bag and followed her out the door.

"Come and meet some of my friends. We eat our lunch under that tree over there."

As they got closer to the tree, some of the children looked their way and whispered to each other.

He knew they were whispering about him, and his face heated. His eyes stung as he watched them stand and move away before they got there. He stopped walking and looked at Chelsea. He did not want to go where he was not welcome.

"Ashok, come on," Chelsea called as she turned back.

Shaking his head, Ashok took a step backwards.

"What's the matter?" she asked as she trotted back to join him. She waved at her friends.

"What about them?" Ashok muttered and pointed to the boys walking away.

Chelsea grabbed his bag. "Those aren't my friends, silly." She skipped away toward the tree, beckoning him to follow.

As he watched her bound away with his bag, he raised his head. What was he doing being afraid of these people?

He was Ashok, the boy Jesus loved. He thought of the eagle his grandpa had made him and his mouth widened in a smile.

Those boys in the class were just being mean. They didn't know him; and if they did maybe they would like him, but even if they didn't, he was determined not to care.

Running the remaining distance to the tree, he joined Chelsea and three other children.

"Hello, I'm Ashok."

"Hi, I'm Shane and this is Rachel and Helen. You can sit by me if you like."

"Thank you," Ashok said shyly, happiness bubbling inside him. They wanted to include him.

He sat on the ground and pulled his bag onto his knee.

"Where are you from, Ashok?" Chelsea took a bite of an apple.

"Mumbai. I am staying here with my grandparents until my father comes for me."

Shane thrust an open bag of potato chips in front of Ashok's face. "Want one?" he offered.

"Thank you." Ashok pushed his fingers into the bag and

took a chip.

Dropping the chip bag back on his lap, Shane took a handful. “I saw Mrs Turner dropping you off at school. How do you know the Turners?” Shane stared at him waiting for an answer.

“Eli Turner is my father. He adopted me and that makes me the Turners’ grandson.” Ashok still could not believe that Baap had chosen to make him his son.

He felt proud to be part of such a good and kind family. He too wanted to be kind. He glanced around the group and wanted to be a good friend to them.

“What happened to your family?” Chelsea asked. “You don’t mind me asking, do you, Ashok? My dad died when I was five and I just live with my mum, so I know about people dying.”

“I am sorry your father died, Chelsea. My sister and I never knew our parents.”

“You have a sister? Where is she?” Chelsea questioned.

Ashok couldn’t believe his blunder. Diving into his school bag, he pulled out his lunch. Why had he mentioned he had a sister? He wished he could swallow back the words.

Opening the sandwich, he glanced down at the soft white bread. Shanti would have loved to eat the bread that Grandma made. The smell that filled the house made him hungry every time she baked.

“My sister died,” he said sadly, no longer hungry.

The punch in his arm shocked him. Ashok’s head snapped back and he jumped to his feet.

“Come on, mate,” Shane ordered. “At least you had a sister. I've just got me and my mum and dad. I would love to have had a sister. What was her name?"

Ashok tried to imagine what it would have been like if he'd never had Shanti, and thinking about her, he smiled. "Her name is Shanti. She may be dead, but to me she will always be in my heart. I love her very much."

Ashok's eyes smarted and he didn't know what else to say.

"Yeah, I think that about my dad too." Chelsea patted the ground beside her. "Sit down and eat your lunch, Ashok. What's on your sandwich?"

Looking at his new friends, Ashok felt bubbly inside. He dropped down beside Chelsea. "My grandma is trying to get me used to eating bread. I like it. In India it was difficult for me to find bread."

Shane nodded as if he understood and munched on a carrot. "My mum insists I have a raw carrot a day. I make a stink about it, but I really like them. Do you think I have good eyesight, Chels?" he asked and opened his eyes wide.

Laughing, Ashok decided to ask for a carrot for tomorrow's lunch.

Chapter 25

The quiet in the plane should have created the perfect environment for Charlotte to rest her head on Phillip's shoulder and go to sleep. Her gaze shifted from his sleeping face to the darkness outside the window.

Something was wrong. She felt it in her spirit and her muscles tensed as she grasped her hands together.

What is it, Lord? Her eyes closed and she breathed in deeply, trying to bring peace to her heart. *Your peace passes understanding, my Jesus. Your goodness reaches far into the night. When you call I will listen.*

Gargi's face flashed through her mind and she gasped and sat forward.

"No, Lord," she whispered. "Not Gargi, please not Gargi." Tears flooded her eyes and the urgency to pray made her tremble. She glanced at Phillip and for a moment she thought to leave him sleeping, then her mouth tightened and she placed her hand on his arm and gave it a little shake.

Phillip shifted and turned toward her. He rubbed his eyes and smiled. "Time to wake up already?"

"No. Sorry. Gargi's in trouble, we need to pray," she stated matter-of-factly. She took his hand and closed her eyes. The sound of someone snoring drifted across the aisle and Charlotte lowered her voice.

"Lord Jesus, we don't know where Gargi is, but you do. We don't know what is happening for her right this minute, but you do. Oh, Father God, be her strength and protect her from the evil one who is out to destroy her. Lord God, help her please." She stopped and swiped at the tears that trailed down her face.

"Yes, Lord Jesus," Phillip clenched his hands. "Charlie and I stand together and ask that you take hold of Gargi's hand and squeeze it so that she knows she's not alone. Touch Gargi and give her wisdom to know what to do. Lead her to safety, we ask in the name of Jesus."

Dipping her head, Charlotte continued to pray. "*Ar la sar mec ca,*" she whispered and allowed God to comfort her.

Phillip touched her arm and leaned over to kiss her cheek. "I agree something's up. As soon as we land I'll phone Eli and see if he's heard anything."

"I've asked him to pick us up," Charlotte murmured. She glanced at her watch. They still had another two hours before they landed.

"She will be all right, sweetheart," Phillip said and rubbed her arm.

Charlotte turned to look out the window. Keeping her head

turned away from Phillip, she closed her eyes tight.

Lord, I know you're with Gargi, I do.

She pressed her hand to her heart and wanted to scream for everyone to wake up and pray. Shanti had died; she'd been helpless to save the child. The thought of Gargi being somewhere and in danger was just about too much for her to handle. She licked her lips. *I cannot do this again, I just can't.*

Not by might nor by power, but by my Spirit.

Easing back into the seat, she leaned her head back and kept her eyes shut. She closed the palm of her right hand until her nails pricked her skin.

I have set you always before me, Lord Jesus, because you are at my right hand. I will not be shaken. Please remind Gargi of this verse. We spoke of it together and I feel she needs it right now. Forgive me for—for thinking the battle was too hard. I trust you, I do. I am yours.

Phillip touched her hair. "Are you okay, Charlie?"

She opened her eyes. "I am now."

~

Gargi tried to relax her shoulders as she waited. They had separated her from the children, and this didn't sit well with her. She'd been a child just like them the last time she'd been taken and hadn't known what to expect. Now she wasn't sure whether the knowledge of places like this was a bonus or made the waiting worse.

Her right hand tingled and she scratched the palm absently. She surveyed the room and was thankful there was no bed or mat present. She raced across the room and tapped her knuckles on the boarded window.

Dust particles floated up from the wood and Gargi stepped back and waved her hand through them.

They wouldn't find her; she had to be realistic. The truck would be long gone, and there was no way Eli would burst through that door in the next five minutes and save her.

She was on her own.

"No, no," she reminded herself softly. "I'm not on my own—am I, Jesus?" She pushed her hair behind her ears. As her arms dropped to her sides, she remembered.

"I will not be shaken, my Lord, because you are right here with me. I am yours and you are mine. Thank you, Jesus, thank you." A soft sensation passed across her body, and she dropped to her knees.

"For I am convinced that neither death nor life, neither angels nor demons, neither the present nor the future, nor any powers, neither—um—neither?" Gargi paused and tapped her forehead. "Lord, I can't remember the rest, except that nothing can separate me from your love. I believe that!"

Hearing the click at the door, Gargi scrambled to her feet.

The man who entered looked dressed to attend a social function. His shirt was made of silk and shimmered softly as he moved. His dark trousers had a seam pressed down the middle of each leg. Gargi hated what he represented. Just by looking at him she knew he believed money could buy anything.

She swallowed and made herself loosely link her hands together. She would not give him the pleasure of seeing her fear.

He rested both hands lightly on top of a highly polished cane. His gaze scorched a path over her face.

Another man entered carrying a chair. Gargi's gaze followed him as he placed the chair beside the man with the cane; their eyes locked for a moment, then he turned and left the room.

Gargi took an involuntary step back and had to stop herself from retreating to the far wall. She curled the fingers of her right hand so she could feel her nails in her palm.

God was with her, as close as her right hand.

Shuffling in the chair, the man got comfortable then leaned back and crossed his ankles. "Good day, it is so nice of you to join us." His voice was deep, and rasping, and made her cringe.

His perfect teeth seemed too white, and Gargi frowned at the falseness of them. She would not talk to him. She would not lower herself to engage this stranger in conversation when she was sure nothing she said would make any difference to the plans he had for her.

"I have met you before, Gargi. Do you remember me?"

Shaking her head, she tried to remember. There had been so many men; could he have been one of them?

His brow furrowed, and he raised his hand to the push away the crease. "I had presumed you dead, but here you are and somehow more beautiful than before. This I find very interesting." He shrugged. "I am pleased by the outcome," he continued as if having a conversation with himself. "Yes, this will make your friend Charlotte very upset when she learns you are lost to her." Throwing back his head, he laughed and spittle slipped down his chin.

"You are puzzled?" He dabbed his chin with a handkerchief.

The mention of Charlie's name changed everything. Gargi steeled herself to show no emotion.

Pulling himself up with his cane, the man labored to stand in front of her. "Take a good look. Do you recognize me?"

She searched his face and tried to remember. As her gaze flicked back to his eyes, a shiver ripped down her spine.

She'd stopped making eye contact in the brothel. It seemed easier not to connect with the men. And when she looked in their eyes, she could see the filth of herself reflected back at her.

His eyes were so cold and—familiar.

The face was different but she knew him. She looked at his left hand on the cane. The small scar above his thumb remained from the time she'd bitten him in defiance.

"I don't know you," she mumbled and dropped her gaze as if in submission.

She couldn't let on that she knew him. If he realized he was still recognizable, then he would become brutal.

"Ha!" He plodded back toward the chair. Rubbing his hands together, he resumed his seat. "Let me tell you of your future."

Gargi wondered what would happen if she charged across

the room and pushed the chair over. Would the other man be waiting outside the door? Even if he was, the satisfaction of seeing Scarface splattered on the floor was tempting. Why had he gone to such lengths to change his appearance?

She folded her arms and glared at him.

She could do this, she knew she could. She'd survived the brothel before and she could do it again. This time she'd be like Charlie and encourage the other girls to have hope.

Eli would find her. He'd found Charlie and he'd find her. It may take him a while, but he already knew a lot of the places to search.

"Tomorrow night you will be transported with the children to a ship. I hope you don't suffer from motion sickness." Scarface smirked. "You have the option of making it easier on yourself, Gargi. I have a buyer who wants you. He believes you are an innocent young woman, snatched from a family of influence, and this excites him. He alone will use you." He rubbed his hand up and down his thigh as if trying to release the muscle.

Gargi stepped toward him.

"Please, don't send me away. I want to stay here in India and—and—serve you." Gargi dropped to her knees in front of him. She had to stay in India. If she left, the hope of rescue would vanish completely. If she left, who would know to tell the authorities to look for the children on a ship?

His hand slammed into her face, toppling her to the side.

Gargi's eyes flooded and she choked back a sob. She gently touched her throbbing cheek.

He seized her jaw and roughly inspected the mark he'd

made. "Now look what you made me do!" Pushing to his feet, he banged his cane on the ground. The door opened.

"Frank, put something on her face and get her out of my sight. She'll be all right by the time she gets there."

"Yes, boss."

"Gargi, as I suggested before, it is up to you to make the most of the situation before you. Once you are at your destination you can pretend to be an innocent and perhaps have an easier life—or live with the consequences."

"That is no choice," she screamed. "I will still be used against my will."

Turning his back on her, Scarface laughed. "Frank, feel free to check out the merchandise before we ship her out. Just don't damage her."

Why hadn't Scarface used her for himself? She shuddered as memories of his brutality made her skin crawl.

Frank rubbed his hands together. "Thank you, boss, I will take great care not to mark her."

Gargi's heart pounded. Frank stood a foot taller than Scarface and was dressed like an American businessman. Gargi knew the signs of physical strength hidden behind expensive clothes. This man was dangerous. His wide-set hazel eyes watched her like a hawk scans its dinner.

Since she'd given her life to Jesus, she had begun to feel like a new creation, cleaned from the filth of strangers' hands.

Her skin crawled as he reached out and touched her arm with his fingertips. She slapped his hand away and stepped back.

"Please help me," she begged, searching his face for any

sign of softness.

"My advice to you, girl, is that you accept your lot and enjoy the journey."

"Are you serious? Enjoy it! How can you live with yourself, working for such a man? You will answer to God for what you are doing."

"I don't work for him. He just thinks I do. That's the fun of it. I'm just keeping my eye on him," he told her as he shrugged out of his jacket. "You're probably asking yourself why I'm telling you this." He stood in front of her and tweaked her hair. "For some reason my employer thinks Khlaid has some value. I don't personally agree with him but have learnt to keep my mouth shut and bide my time."

Closing her eyes, Gargi tried to picture Eli's face. Not all men are animals, she reminded herself. Yet the man in front of her was blind and his blindness would lead to his destruction.

"Frank, do you really think you are winning here? What good is it to you if you gain wealth, power, and yet lose your own soul? You will be held accountable. Let me tell you of Jesus and how he saved me from myself."

He pulled her close to his face. "You're a Christian? Ha-ha," he sniggered.

"It's not too late for you. Please let me help you," Gargi offered desperately.

Uncertainty flashed across Frank's face and Gargi couldn't look away from the softening she saw in his eyes.

Shaking his head in denial, he grabbed her shoulders and stepped her back until she was hard up against the wall.

"Enough talking. I am a busy man."

Chapter 26

Eli scanned the arrivals board and noted Charlie's plane had landed. Normally he enjoyed watching people as they greeted each other at the arrival gates, but the noisy terminal exacerbated the awful thumping behind his eyes.

Rubbing his head he scanned the people coming through the doors.

He simply didn't know how to tell Charlie how horribly things had gone. His chest felt heavy and his eyes burned from lack of sleep. He needed to get some rest, but every time he closed his eyes the nightmare returned and now it was Gargi who reached out for his hand.

"Eli," Charlie called as she ran toward him.

Opening his arms, he gathered her close. "Hello, Charlie."

Charlie pulled back and then searched his face. He could see the strain around her eyes.

"What's happened to Gargi?" she demanded. "Where is

she?”

How could she possibly know?

She crossed her arms. “Don’t give me that look. I know something’s happened. Phillip and I have been praying on and off all night for her. Tell me!”

“She’s missing.” Tears welled in his eyes and his shoulders shook. “I don’t know what to do, where to look for her.”

Charlie’s mouth dropped open. Eli wanted to cry at the look that passed over her face.

“I’m sorry, Charlie.”

Phillip slung his arm over Charlie’s shoulder and pulled her close.

The pain in Eli’s chest intensified as he watched his sister bury her head in Phillip’s shoulder.

Would he ever get to hold Gargi like that? He noticed the engagement ring on Charlie’s finger and had to stem the jealousy that made him wish he could put a ring on Gargi’s finger.

Stepping around them, he busied himself picking up their bags. There would be time later to congratulate Charlie when they shared the news with him. Right now he just wanted to get out of the airport.

“Eli,” Phillip said.

Eli looked at his friend and the sympathy on Phillip’s face was just about his undoing. He shrugged. What could he say that would explain what he felt?

“Eli, I know you love her,” Phillip stated. He laid his hand on Eli’s shoulder.

“I do,” Eli said sadly. He glanced at Charlie. “Gargi told

me she loved me. She was coming back to me."

"Oh, Eli," Charlie cried. "We will find her."

Eli nodded. "I'll find her or die trying."

~

Gargi clenched her stomach muscles in an attempt to stop the shaking that vibrated through her insides. Frank had not been rough with her, but each time he took her a part of her died. Moving across the room, she poured herself a glass of water.

Frank had told her things were just about ready for her trip. The casual tone of his voice had frightened her. She'd tried to convince him to keep her, take her for himself and stand up to his boss. He'd laughed at her and told her she wasn't that good.

She drank thirstily then put the glass gently on the shelf. Bowing her head, she dropped to her knees.

"Lord Jesus," she whispered. "I feel the stain inside me. I don't think I can survive this for long. Please rescue me." She cupped the back of her head with her hands and bent over her knees. Tears streamed from her eyes.

If only she'd not told Eli she loved him. She knew him—and he wouldn't give up until he found her. He too would be a prisoner of her abductors by the mere fact that he couldn't get on with his life.

Gargi used the hem of her sari to wipe her face, took a deep breath, and stood.

She would not feel sorry for herself, she would not give up hope—she would be rescued.

Charlie had focused on those around her in the brothel, and so would she. The children would need her to be strong. They must be so frightened, alone, and unsure of what was happening to them.

If this were her lot, then she would make her Lord proud of her. Each day she would remind herself that she was not of this depraved world but belonged to him.

The door swung open and Frank entered the room with a small box. "Right, come here, Gargi. I have a few things for you."

Cautiously Gargi obeyed and looked in the box.

"A Mickey Mouse watch." He laughed. "This will help you count the days of your trip. It should take around nine days, ten at the most."

"Thank you." Gargi strapped the plastic watch to her wrist. "Can you tell me where you're sending me?"

"What does it matter?"

"Please. Knowing will help me prepare myself."

Shrugging, he placed the box on the bed. "Everything you need is in the container. Water, food, light, and air."

"Container? As in—shipping container?" she asked in disbelief. Wasn't this place bad enough? She stepped away from him toward the door.

"What, you thought you were going to be on an ocean liner?" he snarled. Frank snatched her hand, stopping her retreat.

He crunched her fingers until she screamed.

"You are going to Jeddah, Saudi Arabia. Do not be concerned, we have sent others there. I'm sure you'll enjoy your travelling arrangements." Flinging her hand away, he stalked toward the door. "Get ready, you leave in an hour."

Gargi watched the door slam shut and then dropped her gaze to the box. Her vision clouded over with unshed tears. She sunk onto the bed and gripped the mattress. Uncontrollable shaking took over her body.

The thought of being locked inside a shipping container made her break out in a sweat. She jammed her hands under her armpits and hugged herself. She'd never coped well in enclosed spaces; even being locked in this room she'd felt the walls closing in.

Charging across the room to the door, she rattled the handle. "Let me out of here," she screamed. Forming fists she slammed them against the door until her arms ached.

All her energy drained out of her like water leaving a sink. She slipped to the floor. Her back leaned against the unrelenting hardness of the wall and she sobbed. Gulping down breaths, Gargi closed her eyes.

"I will be all right," she whispered. "I can survive this. I must survive this."

Gargi hugged her knees. Behind her closed lids she pictured many hands reaching out to paw her body.

A shipping container.

Once Scarface had locked her in a wooden coffin for a week. She had clawed at the top until her fingers bled. The small hole above her face had been her only source of air.

The lid would be lifted once a day and strangers would hop on top of her, have their way, then leave. Scarface told her the men's fantasy was to have sex with a dead woman.

After her body had serviced many men, she was yanked out. They forced her to drink a bottle of water, pushed her on a bucket to wee, and then hosed her down. If she didn't willingly step back into the coffin, Scarface would pull her hair out until many clumps of it hung from his fingers.

Gargi was petrified of enclosed spaces.

~

Charlotte stared at the scars from cigarette burns on her right hand. Torture had been a part of her captivity. She picked up a small bottle of Bio-Oil and tipped a little into the palm of her hand. Slowly she massaged the liquid into her skin.

Her fingers remembered rubbing Gargi's feet when she was pregnant. It was then that she'd seen the first softening on her friend's face.

Tears flooded Charlotte's eyes and she gave in to the need to cry.

Poor Gargi had been through so much. Charlotte wrung her hands. Her heart felt ready to explode with longing. *Lord Jesus, Gargi. Sweet, sweet Gargi.*

Great gulping sobs escaped her. She couldn't stand the

thought of Gargi's freedom being taken from her again.

Charlotte wiped her face and tried to stem her grief.

Yesterday, along with Padma and two other girls from Shanti's Rest, she had canvased the streets showing photos of Gargi, begging people to help locate her.

It was just about killing her to sit at her desk and wait for news from Eli. She'd wanted to go with him, but the danger of leaving Shanti's Rest unprotected was too high.

Finding Gargi seemed impossible. She could be anywhere.

How was she supposed to work when all she could think about was her friend?

The girls had been so pleased to have her back that they'd made a banner for her and cooked a special meal.

If only Gargi were here—then maybe the ache under her ribs would let up.

Giving a heavy sigh, she tried to release the tension in her chest. She glanced at the bank statement in her hand and frowned. There were so many expenses to running this place, and she hated that it all depended on having money to keep the doors open.

Throwing the statement down in disgust, she walked out of the office and wandered down the hall to the schoolroom. As she slipped through the door unnoticed, Charlotte watched the girls' keen faces as they did their English lessons.

They were so eager to learn, so desperate to turn their lives around, and this was just a small part of helping them on the road to freedom. She knew she should start thinking about getting ready to meet Eli and Ted at the motel.

It all seemed a little surreal. Trying to raise funds and carrying on with life when Gargi was missing. Charlotte wanted to scream out that it wasn't fair.

Her feet felt heavy as she left the schoolroom and walked upstairs to the bedrooms. She needed some time alone; she had to get her attitude right. Feeling despondent wasn't going to help anyone, let alone her.

Shutting her bedroom door, Charlotte sat on the edge of the bed and closed her eyes. She had to focus on Jesus Christ. She had to hold on to hope.

"You never left me, Lord Jesus. I know you're with Gargi, I do. But I hate that she's missing. All sorts of thoughts enter my mind about what is happening to her and I can't stand it." Tear sprung to her eyes and she allowed them to fall. "In her darkness, be her light I pray. Remind her of your goodness and strengthen her to lean into all that you are. Remind her of the verses we memorized together and make them come alive to her."

Clutching her hands together, Charlotte dipped her head. She'd not realized the pain her family must have suffered when she was missing. The not knowing whether Gargi was alive was the hardest part. If she knew Gargi was dead, then she'd be able to rejoice with her, but the thought of her friend being hurt all over again was agonizing.

She grabbed her head with both hands then shook it. "Charlotte Rose Turner, stop it! Stop it now!" Standing, she stretched her hands above her head. "I will take captive these thoughts and make my mind obedient to you, my Lord. Worrying doesn't show that I trust you—and I do. I don't know how we will find her, but you know exactly where she is."

Her mouth curved and she wiped her face.

The sparkle of her ring caught her attention. The miracle of Phillip's love warmed her.

She'd been forced to be a prostitute, but was now engaged to be married to a wonderful man.

Knowing that Gargi loved her brother made Charlotte want to do everything in her power to make this right. More than anything, her friend deserved happiness. Charlotte wanted to see Eli's ring on Gargi's finger.

Charlotte changed into a clean dress then slipped her feet into her sandals.

Eli had told her that his funds were just about depleted. He'd sowed much into finding her and then in helping establish this home.

As much as she'd tried to convince him to join the staff at Shanti's Rest, he'd refused—yet he needed money.

She lightly applied lip gloss to her mouth. "Lord, how can I help my brother? He gave everything he had to find me, all his savings. He sold his home—everything. And now he has no income and he's just about broke." Her stomach started to churn and Charlotte dropped the lipstick. What was she doing? Worrying didn't help. God would work this out.

~

The moist night air on her skin teased Gargi with a sense

of freedom. She looked around the parking lot and counted five trucks. The warehouse behind her seemed locked up and sinister. No light shone from any of the windows.

There was a lot of activity going on around two of the trucks. No one seemed interested that Frank was dragging her unwillingly behind him.

Gargi dug her heels in and screamed at the top of her lungs. "Help me."

Frank wrenched her forward against his chest. "You waste your breath. These men work with me." He continued walking toward a large truck with a corrugated steel container sitting on the back of the truck bed.

A man came around the side of the truck, and Gargi recognized him as one of the men who had captured her and the children. He flung wide the containers doors and stood back.

Frank grabbed Gargi around the waist, swung her into his arms, and then hoisted her up into the container.

Pain screamed through her knees as she landed heavily. She rubbed the sore spots then slowly stood. She glanced at the roof then spun around to gauge the length of the steel box. The walls seemed to move closer to her.

Twisting her fingers together, Gargi turned and watched as Frank joined her.

He dusted his hands together and then motioned her forward. "Before the children join you I want to tell you what to do."

He stepped to the left side of the container and picked up one of several harnesses bolted to the wall. "You are to strap yourself and the children in these. If you do not brace yourself when the container is being lifted by the cranes, you will be tossed around and—damaged." He cupped her face with both hands. His thumbs smoothed over her cheeks in a gentle caress.

Gargi had to steel herself to remain still.

"It would be a shame to see this pretty face disfigured." Frank stated gruffly. He dropped his hands and demonstrated how to click the strap in place. "The walls have rubber foam glued to them for your protection and also to stop noise from being detected from the outside. Don't waste your breath trying to call for help, no one will hear or care enough to investigate."

Her heart was pounding as though she'd been sprinting. She gasped and tried to suck air into her lungs.

Grabbing her shoulders, Frank shook her. "Listen! I will tell you this once." His fingers dug into her flesh. He picked her up and flung her across the container. She landed on some large cushions spread out on the floor at the back.

Scrambling to her feet, Gargi glared at him and held her stinging elbow.

A frown drew Frank's brows together. "There is enough water here for each of you to have four of these cups a day." He waved the cup in her face. "Do not allow the girls to have more than that as I have calculated it to last only fourteen days—that gives you four extra days if the ship is delayed."

Gargi licked her lips and suddenly longed for a tall, cold, glass of water.

"The food has been separated into days as well. There is plenty to see you through ten days."

Shaking her head in disbelief, Gargi swept her hand over her forehead to wipe away the sweat that was pouring from her skin. Even with the containers doors wide open, the air seemed to be disappearing.

"Th-there's no air in here." She pulled the sari away from her neck.

"Don't be over dramatic, Gargi. You will be fine." Frank pointed to the left wall. "There is also a canister of air secured over there. Only use it in an emergency. This switch is lighting. Make sure you turn it off as it has a limited power source."

Gargi pushed him out of the way and then raced for the door.

She didn't hear footsteps. When she glanced back at him, Frank staggered and recovered his footing but didn't follow her. He folded his arms and waited.

Squatting down, Gargi prepared to jump from the container.

The shuffling sound came from her left and Gargi froze. The children were being heralded toward the truck. Amita was leading them and she held Isha by the hand.

Gargi moaned. She couldn't leave them. She stood.

She wanted to curse Frank and scream that she hated him.

"Lost for words?" he jeered.

A chill touched the base of her spine and she knew she had to forgive him now, while she had the chance. Everything in her wanted to hit back at him but Charlie had taught her that she would only be hurting herself.

Clearing her throat, she reached over and touched his arm.

"I forgive you. I'll be praying for you."

Slapping her hand away, he looked startled. Then he massaged his arm as if her fingers had burned him. His face turned red and he rubbed the back of his neck. "You are the one who will need prayer!" He turned his back on her.

A wave of fresh air passed over Gargi. People were praying for her, she knew it. Her lips trembled. She curved them slightly in a small smile as she prepared to welcome the children.

"Hurry up," Frank shouted to the men lifting the children into the container.

Ignoring Frank, Gargi squatted and opened her arms to embrace Amita. "Hello, sweet child," she said.

Soon crying children surrounded her, and as much as she tried, she couldn't stop the tears from forming in her eyes.

Slamming his open hand hard against the wall, Frank cursed. "Gargi, get them strapped in before we close the doors, otherwise you won't be able to see." He squinted at her. She couldn't look away. His mouth opened as if he were going to say something, but then he shook his head and jumped out of the container.

Gargi reached for Isha. "Girls, listen to me. I want you to go and stand beside a harness and put your arms through the straps. I'll come and click you in."

Picking up Isha, she held her close and felt the girl's warm little hands circle her neck. She helped Isha into the harness and pulled the straps until they were firm. The child's eyes looked too big for her face. Gargi leaned forward and kissed her cheek.

"Be brave precious, you're not alone." She brushed Isha's hair behind her ears.

Moving along the line of children, she secured each child and made sure the foam around her head was firmly in place.

"Girls, once the door is closed it'll be so dark in here that we won't be able to see." Gargi hoped she sounded unconcerned. "When the truck gets to the port a—a crane will pick the container up and place it on a ship. That's why we need to be strapped in so we don't get hurt. As soon as we know the container is secured on the ship, we can undo the harness and get comfortable on the cushions."

After checking Amita's harness, Gargi scooped up the straps to the last harness and slipped her arms through the gaps. She clicked the lock and looked at the man at the door.

He nodded solemnly and stepped back.

As the door closed, Gargi's gaze clung to the last rays of light before the door banged shut. Darkness surrounded them and Gargi struggled to contain the scream that was building in her chest.

The clunk of the steel bar locking them in made their prison seem so final. Panic built inside her and she found it difficult to breathe. Raising her hand, she wiggled her fingers and peered into the darkness, trying to see them.

"I hate the dark," sobbed Amita.

"I want to go home," someone screamed. "I want my mam—Mam!"

The truck jolted forward, causing the harness to dig into Gargi's arm. She closed her eyes, inhaled deeply, and tried to think. She couldn't let panic take over. She had to be the one to help the children cope.

Jesus, show me what to do? Squeezing her eyes tight made red spots waver in front of her. Smiling, she allowed the idea to form in her head, and the tightness around her chest lifted.

"When I close my eyes," she said cheerfully, "I see nothing. What do you see, Isha?"

"I'm too scared to close my eyes," a little voice whispered.

"Is that you, Isha?" Gargi knew it wasn't fear of darkness itself, but the dangers concealed by the darkness that frightened. The what-ifs that slammed through your mind. She shivered.

Isha sobbed. "It's me."

"Do it for me, Isha. Just try it for a minute and tell me what you see."

Gargi's mouth felt dry and she licked her lips. *Please, Jesus, help Isha answer.*

"I—um, I see nothing," the small voice answered.

"Exactly! Nothing. So are we afraid of nothing? No, no, no!" Gargi's fingers curled around the harness. "Girls, now I want you to close your eyes as tight as you can and tell me what you see."

"I see stars," exclaimed Amita.

"Me too," someone yelled and laughed.

"I see a shimmer, and it's reddish," another added.

"Okay, open your eyes. What fun, colors in the darkness," Gargi's eyes welled up. She took a calming breath. "Anytime you're afraid of the dark, close your eyes tight and imagine God flashing his beautiful colors in front of you."

Turning her head in Amita's direction, she tried to see the

child's shadow. The roughness of the harness bit into her neck. She frantically pulled at the strap, trying to create more room. Panic started to rise in her chest. She hated the feeling of being tied up. Then somehow the taste of sweat on her upper lip sobered her. She had to focus. The children needed her. "I have another thing we can do. I'm going to reach my hand out and touch Amita's hand and squeeze it. Then I'm going to say my name and one thing I like, then it's Amita's turn."

Moving her hand toward the child, Gargi felt around until she found the warmth of Amita's outstretched fingers.

"I've got you. My name is Gargi and I like—I love children." She gently clasped Amita's hand then let go.

The scraping of Amita's hand feeling around seemed so loud in the small space.

"I've got you," Amita said, copying Gargi's words. "My name is Amita and I love making mud balls by the paddy fields."

A squeaky voice jumped in as soon as Amita finished. "I've got you. My name is Pia and I love chocolate."

"When did you have chocolate?" someone asked.

"I had a little once, when visitors came to our village. It was sooo good." Pia clapped her hands.

The container creaked as if laughing at her attempt to soothe the girls.

Someone thumped her feet against the wall.

"My name is Daya and I don't want to play this stupid game. I know what you're trying to do. You're trying to make us think of something other than what is happening to us. I just can't," she whimpered. "We are all going to die."

"You are right, Daya," Gargi could smell the raw fear oozing out of them. She wiped her clammy palms on her sari. "We are all going to die one day. But not today—and yes, I am hoping the game will help us think of other things. We all know we are locked in here, but it is what it is, and for now we must make the best of the situation."

"I want to go home," someone croaked.

Gargi hugged her arms and waited.

The air was filled with the sound of sniffles and labored breathing. Gargi felt shattered and longed for the nightmare to be over.

"I've got you," said a wobbly voice. "My name is Neha and I love seeing the sun rise. I like to stand and count the seconds it takes before I can no longer look at it. When I closed my eyes tight it was like looking at the sun, and the red stars that flickered under my lids reminded me of that." She cleared her throat. "I am twelve years old and I can only guess at what will happen to us, but I am thankful that I am not alone."

Gargi listened as the children continued saying their names. This was only the beginning of the journey into the unknown. Nine days in this coffin, then what? She shuddered to think of what lay ahead. She pictured Eli's face and remembered the sound of his voice when she'd told him of her love.

She'd never thought a man like Eli would look twice at her, yet he had. He'd seen the value that God placed on her, and she loved him for that. Her heart called out to him and she longed to touch him once more.

Chapter 27

Four days he'd been searching for Gargi. The last thing Eli wanted to do was to sit in on a meeting with a possible sponsor for Shanti's Rest.

Why had Ted insisted he be here?

Splashing water over his face, Eli closed his eyes and leaned heavily on the basin. Last night had been a nightmare. Isak had refused to allow him to push his way into brothels, and it had seemed he was fighting against him.

The very thought of it taking as long to find Gargi as his search for Charlie, seemed too much to bear.

He was running blind.

Isak had been ecstatic that the lead at Bandra Station had led to arrests. As much as Eli wanted to celebrate with his friend and hoped that they were on the right trail to find Gargi, now it felt like he was swimming around in circles, unsure of which direction to go.

Gargi might not even be in India. If only he had some clue where to look.

Every time he entered a house of slavery, his heart tore a fraction more.

Isak seemed to be handling it better than he was. The smells haunted him. Sickly perfume, sweat and semen. His stomach cramped. Eli hated that last night he'd embarrassed himself by vomiting in the gutter after they'd left one place.

The shrill of the telephone made him tense. Picking up the towel, he buried his face in the soft, white terry cloth and ignored the phone. He knew Ted would be waiting for him, but heck, five minutes; couldn't he wait five minutes without hounding him to hurry up?

Trudging across the room, Eli picked up his jacket and slung it over his shoulders. He glanced around the luxurious hotel suite, which had become his home since he'd moved out of Phillip's, and knew God had gone before him.

Who would have thought that a chance meeting on an airplane would turn into a genuine friendship? He still felt overwhelmed by the generous offer from Ted to host him in this five-star hotel—and that included every meal he wanted. Eli would swap the suite at the bat of an eyelid if he could be back in Phillip's small apartment with Gargi and Ashok.

He'd been so humbled by Ted's generosity and challenged by his words.

As he waited for the elevator, Eli stared into space and heard his friend's voice in his mind. "*Eli, it's the least I can do. I believe in you, buddy. Consider my small contribution as a wage from your God. Will that make it easier for you to lose your pride and accept what you call charity?"*

It was God who provided. Eli knew this; and to be reminded by his friend who had yet to make a decision to trust Jesus was humbling and slightly embarrassing.

Eli grinned. "Get over yourself," he muttered as he entered the empty elevator and pressed the down arrow.

~

Walking across the lobby, Charlotte smiled at the young woman manning the reception desk. The girl beside her was one of the trainees at Shanti's Rest. Ted was so amazing to allow the girls to work alongside his staff as volunteers to learn new skills. His contacts in the local community were opening so many doors for them.

If this man she was about to meet got on board as a sponsor, then maybe she could take on even more girls. As she approached Ted and Eli, the two men beside them stood to watch her approach.

Ted held out his hand to Charlotte. "Gentlemen, I'd like to introduce you to Charlotte Turner, the founder of Shanti's Rest. Charlotte"—Ted motioned with his hand to the two men beside him—"I'd like you to meet Frank Johnson and Mr K. L. Singh."

"Hello, so nice to meet you both." Charlotte smiled.

"Ms Turner." K. L. Singh extended his hand to her, and

his eyes seemed to search her face hungrily.

Slipping her hand into his, Charlotte felt a chill go through her. She pulled her hand away.

"Do I know you?" She swallowed. "Have we met before?" Her skin went clammy at the possibility that she'd—she'd had him as a customer.

"I don't think so, Ms Turner. I'm sure I would have remembered such a beautiful young woman. I have been out of the country until recently, so it is very unlikely that we would have crossed paths here in Mumbai."

"My mistake." Charlotte licked her lips nervously and wondered at her apprehension. She didn't really recognize him, but something about him reminded her of someone.

"Shall we take a seat and then we can get down to business," Eli suggested.

Moving to sit next to Eli, Charlotte took his hand before she sat down.

She glanced across at the other man. "Where are you from, Mr Johnson?"

"Originally, the States, but I've travelled widely and for now this is home." His eyes shifted down to Charlotte's chest, ever so briefly, that she thought she'd imagined it.

Eli clasped his hands together on the table. "So, Mr Singh, what does K. L. stand for, if you don't mind my asking?"

"Not at all. You would laugh if I told you." He shifted in his chair. "My friends have always called me KL. I prefer it to my given name, so that's the name I use exclusively."

"I see." Eli frowned. "KL it is. How did you hear about Shanti's Rest?"

"Frank here"—KL gestured across the table—"introduced me to the idea of becoming a financial backer of a charity as a tax break. We scouted around and I've become very interested in the work you are doing with the girls taken from the brothels."

"Rescued, Mr Singh," Charlotte informed him. "Not taken. *Taken* refers to being forced against your will. The girls at Shanti's Rest come voluntarily."

"Forgive me, Ms Turner." KL rubbed his chin.

Charlotte leaned forward. She unapologetically stared at the man across the table. Who was he?

He locked his eyes on her. "Tell me how best we could invest in what you are doing."

As much as she wanted to look away, it was like she was in a trance and glued to his stare.

"Charlotte?" Ted's voice startled her.

Glancing at Ted, Charlotte cleared her throat. "Um, there are numerous ways to support the work at Shanti's Rest, but the most needed at the moment is financial, as you can imagine, the costs involved in running such a home are ongoing."

"Yes, yes. Money makes the world go round." KL nodded and dabbed at his mouth with a cloth. "Would it be possible to have a tour of the property and see firsthand what you are doing?"

Ted turned to Charlotte. "Charlotte, could you arrange this for us?"

Looking across the room at Eli, Charlotte noticed his frown had deepened. Did he too find it difficult to like the man offering them support? She straightened in her chair.

"I'm sorry, gentleman, but a tour is out of the question. The girls need to feel safe at Shanti's Rest, and I won't jeopardize this by taking strangers through even though we are desperate for funding. If you want to help, give us your money," she said firmly.

Standing awkwardly, KL nodded to his partner. "I think we are leaving, Frank."

Ted hurried to his feet. "Please, KL, forgive Charlotte, she is very passionate in protecting the young women at Shanti's Rest. Maybe we can arrange for the girls to go on a day trip so you can visit the complex."

"I am sorry to have wasted your time, Ted." KL placed his hand on his heart and bowed to Charlotte. "But I find being called a stranger when I was offering thousands of dollars as support very offensive. I would have thought it would have classed me as a friend."

A chill raced up Charlotte's back and she stiffened. "I apologize if I insulted you, Mr Singh. I am very protective of my girls; surely you can understand that taking men through Shanti's Rest is not a good idea when it has been men who have hurt the girls?"

KL leaned on his cane. "I must reiterate that as much as I appreciate what you are doing, for me this is a business transaction, nothing more. I cannot—I will not invest heavily in something I have not seen. Surely you understand the position you put me in?"

"Eli?" Charlotte turned to her brother, who had been quiet throughout most of the conversation. She did not trust these men, but couldn't substantiate the reason why. If Eli told her to do it, then she would go against the feelings that were building inside her.

Standing, Eli folded his arms. “We could give you all the information you need without your visiting Shanti’s Rest. All our other sponsors have been satisfied with this. However, the difference is that they have… a heart for these girls—and as you have stated yourself, Mr Singh, this is just a business deal to you.”

Turning to Charlotte, KL curved his lips. “Perhaps you could convince me otherwise, Ms Turner? I can see you are passionate in what you do. Passion is a good driving force in any venture, I believe.” Shrugging his shoulders, he laughed. “Yes, I think we will do as you say. Suddenly I no longer have the need to visit a building when I have all I need right in front of me. Can you spare me a little of your time to discuss the work you do, Ms Turner?”

“I’m here now. What do you want to know?” Charlotte could hear the wariness in her tone and made an effort to lighten her words with a smile.

“I am pressed for time,” KL apologized. “Maybe on Wednesday the two of us could have a chat over a nice cup of tea? Yes?”

Charlotte tried to think of a reason she couldn’t meet with KL.

Without waiting for an answer, KL turned to Frank. “Write out a check for ten thousand dollars to Shanti’s Rest,” he ordered. He held out his hand to Charlotte. “Until Wednesday, my dear.”

Chapter 28

Gargi kicked her heels against the rubber foam hoping to sound an alarm, but her feet bounced silently off the insulation. Even the door had been insulated against sound. The roof alone was bare tin.

She could hear the girls whispering to each other as if talking aloud would somehow increase the danger.

The truck stopped and she tried desperately to hear what was going on.

A loud boom sounded as something crashed on the roof.

Gargi looked up and held her breath, expecting the ceiling to cave in.

The container jerked to the side.

Screaming broke out and the deafening sound echoed around the enclosed space.

Gargi yelled over the noise. "Grab hold of your harness." She hoped the sound of their terror could be heard from outside the container. Maybe Frank was wrong about the sound-proofing.

She gripped the harness. She remembered seeing a shipping container swinging from a crane on the television. It had swayed back and forth as it was lifted to the ship.

She pictured the large magnet attached to the top of the container.

Jesus.

The container smashed into something. Gargi's head snapped to the left and she bit the side of her tongue. Tears flooded her eyes. Anchoring her feet, she pushed back into the foam and tried to brace herself.

The container swung and everyone screamed again.

Gargi prayed the cable holding the container would not snap.

The swaying motion made her stomach churn. Tightening her hold on the harness, she prayed the crane driver would safely place them on the ship.

She could hear the girls' frightened sobs and wanted to tell them everything would be all right.

A ripping sound, like a zip being opened, startled Gargi.

Thump.

"Oucccch," someone cried out.

"What's happened?" Gargi asked urgently.

"It's Isha—I heard her fall," someone answered.

"Isha, sweetheart, where are you?" Gargi called out.

A soft moan sounded from the floor.

"Isha, can you crawl toward my voice?" Gargi waited for a reply.

The rocking of the container made it impossible for Gargi to keep her legs still. They dangled in front of her and she felt powerless to help the girl.

The child whooshed past her.

"Where is she, can anyone see her?" Gargi longed for a light.

A mighty jolt knocked the breath out of Gargi. Coughing, she swallowed, and tears streamed down her face.

Isha's ear-splitting scream sent a chill down Gargi's spine. Goose bumps covered her arms.

The girls fell silent. Except Isha. She screamed and screamed and screamed.

The sound of Isha being tossed and bounced off the walls like a ball drained Gargi of her own fear. Her fingers hesitated over her buckle. If she got out, could she rescue the child?

There was a loud thud followed by a sickening crack nearby.

Gargi reached her hands into the darkness, her fingers desperate to grab hold of Isha.

Something bumped against her leg and Gargi used her feet to pull Isha closer. Lifting Isha's slight form to her chest, Gargi locked her fingers behind her back.

The child's head flopped back as if unsupported by her neck. Gargi lodged the girl's head in the crook of her arm.

The container crashed and landed.

The walls jarred and even the foam couldn't shield them from the impact. Gargi's body lurched forward only to be halted from falling by the harness.

Her hands loosened and Isha slipped down her legs.

Clawing her fingers into the little girl's clothing, Gargi hoisted her back up.

"Can we get out of the harness now, Gargi?" Amita asked, her voice rising with panic.

Gargi licked the blood off her lips with her sore tongue and tried to calm her heartbeat. "No, not yet," she whispered. "I think we should wait a little longer."

A minute later the container jolted as another container was slammed into place next to them. The boom echoed around them, drowning out their cries. Gargi closed her eyes and counted to ten in her head. The thought of being hemmed in by huge steel shipping containers, weighted down with heavy loads, made her skin crawl.

Please, Lord, don't let them put one on top of us.

The roof shuddered. Gargi blinked to stop her tears from overflowing.

She looked up and imagined the containers sandwiching them in.

The walls flexed as another container was stacked on the growing pile on top of them.

Gargi dipped her head. *Jesus, Jesus.*

Isha's body hung heavily in her arms. She knew Isha was unconscious, but there was nothing she could about that right now so she cradled the child close to her heart.

"The Lord is my light and my salvation—whom shall I fear? The Lord is the stronghold of my life—of whom shall I be afraid?" she declared into the darkness.

Clank.

"Gargi," Pia called. "I've undone my harness, can I come

to you?"

"Pia, sit where you are for a moment. Girls, we need to do this carefully, I don't want any of you to get hurt. If you can unclick the harness, do so and then sit on the floor until I can get the light on. I'm holding Isha, so once I'm free, I'll place her on the cushions."

As much as she tried, Gargi couldn't open the harness while she held Isha. "Amita, can you help me unclick my harness?"

Amita reached under Isha, and Gargi could feel her pushing at the harness. "I can't get it to budge."

"Get out of the way," a girl said to Amita.

Gargi felt a pair of hands dive in around Isha's stomach. The slight weight was lifted away.

"I've got her, Gargi. Can you undo your harness now?"

Gargi shrugged out of the harness and smiled in the darkness. "Thank you. I can't see you. What's your name?"

"I'm Daya."

"Do you want me to take Isha or can you hold her until I get the light on?"

"I'm okay, she's not heavy," Daya murmured. "I think she's bleeding, her arms feel sticky."

Gargi had felt the blood soaking through the child's clothes. "We will clean Isha up once the light is on."

Inching her way to the back left corner, Gargi tried to locate the switch Frank had shown her. She ran her hand over the rough surface of the floor until she came across the power board.

She flicked on the switch and sighed as soft light flooded

the container. Someone clapped.

"Oh, thank goodness," Neha sobbed.

Gargi saw that the girls were helping each other out of the harnesses.

Daya placed Isha on the cushions and sat beside her. Gargi joined her and gazed down at the small child.

The gash on Isha's cheek was oozing blood, and her arm looked bent in an unnatural position, but it was her neck Gargi was concerned about.

She removed the cushion from under the child's head then spread her out on the floor and tried to hold her head firmly in place.

Searching the container with her eyes, Gargi frowned. There was nothing here that she could use to brace Isha's neck.

Gargi shivered when she remembered hearing the loud crack. Peering at the child's lifeless face, Gargi felt overwhelmed by sadness. Tears flooded her eyes and her throat felt clogged.

"Is Isha all right?" a small voice asked.

Gargi met Amita's gaze. "I think Isha may have hurt her neck. Can you hold it like this for me while I find something to strap it?"

Amita sat cross-legged beside Isha and placed her hands where Gargi's had been.

Gargi emptied the cardboard box Frank had given her, then she tore it in half and folded it until she was satisfied.

Moving back to Isha, she slipped her makeshift brace under the girl's neck and prayed it would be firm enough to offer some support.

She stood and surveyed her surroundings. The thump of another container landing made Gargi lunge forward.

Stiffening her resolve, she jutted out her chin and addressed the girls. “I know you are all frightened, but I want you to know something. This is only the beginning of our journey. If we allow ourselves to give up now—we won’t make it.”

“But how long are we going to be locked up in here?” Pia asked.

Tension twisted Gargi’s neck muscles. “I think the journey is about ten days, but we will just have to wait and see.”

“Ten days!” Neha exclaimed and ran to the door. She slammed her hands on the paneling and screamed.

Watching Neha, Gargi felt the added burden of helping these girls. This wasn’t just about her own survival; it was bigger than anything she had ever lived through. Turning her back on Neha, she went to check the food supplies and water. She’d seen a pencil and small notebook in the things that had spilled out of the box. Why had Frank given her these things? Somehow it seemed like a small kindness in the midst of a cruel act. Whatever the reason, she was thankful. She picked up the pencil and opened the notebook.

Day one—Container. Isha’s harness broke and she’s hurt.

Her hand shook and she glanced up at the shimmering light. Frank had said to use it sparingly. How long should she allow the light to be on?

One of the girls came and stood beside her. “I’m hungry.”

Jumping on the spot, Pia crossed her legs and moaned. “I

need to go wee."

Gargi hurried to look in the wooden crate that was strapped to the wall on the opposite side to the harnesses.

Stacked within each other were three buckets. She could only presume these were to be used for toileting. Pulling out one bucket, she took Pia's hand.

"Let's put the bucket over by the door. Do you think you can squat on it by yourself?"

Pia grabbed the bucket and Gargi smiled when she heard the trickling sound and Pia's loud sigh of relief.

The strong smell of urine made her screw up her nose. They needed something to cover the bucket to keep the smell inside.

Going back to the crate, Gargi rummaged around and pulled out some thin blankets. She threw them over toward the cushions and pulled out a stack of paper plates. There was nothing she could use to cover the bucket.

Daya approached her and pointed to the crate. "If we empty the crate, then we can break off the side and use the wood to cover the buckets."

"Daya, that's a great idea! You're a real thinker. How old are you?" Gargi asked as she started unloading the crate and stacking the sparse contents in a pile.

"Fourteen, but I feel—older," she answered.

"You're very beautiful and you don't look older. Thank you for your help. It's good to know I have someone to help me look after the children."

Daya shrugged and straightened her shoulders.

Gargi hid her smile. She scanned the food and picked up a

container filled with cooked rice.

Removing the lid, Gargi sniffed the rice. She knew from experience that rice had to be stored correctly; otherwise it could go off and make you very sick.

Her stomach rumbled.

Pia picked up a plate. “Are we going to eat now?”

Gargi’s gaze took in all the pairs of eyes looking at her and she nodded. If this was all the food they had, then they needed to eat the rice first. She’d have to risk it.

She spread the plates out on the floor, and then shared out the rice. The girls sat and spooned the food into their mouths with their fingers.

Using their hands to eat was natural to them, but with little water to keep clean, Gargi prayed that no one would get sick.

As Gargi lifted the rice to her mouth, she hesitated. She placed the rice back on the plate and pushed it away.

The girls scarfed down their food.

Her stomach complained, wanting food. Picking up the cup, she went to the water and poured herself a small amount. Today she wouldn’t eat. Smiling, she thought of all the good food she’d eaten since leaving the brothel. She could do with losing a little weight, she reassured herself.

“Are you going to eat that, Gargi?” one of the girls asked.

“No. You can share it out.” Pouring water into the other cups, Gargi handed them out. “Once you have finished your food, drink your water, relieve yourselves, then I’m going to turn out the light.”

“Can we leave it on?” Amita asked. “I don’t like the dark.”

“We need to sleep at night and save the light. Once everyone is settled, I'll tell you a story."

She used her hand to wipe the plates. Then stacked them. Even in the brothel they had water to clean with.

Already she was feeling dirty. What state would they be in after so many days without cleaning? One thing she was pedantic about was washing her hands. At the brothel the girls had called her *washer whore*. She didn't care. As the water ran off her hands, she visualized the touch of the men's hands leaving her.

Her fingers trembled. She had to stop thinking so much. It was time to check on Isha.

The child's eyes were still shut and her breathing was labored. Picking up her wrist, Gargi felt a weak pulse.

"Jesus, little Isha needs a miracle right now. Please touch her and heal her," Gargi whispered. "Isha, sweet one. I love you. Jesus loves you and he's holding your hand. Can you feel him? I don't know if you can hear me, but you're not alone." She longed to pick Isha up and cradle her. Instead she placed a blanket over the child's still form.

As much as Gargi wanted to deny it, she knew Isha's spine was broken. The lack of movement in the little body confirmed the danger Isha was in.

It was hard to believe she'd only just met these children. Gargi brushed a stray tear off her face and gazed down at the still form. Her heart pounded and she felt so angry. Everything in her wanted to gather the children close and magically return them to safety.

If Isha survived, what would become of her? Gargi checked the cardboard around the child's neck.

She cocked her head from side to side, trying to relieve some tension. She noticed that most of the girls were settling on the cushions.

Turning, she went to the bucket. With her back to the children, she squatted over the makeshift toilet. Gargi held her breath as the smell whiffed into her nose. Someone had emptied her bowels.

Cringing at the thought of what the container would smell like after ten days, Gargi stood and placed the broken pieces of crate over the top. The few steps it took to reach the light switch didn't alleviate the smell that was hovering around her.

"Everyone settled?" Gargi asked. She had to turn away from the picture the children made, sitting and lying on the cushions. They looked to her for guidance and there was nothing she could do to make this right.

Let the little children come to me.

Her finger froze over the switch. Warmth filled her. If it were the last thing she did, she would introduce these precious ones to her Lord.

Flicking the switch, Gargi dropped to her knees as thick darkness surrounded them. Crawling toward the cushions, she chuckled. "Make room, here I come," she said in a squeaky, funny voice.

Girls shuffled and thumped the cushions as they got comfortable.

Gargi felt the young bodies next to her. "It would be easy to let what is happening destroy us," Gargi told them. "To be unhappy all the time and focus on our pain and this steel prison." Rubbing the arm of the child next to her, Gargi smiled.

Surely praise brings in the presence of God. "No matter what's happening to me, I will not let it overwhelm me."

"How do you do that, Gargi?" Amita asked. "I'm so scared. This is bad enough, but when I think of what might happen to me once those doors are opened—I cannot stop trembling."

"Then don't think about it, Amita. This is the moment you are living in and this is the moment you must think about. Right now!" Gargi ordered firmly. "Can you imagine a wild lily in a grassy field? See the sun's rays warming it. The soft rain watering its roots."

"Mmm," someone whispered. "I can imagine it."

Emotion caught in Gargi's throat. "That flower is just relaxing and it can't make it rain or shine. Maybe there is a gentle breeze or mighty gust of wind. I don't know, but the flower has to accept the weather as it is and make the most of what is thrown at it. We need to do this too. Keep our minds on God and the eternal reward that awaits us. I know bad things are happening, but if you can be devoted to Jesus and rise above the bad things, then your faith and spirit will rise up and make the sun shine."

"I don't think I can," Amita cried. "Poor Isha," she sobbed.

"I like flowers," Daya stated. "I would often stop and smell wildflowers and sometime pick them for my mam. I like the idea of being like a flower."

"Me too," someone agreed.

Gargi wanted to kiss Daya. "Did you know," she whispered, “that in the Bible it says that a person who stands the test will receive the crown of life that the Lord has promised to those who love him?”

“What is Bible?” someone inquired.

“I want a crown of—life,” another girl whispered.

Sighing, Gargi shifted her shoulder and got more comfortable. In a whisper she talked about how she’d met Jesus and all that he had done for her. How even though she had been a prostitute in a brothel, nothing could take away the love of God from her.

Chapter 29

Glancing back at his grandparents, Ashok slid down the sand dune toward the water. Hundreds of starfish lined the beach. Ashok reached down and picked one up. His grandfather had told him that the starfish would have been washed up in the storm last night.

He rubbed his finger over the leathery shell and rested it in his outstretched hand.

The starfish twitched and Ashok held it closer to his face. It was alive. Scooping up another chocolate-brown starfish, he watched the creature's arms sway.

He saw that his grandparents had set up an umbrella and his grandma was sitting in a beach chair talking to Grandpa.

Placing the starfish in his bucket, he picked up another, and then another until the bucket was full.

He plopped down on the warm sand. Pulled off his sandals and placed them neatly together. Taking care not to step on any of the scattered creatures, Ashok waded into the waves until he was up to his knees. He submerged the bucket and bent over to watch the starfishes crawl away.

Leaping through the waves, he lunged back toward the stranded starfish on the beach and filled his bucket again. Ashok saw his grandfather walking toward him.

"There are an awful lot of them," Bill said and handed Ashok another one.

Ashok felt his chest tighten.

"You can't save them all, lad."

"I know. But can you help me save some of them?" Ashok begged. His heart was pounding and he had to do something. Each starfish mattered, just like Shanti mattered. Just like Gargi mattered, just like he mattered.

Bill took off his shirt and knotted the sleeves together. He pushed his arm through the loop he'd made and began picking up starfish and placing them in the shirt.

Ashok jumped up and down. "Grandma," he yelled. "We are saving the starfish."

Striding back into the water, Ashok laughed. When he turned back toward the beach, he saw Grandma was helping.

Tears sprung to his eyes and he caught his breath. Looking out to sea, he watched the waves crash. "Jesus, thank you for my grandparents. I miss my baap, but I am happy here. You see me, don't you, Jesus?"

A warm breeze swirled around him, tickling his face. He licked his lips and tasted salt. He tried to catch more of the ocean in his mouth.

Taking a starfish in his hand, he lowered it into the water.

"You're free. Go live another day." He swished his hand through the white foam. He liked the cool feel on his warm skin. "Jesus, wherever Gargi is, help her know that you are taking care of the starfish."

~

Stretching, Macy sighed and ambled up the beach to have a rest. A day in the sun had turned into backbreaking exercise of rescuing as many starfish as they could. Fortunately others had joined them, so she didn't feel too bad leaving the boys to it.

She dusted sand off her chair then eased herself into the seat. Reaching inside the cooler, she pulled out a bottle of chilled water and took a long swig.

The beach was one of her favorite places. As she looked at the cloudless blue sky waves of warm air settled on her.

Oh, to have the energy of a young boy. Ashok didn't seem to slow down. She so admired the endurance of grandparents who brought up their grandchildren. As much as she enjoyed the boy, she was exhausted.

Life with just Bill was easy. Sometimes they didn't bother having a proper dinner, just filled up on a cup of tea and toast. She felt it important to cook a healthy meal every night for Ashok. He was a growing boy and needed his nutrients.

She pulled her hat farther down to protect her face from

the sun and closed her eyes. Having difficulty sleeping was paying its toll; she felt so frustrated that the night flushes were keeping her awake.

Last night Bill had snored away and she'd given up trying to go to sleep and read until 1:00 a.m.

Rubbing her eyes, she listened to the sound of Ashok's laughter and pictured his happy face in her mind. If Eli found Gargi—*when* Eli found Gargi, Macy corrected herself. She sniffed back the sadness that came with the thought of the precious girl being missing.

Macy wanted Gargi here. Safe. Married to her son and a mother to Ashok.

She never thought she would love a child that wasn't her blood as much as she loved Ashok.

Wringing her hands, Macy longed to hold Gargi close to her heart. She wanted to make things right for her and show her what a mother's love was like.

She clutched her chest. Would the pain never go away? Would their lives ever return to a semblance of normality?

"Grandma, Grandma," Ashok yelled excitedly as he ran toward her.

Wiping the moisture off her face, Macy forced a smile.

Ashok stretched out his hand and showed her the perfectly shaped orange fan-shaped shell.

"Oh my. It's simply beautiful, Ashok."

"I want you to have it, Grandma," he stated proudly.

"Are you sure, sweetheart? You found it, maybe you should keep it."

Ashok's mouth spread wide in a grin. "I like it very much,

that's why I want you to have it. It is very pretty and I know girls like pretty things. I love you, Grandma."

Macy's eyes watered as she took the shell. "I will treasure it forever. Thank you." She stood, then opened her arms, and Ashok dived into her embrace.

Her hand rubbed his back. She couldn't stop the tears that slipped out onto her cheeks.

"Are you okay, Grandma?"

"Mmm" She was too choked up to talk.

Stepping back, Ashok frowned. "Then why are you crying?"

Macy cupped his sweet cheek. "Happy tears. I love you so much and am so thankful that you are my grandson."

"Really? I don't understand tears when you're happy. I laugh when I'm happy. Girls are strange." Ashok nodded his head as if he had just discovered a new truth.

"You're not wrong there," Bill agreed as he joined them.

Macy patted Bill's arm.

"Grandma, do you think God is happy with us for saving the starfish?"

"Oh, yes." Her grandson's desire to please God made her feel soft inside. "It's important to do what you can. I'm very proud of you."

~

Padma smoothed out the rumples on the sheet then tucked the linen edge under the mattress. Charlie handed her a colorful hand-knitted blanket.

She spread it over the bed, liking the warm welcoming colors and soft textures. Mrs Turner had sent the wool blankets to Shanti's Rest from Australia. Each blanket was made by someone from her church.

Padma enjoyed getting the rooms ready for a new girl. It was something she could do that showed she cared. Earlier she'd put a small bunch of tuberosa flowers in a vase. The strong, sweet scent reminder her of grapes.

Charlie sat on the edge of the bed. "Please, Padma? I don't want to meet with this man on my own. For some reason he gives me the creeps, and I don't know how to explain it to Ted without seeming paranoid."

"You cannot let every man you meet throw you into a spin, Charlie. You are the one who told me that not all men are evil."

"Yes, I know," Charlie admitted with a grin. "That's why I want you to come with me. Check out my response and reassure me that he's okay."

Padma glanced at her watch. She didn't want to tell Charlie that she trusted her instincts and that the man probably was a creep. "Where are we meeting him?"

"Oh, thank you!" Charlie threw her arms around Padma.

Padma laughed. She was always surprised by Charlie's demonstrations of affection. At first she'd struggled to return the hugs, but now she looked forward to them.

"I told Mr Singh we'd meet him at the hotel at ten this

morning. He suggested someplace else but I wanted to be somewhere I know and with people around us. I also refused his offer to pick me up."

"I can be ready in half an hour." Padma glanced at Charlie through her eyelashes. She desperately wanted to talk to her about Tanvir, but didn't want to burden her friend with her problems.

Charlie raised her eyebrows. "What is it, Padma?"

Shrugging, Padma waved her hands. "Tanvir puts pressure on me to live with them. My brother is most insistent about it being his responsibility to take care of me since our parents are no longer alive. This is more difficult than I thought." She clutched her arms around her stomach. "I keep thinking that the more my family gets to know me, then they—um—they will eventually reject me."

"Padma, we have talked about this. You have to start liking yourself. You are a beautiful woman and they love you."

"This is easier said than done, my friend. I tell myself it will all work out, but I fear such a rejection." She pinched the bridge of her nose. If only she could embrace love.

Tears pooled in Charlie's eyes. "Why do you insist on living in the future and not enjoying today? Love them back. I see you wanting to withdraw from them because you fear their rejection. Instead you're the one who is rejecting them."

"No, no! I would never reject them, I love them."

"What do you think it looks like from their point of view? You refuse their every invitation—often you don't return Tanvir or Oni's calls. You are an aunty, for goodness sake!" Crossing her arms in front of herself, Charlie stared at her.

"How do you think little Padma will feel as she gets older, knowing you didn't want to be her aunty?"

Dipping her head, Padma blinked back tears. She couldn't stand the thought of her niece thinking she didn't want to be involved in her life.

"You are right, of course. I must make some changes. Life is anything but simple. That you could forgive me still amazes me."

"Padma." Charlie stepped toward her and touched her shoulder.

Padma's throat thickened.

Charlie wiped moisture off her own eyelashes. "Don't keep going over old ground. You're my friend and I love you. Jesus loves you—and until you get this through that pretty head of yours, you'll continue to go round in circles."

"Circles?" Padma gave Charlie a half smile. The more time she spent with Charlie, the less she could deny her friends God. And Tanvir didn't preach at her as she'd expected. He just wanted to be a part of her life.

"Gosh," Charlie grabbed Padma's hand. "We have ten minutes to get there. Hurry, go get ready. I've got the feeling Mr Singh doesn't like to be kept waiting."

Chapter 30

The soft moaning woke Gargi. At first she thought it must be Isha but then realized the sound was coming from farther over on the cushions.

Crawling across to the floor, she turned on the light and straightened to stretch out her back.

"Gargi, my stomach hurts," Pia sobbed. "I'm going to be…" Her hand covered her mouth and she lunged off the cushions toward the empty bucket beside Gargi.

Pia dunked her head into the bucket and her whole body jerked as she heaved.

Holding the girl's hair away from her face, Gargi tried not to gag at the foul smell that rose to her nose. She glanced across at the other girls to give them a reassuring smile and noticed other pale, unwell faces.

"It's okay, Pia. I've got you," Gargi soothed.

Pia flopped down beside the bucket and wiped the back of

her hand over her mouth.

"Get out of my way," Neha screamed, grabbing the bucket.

"Oh no," Gargi moaned as she twisted to help Neha. Her hand supported Neha's forehead. Gargi cooed softly as Neha vomited.

Angling her head, Gargi looked at the girls on the cushions. "Does anyone else feel like they're going to be sick?"

Several heads nodded and Gargi's stomach twisted. It had to be the rice. Why didn't she listen to her instincts and not let them eat it?

"I'll get the other bucket ready," Daya muttered.

"Do you feel okay, Daya?" Gargi asked hopefully.

"I feel a little queasy, but I don't think I'm going to throw up." Daya patted her stomach and shrugged. "I'm tough."

"My stomach feels like it's cramping," moaned Neha as she curled into a ball.

"Anyone who doesn't feel like you're going to vomit, please pick up your cushion and move over there." Gargi pointed. "Quickly, girls," she snapped. She hated the sound of her voice, but how on earth was she going to take care of this mess? The smell alone would only get worse as the days ticked by, and she knew by experience that the girls who vomited would need to drink more water to stay hydrated.

Ripping the end of her sari, she tipped a little of their precious water onto the fabric and went to wipe Pia's face.

"I'm so thirsty, can I have some water, Gargi?" Pia begged.

"Soon, Pia, soon." Avoiding Pia's eyes, Gargi sat behind

her and plaited her hair away from her face. She used the end strands of hair to make a knot and hoped it would hold. She turned to Daya. "Can you help me plait everyone's hair?"

Daya nodded. She sidled up to a girl and caressed her hair.

Gargi watched as she busily plaited the girls' hair and was surprised when she started to hum. As much as the girl snapped at everyone, there was something about her that Gargi liked. The hard shell hid a soft interior, and Gargi wanted to protect her from becoming hard on the inside.

"Daya," Gargi called.

The girl turned and looked across the gap between them, her eyebrows raised in question.

"I love you. You remind me of myself when I was your age. If I had a sister, I'd want her to be just like you." Smiling, Gargi blew her a kiss.

Daya's eyes flooded. "I would be pleased to have you as my sister."

"Sisters, then," Gargi stated.

~

Khlaid snapped the pencil and threw it across the office. He should be concentrating on his planned abduction of Charlotte and enjoying the excitement of finally having her back where she belonged. Now he had Frank breathing down his neck.

The knocking on the door made him scowl.

Frank entered without waiting for permission, and this annoyed Khlaid even more. It was times like this that he wished he had full mobility and he'd show the stuck-up white boy who was boss.

"Sir, I've been on the phone all morning and the storm is not letting up. We need to do something. It's been a week and there is no way the water and food supplies in the container will see them through to the end of the journey."

"What do you expect me to do? Go to the authorities and tell them I have a shipment of slaves in transit that could possibly die because the stupid shipping line can't weather a storm and stick to time schedules?"

"You cannot let them die," Frank snarled.

"Why the sudden concern? They are merely merchandise." Khlaid mocked Frank's behavior and shrugged his shoulders. He would not let his fear of failure weaken his position with this man.

"It is time to play your next card. Contact the captain. You know this is an option," Frank challenged. "The buyers have been requesting delivery dates. They are not happy that the shipment has been delayed. You need to ensure the girls are in good condition upon arrival."

Rubbing his eyes, Khlaid sat back and sighed. He waved his hand in dismissal.

Frank stood silently in front of Khlaid's desk and crossed his arms.

Khlaid swallowed the growl that rose up his throat. He wanted to push his fist into the guy's face. How dare he stand there and mock his authority?

"Get out," he screamed. "You have your orders. I will take care of the shipment. We have a little time to see if the ship catches up on lost time."

"I will be reporting this." Frank cursed, spun around, and charged out the door.

Picking up his glass of water, Khlaid took a slow sip. His hand shook, so he tightened his fingers around the cool glass. Things would work out in his favor, they always did. The consignment would get there on time.

He readied himself to meet with Charlotte.

~

Padma had left Charlie sitting on the sofa in the reception area and went to the bathroom. She glanced at her reflection in the mirror and liked what she saw. She looked—fresher. She traced the lines around her eyes. The frown that had been her constant companion was gone. She was starting to believe there was a good future ahead for her.

She'd move in with Tanvir and his family. Her family.

Drying her hands, she turned to leave and hesitated. She smiled at her reflection. "You are real, Jesus. I believe this. I see you in the people around me. Is being saved really as simple as believing?"

The door behind her opened. Dipping her head, Padma

edged past the woman who was entering the bathroom and grinned. Her steps felt lighter somehow, as if she were walking on air. Maybe admitting she believed in Jesus was the first step. As soon as she got some time to herself, she was going to read some of the verses Charlie had highlighted in the Bible she'd gifted her.

She returned to the reception area. The man standing in front of Charlie had his back to Padma, yet there was something about the way he was standing that—triggered something in her. She halted.

Sweeping her gaze around the room, Padma hated the way her peace disappeared as if sucked out by a vacuum cleaner. She had to force herself to step forward.

The problem with having worked in a brothel was that there had been so many men. Faces that seemed vaguely familiar reminded her of the past.

Stiffening her spine, she determined not to be intimidated by the man offering them financial support. He either got on board because he believed in their work, or she would flick him off like an unwanted fly.

A giggle rose within her and she tried to suppress it. How she'd changed. She felt more confident and loved because she was finally beginning to like herself.

"Hello," she said boldly and laid her hand on Charlie's arm. She turned toward the man.

His eyes hardened for a moment, and then he bowed before her.

A chill touched the base of her spine and her mouth went dry.

"Padma, I'd like you to meet Mr Singh," Charlie stated politely, and Padma could tell that Charlie was not relaxed by the tone of her voice.

Mr Singh held out his hand toward her. Padma wanted to ignore the gesture.

Her mouth clamped shut to stop a rude comment escaping. She placed her hand in his and glanced down at their joined hands. The feel of his flesh touching hers creeped her out. The inner trembling made her feel physically sick.

Pulling her fingers free, she stopped herself from wiping her hand down her sari. Glancing at Charlie, Padma decided to take control of the meeting. "Mr Singh, Charlotte tells me you are thinking of investing in the work at Shanti's Rest."

"Yes. I have already written out one check. May we be seated? I have difficulty standing for long periods of time." He audibly swallowed. "I have this um—war injury." Mr Singh laughed softly and rubbed his leg.

"I'll order refreshments," Charlie offered. "Please take a seat, Mr Singh. Padma, perhaps you can share some of the work that takes place at Shanti's Rest."

"Of course." Padma turned to lead the way across the lounge. She didn't like him. When she reached the cream couches, she turned to watch Mr Singh's approach.

His face wasn't familiar, but everything else about him told her clearly who he was. That Khlaid would think he could hide from her made her want to spit in his face. He may have changed his appearance, but his eyes were the same and the feel of his hand on hers had sent the same shivers up her spine. The tilt of his head as he moved and the way his shoulders sloped as he walked. All these things confirmed what she knew to be true.

Charlie joined them and sat next to Padma.

"I believe you were right, Charlie," Padma stated calmly and faced Khlaid. "Did you know, *Mr Singh*, that Charlotte has the ability to judge people and see through to the truth behind their eyes?" She wanted to scream out his real name and expose him for the animal he was.

"A good ability I am sure," Mr Singh agreed. "You can see that I am a genuine supporter I hope, Charlotte?"

Padma widened her eyes, trying to send a signal to Charlie.

Charlie tried to laugh. "I am sure you are genuine in your kindness, Mr Singh. I think what Padma is trying to say is that—"

Sitting forward over her knees, Padma interrupted. "What I am saying is that there is no way in hell that we will take any money from you." She sprung to her feet and yanked on Charlie's arm to make her stand.

"Padma!" Charlie gazed sternly at Padma. "Please forgive my friend, Mr Singh. I'm not sure what's gotten into her."

"Charlie, this man is a fraud." Padma sneered and leaned closer to him across the table. She couldn't take the deception any longer. "You may be able to change your face, Khlaid. But I'd know you anywhere."

All the color left Charlie's face. Her forehead furrowed and her eyes widened in surprise.

Coughing into his hand, he shook his head. "I do not know of whom you speak." He stood and leaned heavily on his cane. "I think I will be going. There is no way I will continue to support such an—an unbalanced group of people." Stumbling, he turned and walked away.

The shaking set in the minute Khlaid left them. Padma gripped Charlie's hands. "What shall we do? I know it's him," she said.

"How can it be? He's nothing like Saul."

"It's him, you know it is. He's up to something—we need to call Eli."

Charlie sat back down. She pulled a cushion from behind her back and hugged it. "I agree that I don't trust him, but how can you be so certain it's Saul—Khlaid?"

The shaking began in Padma's knees and she collapsed on the couch beside Charlie. She wasn't brave like her friend. She'd given her life over to Khlaid once before and the thought of him taking control of her again terrified her.

"We don't have time for this discussion, Charlie. Call your brother, please," Padma begged.

Chapter 31

Ashok's voice on the other end of the phone sounded excited and Eli couldn't help but grin. These calls with his son had become the highlight of his days. Somehow the boy grounded him and gave him a sense of purpose. Ashok needed his baap to come through for him. Eli knew he couldn't wallow in self-pity and ignore his responsibilities.

"Baap, do you think that one day we will live in Australia for good?"

"Would you like to?" Eli asked instead of answering his son's question.

"I miss India, but I never had a home there. We lived with Uncle Phillip. But here I have my own room and I have made friends."

"I honestly don't know what the future holds, son. I miss you and want you with me, but for now I'm glad you are happy there."

"Please tell me what is happening. I miss Gargi. Any news about her?"

Staring into space, Eli blinked several times. Today it was like a tap had been turned on inside his head. He wiped the moisture from his eyes then forced cheerfulness into his voice.

"No news yet, but I'm sure she's fine. God has a way of looking after us, although sometimes we don't understand."

"You will find her, I believe this," Ashok stated. "Did you like the picture I drew you?"

"I love it. I'm having it framed, it's so good."

"It's not that good," Ashok chuckled.

Eli smiled and tried to picture the boy's face. "Ashok, thank you for the drawing. I love you, son."

"I love you too." Ashok's voice wavered.

"I'll call you in a couple of days." Eli didn't want to hang up. He wanted to hold on to the connection and refuse to let go of what was real to him.

"Baap, I will look forward to talking with you again. Bye."

Stunned at his son's confidence in him, he put down the phone and went into the small kitchen to pour himself a drink.

Hearing the boy was content made it easier. Eli envied his parents and for a moment wished that he could swap places with them. Australia seemed so far away; the home he'd grown up in, like a long-lost dream.

Isak had ordered him to take a day off and stay home. "Rest and get some sleep" had been his exact words. Eli knew he was getting grumpier by the day. As much as he tried to control his words, he snapped at everyone. His nerves were at breaking point.

Another girl had been rescued last night and was with Charlie now. Shanti's Rest was bursting at the seams. Charlie insisted they needed to keep working. That Gargi would not want them to lose sight of the prize.

Every girl rescued sent out a message of hope to the others. Charlie wanted to start a campaign advertising what they were doing and extend the work to other cities. A great idea, but the logistics worried him. They'd need to increase their fundraising efforts.

His stared into the glass of water and absently swirled the liquid around. He took a small sip then placed the glass on the bench.

His shoulders ached with tension. If he had his way, he'd have an army storming the gates of every brothel in the city. What pleasure he'd get in locking up every person who thought he had the right to turn people into slaves.

The more he thought about it, the more he seethed.

He couldn't mope around the hotel, waiting for another day to arrive. He tipped his head to the right then to the left trying to unlock a knot.

A run. That's what he needed. He pulled on socks then bent over and pushed his feet into his joggers.

Walking down the street, he stretched his legs and tried to get enthusiastic about upping his pace. His energy level felt like zero and each step seemed labored. It seemed pointless.

The last two years of his life had been nothing but pain.

His feet moved of their own accord and he listened to the

thud of his shoes on the road. He liked the feel of his muscles kicking into action.

Ashok's face flashed through his mind. He didn't want to focus on how good it was to be the boy's father. He wanted to allow himself a moment of self-pity.

Squinting his eyes against the sweat that dripped down his forehead, he clenched his jaw. If his father were here right now, Eli knew his dad would ask him where his peace had gone. His dad had taught him well. His words still rang in his ears even now.

He increased his speed and tried to block out the sermon that was pushing at his brain.

"When your heart is fixed, Eli, trusting totally in God, then it is kept at peace and is not afraid."

Stopping, he bent and gripped his knees. Moisture dripped off his face onto the pavement and he watched as the splats spread, drying on the heat of the road.

Peace? How could he have peace when—when he loved her? What if he never found her?

My peace I give you.

Folding his arms defiantly, Eli braced his feet.

"Where is your peace?" he shouted into the traffic zooming past him. "I don't feel it!"

Did God expect him to blindly accept that Gargi could be lost to him forever? It was all very well claiming you had the peace of God, but when it came to the crunch—when your very life counted on it—what then?

"Answer me. What do you expect of me?" He flailed his hands in the air.

A car screeched past him, narrowly missing his legs. Eli stepped off the road. The unobservant driver had been on his cell phone.

Eli started walking back the way he'd come. He felt pressed in on every side and couldn't see a way through the fog that clouded his vision. God's peace was a gift. He knew that. He also knew he had to accept it; yet part of him wanted to rebel against such a total acceptance of things he could not change. It felt like he was on a roller coaster, one moment totally committed to the ride and trusting in the apparatus, the next moment screaming to get off.

He swung his arms faster, increasing his pace. When he'd first met Gargi, he felt an instant connection. She shyly met his gaze and instinctively he wanted to protect her. She deserved so much more than life had given her, and he wanted to be the one to lay it all at her feet.

He tried to regulate his breathing. The noises around him faded and melded together as he reflected on the past. He should have trusted in her love for him and not let her go off by herself. If he'd gone with her, they'd be together now.

Stupid, plain stupid!

She is not yours, Eli.

His heart pounded and tears flooded his eyes. He'd learned this lesson before with Charlie. He'd had to release his sister totally into God's hands.

Could he do this again?

Did he want to survive the pain of losing Gargi?

What option did he have? While he still had breath in his lungs, he had to carry on, he had to choose to believe in a brighter tomorrow. He had to hope.

"Forgive me, Lord. I am but a man. Forgive my struggle and help me." He forced away the haunted image of how Gargi had looked when he'd first met her. His vision blurred as he watched clouds zoom above him. He fixed his eyes on the unseen, on the truth of God's presence.

Never will I leave you.

Exhaling loudly, he let his shoulders relax.

"You're with Gargi, I know you are."

He'd do what he could and leave the rest to God. God saw everything. Gargi was not alone.

He visualized Jesus handing him a cloak, a garment of peace. Warmth covered him and he determined to stay in this place of trust. If he walked into the shadows, then he'd take the light with him.

He paced himself, no longer in a hurry.

When he arrived at the hotel, he skirted around the back of the building to avoid the patrons. As he waited for the staff elevator to arrive, he swiped sweat off his forehead with the back of his hand.

As soon as the elevator arrived, he stepped in and pressed his floor number and the close door button. He didn't want company. Not knowing what his next move was didn't faze him. God would show him.

The doors opened and he strode down the hall to his room. Swiping the electronic key over the lock, he entered his suite.

As he stepped over the threshold into the room, his foot landed on a white envelope, which must have been pushed under the door.

Eli slipped his finger under the flap of the envelope then withdrew a typed sheet of paper.

I don't want to care, but I do.

Gargi touched me by her forgiveness and I find her face now haunts me.

You will find her and others in a shipping container headed for Saudi Arabia.

Ship's name: Jag Tan.

Container number: CTQU9257607.

The burden is now yours.

Eli sucked in a deep breath.

He charged into his bedroom and hastily changed clothes.

Snatching up his phone and car keys from the table by the door, he ran out of the apartment.

~

Gargi's fingers shook as she handed Pia the shallow cup of water. She desperately wanted to pour the contents down her own throat. Running her tongue over her dry, cracked lips, she tried to moisten them. It seemed that her tongue had dried up on her.

"Thank you," Pia whispered. The words were so hushed that Gargi had to duck her head close to Pia's face to hear her.

The swell of the ship made it difficult to stand and Gargi

swayed as she staggered to return the cup. The water jug was just about empty and she felt sick to her stomach with the thirst that was screaming within her. She'd not had a drink for two days and knew she couldn't hold out much longer.

The girls had been so dehydrated after the food poisoning that she'd relented and let them drink more than their daily quota. Waves crashed against the side of the container and several girls gasped.

Squatting down where she was, Gargi hugged her legs and rested her forehead on her bent knees.

At first being out at sea had been reassuring. Gargi thought the sooner they reached their destination, the sooner they could get out of this stinking box.

She felt so dirty.

Everyone was urinating less but the buckets were full to overflowing with unspeakable waste.

She'd smelt bad things in her life but this stench grew worse each day. It was like a decaying carcass and just the thought of it made her gag. Her throat burned from the seasickness that had brought bile up from her stomach.

Gargi longed to wash her hands and hated the irony of the waves outside mocking her need to get clean. Even saltwater would be better than none.

If only there was a lull in the storm. Clutching her stomach, she bent over. The waves were relentlessly bashing into the container and the roaring sounds made her imagination go wild.

She grimaced as she recalled someone once telling her that the ocean bed was littered with shipping containers lost in storms.

At one stage it sounded like a container above them had shifted, and the grinding sound from the roof had brought fears of their container slipping from the ship into the sea.

She glanced up at the small air vents and wished they actually provided some clean air. The tiny holes seemed to have clogged up, letting little air through into the foul-smelling container.

Her throat felt thick and she took a shallow breath.

They'd had to resort to having turns using the air canister. The putrid smells coming from the buckets and the dampness that seemed to hang off them all, were making it hard to breathe.

The light wavered and her head jerked up. *Please don't go out, please*. She prayed silently.

"Gargi! Isha isn't breathing," Amita cried.

Slowly turning her head in Amita's direction, Gargi wanted to deny the words she heard. The little girl hadn't opened her eyes once. She'd not eaten anything, and it had been almost impossible to trickle water down her throat.

It took all Gargi's energy to push up from her position on the floor and crawl to Isha. She pressed her fingers into the child's wrist to search for a pulse.

The tiny girl's arm was limp and cool to the touch. There was no flicker of life under Gargi's fingers.

Her stomach plummeted with the finality of it.

Gulping back her grief, Gargi stiffened her spine. She had to be the one to reassure the others. There was no one else for them but her. Yet all she wanted to do was curl up into a ball and deny the hopelessness of it all.

"Is she dead?" Pia cried.

"Yes. Isha has left us," Gargi said in a husky voice. "Jesus has taken her to—heaven. She's not in any pain now."

No one spoke; and as much as Gargi wanted to cry, she didn't have the energy. She blinked, trying to clear her vision, but it remained blurred.

Lifting a blanket, she covered Isha then sat back on her heels.

Who would be next to die? As much as she hated to think about it, Isha may have had the easiest death. Resting her chin on her chest, she closed her eyes and examined the struggle within her heart.

It was not over. She would not give in to the heavy weight that pressed down on her lungs, twisting and turning and making it difficult to breathe. She opened her eyes again to look at these girls who depended on her for hope.

"Amita, Daya, can you come here, please."

Neither girl spoke as they sat down beside her, and Gargi wished she didn't have to burden them with the truth of their situation. They were so young.

"We don't have enough water to go the distance," she whispered. "The food is gone, and because of the storm I'm not sure how many days before we arrive in port… and then I don't know how long it will be before someone comes and opens the doors."

Amita gripped Gargi's arm. The feel of the child's fingers on her skin was reassuring somehow. "Gargi, you need to have some water. Please—we need you."

"I will have some soon," she promised. "I'm not worried about the food running out. I'm sure we can all survive without food for a few days, but without water…" She glanced at Amita. The girl's face glistened with sweat and Daya's complexion was no better.

Gargi lifted the weight of her hair off her neck, hoping for some relief from the heat. When the rain stopped, the container heated up like a furnace; the more they sweated, the more water they would need to stop dehydration setting in.

At night they were freezing, and during the day the metal walls seemed to burn off all the moisture left in the air.

"I've told you Jesus loves you, I've told you how I'm not afraid to die," she whispered to try and save her energy.

"Hush, Gargi," Daya ordered. "You think we want to listen to you talking like this? You call us sister then talk of dying. Do not do this to us," she snapped.

Pulling herself up into a sitting position, Gargi nodded. "I'm sorry. I just wanted to reassure you."

"I'm getting you some water," Amita proclaimed. She went and poured a small amount into a cup.

"Drink," Daya ordered.

Gargi's mouth felt so dry and sticky. She was so tired. It would be so easy to close her eyes and shut out all that was around her. A small smile lifted the corner of her mouth and she grimaced as the crack in her lip stung.

The girls loved her and wanted to look after her. She could feel the pounding of her heart in her chest and knew she needed to focus.

She blinked several times. Was there someone else in the

container with them? Liking the idea of an angel being present, she allowed her mind to picture a mighty warrior spreading his wings and flapping them to create a breeze for them.

"Can you feel the air moving?" she croaked.

Shaking her head, Daya reached over and lifted the cup to Gargi's mouth. She wanted to refuse to drink, but she swallowed the small dribble of water greedily.

"Thank you," she whispered.

"How long can we last without water?" Amita asked.

"As long as we have to." Daya's forehead creased and Gargi wanted to reach out to smooth the worry away.

Wishing she didn't have to correct Daya, Gargi shook her head. "The body needs water to survive. I think three days is about how long you can live without water. Not only do we not have enough water for all of us—but the heat during the day and the icy cold at night are sucking more moisture from our bodies."

"My skin is driving me mad," Neha complained from behind them. The sound of her scratching made Gargi turn to her.

"Don't scratch, precious," Gargi begged. "I know your skin is itchy and I don't know why this is happening to us. But can you pat away the itch rather than scratch?"

Gargi tried to create some saliva in her mouth, but the little water she'd swallowed hadn't made a difference.

Daya slid up to her and rested her head on Gargi's shoulder.

It took an enormous effort, but Gargi raised her hand and

brushed Daya's hair. If anyone were to survive this nightmare, it would be Daya. She tried to encourage the smaller children and worked hard to help clean their small space. She was brave.

"Eli Turner," Gargi whispered.

"What?" Daya murmured.

"Eli Turner. I want you to remember this man's name. He's such a good man and I love him. If I don't make it, or even if I do and we get separated, I want you to remember his name."

"Why?" Amita bent forward to listen.

"Because you have to find him. If ever you get the chance to escape, try and get a message to him. He'll help you."

"It would be impossible," Amita said dejectedly.

"No, not impossible," challenged Daya. "What did you say about all things being possible, Gargi?"

"You remembered? I'm not sure of the verse right now, but God will never leave you. He's here right now. Live well, be kind." She coughed and the action hurt her chest. "Eli Turner," Gargi urged. "Remember his name." Closing her eyes, she welcomed the darkness. "Daya, can you turn the light out? Maybe if we try and sleep, this storm will pass and then we can talk some more."

As darkness surrounded them, Gargi sighed. Her tongue felt swollen and cracked, and she knew she couldn't last too much longer without water. The air was pungent around them and she longed to feel the ocean breeze on her face.

Jesus, my Lord.

Her heart was sad for what could have been. She wondered if she'd ever have the opportunity to show Eli how much he meant to her. She pictured Ashok's sweet face and yearned to make things right with him.

Please, Lord. If she had the chance, she'd be his mother in a minute. If she had the chance, she'd have all these children here as her own.

"Gargi, can you pray? I always feel better when you pray," someone said.

Gargi rubbed her forehead. It was easier to pray in her mind than to try and form words on lips that seemed to have forgotten how to move. *Lord, help me comfort them through your Word.*

Gargi's voice sounded croaky, but as she started talking, it seemed like honey slipped down her throat and soothed away the crackle.

"Then the angel showed me the river of the water of life, as clear as crystal." Gargi marveled at the words. She didn't know where they were coming from, but it was like she could hear them echoed in her mind. "As clear as crystal," she continued, "flowing from the throne of God and of the Lamb down the middle of the great street of the city."

"I can hear the sound of the river," Pia whispered.

Gargi listened and imagined the sound of the waves hitting the walls around them becoming the sound of water, clear as crystal flowing down a heavenly river. Saltwater becoming freshwater, and there would be a huge number of fish. Where this river flowed—everything lived.

"I hear it too," Amita laughed.

"Tell us more," begged Daya.

More, Lord.

Warmth surrounded her and Gargi wanted to laugh. What the enemy intended as their prison suddenly became a holy place.

"On each side of the river stood the tree of life, bearing twelve crops of fruit, yielding its fruit every month. And the leaves of the tree are for the healing of the nations. No longer will there be any curse."

"Is this real?" Daya asked. "I so want it to be real. I don't understand it, but I can picture the trees filled with fruit."

"It's real," Gargi confirmed. She raised her hand and imagined waving it through the cooling, crystal water. She could plainly see fish swimming next to her fingers. For a moment she thought she could feel the chill of the water on her hand.

"The throne of God and the Lamb—Jesus is the Lamb, girls. I understand now, for the first time, why the Lamb."

She could see the Lamb and his eyes beckoned her. Loved her.

Jesus.

Blinking into the darkness, she tried to clear her vision. "It is the Lamb who takes away the sins of the world," she murmured.

"I don't understand," Pia said and her voice sounded too loud in the soft air that surrounded Gargi.

"A long time ago," Gargi whispered, "lambs were sacrificed as a way of cleaning people from their sins. It didn't really work though, because people kept sinning and then they needed another sacrifice, then another. God has to punish sin"—she coughed painfully into her hand—"so he sent his son, Jesus, to take our sin upon himself. Jesus died on our behalf on the cross, and I think he is the Lamb. Yes, I know he is the Lamb."

Gargi squeezed her eyes tight, focused on the colors swimming around her. She slumped deeper into the cushion and declared into the darkness, "They will see his face, and his name will be on their foreheads. There will be no more night. They will not need the light of a lamp or the light of the sun, for the Lord God will give them light."

"I want his name on my forehead," Daya exclaimed. "Jesus, be my Lamb, forgive me," she called out urgently.

"Me too," Amita sobbed.

Pia curled into a ball and hid her face in the cushion.

Gargi's heart skipped a beat. There were times when she noticed such fear on Pia's young face that even the darkness of her skin paled. One so young should not have to think about danger and death.

She wanted to make promises she couldn't keep to this child.

The little girl was so thin and much smaller than Shanti had been, maybe only six years old.

Gargi remembered Amita telling her that Pia never knew her parents. Her mother had died in childbirth. Pia had lived by collecting the rubbish from around the village. The child had no family. No wonder she'd all but given up.

Gargi longed to be Pia's mam.

Chapter 32

As much as he wanted to deny that he was in trouble, Khlaid felt like a fly caught in a spider's web. He couldn't run, because the strands of the web had him trapped; and every time he tried to escape, it felt like a noose tightened around his throat.

He cursed Frank. He knew the man had reported to his superiors about the trouble with the shipment. Already the buyers had withdrawn funds from his account and he'd been unable to stop them.

Now he was faced with the problem of contacting the captain and agreeing to his terms. This was his first experience with international shipping and he regretted not sticking with what he knew.

Frank had insisted Khlaid contact the captain two days ago, but he'd hoped the storm would abate, allowing the ship to catch up on lost time. It hadn't.

To involve the captain meant a cut in profits and a loss of merchandise. The captain would take two of the best girls from the consignment.

His contacts on shore had informed him they were not going anywhere near the ship. They had cursed his stupidity in not supplying more water and food for the captives. He clicked his jaw.

Frank had argued to stock up with more supplies.

Khlaid's eye began to sting and he yelped in pain. He scowled and pushed his hand into the spot that hurt.

Cursing, he sat down and pulled out a small mirror from his desk drawer. A blood vessel had burst, and the white of his eye had fiery red veins distorting the color.

Sitting back, he closed his eyes.

He had been wrong to not listen, but Frank had annoyed him with his demands—and that had made Khlaid more determined to have things his way.

This mess wouldn't be upon him now if he hadn't needed to prove a point with Frank—that he was the boss.

Now he had no idea where Frank was.

Khlaid had left messages for his employer to phone him, but no one was talking to him. The only response he'd received was that he had better clean up his mess or they'd clean him up.

If he was going down, then Padma and Charlotte were going with him. He couldn't believe that slut Padma had recognized him.

Fury ignited within him and his body shook with the force of his anger.

The door opened and two men entered.

Khlaid's insides burned. If these men could collect enough girls to soothe his impatient buyer, he may be able to get out of this alive. "You know what to do," he snarled. "Go and get them."

One of the men stepped forward. "Boss, we can get you a new shipment of girls—but we want our money up front."

"You doubt me?" he sneered.

They stood solidly in front of him.

"Get out," he bellowed. "I will get someone who doesn't question my authority."

"You place the money in our hands, and we will have the girls for you in three hours. But it's as we thought, you are over." Turning, the first man motioned to the door with his jaw. Both men left without another word.

"I—am—not—over," Khlaid shouted at their retreating backs.

The door slammed and he collapsed into the chair. What was he to do? He'd spent some of the advance already and if he didn't supply, then… He shuddered to think of what would happen to him.

Running his tongue over his teeth, he realized he missed the gap that had been filled. How often had he unconsciously pushed his tongue into the hole between his teeth when he'd been worried? Now his tongue slid over the smooth veneer and it didn't feel right.

He wanted his old appearance back. Who was he to think he could be someone else when all along he was who he was?

Picking up the phone, he placed the unavoidable call to the

captain. The smug tone of the man's voice over the crackly line only reinforced Khlaid's anger.

"Can you access the container?" he screamed into the phone.

"Of course. We plan for these developments," the captain replied. "You think a ship this size has no order? Your container is in bay fifty-three as planned."

Slamming the phone into its socket, he accepted the inevitable. There would not be so much profit, but he'd be okay.

He ground his false teeth. His thoughts flustered him. Charlotte had tried to be kind to him. What was it about her that continually gnawed at his gut?

Picking up his car keys, he absently twisted them in his hand.

Had Charlotte helped Gargi escape the brothel? If she had, could she have left instead of Gargi—but chosen to stay?

Why would she do that? He raised his fingers to the hidden scar on his hairline that had stretched his skin and changed his appearance. His fingers became frantic and his nails tore at the itch.

He remembered Charlotte begging him to help her rescue the little girl.

Shanti's face swam before his eyes. She was small, beautiful, and quiet. The boss had hurt her bad, yet she'd hardly said a word. In the end she'd died and everything had collapsed. Charlotte had spoken to her God and his legs had become like jelly under him.

His eyes widened.

Why hadn't he thought about this before? He had been so

angry by what had happened to him that he'd wanted revenge.

He still wanted revenge. Wanted to—to what? Hurt Charlotte like he'd been hurt. What good would that do? It wouldn't change anything.

Charlotte's God had power.

A small trickle of blood dripped from his scar and ran down his cheek. He wiped it with his finger. Staring at the blood smear on his finger, he wondered at all the blood he'd spilt. He enjoyed inflicting pain and the power it gave him.

Rubbing his index finger together with his thumb, he liked the smooth feeling between his fingers.

If her God could make him a cripple, then why didn't he save Charlotte before she was turned into a whore?

Surely such a God couldn't be trusted. Her God wasn't real; he was just a figment of her imagination.

He opened the office safe and removed the remaining money stashed there and pocketed a gun. It would be enough to set up a place for Charlotte.

Khlaid picked up his cane and strode with purpose out of the building.

He'd walk into Shanti's Rest like he owned it and take Charlotte. The captain would secure the shipment and life would go on as planned.

Patting his pocket, he felt the gun and hesitated for a moment. He lifted the cane and stiffened his leg. He was no cripple. The doctors had said there was nothing wrong with him.

Khlaid hurled the cane across the street and smiled as it

bounced and landed.

He was the master of his own life; no one would tell him what to do. He slipped his hand into his pocket and wrapped his fingers around the gun.

Stepping out onto the road, he glanced for approaching traffic before he ran toward his car.

His legs felt strong and powerful.

Laughing, Khlaid slid into his car and released a shout of joy.

He was the boss.

~

Ashok liked his friend's kitchen. There were so many shiny appliances on the bench tops that he thought Shane's mother must spend a lot of time cooking. His mouth watered at the size of the cookies in the jar on the bench.

He averted his eyes when Shane's mother cupped his friend's jaw with her hand. There was something intimate about the gesture, and the way she glanced down at Shane stung Ashok's heart.

He wanted a mother.

He wanted Gargi as his mother. He knew that his baap loved her, and Ashok believed she loved both his baap and him. Why did adults make it so difficult when things really were quite simple?

Shane giggled and Ashok glanced toward him. His mother pushed her fingers into his sides and tickled him, then she chased him around the room.

Ashok gnawed at the soft inside skin of his cheek. He'd never been tickled.

Grandma was always hugging him, but it wasn't the same as having a mother. Grandma and Grandpa were old and got tired sometimes.

His eyes smarted and he blinked several times.

"Ashok, do you want to sleep over?" Shane asked.

"Sleep over?" Ashok had never heard these two words spoken in such a way. Sleep over the top of what?

"Yeah. You could sleep in my room with me or we could put up the tent in the yard. It'll be fun."

Sleep over *at*. Now he understood. "I would have to ask my grandma," Ashok stated seriously.

"You don't sound very excited about it," Shane grumbled.

"I would very much like to sleep over with you, my friend. This I have never done before."

"You are so funny. Don't be so serious, we'll stay up all night and tell scary stories."

"I don't like scary stories. No, I like happy stories. Can we tell happy stories?"

"What's the fun in that?" Shane asked, disgusted with the idea.

Standing, Ashok felt the frown pull his forehead. He tried to smile but his lips felt thin. He stared into Shane's eyes.

"I am sorry, but I will not sleep over if you want to tell bad stories." He crossed his arms in front of him.

Shane's mother laid her hand on Ashok's arm. "Ashok, what Shane means is make-believe stories. Fun stories," she explained.

Ashok looked at Shane.

Shane laughed. "You know, about monsters and things."

Dipping his head, Ashok felt like crying. He didn't like monsters. "My sister was murdered by a monster," he muttered.

"What?" Shane's voice seemed to boom around the room.

Ashok decided to tell them. He sat back down. "My little sister was snatched out of my arms and taken to a bad place where men hurt her. In the end she was stabbed with a big knife and died in my arms."

Shane's mother gasped.

The scraping sound of the chair being pulled out made Ashok look across the table. "That sucks," Shane said. "Sorry, mate."

"That's all right. You didn't know." Ashok heard the tremor in his voice and felt foolish. He tried to smile.

"I know what we can do." Shane jumped up. "Mum, can we have a movie marathon? Please?"

"If Ashok's grandmother says it okay, then yes."

"Who's your favorite Transformer?" Shane questioned Ashok.

Ashok shrugged. He didn't want to tell Shane he had no idea what he was talking about.

"Come with me and I'll show you my collection."

Entering his friend's bedroom for the first time was like moving into a different world. Each wall was painted a different color and the wall painted black had posters of huge machines that looked like they were alive.

"That's Bumblebee. He's my favorite Transformer." Shane stood before the poster and ran his finger over the shape of the robot.

"Transformer?" Ashok asked, puzzled.

"Yes. It's a movie and…" Shane swooped across the room and came back with a yellow car. "Watch this."

Ashok's mouth dropped open as the toy changed into the robot in the poster. "Oh."

As the night wore on, Ashok yawned. The movies were great and he wanted his own Transformer. But he didn't want Bumblebee, he wanted Optimus Prime. He was the leader and Ashok liked him the best. Optimus Prime was brave and somehow kind.

"Time for bed, boys."

Shane stood up and stretched. "Okay, Mum. Come on, Ashok."

Throwing the pillow down to the end of the bed, Ashok pushed his hand under his head. He couldn't get used to sleeping with a pillow and preferred to lie straight in the bed.

"I like you," Shane whispered. "It's good having a new friend."

Swallowing past the lump in his throat, Ashok peered into the darkness. "I am glad also that you are my friend. It is good fun to have a sleepover."

"Are you tired?" Shane yawned several times.

"Yes, very. You?"

"Mmm. Normally I'd want to whisper for hours, but I'm

beat. See you in the morning." Shane turned over.

Ashok listened to his friends breathing as it got heavier. He wished he were Optimus Prime and could go and fight the battles of the world. If he were the robot, he'd go and pluck Gargi from wherever she was and bring her here to be with him.

Every time he had a moment to himself, he couldn't stop thinking about her. If she were his mother and married to Baap, people would presume they were a natural family because Gargi's skin was dark like his.

He got sick of explaining that Baap had adopted him. Why did people need to know such details over here in Australia? In India these things were unimportant. The important things were finding food and shelter.

Gargi understood what it was like to have been abandoned by her parents. It was important to Ashok that Gargi had known and loved Shanti.

Jesus, I can't talk out loud right now, I don't want to wake Shane. Thank you for my new friend.

Lying on his side, he reached out and touched the wall. He spread his fingers until his palm lay flat on the cool surface.

Please, Lord. Can you—he turned onto his back—*Jesus, can Gargi be my mother? I love her, Baap loves her.* Peering into the darkness, he shivered. *Lord, I know that Gargi's missing, but you've shown me that she's not missing to you. Bring her home to me. I want to show her how much love I have in my heart for her.*

He pulled his knees to his tummy. His chest stung with tension and he knew he should be thinking about nice things to help him sleep, but he just couldn't. He worried his lip with his teeth and wanted to scream with frustration.

Jesus, you took Shanti to heaven and I know I can't stop you from wanting Gargi, but can I have her? Pleeeease? Tears welled in his eyes.

Where was she? Sitting up, he swung his legs over the side of the bed and he rocked. Something was up, he just knew it, and the thought of Gargi being in trouble hurt so bad. He didn't know what to pray, all his words seemed useless.

He knelt on the floor and leaned his elbows on the bed. His hands steepled together.

"Wherever Gargi is," he whispered. "Jesus, keep her safe. Let her come home to Baap and me."

"You okay, mate?" Shane mumbled.

Ashok spread his legs out in front of him. "No. Do you pray, Shane?"

"No, never have."

"Can you start now?"

"I don't know how."

"It's just talking to God. My friend needs me to pray for her, I feel it in my heart. Her name is Gargi and I want—I love her."

Shane climbed out of bed and joined Ashok on the floor. "Do I close my eyes?"

Chapter 33

Phillip felt the shift inside him as if someone had flicked a switch on his dreams and aspirations and turned him in a different direction. He was glad he'd decided to walk the two blocks to Shanti's Rest because he wanted a moment to himself.

For years he'd wanted another doctor to join him at the clinic. Now that one had come he found the workload lighter but more—trying.

He felt restless, as if he were in the wrong place.

His steps felt sluggish and he stopped to survey the street. Women were setting up their stalls in front of the parked cars.

He skipped through the flowing traffic to the other side of the road.

The people of India were amazing. They made do with what they had and were so industrious. Women spread out their mats and piled their brightly colored fabrics out in front of themselves.

Woman after woman sat cross-legged and carefully judged the distance of the car wheels before arranging her product neatly.

If Mumbai was anything, it was colorful.

The women were beautiful and their smiles as they welcomed shoppers and tourists touched Phillip's heart.

These people deserved good things. They never complained about sitting on the hard concrete for hours, waiting for the odd sale that would make the day worthwhile.

Two women laughed together and he felt displeased with himself. Here he was wondering what was next for him and these women just accepted their lives and worked.

Did they have dreams, or was their whole life about survival? Getting food for the family being their biggest goal?

He felt his time in the clinic was coming to an end, and this puzzled him. He'd thought he would be working there until he was old and grey. That a shift was happening inside of him excited him somehow but also nagged at his sense of responsibility to take care of the children.

Reaching into his pocket, he pulled out his wallet to check how much money he had. He never had much cash and had willingly given Eli all his savings to help fund his search for Gargi.

It wasn't as if it had been much. Five thousand dollars had taken a long time to save on his meager wage, but he'd always been okay with having no surplus as long as he had no debt.

Now that he was engaged to Charlie, things had changed.

He wanted to take care of her. Buy a bigger apartment so that they could set up a home together. The look on Charlie's face as he'd slipped his ring on her finger had made the money he'd borrowed from his father seem incidental. But now that his father was constantly at him about how he was going to pay it back, the debt seemed to weigh him down.

It was as if his father wanted to use the debt as a way to manipulate Phillip back to the States and full-time practice. His father was loaded and didn't need the money, but what he did need was Phillip to play ball and do as he was told.

Slipping the last note out of his wallet, he strolled amongst the stalls to buy a gift for Charlie. He scowled at the thought of how much his father could help the poor if he weren't such a tight-fisted man.

His face heated. It wasn't his place to judge his father.

Squatting, he fingered the soft fabric and smiled at the old woman nodding her head at him.

"Good choice." Her smile revealed missing front teeth.

Phillip smiled back. "How much for this?" Picking up the bright red fabric, he pictured Charlie in it.

She named a price and gave him an even wider smile. The money in his hand could buy three pieces of fabric and also his lunch and maybe his dinner.

"I'll take it, thank you." Passing over his money, he took the paper bag she handed him and stood up.

The woman searched around for change and he lightly touched her hand and shook his head. "Thank you."

Phillip walked away. He didn't want her words of gratitude. Even though his bank accounts were just about empty, he had so many possibilities in front of him. A rich man was one who knew what he had was sufficient.

Phillip didn't know what God had for him around the corner, but he did know that with Charlie beside him it would obviously be connected to Shanti's Rest. That was just fine with him.

It was like a weight had been lifted off his shoulders. He would continue at the clinic until he had clear direction from God that he was to leave.

Whatever the future held, he knew his gift was to help the sick.

He loved the idea of having more time to invest in the work at Shanti's Rest. As he walked, he slowed his steps and listened intently to the street noises. He'd enjoyed visiting Australia and seeing where Charlie grew up, but India was home. That Charlie also felt this way was an added bonus.

India was in his blood; if he lived his whole life here, he'd be content. As he approached the open gates at the entrance to Shanti's Rest, he frowned. He thought they'd decided to lock the compound's gates.

A spark of anger tightened his chest. Charlie had argued about this and he could see her point of view. She wanted it to be an open door for girls wanting to access help, but what good was help if the place they were walking into wasn't safe?

Striding down the road, he knew he and Charlotte would have words. Saying that his fiancée was stubborn when she believed in something was an understatement. He loved the fire that sprung into her eyes when he teased her. His anger slipped away as quickly as it had come.

Maybe he'd have a little fun before he gave her his gift.

His lips curved as he chuckled.

~

Gargi's arm's ached from holding the child. First Isha, now this little one. Her heart ached as she looked down into the still, small face; Gargi knew she'd slipped quietly from life into eternity without a murmur.

Gargi rested her head against the wall then closed her eyes. How many other women and children were shipped around the world in floating tombs?

How could God close his eyes to such injustice? Her chest tightened and she wanted to scream that no one cared. It was wrong, so unfair that these little ones had no one looking for them, no one crying out their names for the world to see what the moving darkness hid.

She swept the child's hair back behind her ears. Her name was Kala. She'd been the quiet one, never asking for anything, just watching.

Gritting her teeth tightly together, Gargi felt such anger that she wanted to hit something. She hugged her still burden close to her chest and crawled across the floor to the door. She placed Kala gently against the wall and positioned her arms at her sides. Squatting back, Gargi sat on her ankles and dipped her head.

Amita sidled up to her. “Is she dead?” she whispered.

“Yes,” Gargi answered in a flat voice. She wished she were stronger. The thin strand of thread holding her faith together seemed to be tearing.

She wanted to tell Amita that everything would be all right, but the truth was she didn’t believe it. Most of her life she’d been in captivity and the memory of the small window of freedom she’d experienced was fading from her mind.

Charlie had told her that when your faith grows weak, you need others to hold you up.

That you needed to ask for help.

Gargi’s gaze locked on Daya’s. The girl’s large brown eyes stared calmly across at her and seemed expectant, as if Daya believed Gargi would say something that would fix things.

Gargi stood and folded her arms loosely. “I don’t know why bad things happen to good people. I don’t know why God allows little children like Kala to die at the hands of evil men.”

“I hate them,” one of the girls cried.

“Hush, precious one.” Gargi shuffled to sit in the middle of the cushions. Her hands pulled tight into fists and she wanted to smash something, preferably Scarface’s smug face. Kala’s death seemed so pointless. But maybe that was okay with God?

Shaking her head, Gargi groaned.

Lord, forgive me. I know it’s not okay with you—but I’m hurting here.

There was no way she could manage to stay calm any longer. She had to fight for what was right.

"Don't hate people who are blind to the path they are taking," she stated strongly. "They are walking toward their own death. It makes me so angry that we are locked up in here. It really does, but I'm not going to give up!"

"Why doesn't God help us?" Amita mumbled. "I believed what you said about him, Gargi. I asked Jesus to be my friend, yet nothing has changed."

Gargi's lips stung as she tried to smile. "Everything has changed." As Gargi heard her own words, she knew it was true. "Forgiveness is the key. Jesus has forgiven us our sins and as we forgive others, including the unseen faces of the people who have bad plans for our lives, then…"

"Then what? We die?" Amita asked.

Daya grabbed Amita's hand. "I did not believe in anything until Jesus. Now I see him in the love Gargi shows us. In you, Amita, my sister."

Amita sobbed. "Kala is dead, who will be next?"

"Girls." Gargi drew in a haggard breath. "Death is not the end."

"How can you be so sure?" Amita drew her arms protectively around her stomach. "It feels like the end when you see all the life gone from Kala's face."

Gargi knew deep in her spirit that death was in fact the beginning of real life. "I just know, here." She placed her hand over her heart. "I also knew a beautiful girl called Shanti. She came to believe in Jesus and died a terrible death by an evil man." Gargi tried to remember what Ashok told her Shanti had said before she died. "Her brother held her as she died. He told me that she asked him if he could see Jesus. She told him not to be afraid, that she was all right."

"I can feel his presence," Daya said.

"If you die before me, Gargi, can you come get me?" Amita whispered.

Gargi leaned over and kissed Amita's cheek. "Rest, Amita. Don't focus on dying. You are alive now—that is what's important. Now, sleep."

Gargi stared up at the flickering light and was glad she'd decided to leave it on. What did it matter if it ran out? The sounds of the children sleeping made her wish she too could slip into the oblivion sleep offered.

She knew it was only a matter of time, maybe hours, but she hung on to every shallow breath. Closing her eyelids, she yearned for some form of liquid to moisten her eyes.

Her fingers twitched and she loosened her hold on the notebook. She hoped Eli would somehow get possession of it and read the words she'd written about her love for him and Ashok.

She tried to count in her head the number of days they'd been locked up but struggled to hold on to her thoughts.

The incessant itch on her skin was worse. She rubbed her head on the cushion and tried to ignore the need to scratch. She just didn't have the energy to raise her hand.

Poor little Pia suffered the most. She'd scratched so much that her skin was raw with infection and Gargi prayed that Jesus would end Pia's suffering soon.

Daya's head was close to hers and their gaze met.

Gargi wanted to say Daya's name, but her lips were so swollen and cracked that she'd stopped talking unless she had to.

"Gargi," Daya mouthed. "I love you."

Gargi tried to smile. Had she moved or had she imagined moving? Confusion floated around her and she felt light-headed. Distant from those around her.

Breathe, daughter.

Gargi's chest heaved and pain screamed through her lungs.

Her body jolted, pulled by an unseen force.

One more breath. She had to try, not give in.

The door creaked and Daya pushed up on her elbow.

Amita slipped across the cushions and took hold of Gargi's hand. "Someone's opening the door," she whispered.

Daya took her other hand. "God has saved us." She brushed her lips over Gargi's face and turned to face the door.

The doors swung wide.

Wet, salty air gushed into the container.

Gargi parted her lips. Her lungs expanded and she inhaled deeply.

Three men stood swearing and holding their hands over their noses. A man hovered around them and screamed orders. "Throw the buckets and the dead overboard! Transfer the living to the accommodation bay. Hose out this hellhole and get it ready to house them again."

As the men swooped toward them, Gargi watched helplessly as they lifted Isha's and Kala's bodies and bundled them together in a sack. She closed her eyes to the sight and reminded herself that they had already left this life and were with Jesus.

"He's a fool to have waited this long," one of the men commented. "They'll recover but will fetch a much lesser price."

A large man stood over Gargi and lifted her. Gargi stiffened her neck to stop her head from flopping back and let her cheek rest on the rough surface of his shirt. The scents of body odor and salt were nice compared to what she'd breathed in day and night. She wanted to ask for water but part of her didn't want to come back from the place she'd been heading.

Waves pelted the deck, and the man carrying her hugged her close. "Don't worry, girly. I'm used to walking the waves. You'll have fresh water soon and be as good as new."

Chapter 34

Slipping the engagement ring off her finger, Charlotte admired the setting. Phillip had chosen the perfect design for her. She could never wear anything ostentatious, she liked simplicity.

As she pushed the diamond back on her finger, she circled her desk. This little room had become a special place to her. She'd never thought an office could be a prayer closet, but it was. When the door was closed, no one came in; people knew not to interrupt her no matter what.

"Jesus, thank you for this place, this time." Charlotte returned to her desk and sat down. Her fingers caressed the top of her Bible.

"Bless the Lord, O my soul, and all that is within me, bless his holy name! Bless the Lord, O my soul, and forget not all his benefits, who forgives all your iniquity, who heals all your diseases, who redeems your life from the pit."

She shut her eyes, wanting to block out all distractions. She focused on the name of Jesus. How often had she pictured herself being held up by the hands of God?

"Jesus, it hurts thinking of Gargi being in captivity. She's been through so much already, yet I know that wherever she is, whatever is happening to her—you are with her."

A tear slipped down her cheek and she wiped it away. "Jesus, I've learned to trust you no matter what. Things happen and there is nothing I can do about them, but I can trust you. I long to hold Gargi in my arms and tell her it will be all right, but I just don't know whether it will be or not."

Her nose started to run. Sniffing, she opened her eyes and pulled her Bible to her chest. "Your Word promises me peace and I claim that now. I trust you with her life. I pray in your name, Lord Jesus. Pour strength into Gargi's body, peace into her mind, determination into her spirit to fight and never give up."

The thought of never seeing her friend again because evil had been allowed to have its way angered her. She thumped the Bible down on the desk and screwed up her face.

"I won't accept it, Lord. You say in the book of Mark that whatever I ask for in prayer, and believe—that I have received it, that it will be mine. I ask, believing I will see Gargi again."

She relaxed back into her seat.

She *would* see Gargi again.

She knew the truth. They would spend eternity together. When she'd prayed the prayer she'd meant in this lifetime, not eternity, but now she wasn't so sure.

Picking up a pencil, she started to write out verses on prayer in her journal. She circled many others as an idea formed. She'd start up a prayer strategy for Shanti's Rest.

She knew people prayed, but what if they were given specific prayer requests to help them focus on key areas? Tapping the pencil on her chin, she pondered what the needs were.

Her pencil scribbled over the page. Education about the danger of traffickers. Prayer for the release of prisoners. Prayer for people like Saul.

Her fingers tightened on the pencil. Saul had done things to her that should make her hate him. She'd wanted to at one stage, but had released his hold over her to God.

Saul was lost, dead to all God had for him. Was there still hope for him?

If she could, would she save him? Reach out to him again as she'd tried to once before? Part of her wanted to dust her hands of all responsibility.

"Lord Jesus, Saul needs you. I don't hate him, yet if I never saw him again—I'd be okay with that."

For all have sinned and fall short of the glory of God.

Linking her hands, she dipped her head.

All included Saul. *All* included her.

Charlotte accepted the message. She too was a sinner and in reality no different than the worst of the worst.

Each day was a new opportunity, each breath a new chance to make things right. With Phillip at her side.

She felt all soft inside. Never in her wildest dreams had she thought she could love a man as much as she loved Phillip. The more time they spent together, the more relaxed she became. She'd thought she knew him, but there was so much more to him than she'd ever imagined.

His eyes sparkled when he was excited or planning a surprise for her, and they darkened when he was angry. He was passionate about injustice, and she marveled that he'd spent so many years helping at the mission's clinic.

Her fiancé was sold out for kingdom purposes. God knew she needed to be on the front line. Her life was forever changed by what she knew. She was in an army fighting for what was right.

At some stage in the future, a long way off, maybe she would be able to settle down to a quieter life, but for now she needed to see girls rescued—and Phillip wanted this too.

The banging on the outer door surprised her. Someone must be really thumping the door for the noise to reach her.

Part of her wanted to jump up and go see what all the commotion was about, but then she pulled her mind back to focusing on her time with the Lord. Padma would handle it.

"Jesus, about Padma. I don't know if she's made a decision to follow you yet. I see such softness on her face and love the changes so evident within her."

Who would have thought that Padma and Tanvir would find each other? Brother and sister—amazing! The plans of God were like a tapestry.

Her heart dropped as she thought of her brother. Eli needed such covering right now. She couldn't imagine how hard it must be for him to be once again searching for someone he loved.

She knew firsthand what could be happening to Gargi. Charlotte wanted to gather Eli close and promise him things would work out for the best.

What he needed most right now were people to stand with him and storm heaven for Gargi's return.

Words slipped from her mouth and she dropped to her knees. She allowed her spirit to pray and lowered her head to the floor. Tears flooded her eyes and she let them flow freely.

Each tear, a message of her love for Eli and Gargi. "Collect my tears, Lord. Hear my cry. In your righteousness, rescue Gargi and deliver her from her enemies. Turn your ear to me and hear my prayer. You are my rock of refuge to which I can always go, give the command to save Gargi…"

The office door burst open and Padma stumbled in, screaming.

Charlotte's mouth dropped open as the man she now knew was Saul slammed the door behind them.

"Hello, angel face," he sneered.

Charlotte stood. She took a step toward him and made herself smile. "Why hello, Saul. I was just praying for you."

"Have you forgotten so soon what I said I'd do to you if you called me that name again?"

"I call you Saul because there was a man in the Bible called Saul and he had Christians killed…"

"Enough," Saul demanded. "I read about the king who lost his kingdom and went mad. You think I'm a fool?"

"No, not a fool. Just stubborn. I refer to another man named Saul. A man who had Christians killed but one day met with Jesus and believed. He changed and became a mighty man of God. This is my prayer for you."

Khlaid pulled out a gun. The small pocket pistol rested easily in his hand.

Charlotte stopped herself from stepping back. She knew this type of gun. Eli had given Gargi one. It had no hammer; you could just point and shoot. The safety was in the long trigger discharge.

She had to get him talking. Stall for time. Raising her chin, she stared at him defiantly.

"You don't scare me. Have you forgotten what my God did to your legs? You stand there as if you are in control when in truth there is nothing you can do to me that will destroy me."

"Shut up!" he hollered. "I'm in control here. I've already disposed of your security guard and nothing will stop me from getting what I want." Throwing some long cable ties at Padma, he sneered. "Tie those around Charlotte's hands," he ordered.

Padma caught the plastic ties and glanced at Charlotte.

Charlotte rolled her eyes at Padma.

Khlaid charged across the room and waved the gun in front of Charlotte's face. "You mock me," he screamed.

Charlotte heard the small waver of doubt in his voice.

"Relax, Saul." She touched his arm. "Do you want to give me the gun? You cannot win this."

Khlaid stepped back from Charlotte. His hand snaked out and grabbed Padma by the hair.

Padma's head snapped back and she screamed.

He slammed the muzzle hard into Padma's temple.

Padma moaned. Her shoulders stooped and Charlotte wanted to grab for her before she fainted.

The change in Padma's expression frightened Charlotte. Her eyes widened in outrage and she pulled savagely at Khlaid's hand.

Charlotte stiffened at the look of stark anger in her friend's eyes.

"Don't do anything foolish, Padma. Stay still," she begged.

The door flung open, crashed noisily against the wall, and then swung back on its hinges.

Phillip charged through the door to stand in front of Charlotte.

"Let go of Padma," Phillip ordered.

Everything seemed to play out before Charlotte as though she were in a slow-motion movie. Phillip's voice sounded adamant and sort of final.

"I'm the one with the gun." Khlaid cursed. "Get back from Charlotte, she's coming with me."

"No—she—is—not," Phillip said, stretching out each word. "You are not leaving here. Move away from Padma before you live to regret it."

Laying her hand on Phillip's arm, Charlotte stepped around him. "Saul, please do as he says," Charlotte urged. "I don't want anything to happen to you."

"You don't care about what happens to me," Khlaid snarled. "Maybe you care more about this man than your friend here." He whipped the gun around and aimed it at Phillip's chest.

Phillip pushed Charlotte farther away and folded his arms as if he were completely relaxed.

Padma laughed and everyone looked at her as if she'd lost her mind.

She rubbed her head where the gun had been and shrugged her shoulders. "This is just ridiculous," she stated in a bored voice. "Charlie, Phillip—could you please leave? I have a few things I'd like to say to my husband." She stepped directly in front of Khlaid and took hold of the gun's barrel.

The sight of Padma's fingers tightening over the cold steel of the gun sent shivers down Charlotte's spine. Her friend's face appeared calm, too calm.

"Charlotte, do as she says," Phillip ordered.

"You too, Phillip," Padma said without moving her gaze from Khlaid's.

Khlaid sneered. "You have a death wish, Padma? Don't think I won't pull the trigger."

"I'm not afraid to die," Padma murmured. "I've made my peace with God, but have you, Khlaid? If you die today, are you ready to face eternity in misery?"

Charlotte stepped toward the door then hesitated. She couldn't leave. Her mouth opened and she wanted to say something that would change the situation.

"Come on, Charlie." Phillip propelled her toward the door.

Charlotte glanced back at her friend. If she stepped through the door and left Padma there, would Saul pull the trigger?

"I'm sorry, Phillip," Charlotte stated as she pushed past him to stand in the center of the room.

"Saul, please put the gun down. We *can* work this out." Charlotte longed to shake some sense into Padma. You don't hold on to a loaded revolver's muzzle. If only she could distract Saul enough to allow Phillip to storm him. "Padma, you say you've made your peace with God? When were you planning on telling me this?"

"You have been out of the country, Charlie. Khlaid, do you know that Jesus Christ can give you a new life?"

Khlaid lunged forward, shoving Padma to the floor. Whirling around, he grabbed Charlotte, pulled her hard up against his chest and locked his mouth over hers.

The gun exploded.

Something warm and wet seeped through Charlotte's blouse. She raised her hand in shock as she fell backwards.

~

Even though they'd hosed out the container, Gargi could still smell the filth. The men who'd showered them had been indifferent to their injuries. Stumbling across the slippery deck, Gargi panted as she carried Pia. Her foot caught on a coil of rope and she lunged forward and speared her knee on the sharp edge of the container.

"I'm sorry, Pia," she moaned. "Are you all right?" Standing, she helped Pia into the container. Her knee stung and she felt the trickle of blood running down her leg.

The cushions were gone and there was not even a blanket in sight. Licking her lips with her alien tongue, Gargi wondered how long it would take for her body to respond to the liquid she'd been given.

Easing down on the floor beside Pia, Gargi exhaled a long breath. She was exhausted. The energy she'd spent being showered and moving across the ship had drained all her strength. As she leaned her head on the foam wall, Gargi watched the other children re-enter their cage.

Amita slipped down beside her and reached to take Gargi's hand. "Will they close the door again?"

Gargi wanted to reassure her but refused to offer empty promises. The pain in her body was nothing compared to the agony of her despondence.

She felt robbed. Her eyes had been focused on heaven and she didn't want to be back in this container and living. She didn't want the responsibility of keeping the children strong so others could abuse them.

She wanted out.

Closing her eyes to the sight of the children settling around her, Gargi battled with her desire to let go of hope.

Daya joined them and crossed her arms. "We need to prepare ourselves. That man over there—" She pointed to the sailor leaning against the rail of the ship, "—he said the captain would be coming to pick two of us to sell for himself."

Gargi heard the words, but she didn't want to acknowledge what they meant. She tried to push the pictures that surfaced in her mind away. Yet part of her opened the door to the memories.

As the horrendous things that had happened to her as a child taunted her, she slipped farther down the wall. She could feel the rough hands pulling at her body as if they owned her. Crude words echoed around her, pouring filth into her mind. Invisible chains tightened around her heart and held her captive and told her she was nothing.

"Daya," Gargi whispered, trying to come back from the dark pit that beckoned her.

"There is nothing you can say, Gargi," Daya declared with a shrug of her shoulders. "You know the captain will pick me and probably Amita. We are the ones who have survived this nightmare the best."

"Pray." Gargi mouthed the word and closed her eyes. She couldn't change what was, but she could pray. She wasn't helpless, she reminded herself. She had strength within her that could move mountains.

Renew me, Lord. Peace washed over her like fresh water, and she straightened her shoulders. This was not over, she was not dead, and she had to stop thinking like she was. Ignoring the pain that pulsed through her body, she pulled herself to standing.

"Come here." Gargi motioned for Daya to come close.

Shaking her head, Daya stepped farther away from her and leaned against the container's door. "Gargi, I am going to suggest he take only me and keep me for himself. I will serve him well and that may give you a chance of escape once you are on land. You cannot stop me from doing this, my mind is made up."

"You think by sacrificing yourself they will leave us

alone? Daya, we are all slaves here. And as much as I love you and appreciate what you want to do, it won't make a difference to the outcome."

"Just because you're older than me, Gargi, does not mean you know everything!" Daya blurted out. "You're sick and need more time to recover. I am strong and younger and I'm telling you to sit back down and look sick—because you are!"

Chapter 35

"What do you mean you can't locate the ship?" Eli asked sharply. "You assured me you would have the information I need today."

"Mr Turner, as you know, all ships are fitted with a maritime automatic identification system which transmits the ship's position for obvious reasons." The small man shrugged his shoulders and glanced at Isak nervously.

"Yes, yes I know," Eli wanted to grab the man's shirt and shake him. He didn't want conversation, he wanted action. Clenching his fists, Eli tried to control his anger.

"Um, it seems the ship's gone incommunicado."

Eli threw his hands up in frustration. "What? You're telling me that a cargo ship can just disappear?"

"Yes. It may be the storm, or someone has turned off their transmitters."

"I have a plane chartered and time is crucial. I want a location now." Eli knew he was being unreasonable, that it wasn't the man's fault, but something had to give before he exploded.

Isak stroked his chin. "Eli, calm down," Isak commanded. "This man is trying to help us. He's just an employee of Marine Traffic." Slapping the small man on the back, Isak ducked his head down and smiled. "Can you tell us the ship's last known location?"

The fellow's face brightened. "Yes."

~

Lunging across the room, Phillip dragged Khlaid off Charlie. His breath came fast and he could feel his heart pounding. His fingers went white as his hold on Khlaid's arm tightened.

He hyperextended the guy's elbow to prevent escape. The sound of the creep hissing made him exert more pressure to the wrist.

Charlie sat up and Phillip's eyes widened when he saw the blood on her shirt.

"Are you okay?"

"Yes." She looked down at her shoulder. "I think it only grazed my skin."

"Where's the gun?" He twisted around to stare at Padma.

"Phillip, let go of him," Padma commanded. Moving around the desk, she dragged the chair to the front of the desk and pushed it toward Khlaid. "Sit."

"I'm not letting him go. Charlie, pass me that tie."

Khlaid slammed his head back into Phillip's face.

Phillip heard the crack of his nose breaking before he felt the pain. He staggered back. His hand cupped to catch the pool of blood streaming out of his nostrils.

Khlaid's hand flew out and slapped the gun out of Padma's hand and onto the floor.

Charlie crawled across the floor and flicked the gun under the desk.

Straightening, Phillip wiped his hand down the side of his leg and took a menacing step toward Khlaid.

Khlaid chuckled and folded his arms. "Did you know I am responsible for your friend Gargi being sent to sea? I miscalculated the amount of water they would need if the ship were delayed in any way. She's probably dead by now. A horrible way to die, I've heard. The body shrivels up from the inside with the absence of water."

Phillip's eyes smarted. He wanted to stop the flow of Khlaid's words.

"There were twenty in the container." Khlaid sniggered.

"Shut up," Phillip screamed.

"Frank—you remember Frank don't you, Charlotte?" Khlaid licked his lips suggestively. "Frank sampled Gargi several times to make sure she was up to the job ahead of her. Do you think your brother will still want her now?"

Phillip's head felt like it was going to explode. He charged across the room and slammed his shoulder into Khlaid's chest. Khlaid was taller than him and as hard as a brick wall.

Phillip dug his feet into the rug and pushed like he was tackling an opponent in a game of football. He staggered across the room until they both toppled to the floor.

Fire burned through Phillip's veins and he smashed his fist into Khlaid's face.

The man under him shook his head and had the gall to smile.

Clenching his fingers, Phillip smashed the smile from the mocking face.

Again he lifted his arm to strike. Khlaid blocked his swing and dived out of the way.

Khlaid spat blood out of his mouth. With a snarl he lunged for Phillip.

Fists raised, Phillip sprung to action. He ducked his head into the creep's muscly shoulder and pummeled his stomach. The pain in his nose was excruciating.

He spat out blood and prayed for strength.

Creating space between them, Phillip put all his force behind his next hit.

Khlaid swayed backwards before he collapsed in a heap.

"Phillip, stop!" Charlie screamed.

Breathing heavily, Phillip glanced at Charlie, and her eyes beseeched him to listen.

"He deserves to die for all he's done," Phillip snarled.

"You are not his judge," Charlie countered. "Get off him."

"No! I'm going to end this."

Coughing, Khlaid turned his head. "You don't have the guts to kill me, sissy boy."

Heat flushed through Phillip's body and his muscles

tensed. He braced his feet as he tried to get control of his anger. Everything in him wanted to continue pounding Khlaid's face.

Be merciful.

"You lie there and have no regret about the things you've done, the people you've hurt," Phillip spat.

He pushed his fist down hard on Khlaid's shoulder. He didn't want to be merciful.

Khlaid winced then gave a cruel laugh. "I know why you want Charlotte. Her body was like honey in my hands."

"Shut—the—hell—up!" Phillip screamed. Fury made him see red and he pulled Khlaid to his feet and shook him violently.

Khlaid's hands snapped out and he shoved Phillip back.

"You just don't get it, do you?" Khlaid huffed. "You can put a ring on Charlotte's finger but she will always be mine—I had her first." He stumbled to the chair and crumbled into it. Blood seeped from his left eye and he lifted a shaky finger to wipe it.

Tensing, Phillip's hands balled and his knuckles stung. He glared across the room. The thought of Khlaid's hands on Charlie, touching her and hurting her, sent a spear of pain through his chest.

Roughly yanking Khlaid's arms behind his back, Phillip secured them together. Then he tied his feet to the chair legs. Once he was satisfied Khlaid wasn't going anywhere, Phillip took a step away from the chair.

He lifted his foot and gave the chair a kick, sending it and Khlaid to the floor.

Charlie came and stood beside him. Her face had lost its color and Phillip could see the strain around her eyes.

She laid her hand on his arm. He wanted to shrug it off. It was his place to avenge her, make it right.

The hand on his arm pressed slightly and he felt Charlie tremble.

"You're wrong, Saul," Charlie said. "I'm not yours. Never have been and never will be. You have no hold over me. You see… I feel sorry for you. And… I forgive you."

Charlie leaned heavily against Phillip and he pulled her close. The smell of blood reminded him she'd been shot.

"Charlie?" His gaze dropped to her right shoulder. The dampness told him that she was still bleeding. How could he have forgotten? He'd allowed his anger to overrule his brain.

He carried her to the desk and set her on top of her papers.

Padma stood looking down at Khlaid.

Shuffling, Khlaid groaned. "Padma, help me up," he hissed.

"I don't think so," Padma replied sweetly. "And by the way, I want a divorce."

There was a commotion at the door and two policemen entered and took hold of Khlaid's arms and picked up the chair.

A number of girls stood around the door, watching. Phillip could only assume that one of them had called the police.

An officer freed Khlaid's legs. "Khlaid Mallick, you're coming with us. We have a warrant for your arrest concerning the trafficking of women and children." The policeman turned to Phillip. "When you are ready, sir, I'd appreciate your coming down to the station to make a statement concerning what's happened here."

"Of course." Phillip nodded but kept his attention on Charlie. His fingers shook as he opened her shirt to check her wound. The bullet had nicked the flesh at the top of her shoulder.

"Padma, can you get me the first aid kit? And Charlie needs a blanket, she's starting to shiver." He brushed his lips over Charlie's mouth. "I'm going to press the wound, sweetheart. It will hurt, but I need to stop the bleeding."

Charlie nodded.

"Thank goodness the bullet just skimmed your shoulder. This could have been a lot worse."

"Here you go." Padma placed the first aid box beside him and draped the blanket over Charlie's legs.

Tilting her head, Charlie stared at Phillip as he bent over her. He could feel her eyes boring into his face. He couldn't look at her.

As he ministered to her wound, he noticed his knuckles. The pain throbbed up his arm and he knew he'd probably dislocated a couple of his fingers. Never in his life had he been so violent.

"Phil," Charlie urged.

He ducked his head. He didn't want to see the contempt in her eyes.

"I love you." She reached out to him and he cupped her hand in his and kissed her fingers.

"Charlie." As he gathered her in his arms, he allowed his tears to flow.

Laying her head on his shoulder, Charlie sighed. She

raised her hand to his face. "You know you have to forgive him, don't you?"

"Yeah, and I will, just not yet."

"Sooner would be better than later," she murmured.

Clearing her throat, Padma touched his arm. "Phillip, do we need to take Charlie to the hospital?"

"It's okay, Padma. Charlie is going to be fine," Phillip reassured her. The wound would heal quickly; although all bullet wounds were serious, he felt sure God had deflected the bullet so that it hadn't done any lasting harm.

Chapter 36

Daya was thankful they had returned the cushions to their container. She breathed in deeply and listened to the sounds around her. Even though the container was soundproofed, she could hear the sea. She imagined the waves lapping against the side of the ship and shuddered. The other girls appeared to be asleep. Their heavy breathing made her envious. Sleep shut off reality.

Closing her eyes, she tried to stop herself from thinking. All her life she'd known she was beautiful. Her father had told her over and over again that she was his princess. He'd explained to her that because she was so beautiful, one day a man would come and want to make her his wife, but that man would have to prove himself to her father before he would bless the handing over of his eldest daughter.

She'd felt loved by her parents and had adored her little sister.

Tears welled in her eyes and she pushed her face into the cushion to muffle her sobs. She missed her parents so much. If they were alive, they'd never have let her uncle sell her.

She bit on a fingernail. She couldn't block the memory of watching little Isha being raped.

If her sister had survived the accident that killed all her family, she too would be aboard this ship, destined for a life of—of what?

She shuddered. It would have broken her heart completely in two if she'd had to watch her sweet sister go through what she'd witnessed Isha enduring.

She glanced into the darkness across to where Gargi lay amongst the cushions.

"Gargi, are you awake?" she whispered.

"Yes. Can't you sleep either, Daya?"

"Can I ask you something?"

"Mmm," Gargi answered sleepily.

Wiping her eyes, Daya tried to still the tremors that had taken over her body. She'd always been strong and confident, but since she'd been forced to live with her uncle, her life had been turned upside down.

"I don't think I can… do this. Just the thought of a man touching me—" Daya shut her eyes tight. "What can I do to—to live?" She held her breath while she waited for Gargi to answer. Time thickened into silence around her.

"You have to hold on to your faith and live one day at a time," Gargi said simply. "Do not focus on tomorrow, trust God in everything, and never give up."

"Isha died," Daya's voice cracked. "Will it be like that for all of us?"

"No. Daya, you are strong and will get through this. Isha was only four years old. Her body could not cope with—with the things that happened to her. And maybe she would have survived if she hadn't fallen from her harness."

"Kala died too, Gargi. I know she was sick, but do you think she died of a broken heart?"

"I don't know what caused her death. Maybe she wasn't as healthy as we were at the beginning of our journey."

Daya pulled her blanket closer to her face. "I have never thought about sex," Daya stuttered and her face flamed. "Um, the first—first time for you, did it—did it just about kill you too?" Daya asked in despair.

Gargi crawled across the cushions to her.

Daya eased herself into Gargi's arms and rested her head on Gargi's chest. The sound of Gargi's heartbeat was comforting and she counted the beats as she tried to calm her own racing heart.

Gargi rubbed Daya's back gently.

Closing her eyes, Daya waited for Gargi's reply.

"It will hurt you because the man who takes you will not love you. I have come to believe that if the man is your husband and you love each other, then it will be different."

Gargi sighed loudly. "Daya, you will be treated like an animal, a thing to be used and discarded—but it will not destroy you. You must not let it."

"I would rather die than have this happen to me. I wish I had died with my family," Daya declared in defeat.

"You must not say that," Gargi said sternly. "You must

live and not give up!"

Hanging her head, Daya hated that she felt so weak. She didn't want to disappoint Gargi. The warmth of Gargi's body made her feel… safe.

Maybe having someone love you, someone who believed in you, was all it took to get through.

"I have met your Jesus, and I love him," she whispered. "But what if I can't hear him? What if I grow to hate the people who hurt me?"

"You are describing what I was like before I gave my life to Jesus. When I was in the brothel, I didn't have any hope, but my friend Charlie showed me what real strength is. I hated everyone and had become so angry and bitter. No one was my friend and the other girls were afraid of me. I thought this was the way to cope, to isolate myself from feeling."

Clutching her hands together, Daya felt the roughness of her nails. Her mother had begged her to stop biting them and made her rub oil on the uneven, rough edges. There were so many little things her mother had done for her that only now she recognized as acts of love.

The feel of Gargi's hand smoothing her hair made her want to cry. She'd tried to be tough and not let the younger children see her fear, but now the time was getting closer to when they would leave the container, and she wanted to stay in the darkness and hide.

"Daya, my friend Charlie showed me how to be strong and live each day well."

"How?" Daya snuggled farther into Gargi's shoulder.

"She prayed for each person who hurt her. Sometimes this

didn't work, but afterwards she would ask God to forgive them for what they did to her. She'd ask God to help her be merciful to others."

Tilting her head, Daya looked up at Gargi. If she could stay with Gargi, she would be okay. She snaked her arm under Gargi and hugged her. "Do you think we will stay together?" she asked hopefully.

"I'd like that. But if we are separated, can you do something for me?"

"Anything, I will do anything for you, Gargi." Daya took hold of Gargi's hands.

"Can you read, Daya?"

"Yes. My parents believed in an education and it wasn't until they died that my life became… difficult."

"If you can, try and get your hands on a Bible. Read and memorize what you can and believe what you read."

"What if I can't get a Bible? What if no one around me believes what we believe? How will I be able to hold on to what the Bible says?"

Gargi pressed her lips to Daya's cheek. "I have been a Christian such a short time myself and I don't know many verses. Most of what I know is what Charlie taught me. But what I do know is that Jesus lives within my heart and the Holy Spirit is with me."

"Is the Holy Spirit with me too?"

"Oh yes, little one. When you believe in Jesus Christ as your Lord, you will never be alone again."

Daya touched the spot that Gargi had kissed. Her heart yearned to be back at home with her mother. Her mother had been a little older than Gargi, but they both had the same kind nature.

Tears slipped down her cheeks, and she tried to cling to the hope that she and Gargi would remain together. She no longer wanted to offer herself to the ugly captain.

"Even if you don't have a Bible, God will speak to you, show you what to do. It will all work out okay in the end, you wait and see," Gargi reassured her.

The walls creaked and the sound was so familiar that it seemed comforting. "Even though it's been awful here, I don't want to leave." Daya wanted to hold on to the safety she had in Gargi's arms.

Gargi cupped Daya's face and whispered, "Remember we are family and even if we're not together, you will always be with me because I love you. Will you pray for me, Daya?"

"Yes, every day," Daya promised.

"I have seen you love the other girls and give them your food. You are a beautiful girl. Keep thinking of what you can do to help the people around you. This will also distract you from your own problems."

"I will try."

"Think about good things. If we are slaves, we must treat the people who own us with dignity and respect. Now close your eyes and try to sleep," Gargi ordered. "Soon the others will be awake, so we need to try and rest now."

Daya stared into the darkness. Even though it was difficult to understand how God the Father, Christ Jesus the Son, and the Holy Spirit were one, she believed it.

Could God hear her thoughts? *Will you hold me tonight,*

Jesus?

For I am the Lord your God who takes hold of your right hand and says to you, Do not fear, I will help you.

Closing her eyes, she relaxed.

~

That no one was interested in storming the ship before it arrived in port infuriated Eli. Even Isak had insisted that he calm down and accept what he could not change.

Walking briskly with his head down, Eli liked being outside. The air felt hotter than he was used to and perspiration dripped down his back.

There was no way he was going to sit around and wait two more days for the vessel to dock.

The narrow street reeked of pungent spices that shopkeepers were selling. He sauntered down an alleyway and kicked at some loose stones scattered along the path.

The houses were in pretty bad shape and leaned towards each other high above the alleyways. He liked the intricate woodwork casements that enabled the people inside to see who was passing below.

He noticed a group of women crossing the road. He took in their burkas. The garments they wore were so loose that they hid their shapes completely. Two of the group had veils over their faces and all he could see was their eyes. He could get himself—and the women—in trouble if he continued to stare, so he shifted his gaze away from them.

Did the men of this country think making their women dress like this would stop foreigners from staring? It seemed strange to him that many of the men walking the street were dressed like westerners, wearing clothes similar to his, yet their women were dressed differently.

Eli strolled toward an old man in traditional clothing, selling fruit from a faded red rug on the ground. Large watermelons were stacked neatly and kept from rolling by small pieces of strategically placed Styrofoam.

Indicating with his hand to the apples and oranges, Eli bought one of each. He handed over the money the man requested and sauntered away to lean against a building and peel his orange.

While he was on Saudi Arabian soil, he was tied to their laws. The police assured Eli they would act quickly and that they were preparing security teams. Also that a Mujahideen battalion, along with the Commission for the Promotion of Virtue and Prevention of Vice, would take care of the matter.

Pushing away from the wall, he continued to walk. It wasn't that he doubted the legal authorities' ability to storm the ship. It was just that every day they wasted could mean death to Gargi and the children.

The surface of the path had become rougher and the people milling around seemed to be watching him. Eli stopped. He didn't recall walking so far from the hotel.

Swallowing a segment of orange, he watched as a man approached him. Glad of his sunglasses, he averted his head and pretended disinterest in the approaching stranger.

"You are Eli Turner?" the stranger asked.

"Yes." Eli raised his eyebrows.

"My master would like to talk with you. It seems you have something in common and he thought he might be of some assistance to you."

"Who is your… master?"

"He is a man of much power and there are—let's say—some things he will not tolerate and other things he will turn a blind eye to. Yes, that is what he is like."

"I'm not going anywhere with you unless you tell me what this is about." Eli folded his arms. The man didn't seem threatening, but things could change in a second.

"My name is Ahmed Hakimi and I will tell you my master's name if you decide to come with me."

"Ahmed, what do I have in common with your boss?"

"We have heard rumors about the women and children aboard the cargo vessel, yes?"

"Yes."

"My master's only daughter was taken two years ago from outside her school. She was never found, and although my master is a hard man who lives on the edge of the law…" Ahmed shrugged. "That is enough information. Are you coming with me or not?"

Shoving his sunglasses to the top of his head, Eli peered into Ahmed's eyes. The man was of medium height and stood calmly, waiting, as if he were in no hurry and didn't particularly care one way or the other.

"I'm coming," Eli answered and pulled his glasses back in

place.

~

The captain stepped into the container and stood with his legs wide apart.

Gargi forced herself to make eye contact. Standing, she loosely linked her hands in front of her. What she wanted to do was spread her arms out wide and shield the children behind her.

His gaze travelled slowly down her body and returned to her face. The side of his mouth curved in a sickening smile and he ran his tongue over his upper teeth.

Gargi wanted to avert her eyes but jutted her chin out in defiance. After Daya had gone to sleep she'd prayed, and it was as if God had shown her a great mystery.

Regardless of what happened to her, Christ was in her. It was that simple. No fanfare. No more, no less.

The captain took hold of her chin. His dry, rough fingers scratched her skin as he tilted her face.

"Yes, I can see why a man would travel the ocean to find you." He dropped her chin. "It appears your boyfriend is in Jeddah awaiting the arrival of my ship. My sources tell me that upon docking, my ship will be boarded and searched."

Hope rose in Gargi's heart.

Eli. Tears flooded her eyes at the thought of him travelling so far to find her. Blinking, she focused on what the captain was saying.

"Stand up." He pulled out a cigarette then placed it between his lips unlit.

Gargi nodded to the children and bent to help Pia. The child was not faring well. It was like she'd lost the will to live. "Girls, remember all we have talked about. Stay strong." Tears threatened to fall, but Gargi was determined to encourage her girls.

The captain waved at one of the men to take Pia from her.

Gargi didn't want to release the child but had no choice.

"It's all right, girly. I'll be gentle with the little scrap," the elderly sailor assured Gargi as he eased Pia into his arms.

She realized it was the same man who had carried her out of the container and dribbled water into her mouth until she was able to drink properly.

Turning back to the captain, she folded her arms. "If you help us, I will speak on your behalf and tell the police how you saved our lives by giving us water and food," Gargi promised.

"You fool, girl," he snarled. "I'm in charge here. Line up."

Amita slipped her hand into Gargi's and kneaded her fingers. Daya rushed to stand on Gargi's right and joined her hands with Gargi and the child next to her.

"I'm scared," Amita murmured.

Gargi looked down the line of children. Two fewer than they'd started with. With their hands linked they stood as one.

The captain took his time advancing down the line. He ducked his head to stare into the face of each person. He forced mouths open and checked teeth and then sighed.

"So hard to choose from such a motley crop of livestock." Scratching his chin, he returned to stand in front of Gargi. His gaze dropped to her hands grasping Daya's and Amita's.

The captain came so close to Gargi that she could smell his stale nicotine breath.

"You are a beautiful specimen—but too old." He flicked the cigarette away then cupped her face. His fingers dented her skin. Pulling her forward, he licked her lips and then up the side of her face.

She arched her spine then thrust her head back. She had to steel herself from letting go of the girls' hands. Her fingers itched to wipe his spittle off her skin. Her eyes locked on his and he winked.

Slowly, as if to increase her pain, the captain placed his hands over each of Gargi's hands and yanked Daya and Amita to his sides.

"I think these two will do nicely." He hugged the girls' under his arms and pulled them close to his body.

A small sob escaped Amita and she closed her eyes. Daya's shoulders drooped and her eyes flicked from the captain to Gargi.

Heart thumping wildly, Gargi sidled closer to the captain and raised her hand to caress his cheek. She ran her index finger under his eye and down to his mouth.

"What a shame," she purred. "An important man like you, I would have thought you would be more interested in an experienced woman like me, someone who could show you a good time."

The captain chuckled. “Tempting, but this is business.” He dragged the girls toward the door and spoke to the men waiting for his instruction.

Running after him, Gargi grabbed the captain’s arm. “Please don’t separate us. I beg you.”

He whipped his hand across her face.

Gargi’s neck snapped back and she staggered to the floor. Her eyes watered. The pain in her face was nothing compared to the way her heart hurt.

Standing, she approached the captain. “Sir, may I speak one last time to my friends?”

He snarled. “Forget them. They are gone from your life. I have a speed boat waiting to take them as we speak.”

She ducked past him and lunged at the girls. “Daya, Amita—don’t give up. Never, ever, give up. Wherever you go, whatever happens to you, hold on to Jesus. I love you both so much. Pray for me as I will pray for you.”

Two men veered menacingly toward Gargi and yanked the girls away from her.

Gargi froze knowing there was nothing she could do. Trying to fight the men any further would only end up causing the girls more grief.

Her eyes met Daya’s and the look of despair in her friend’s eyes was just about Gargi’s undoing. Forcing herself to smile, she placed her hand over her heart.

“Remember all we’ve talked about,” Gargi called.

Daya pulled at the hand of the man dragging her. “Wait,” she demanded.

The man stopped and let go of her.

Running back to Gargi, Daya threw her arms around her and clung tight.

"I love you, Gargi. I will never forget what you've taught me." Daya's voice shook. "I will make you proud. Make Jesus proud."

"I know you will. If I can, I will find you. I can't promise, but if I ever get free, I will try." Tears flowed down Gargi's face and she kissed Daya's cheek. "Daya, I'm already proud of you."

Swiping the tears from her face, Daya followed the man out of the container.

The moment they were out of sight, the trembling started. Gargi hugged her stomach and tried to still the pain that was charging through her like electricity.

Would she ever see the girls again? The look of resolve on Daya's face as she'd accepted their separation had been so solemn.

These girls had become her children and she'd not been able to keep them safe. Sinking to the floor, she bent over and wept.

"Get up," a seaman demanded.

Forcing her legs to obey, Gargi did as he ordered. The other children scurried close to her and she set her shoulders straight and stood tall.

Five men charged into the container and forced the girls to move to the back corner. "You will do as we tell you. We have little time to get organized."

Closing her eyes for a moment, Gargi prayed for her friends and she blocked out the noise of the men barking orders and the sounds of the children crying.

Chapter 37

Eli's fingers itched to pull his mobile phone out of his pocket and alert Isak to what he was doing, but he sat silently next to Ahmed.

He wondered where the driver was taking them. They'd been driving for an hour and he'd watched the neighborhood change from old city to a place of affluence.

Eli cocked his eyebrows to Ahmed. "You said you would tell me the name of your employer if I came with you."

"Sheikh Saeed Tahan," Ahmed informed Eli. "My prince is expecting you as his guest and I suggest for your—how do you say—well-being? Yes that is it, that you be extremely grateful for an audience with him."

Ahmed turned away and folded his arms stiffly, clearly not wanting to engage in conversation.

Staring out the tinted car window, Eli took no notice of the scenes flashing past him. Was his life always going to be like this? Stepping into unknown situations where he could easily disappear from the face of the earth, never to be seen again.

He pictured his life before India. Now he realized how bored he'd become with crunching numbers to meet monthly deadlines. The thought of going back to working in an office held no appeal even if it also held no danger.

India had gained him a son and he'd met the woman he loved. If he found Gargi, would he be able to settle down to the bland life he'd once lived?

"We are here," Ahmed said and unclicked his seat belt.

The car stopped at a security gate and a camera scanned the car. The gate opened and the car glided through.

Eli's gaze followed the curving driveway up to a white palace. There were men wearing white robes, walking around casually, yet Eli sensed their relaxed posture was deceptive; they were ready for any situation that might befall them.

"Follow me." Ahmed circled the car and led the way toward the entrance of the palace.

The sound of Ahmed's shoes klop-klopping on the glassy tiles beckoned Eli to hurry after him. Despite the gravity of the situation, he couldn't help but admire the opulent furnishings and artwork scattered around the foyer.

Tall vases were displayed on stands and he was sure the van Gogh on the wall was an original.

"Wait here," Ahmed commanded. "Someone will come for you when the prince is ready to see you. You will be brought refreshments." Bowing, Ahmed backed away and left the room.

Eli moved across the room to the large window. He

pushed the sheer net curtain aside to peer through the glass.

Manicured trees and formal gardens stretched before him. His gaze dropped to the trimmed lawn. Not a blade looked out of place. It seemed almost artificial.

Turning, he surveyed the room. Obviously a sitting room of sorts. Plush loungers circled an oval handcrafted teak coffee table, which sat on a red Persian rug. An intricately engraved brass incense burner stood one foot tall on a pedestal. Eli knew the smell of agarwood and liked the strong and sharp aroma that filled the room.

The door opened and a man entered. He wore the traditional white ankle-length robe with long sleeves, and it seemed as if the collar had been stiffened.

Eli watched as the man placed a glass jug on the table. Ice clanked as he lifted the jug and a tall glass.

“May I pour for you, sir?” The man’s tanned oval face turned to Eli and bushy eyebrows rose in question.

“Thank you.” Taking the glass from him, Eli took a sip and realized it was pineapple juice.

The man left as quietly as he’d entered, and Eli sat. How long would the sheikh expect him to wait? Placing the glass on the table, he leaned his head back and sighed. It had been a long day and he felt weary. He allowed himself the luxury of letting his eyes close.

“Mr Turner. Please come with me.”

Eli felt disoriented. He’d wanted to rest his eyes for only a moment but must have drifted off to sleep. The filtered light through the window showed that at least an hour had passed.

He rose, then followed the man down a number of passages. They stopped outside a door with a man standing sentry.

Stepping toward Eli, the man indicated without words for him to raise his arms.

Spreading his arms and legs out, Eli allowed the man to pat him down.

The guard stepped back and resumed his statue-like position.

The man Eli had followed knocked and waited.

The door opened. Eli stepped inside an ornate and beautiful room, which he presumed was the sheikh's office. Ahmed beckoned him forward.

A massive hand-carved desk sat pride of place in the center of the room. The man behind the desk stood to greet Eli.

"Mr Turner, it is my pleasure to meet you. Thank you for coming." The prince was dressed in casual clothes and his hair was cut short. Eli guessed him to be closer to forty than thirty. He extended his hand and Eli reached out and shook it.

Ahmed bowed stiffly. "Mr Turner, Prince Saeed Tahan."

"Prince Saeed, I understand you think we can help each other." Eli could see Ahmed stiffen beside him but didn't care. They'd brought him here for a reason and he didn't have time to play stupid games before they got down to business.

"You wish to insult me by not engaging in pleasant conversation, Mr Turner?"

"I mean you no disrespect, sir. I'm sure if you require pleasant conversation, there are plenty of people who are willing." Eli met the prince's steely gaze and waited for his reaction to his forthrightness. He hadn't meant to be rude, but the toll of the afternoon was getting to him. If this came to nothing, then he had wasted another day.

The left side of the prince's mouth lifted. "Leave us, Ahmed," Prince Saeed commanded. "Eli, may I call you by your given name?"

"Yes, of course."

"Come, my friend, sit and I will explain my reason for wanting to see you." The prince sat on a leather couch and waited for Eli to join him.

Though he was sitting across from a man who seemed to own some type of small kingdom, Eli found himself relaxing. He liked the way the prince met his eyes and he didn't feel threatened.

Resting his hands on his knees, the prince leaned forward. "I have heard that you want to board a certain ship and search it for trafficked children."

"Yes. I believe there are women and children locked inside a shipping container. By the calculations I have been given, the water and food would have long run out."

"This is why you do not want to wait for the correct authorities to board the ship, yes?"

Eli felt the urgent need to do something. He leaned forward to narrow the gap between them. "Can you help?"

"Are you prepared to go this minute to the ship?"

Squinting in surprise, Eli straightened. Evening was approaching, and the fading light would make things more difficult.

"Prince Saeed, I am keen to go, yes. But can you tell me why you would want to get involved when this may put you at risk of breaking the law?"

"The law is set to protect the innocent, and I'm afraid that the slowness of our authorities has often let me down." Sighing, he stood and picked up a framed photo of a woman and a small child.

"This is my first wife and our only child. My daughter is lost to me and this burns a hole in my heart. When I hear of other young ones being taken and used in such ways—I imagine my precious child and it rips my heart open." His hands clasped together and he inclined his head towards his chest.

Eli warmed to him. Both a prince and a common man can be affected equally by grief.

"I am sorry for your loss. I understand the pain you must be feeling. I too lost my sister and she was subjected to unspeakable things. God was good to us and we found her. I will pray that you will also find your daughter."

"Save your prayers, Eli Turner. My daughter is dead. They found her body a year after her abduction, and it was photographed and sent to me by strangers who wished to torment me."

Compassion for the man filled Eli and he stood and placed his hand on the prince's shoulder. "Then I will pray for you."

Saeed's eyes narrowed.

Eli dropped his hand and stepped back.

"Thank you for your concern. Allah be praised." The prince placed the photo back. "Each child we rescue is one less that gets destroyed. I am a man of power and much influence. The things that I order to be done are obeyed and not questioned."

"You are a caring man."

Saeed stood taller. "You wish to go with my men to the boat?"

"Yes."

"You do not mind boarding a vessel at sea illegally?"

Eli considered his question. He needed to stay within the law, this was an absolute for him.

"You need time to consider your answer, my friend?" Saeed's eyebrows drew together. "I thought this quest was urgent for you. Maybe I was mistaken in the type of man you are. I will arrange your transport back to your hotel."

"You weren't mistaken. I will do what I have to, to save them."

"Good. I have been watching this vessel and have had my suspicions about the captain before. Tonight, if what you say is true, we will have proof that he is a trafficker and we will take care of him."

Frowning, Eli surveyed the prince's face. "I wish to rescue the women and children. You cannot be sure that the crew on the ship are even aware of the presence of trafficking aboard their vessel."

"Enough talk. I have my ways of finding out such things. Ahmed will go with you and assure your safe return."

The door opened and Ahmed entered and bowed to the prince.

Saeed nodded to him. "You have your instructions, Ahmed."

"Yes, my prince."

"Eli Turner is a friend of mine. Keep him safe." Prince Saeed stepped toward Eli and held out his hand.

Chapter 38

Macy's gaze sought out Ashok standing beside Bill. Her grandson loved going grocery shopping with them and especially enjoyed pushing the shopping trolley around the supermarket.

Not once had Ashok asked her to buy him something from the shelves. She remembered Eli at Ashok's age. He'd badger her until she'd buy him some sugary treat, then she'd pay the consequence as he bounced off the walls full of energy.

Her eyes smarted as she followed Bill. They had so much at their fingertips that it seemed obscene somehow to try and decide which type of shampoo she wanted to use this week.

It wasn't that she felt guilty having so much disposable income, it was just that now more than ever before, she was aware of the need of others.

She felt she had to play a part, even a small part, in helping.

She couldn't save the world; that was up to Jesus. But as she looked at her grandson she knew she had to love him more. Make him realize how important he was to her.

Moving alongside him, she picked up his hand. "If you could have anything from this shop, what would it be?"

"I do not need anything, Grandma."

"I know that, sweetheart. But if you could buy anything, what would it be?"

"I do not know."

Pulling out a twenty-dollar bill, Macy handed it to him. "I want you to walk around the aisles and spend this on yourself. Grandpa and I will finish the shopping."

Ashok dropped his gaze to the money and smiled. "Anything?"

"Anything," she answered. "Off you go."

He sprinted away.

"No running," Macy called after him. He skidded and slowed his pace, and Macy smiled.

Bill touched her shoulder. "What are you doing, Macy?"

"I just want him to have a little fun. Have you seen the sadness on his face lately?"

"Yes. He's missing Eli. You can't buy him happiness. The thrill of having the money to spend will only be a temporary fix."

Macy knew he was right, but she hadn't meant to fix anything. Annoyance that he would think this was her desire made her want to snap at him.

She took a long breath and forced herself to speak gently. He was just speaking his mind. Her reaction to his words was her problem, not his.

"It's not my intention to try and *buy* Ashok happiness. That you'd think I'd try and do that is just stupid." Holding up her hand, she stopped him from interrupting her. "I'm not saying you are stupid, darling man. I just want him to experience trying to decide what to buy with twenty dollars. It's a good lesson for him."

"I see," Bill murmured. "How about a quick kiss while the boy's distracted?"

"Bill! We're in the supermarket," Macy replied with a smile.

"So? Come here, you gorgeous woman. I love you more each day." Bill glanced around as if checking to see if anyone was watching, then he pulled her into his arms and kissed her full on the lips.

Laughing, she pushed him away. "I love you too. Now what type of deodorant do you want?"

~

Standing in the confectionary aisle, Ashok licked his lips in anticipation. There was so much to choose from that he couldn't decide. His grandma had walked past him and told him to take his time, that they were going to go through the checkout, put the groceries in the car, and meet him across the road at the café when he was ready.

He pushed his hand into his pocket and fingered the crisp twenty-dollar note. Never in his life had he been given money he could spend on *anything*.

Wandering away from the candy, he entered the toy aisle. A small doll caught his attention and he pictured Shanti playing with it. He lifted its arms up and down and smiled.

After he had placed the doll back on the shelf, he looked at the books and toy cars. When he spotted the Transformer, he whooped in excitement.

It was Optimus Prime, his favorite.

Picking it up, he checked the price. Sixteen dollars; he'd have change. He wished it wasn't in a box so he could touch it.

Ashok stopped to consider whether it was wise to buy the toy. Twenty dollars was a lot of money and he didn't want to waste it.

But he really wanted the robot.

His stomach started to churn and he wished his grandma hadn't given him the money. Putting the toy back on the shelf, he continued walking and gazing at the items in each aisle.

The best idea was to take his time and make a wise decision. He wanted the Transformer, but he'd never had the chance to spend such a lot of money.

He stopped and read a sign that said Medicine and Health Care. Picking up a sealed bandage, Ashok recalled the doctor he'd met in India. The doctor had stitched up Shanti's knee when she'd cut it running from a stray dog.

Squeezing the bandage in his hand, Ashok remembered

Doctor Paul and his wife, Wendy. They'd been kind to Shanti, and Ashok had asked if he and Shanti could go to America and live with them.

Shaking his head, Ashok tried not to be sad. He hated the thoughts that screamed through his mind. If Doctor Paul had said yes, then maybe Shanti would still be alive.

A thick lump swelled in his throat as he pushed the crinkled bandage back onto the shelf. Doctor Paul had given him many rupees and told him goodbye.

Money sometimes wasn't enough.

Screwing up his face, Ashok remember how quickly the money had disappeared on food.

Slowly dragging his feet on the shiny floor, Ashok looked down at his shoes.

Shoes his grandparents had bought him. His heart raced and he grinned. Spinning around, he charged back to the checkout and picked up a basket. He'd need it for what he was going to buy.

In the biscuit aisle he chose his grandma's favorite biscuits and checked the price. Placing them carefully in his basket, he went to look at the gardening magazines. Grandma liked looking through these; he'd heard her say she'd like to buy another one someday soon.

Ashok added up the money he'd spent so far. Counting on his fingers, he worked out how much he had left. If he had change after getting Grandpa something, he'd buy the magazine as well.

He felt so happy and wanted to share his excitement with someone.

An elderly lady smiled at him before she went out of sight around the corner of the aisle.

His grandpa had worn socks yesterday that had holes in the toes. Clicking his tongue, Ashok laughed and skipped backwards to where he'd seen lots of socks hanging from hooks on a wall.

He chose a pair of thick, black socks. He decided they were the right size and dropped them into his basket.

He knew he had a further nine dollars to spend. The magazine was four dollars, which would leave him enough to buy a card.

Once he'd found the card he liked, Ashok thought about the words he'd write on it. This was his chance to tell his grandparents how much love he felt for them in his heart.

He felt all bubbly inside as he handed over the money to pay for his gifts. He couldn't stop smiling.

As much as he'd wanted Optimus Prime, he knew he'd had more fun working out what to buy his grandparents than he ever would have had playing with a toy.

The lady serving him put his items in a clear plastic bag. She handed him the bag and twenty cents change.

As he took the bag, Ashok glanced at her and hesitated. "Do you think you could put my shopping into another bag that you cannot see through? I have bought gifts for my grandparents and I don't want them to see them until I have wrapped them."

"I don't have another bag. Sorry. Move along," she said.

There was a line of people milling up behind him. Ashok took his things quickly from the counter.

"Boy," someone called out.

Turning, Ashok recognized the old lady he'd seen in the aisle. She was beckoning to him.

He noticed she had a full shopping trolley. Maybe she needed help with getting her groceries to her car. He'd offer to help before he went to the café to meet his grandparents.

"Hello, Ashok. You don't remember me, do you?" she asked.

Ashok frowned. "I do know you, but I'm sorry I cannot remember your name or where I have met you."

"I go to the same church your grandparents go to. You can call me Henny, short for Henrietta." She leaned on her walking stick. "Now what's the problem with this bag?"

Telling her the problem, Ashok shrugged. "I will just give my grandparents their gifts when I meet them at the café."

"No, no. What fun is there in that? What we need to do is get some wrapping paper and wrap them now."

Ashok opened his hand and showed her the twenty-cent piece. "I was going to use some of my drawing paper and Grandma's tape to wrap them when I got home."

"Come with me," she ordered and shuffled toward a counter with a smiling lady behind it.

"Ashok, put your items on this counter." Henny turned to the lady. "Dear, this young man has bought some gifts for his grandparents and they are waiting for him across the road."

"How can I help, madam?"

"Ashok, go and get a roll of wrapping paper that you like," Henny ordered. "Then this young lady will wrap your gifts for us."

Ashok shuffled his feet. “Um, Henny, I think I’ll go now,” he mumbled.

“Boy, do as I tell you.” Henny ruffled his hair and gave him a slight shove.

Ashok glanced at his things on the counter. He didn’t have enough money for paper; he’d checked out the cost before he’d decided to wrap them at home.

He went to do as he’d been told. Once the shop lady asked him for his money, Henny would understand he couldn’t pay for it and then let him go.

The roll of paper he chose was gold and had blue stripes running through it. It would have been nice for both his grandparents, if he’d been able to buy it.

After he had placed the paper on the counter, Ashok stood back and watched as the shop lady took it and ran it under a scanner. Henny passed her some money. Out came some scissors and tape, and the lady got busy wrapping his gifts.

Staring at Henny, Ashok couldn’t stop smiling.

“You are a nice person, Henny. I am thanking you.” He bowed and held out his hand.

Laughing, Henny grabbed him. “Give me a hug, you sweet boy.”

Her arms circled him and he giggled.

“All done.” The shop assistant pushed the gifts across the counter.

“Thank you,” Ashok said loudly. “May I help you with your trolley, Henny?”

“I was hoping you would offer,” Henny said, and Ashok could hear the laughter in her voice.

He liked her so much. It was good to have a new friend and he hoped he could see her again. Placing his parcels in her trolley, he led the way out of the supermarket.

Henny stood beside him as he carefully placed bag after bag into her car boot. He could feel her eyes on his face and it felt like she was waiting for something. Maybe she expected him to drop one of her parcels.

Taking extra care, Ashok bent to pick up the last bag. He saw what was inside and his hands stopped short of touching it. His mouth dropped open and he twirled to look at Henny.

Her face was glowing with warmth, and the lines around her eyes told him that she was enjoying his surprise. She reached out and flicked his mouth shut.

"Go on, take it—it's for you."

Reaching into the bag, Ashok pulled out Optimus Prime. His eyes watered and his chest tightened. He didn't know what to say.

"I'm sorry, Ashok. I was watching you and saw the way you put the toy back on the shelf. Sometimes when you sacrifice what you want, to bless others, you get what you want too."

Opening his mouth, he tried to say thank you, but the words stuck in his throat. He made a coughing sound to try and loosen the emotion that was choking him.

"Thank you," he blurted out. Something burst inside him and he jumped up and down. "Thank you, soooooo much." Laughing, he leaned on the car and ripped the packaging off the robot. "Henny, wait until you see how Optimus Prime turns into a car. My friend Shane has the Transformer movies and we watched them all. Wait until I tell him that you gave me one." He couldn't stop talking, he was so excited. "Wait until I show Grandpa. Oh, Henny—you make me so happy."

"You deserve to be happy. Now off you go, your grandparents will be waiting."

Chapter 39

The sixty-foot launch was sheer luxury and glided through the water effortlessly. Ahmed relaxed beside Eli in the leather seat and calmly sipped a glass of bourbon.

Glancing at his watch for the fifth time, Eli couldn't believe that in twenty minutes or so he'd be aboard the vessel and holding Gargi in his arms. He refused to believe any other possibility.

She would not be dead.

"Mr Turner, relax. You may stay here if you wish. My orders are to keep you out of harm's way."

Eli stood then crossed the stateroom to the open door and breathed in the salt air. The farther away they got from the city lights, the darker the sky became. Men waited on deck with loaded machine guns. Eli turned to face Ahmed.

"I don't want anyone killed. As far as I know, the crew on this ship don't even know there is a container with people in it."

"Do not concern yourself with such details."

"Ahmed, it is not necessary to use force. I appreciate all the prince is doing to help me, but this is my decision. I do not want any gunfire."

Raising his glass, Ahmed saluted Eli. "My prince is allowing you to be part of this mission. The vessel *Jag Tan* has been on our radar long before you turned up."

"Even if that is the case, I respectfully ask you that no one be hurt."

"Do you think we are animals? That we simply kill people because we enjoy it? We are a civilized people, Mr Turner. We value our women and children and will go to any means to protect and avenge them."

"Revenge does not belong to you. Hatred will end up killing you." Eli searched Ahmed's face. He needed to make this man realize that God was the one ultimately in control of all life and that the power Ahmed thought he had, was paper thin.

"Do you have a family? A wife, children?" Eli asked.

"Yes." Ahmed banged his glass onto the table.

"If you were killed tonight, do you think your wife would be happy that you died avenging strangers?"

Ahmed stood and stared down his straight nose at Eli. "The question is redundant. My wife understands what I do is of grave importance. My prince would see it as an honor to take care of my family."

"That's a lot of bull and you know it. Money can't replace a husband or father. There are men on the *Jag Tan* who have families waiting for them to return. It is no different."

"Enough. Ready yourself." Ahmed spun away and left the stateroom.

Eli stared through the salt-smeared window at the figures silhouetted on the main deck.

His lips moved in a silent prayer. *Lord, forgive me if I have made a mistake in joining the prince's men.* He stepped onto the deck and braced his legs against the sway of the waves. He glanced up the staircase to the bridge deck and wondered if he'd be welcomed up there. Ahmed had told him they'd located *Jag Tan* on their radar and were fast approaching her port side.

The launch rocked up on the crest of a wave and then sunk down, hiding the lights of the approaching ship from his view. The closer they got to the ship, the more Eli wondered how they'd board.

Eli gripped the rail. He leaned his hips firmly against the wire lines running horizontally from steel tube to steel tube. Slanting his head, he watched the blinking red light indicating portside at the bow of the container ship.

The air was thick with sea spray. Eli licked his lips and tasted salt. He loved the sea and had dreamed of hiring a catamaran and sailing around the Whitsundays, whale watching.

He'd let go of that dream in an instant if it meant Gargi were with him. The thought of her being locked up and coping with rough seas from inside a tin box made him gag. His fingers clenched the rail until his bones ached.

The launch slowed and the crew sped into action. Fenders were thrown over the side to protect the launch's hull. Ahmed joined Eli at the rail.

"How are you planning to board?" Eli questioned. The huge vessel loomed like a skyscraper before them.

Ahmed pointed to the starboard side of the *Jag Tan* and Eli leaned farther over the rail to see.

A rope ladder with wooden rungs bumped against the side of the vessel.

"You have someone on board expecting us?" Eli grabbed hold of Ahmed's arm.

"Mr Turner, release my arm," Ahmed requested calmly. "We have been in radio contact with the captain for the last ten minutes and it is in his best interest to cooperate."

~

Khlaid bowed his head and stared down at his hands resting on the old, scarred table. The starkness of the police interrogation room only highlighted the end to him.

The questions had been unrelenting, one after the other thumping through his mind like a sledgehammer breaking up concrete.

That the police detested his weakness meant nothing to him.

He was done.

He'd been wrong. Made choices that led to his own destruction.

Leaning his elbows on the table, he cupped his head. He liked the silence and wanted to stay in this room as long as possible.

He flicked a glance at the window. He knew they watched him.

What more would they want from him before they transferred him to a cell in Arthur Road Jail?

He'd confessed. Told them everything.

They didn't care about him; he was nothing but a means to an end. Their goal was to close down one trafficking operation, to celebrate their success in the media. They would hide the fact that half the police force was corrupt, often closing a blind eye for the money that exchanged hands.

Narrowing his eyes, he wanted to scream as his skin pulled across his forehead. It had been his employer's idea to change his appearance. He'd subjected himself to months of pain because of false promises, and now when he looked in the mirror he saw a stranger.

He was glad he'd informed on the swine. Payback felt bittersweet.

Roughly scratching his head, he sought the uncomfortable sensation on his scalp. When he achieved it, he pulled his hand away and looked at the blood under his fingernails.

He pushed his right index fingernail under the bloodied nails, and then he scraped the substance out and flicked it onto the floor.

How much innocent blood did he have on his hands? Shuddering, he gasped.

He'd done the right thing, helping the police.

His gut churned. Bending over, he moaned. Since when did he care about what was right?

It was Charlotte's eyes that haunted him. Soft, forgiving, filled with—compassion.

He'd wanted her, needed her so that he could feel—anything.

Balling his hands into fists, he drove them into his eyes.

She was an angel. Soft. Caring. So, so beautiful. Nothing stopped her love.

Khlaid snapped his head back and cursed his stupidity. He'd sold her. Made money that now soiled his hands.

Frantically rubbing his palms up and down on his legs, he panted as air filled his lungs and hissed around him, whispering his guilt.

You did it.

Guilty. Guiltttty.

Blood—on—your—hands.

He jumped up, knocking over the chair.

Blood on your hands. Blood on your hannnnds.

Murderer.

Innocent bloood.

Charging across the room, he slammed his fist on the door. "Let me out of here." He pounded the solid wood.

Shadows whooshed around him like living things. Spinning, he searched the corners of the room.

His skin prickled and it felt like needles stabbed every exposed surface of flesh.

"I'm sorry," he screamed.

Dropping to his knees, he cried. "Charlotte, I'm sorry. I

love you."

Sobs racked his body.

He'd betrayed her.

"Like Judas betrayed Charlotte's Jesus." He scratched wildly at the back of his neck.

He'd read about her Jesus as he'd searched the Bible for the man Saul.

He was not Saul. Never would be. Tugging at his hair, he got up off his knees and paced across the room.

He was Judas. Traitor, scum, fool.

Die.

His breath quickened and his chest tightened. He'd taken blood money.

Children's blood.

Khlaid slammed his head against the wall and rocked back and forward.

Charlotte's precious blood.

Throwing his head against the wall, he savored the pain.

Your wife's blood.

Padma had loved him at the start. A hoarse cry tore from his throat. His voice mocked his pain as he once again crashed his head into the wall.

He screamed for release from the torment.

A little girl with deep brown eyes mirroring her fear.

Shanti's blood.

Three more times he slammed his forehead into the wall.

His head exploded with pain. Bile rose in his throat. He gagged and gulped it back down.

Blood trickled down his face and he reached up and

rubbed his fingers in it.

Redemption. Blood for blood.

Khlaid staggered over to the chair and dragged it to the door. His hand shook as he wedged the chair back under the door handle.

Surveying the room, he tried to decide what to do. Even if he continued to slam his head into the wall, he knew this wouldn't kill him. He was too thick skulled. This had often worked in his favor in fights, but now what he wanted to do was end it quickly.

He jumped onto the table then steadied himself. He reached up and pulled on the light fixture. The plastic shade came away in his hand. The wire powering the light was too short to be of use.

Biffing the shade across the room in disgust, he eased his body from the table.

His head pounded and he closed his eyes against the pain. There was nothing in this room to assist him. It was as if the room was secured from escape of any type.

He glared into the window and wondered if there was still someone behind the smeared glass. Rubbing his finger into the blood clotting on his forehead, he slouched to the window and used his finger as a pen, intent on leaving a final message.

Pleased with the eligibility of his words, he wiped his hand on his pants.

He moved to the center of the room, turned the table onto its side and pushed it up to the wall with the tabletop away from the wall.

Sliding down the wood, he leaned heavily against the table. He removed his shirt and ripped two pieces from the fabric.

His eyes glazed over as he rolled two small cylinders of cloth and put them aside. Then he bunched up the third piece of shirt and made sure the material was in a thick wad.

His hand shook as he placed the wad on his knee.

Carefully he stuffed the first small cylinder up one nostril, and then wedged the second cylinder up the other nostril.

His mouth automatically opened and he took a shaky breath. Bringing his knees up close to his body he fought to stop himself from yanking out the material.

Khlaid picked up the thick wad of material, leaned his head back, and closed his eyes.

The bunched-up material fell apart and he cursed.

He fed the material into his mouth, packing it tight.

His tongue fought against the obstruction constricting its movements.

Lunging forward, Khlaid heaved.

His eyes opened. He could feel the panic beginning to claw at his chest.

How long would it take for him to die without air? Fire surged through his body as he thought of how heartless he'd been when Frank had wanted to provide more water in the container.

His lungs screamed.

Locking his jaw, Khlaid tried to relax his shoulders.

Focusing on his heart, he imagined the muscle pounding his rib cage. It wouldn't be long.

Die. Escape.

There was something calling him. Reaching out, beckoning him to reconsider.

Shaking his head, he knew his path.

Sadness filled him. He felt cold, alone.

In the distance he thought he heard banging, but his mind was foggy.

His body jerked, tried to suck in air.

The material held.

Chapter 40

Tanvir stood watching her and Padma's eyes smarted. Did he always have to look at her with such knowing? It was the way he waited, not putting any pressure on her, that unnerved her the most.

Sighing, she gave up the pretense that everything was all right. She stepped closer to him.

"Sister." The welcome in his voice was like a homecoming.

"Brother," she whispered.

His hands drew her close. Taking nothing, yet offering her an acceptance that bordered on the surreal.

"Are you ready to talk?" he asked.

So much had happened, and it felt like her heart was ready to explode with the pressure of holding her pain inside.

What could she say? How could she tell him of her guilt? She ducked her head, avoiding his glance.

"My sister, let us take a walk." He took hold of her hand and gave her no option but to follow.

Clicking, and locking the house door, Tanvir walked at a slow pace and placed her hand on his arm. The sound of their footsteps crunching on the gravel somehow comforted her.

She was not alone. Lengthening her stride, she matched his pace.

As they turned the corner and headed toward the small green area surrounded by buildings, Tanvir turned, took her hands, and kissed her knuckles.

"Come, we will sit."

Her stiffness eased. She glanced up at the branches of the only tree surrounded by grass.

"There was a tree at the brothel like this one. It was in the center of the compound."

Tanvir touched the tree and sat on the grass, leaning against its trunk. "Was it a nice tree?"

Ignoring his question, she closed her eyes and pictured Charlie and Shanti playing with the stones in the dirt. They hadn't known she watched them. But she couldn't stop herself. They'd seemed so free in those moments, and the sound of Shanti's sweet laugh had now become the nightmare that kept her awake.

"I could have saved her," she said in a flat tone. "Shanti begged me to help her get back to her brother—but I slapped her around and helped them ready her for—"

"I am sorry for your painful memories," Tanvir interrupted. "But God has a plan."

"How can you say that? Shanti died!" she screamed in anguish. She blamed herself for so many lives torn apart. She had been weak. Trying to protect herself by not getting involved.

Tears gathered in her eyes, but she scowled at them. Tears were not an option. She would not fall apart. She would address this pain that was clawing at her soul—trying to steal what she now believed.

Tanvir clicked his tongue. “Yes, Shanti died. Tragedy happens. I look forward to meeting her.” He gestured to a house sparrow. “She is now like that bird, flying free.”

Waves of doubt rolled through her. He was so sure of his faith.

Dropping to the ground beside him, she smoothed her sari. She had told Charlie that she’d found peace with God, and this was partly true.

How could she accept all that Jesus offered her? She believed, she really did. But there was something holding her back from taking the final step of letting go.

“Tell me,” she begged.

Tanvir chuckled. “At last.”

She gave his shoulder a gentle push and smiled. He kissed her cheek. His warm gaze embraced her. He made himself more comfortably against the tree’s trunk.

“What do you know about the death of Jesus Christ?”

“Charlie told me Jesus died for my sins. That if I open my heart to Jesus, then he will forgive me and I will be his.”

“Yes, that is true,” he reassured her. “It is a simple yet complicated act of faith. Asking Jesus to forgive you, accepting that he has, believing he is with you and that he loves you."

"It seems wrong to be forgiven so easily." Squinting up through the branches, she wished she could relive her life and make different choices.

"It wasn't easy," he stated sadly.

She turned to look at him and wondered what he was thinking.

He cleared his throat. "Sorry, I am always overwhelmed when I think of what our Lord did." Easing his shoulders further back, her brother's face transformed before her. The softness around his eyes beckoned her, and she leaned forward to listen to his softly spoken words.

"Jesus went willingly to the cross. He was innocent of all wrong and at any time he could have stopped what was happening—but he didn't." Tanvir turned, and his gaze captured hers.

"He was beaten and tortured, but he didn't say a word. Like a lamb taken to be slaughtered, he took it all in silence."

Closing his eyes, he paled.

Without opening his eyes he continued. "Crucifixion was a terrible, cruel, miserable death. The cross was laid on the ground and Jesus's hands and feet were nailed to it. Then it was hoisted upright so that the weight of his body hung on the nails till he died in agony."

A sob caught in her throat. She couldn't block the graphic picture from forming in her mind and wanted to tell Tanvir to stop. Her chest tightened and she gripped her hands to stop them from trembling. But she must hear this. "Go on. I'm—I'm listening," she said shakily.

"Jesus Christ went through all that agony, all the shame that was connected to such a death, so that he could purchase for us an everlasting life."

Taking her hands, Tanvir leaned closer and kissed her cheek. "You say it seems wrong to be forgiven so easily. No, my sister, it was not easy, anything but."

She locked her fingers around his and searched his face. Would he understand her confusion about Khlaid if she tried to explain it to him?

Letting go of her hand, Tanvir patted her shoulder. "Do you understand what you need to do, to give your life to Jesus, my sister?"

Nodding, she drew her knees to her chest and rested her forehead for a moment.

"Will you pray with me?" he asked hopefully.

Angling her head, she looked at him then warily raised her chin. "I will pray with you, but first I need to talk to you about Khlaid."

Tanvir crossed his ankles and put his hands behind his head. He seemed so relaxed and she longed to be like him. Nothing seemed to steal his peace.

"I hated him," she confessed. "He is—was evil and mean, but at one time I loved him."

"It is good to love your husband; however, you deserved to be loved in return and treated with respect and kindness."

Her eyes flooded. "I can't believe he killed himself. I don't know what to think." Standing, she paced in front of Tanvir and wrung her hands. Stopping, she threw her head back and blinked up into the glare. "The last thing I said to him was that I wanted a divorce. Many times I wished him dead."

Tanvir stood and dusted off his pants. He stepped toward her but didn't touch her or say anything. She liked that he understood her and didn't say empty words that would try and make her feel better.

Shuddering, Padma momentarily closed her eyes. "I find it impossible to believe he repented, yet the message he wrote in his own blood on that window—"

"I didn't know he left a message. What did it say?"

She glanced past her brother into space. "He wrote, 'I have sinned and spilt innocent blood. Forgive me'."

Tanvir scratched his chin. "It does sound like he confessed, but did he confess to God?"

Narrowing her eyes, Padma pressed a finger into her eyebrow where a solid ache was making it difficult to think. "Isn't acknowledging you've sinned enough?"

Tanvir frowned. "I don't think so. Give me a moment to consider this, my sister." He bowed his head.

"I think I understand," he exclaimed with a sad smile. "If I steal something precious from you and you find out, and then I apologize and say I'm sorry, maybe ask you to forgive me, that is one thing." He moved his hands expressively. "But if I do not personally ask Jesus Christ to forgive my sin, then I have still sinned."

"Oh." Padma felt her insides shrink. How often had she said a grudging *sorry* to Charlie or someone else and then considered it over? She'd never thought to say sorry to God.

Nausea rose in her throat. Clutching her stomach, Padma bent in half. She was a sinner. Even her hatred was a sin against God.

"Um, Tanvir?" She sunk to her knees.

Tanvir knelt beside her and gently rubbed her back as she sobbed.

"How do I pray?" she gushed out hoarsely.

"I will pray and you can say the words after me. Will that make it easier for you?"

"Yes, yes." She closed her eyes. Her throat constricted until she didn't think she could speak. Inhaling deeply, she waited.

"Lord Jesus, I understand I have sinned against you and others," Tanvir stated clearly.

Padma repeated the words and pressed her hand over her eyes as Shanti's face flashed across her vision.

"Forgive me all my sins. I give you my life, my now, my tomorrow, my all."

Sobbing, Padma uttered the words. "I am sorry for my sins, Jesus. So very sorry." Her body shook with emotion.

"Padma, in the book of Romans it says that if you declare with your mouth Jesus is Lord and believe in your heart that God raised him from the dead, you will be saved. Can you do this?" He gently wiped tears from her face.

"Yes," she exclaimed. "I believe. I believe." Pushing to her feet, she raised her arms. "Jesus is Lord! He is alive! I believe." She laughed and spun around and flung her arms around Tanvir.

Chapter 41

The cushion had moved during the night and Gargi moaned as she shifted her hips. She'd slept most of the night on the wooden floor of the container, and pain shot up through her legs as she stood.

Her heart yearned to do something, anything that would change their situation.

Pia had lain in her arms all night and her little hand had played with Gargi's hair. If only Pia would talk; it had been days since she'd spoken and Gargi was worried. It was as if the child were shutting down bit-by-bit and pushing reality from her mind by not talking.

How would Pia survive if she didn't release her fear in some way? Gargi's teeth caught at the fullness of her bottom lip. She longed for Pia to be safe.

Gargi pushed her hair behind her ears. Her fingers trembled and she linked her hands together.

A scraping noise by the door sent a shiver through her and she stiffened. Was this it? Were they coming for them now in the dark of night?

If only Eli had more of a chance to rescue them. But with the captain aware of Eli's plan, there was no way he would dock with them on the ship.

The door swung open and a man carrying a torch stepped into the container. The door was slammed shut behind him.

Heart pounding, Gargi stood.

Light bounced through the darkness from the torch and illuminated a gun in the man's hand. Gargi gasped. All sorts of thoughts ran through her mind. Had he come to use them before they left the ship?

Her fists tightened. She'd fight him before she let him touch one of her girls.

"You." He pointed to Gargi. "Get here." The gun was pointed at her chest and he motioned to the floor beside him.

Doing as he ordered, Gargi crawled toward him and sat on the floor in front of him.

"I will shoot you if anyone makes a noise. Not a sound. Do you understand?"

"Yes," Gargi whispered.

The man leaned against the wall and splayed the beam of light across the sleeping children.

Pia's eyes were open and she stared at the man as though in a trance.

Turning to the man, Gargi whispered. "May I hold her? She's only little." Even though Pia seemed unresponsive, Gargi needed to offer her comfort.

"Get her. Quickly."

Holding Pia to her chest, Gargi stroked her hair. "It's okay, sweet one. I've got you."

The man poked the gun into her neck and motioned with his finger to remain quiet. He switched off the torch and the container was thrown into total darkness.

Pia snuggled farther into her chest and Gargi wondered if the child could hear her heart racing. What was happening?

It was the middle of the night and they were still at sea. The ship's engine had become a soft hum. Gargi could still feel the vibration from the engines but she knew the ship wasn't moving.

Were they preparing to off-load them before they got to port? If they were, why was the seaman demanding they stay quiet?

She craned her neck, trying to hear what was happening outside the container.

~

Eli gripped the rail as Ahmed's men scampered up the ladder to the deck of *Jag Tan*. Their rifles swung over their shoulders and some carried guns poked into their belts.

The faces looking down at the launch were those of tough, seasoned sailors. Eli wondered at their compliance in letting them board.

"Mr Turner, after you," Ahmed ordered and stepped aside for Eli to pass.

The moist sea air had made the ladder slippery. Grabbing hold of the wooden rung, Eli placed his foot on it and then wrapped his hands around the vertical ropes. He hoisted himself up cautiously.

The ship pitched, and the ladder swung out, sending Eli airborne. He gripped the rope tighter and scrambled to regain his footing.

The wind seemed to develop hands that pulled at his arms until his muscles burned. Waves crashed below and mist drenched his clothes. He squinted to stop the sea spray from blinding him and braced for his body to bang against the ship as the rocking of the waves righted his position.

His body slammed against the hard metal, and his breath gushed out. Somehow he managed to hold on to the ladder. Feeling around with his feet for frantic moments, he finally found the wooden rung. He sighed with relief as his feet resumed their position and he continued to climb.

A hand reached out to help him over the rail and he thankfully gripped the calloused fingers.

"Appreciate your help, thanks," Eli muttered and edged away from the rail to allow Ahmed to board.

Eli counted six crewmen scattered around the deck.

"The captain is expecting you on the bridge," a seaman growled. He turned abruptly to lead the way.

Ahmed spoke a command to his men in Arabic and beckoned for Eli to follow. Entering the bridge, Eli noticed the thick layers of salt and dirt on every object. This ship was a working vessel and was in stark contrast to the million-dollar launch he'd just left.

The smells of grease, oil, and salt, along with the odor of sweaty clothes congealed with cigarette smoke made him want to cover his nose.

The captain turned, folded his arms and smiled. "Welcome aboard the *Jag Tan.*"

Ahmed stepped forward. "Captain, I appreciate your cooperation."

"You gave me little choice. However, please convey my regards to Prince Saeed."

"You always have a choice, my friend," Ahmed challenged.

"I have nothing to hide," the captain snorted. "This is a complete waste of time. I run a clean ship. If there are any—as you say—women and children on board, I am unaware of it."

Ahmed uttered instructions to his men. Guns were pointed at the seamen, and Ahmed beckoned for the captain to lead the way.

Grunting, the captain ducked his head as he stepped through the door. Pausing by the ship's rail, he spat into the ocean. He made a display of wiping his chin then turned to Ahmed.

"What container do you want to search? You do realize that each container is stacked in such a way that some may be impossible to open?"

Ahmed stiffened. "Let us hope for your sake that we can access the shipping container we wish to open. I see you have a crane on board. However I wish to do this as quickly as possible."

Listening to the conversation going back and forth between Ahmed and the captain, Eli wanted to tell them to stop wasting time.

He was so close, he knew it.

Shuffling his feet, the captain held out his hand to his first officer, who passed him a thick document.

"This is our inventory," the captain stated in a bored tone. "You have your container's code?"

"Mr Turner?" Ahmed questioned.

Quoting the numbers he'd memorized, Eli stepped close to the captain and looked over his shoulder as he searched the inventory.

The captain gave a slight nod. "You're in luck. We can easily access this container. Bay A. Follow me."

Anticipation surged through Eli and he wanted to run to the container and fling open the steel doors.

Whatever he found would be better than not knowing.

A seaman struggled to unlock the clasps holding the lever in place. "Step back, allow room for the doors to open," he ordered.

"The sea mist will coat the levers and make them difficult to open," the captain told them smugly. "It's the salt, covers everything." He clucked his tongue and snickered.

The mechanism creaked. The seaman yanked the door open, letting it slam back against the container stacked beside it.

Eli pushed past Ahmed and stepped inside. "I need light,"

he yelled.

A stream of light bounced off the walls, and Eli hammered his fist against the metal.

"Empty," he exclaimed through clenched teeth. Facing the captain, he clenched his fingers. "Where are they?"

The captain rubbed his chin. "An empty container?" he mocked. "I don't understand why someone would go to so much trouble to ship *air* halfway across the world."

Grabbing the front of his shirt, Eli shook him. "What have you done with them?"

Ahmed stepped forward and tapped Eli on the arm. "Calm down, Mr Turner. We have not finished here."

Eli shoved the captain away then returned to the container.

The ship's lights cast shadows around them, and he beckoned to one of Ahmed's men to aim his torch at the lever.

When he ran his finger over the steel, it came away clean. "Ahmed, there's no salt on this. I'd say it's been wrenched open more than once during the journey."

Taking a torch from the man next to him, Eli stepped into the container. The dank smell assaulted him and he covered his mouth and nose. You could not hide the smell of death in this place. He charged to the back and he searched every corner.

Eli touched the padded walls. Harnesses hung from them at regular intervals. He picked up one of them and his fingers tightened over the clasp. A picture was forming in his mind, and he didn't like what he was seeing.

Determined, he continued his search.

A small pool of water lay on the floor in the back left corner.

He dipped his finger in and then raised it to his nose and tasted it. Fresh water, not salt. The container had been hosed out recently.

"They were here," he exclaimed.

The captain shrugged his shoulders and turned to Ahmed. "I can see Mr Turner is correct. I will take immediate action to see if these stowaways are still on board my ship. I assure you I had no knowledge of any of this."

Ahmed barked out an order to his men in Arabic and they scattered across the ship to search other containers.

Eli leaned toward Ahmed in question.

"Stand aside, Mr Turner."

Stepping toward the captain, Ahmed waved his hand. Two of his men grabbed the captain and dragged him to the railing.

"You think it is necessary to keep you alive to search this ship? My prince has heard stories about you. Unless you are very helpful, your time has come."

"I have done nothing," the captain snarled.

It was like something snapped in Ahmed's steely control. Eli's eyes widened as the man pushed the captain to his knees.

As much as Eli wanted to find Gargi and the children, they had no proof that the captain was personally involved. Anyone could have used this ship as a tool.

"Wait," Eli commanded. "He could be speaking the truth. We need to complete our search. All I want is my friend and the children."

Ahmed's eyes seemed to darken. The dark brown depths turned to black and Eli wondered at the reason for the change.

Ahmed turned to face Eli. "All right."

Someone touched Eli's arm. One of Ahmed's men beckoned him to follow.

"Go, Mr Turner," Ahmed suggested. "I will escort the captain back to the bridge."

Carefully following the man on the slippery deck, Eli prayed their search would be successful.

"Noooooo."

The scream sent shivers down Eli's spine and he spun around.

The captain was struggling against the hands that were hoisting him up and over the side of the rail.

Eli raced toward the rail to stop what was happening.

A man appeared from nowhere and pressed the hard barrel of a gun into Eli's chest. "Stay."

Stiffening, Eli watched the scene play out in front of him. These men treated violence and death like an everyday occurrence. They dangled the captain over the edge and let go of one foot.

Eli could hear the sound of the captain's fingernails clawing at the side of the ship. His foot slipped through the wire rail and he tried to lodge it to secure a hold.

"Now, captain," Ahmed said. He glanced out to sea as if on a leisure cruise. "Are you sure you have no information you wish to share with me?"

"I know nothing. I promise you! Please, I beg you, pull me up."

The men holding the captain let him slip farther down the side of the vessel. The terror-stricken scream that came out of the captain's mouth forced Eli into action. His heart went into overdrive and he rushed to Ahmed's side.

"Stop!" He could feel a pulse beating furiously in his neck. "Lift him up, his life matters!" He reached over the railing and started yanking the captain's leg.

Ahmed stepped back. "As you wish, Mr Turner." He waved to his men to help.

A deep sigh of relief escaped Eli. Would they have casually dropped a human being overboard with no care of his life?

Something changed within him. He no longer wanted blood for blood. A profound sadness cramped at his shoulders. This life was so temporal. Didn't they understand that this wasn't a game and that they were answerable for their every action?

The captain swayed on his feet and grasped the rail.

After a moment, Eli saw him straighten and whip out his hand to slap Ahmed across the face.

Ahmed staggered and yelped.

The captain clicked his fingers. Two men appeared with machine guns pointed straight at Ahmed's head.

"You think I would allow you to come aboard my domain and order me around? You will pay for dangling me like a loose sheet out for drying." He jerked his head. "Kill him."

Gunfire exploded and Eli ducked down behind some rope. The man that had been holding his arm fled and took cover.

Ahmed crumpled to the deck. Blood seeped out into a pool around him.

Panic surged through Eli. He ran. His heart pounded as he sped along the deck.

An aged seaman half-hidden behind a heavy pulley waved his hand urgently. "Quick, this way,"

Skidding to a stop, Eli changed direction and followed the man down a set of stairs. Holding onto the rails, he tumbled down the stairs and grabbed the man's arm.

"Who are you and why are you helping me?"

"You saved the captain. Didn't let the sorry excuse for a man drop to his death. I don't agree with what the captain's been doing on this ship, but I believe God decides when we die. I liked your compassion, lad." He slapped Eli on the back. "Hurry, we don't have much time. We need to get the children."

Eli stared at the stranger's strong shoulders and balding head. The man was older than Eli had first thought, but there was nothing aged about the way he maneuvered the tight corridors and led the way through the passages.

Stopping, the man turned and held his finger to his lips. He pointed.

Time seemed to stand still as the sound of gunfire hitting metal and screams echoed above them.

"It's clear. They moved the children to another container. It's in Bay C, but Jed's in there with them and he's got a gun. You have to stay out of sight until I can convince him to come out."

"Thank you," Eli muttered. The man had mentioned children, but what about Gargi? Was she with them or was she… gone?

The man grinned, showing that he had a missing front tooth. "Come on, boyo, God's got your back."

Eli had to know his name. "Who are you?"

"I'm nobody important, just an old man making a living. Name's Matthew, if you need to know."

"I'm glad to meet you, Matthew."

"Ha, this way."

The metal steps amplified the sound of their footsteps, and Eli was sure if there were anyone directly above them, they would be alerted to their presence.

"Wait here," Matthew ordered.

Eli squatted and watched as Matthew scampered up to a platform that had access to three containers facing port side.

Tapping on the middle door, Matthew cupped his hands and spoke into the solid metal.

Straining his ears, Eli tried to hear what Matthew was saying. Glancing around nervously, Eli stepped from his hiding place and pressed close to the side of the first container.

"Jed, I'm opening the door. Don't shoot, it's Matthew. Captain wants you on deck."

As the door opened, Eli stayed in the shadows and watched.

A man stepped out and waved a gun in Matthew's face. "You alone, old man?"

"Don't 'old man' me, you fool. Get up to the bridge before the captain has both our heads."

"What about them?" Jed pointed back into the container.

"Give me your gun. I'm to take over from you. Must think I'm too old for the action topside and needs a muscle machine like you." Matthew laughed and slapped Jed on the back.

"You will need this." Jed threw a torch to Matthew. He turned and sprinted off in the opposite direction to Eli.

Stepping out of the shadow, Eli felt his nerves take flight.

Matthew disappeared into the container and Eli ran to join him.

The shape of bodies huddled together in the back corner made his heart rate accelerate. "Matthew, the torch," Eli whispered.

Click. The beam of light glided across the faces of the children and settled fleetingly on Gargi.

Eli's mouth dropped open and his chest tightened, making it difficult to breathe.

He hadn't expected to find her.

Tears welled and spilled.

"Eli?" She stood and he raced to her.

Kissing her face, he folded her protectively to his chest. His throat clogged and he couldn't speak.

He felt the tremor travel through her body and his arms tightened. He'd prayed so much for this moment and now that it was here he felt overwhelmed by the feel of her in his arms.

"Hate to break up the party, but time to go." Matthew went to pick up a little girl, but the child scampered back.

"I'll take her," Gargi whispered, pushing out of Eli's arms.

Taking a quick count, Eli felt his heart skip a beat. He had fifteen children and Gargi to get off the ship.

Turning to Matthew, Eli widened his eyes in question.

"It's not going to be easy, but not impossible," the old man murmured confidently. "We have to get them on the launch and hope for the best."

Gargi staggered sideways under the slight burden of the child's weight.

"You'll have to make her walk," Eli ordered, indicating to the child in her arms.

"No, I'm carrying her," Gargi argued.

"What's her name?" Eli snapped. Time pressed in on them. They had to go.

Gargi lifted the child closer. "Her name's Pia."

Taking Pia's hand, Eli tickled her fingers. "Hey, sweet-heart. You can walk for me, can't you? Gargi will take your hand and we'll be able to move faster that way. What do you say?"

The wide, sunken eyes that stared at him caught hold of his heart. The hollow cheeks covered with red welts and the blinking fear reflected in the brown depths of her eyes gripped him in such a way that he wanted to promise her the world.

"You can do it," Eli encouraged. Taking her from Gargi, he placed her on her feet and laid her hand in Gargi's. He smiled and gently caressed her shoulder.

"Little ones," Matthew spoke softly. "Quiet as wee mice. Two at a time, I'll go first, then Eli. Girly"—he turned to Gargi—"you will go last and push them along."

Matthew slapped the gun into Eli's chest. "Don't think I could fire this, best you take it."

Holding the gun in his hand, Eli wondered if he could pull

the trigger and end a life to save a life. His mouth went dry and his fingers pressed hard into the metal of the gun. He stepped after Matthew and beckoned the children to follow.

The ship was silent and that was more troubling than the sound of gunfire.

Matthew held up his hand for them to stop. "I'll go first," he mouthed.

Eli waited for the signal to follow. Seconds ticked by and he knew something was wrong. Glancing back over the children's heads, he met Gargi's gaze.

"Stay here until I come for you," he whispered.

Gargi nodded and held her hand over her heart.

He lifted the gun, crouched low, and slunk after Matthew.

Moving at a slow pace and staying as low as he could, he crept closer to where Matthew stood.

Eli heard them before he saw them.

"What you doing, old man?" A seaman pressed a gun into Matthew's side.

"What does it look like?" Matthew spat on the deck. "I'm looking for the captain. Is the trouble over topside?"

"You yellow or what? You take flight at the sight of a little blood?"

"That's me. Get that gun away from me." Matthew cursed and pushed the man's shoulder.

"I don't trust you. You're coming with me to the captain. One wrong move and I'll kill you and say you were a casualty of the storm," The seaman grabbed Matthew by the ear and yanked.

Stealing around behind them, Eli curled his fingers around

the gun's muzzle. Raising his arm, he slammed the gun as hard as he could into the side of the man's head.

The man staggered backwards and dropped.

The sight of blood oozing out of the wound he'd administered made Eli angry. He'd changed so much over the last year. He was now a man who would take action to save those he loved.

Matthew snatched the seaman's gun and flung it over the ship's railing.

Sprinting back the way he'd come, he helped the children past the prone body and quickly up the stairs to the next deck.

Motioning the children to group behind the capstan, Matthew drew Eli aside. "I'm not sure what's going on. It's too quiet on deck, but we have to chance it."

"Can you see any of the men I boarded with?" Eli asked and turned his back to Gargi and the children.

"No. If they're dead, they've probably been chucked overboard." Matthew rubbed his chin and pointed to a coil of rope. "We'll have to lower the children by rope. I'd bet money on it that there are a couple of the captain's men on the launch. Either that or he will cast it off with the bodies on board."

"No time to surmise. We need to move—now," Eli hissed.

"You go down and I'll lower the children to you. That way if anything goes wrong you'll have a better chance to escape."

Shaking his head, Eli tapped Matthew's shoulder. "No disrespect, old man, but you're going down first. Then Gargi, so she can help you pull the children aboard." Eli knew what

Matthew was attempting to do. He was trying to watch their backs. But he couldn't let him.

"I'm stronger than you and it'll be easier for me to carry the weight of the drop, plus I have the gun if there's trouble up here."

Matthew nodded. "Your call. Right, I'll go down. If there's company on the launch, I may need a little assistance. I'll indicate like this." He held up his hand high above his head and chuckled. "Or you may just hear me scream."

"On the count of three," Eli whispered.

"One, two, three," Matthew hissed and took off toward the rail. He swung himself over the side and scaled down the ladder in seconds.

"Eli," Gargi whispered.

"Ssh." Eli motioned with his finger and then held his palm out to tell her to stay put.

Lying on his stomach, Eli commando crawled to the railing and peered over the side at the launch.

Matthew was in conversation with a man who had a gun slung casually over his shoulder. They appeared relaxed and Eli watched for the signal.

The idea of going down to the launch to help Matthew and leaving Gargi and the children on board the vessel alone didn't sit well with him.

Slapping the seaman on the shoulder, Matthew flung his head back and laughed then turned to head back toward the ladder. Stopping as if to say one more thing, Matthew swung his arm out and his fist caught the man under the chin, sending him flying.

Watching from above, Eli was impressed with the way Matthew dragged the man below and could only guess what he'd done with him.

Sliding back to Gargi, Eli whispered his plan.

She glanced at the children and frowned.

Eli saw her bite her lip. "I need you down there to help Matthew," he explained. He slung the rope around her waist and then tied a secure knot.

"I don't like this," she hissed.

"You can argue with me later. Hurry, I'm going to start lowering Pia the minute your feet touch the deck. Don't wait for Matthew to join you, loosen the rope, like this," Eli's hands demonstrated how to widen the gap. "Then lift it over her head. I will already be lowering the next child."

Gargi stood on tiptoes and kissed his mouth. "Don't you dare let anything happen to you, Eli Turner. I love you."

"Gargi." Eli hesitated.

"Hush." She touched his lips with her finger. She flung one leg over the rail.

Eli picked her up and eased her over the side onto the ladder.

"Hold the rope and I'll feed it as you go."

He watched her reach the deck then turned to get Pia.

The child lay loosely in his arms and he tightened the rope securely around her waist and shoulders. She hung like a limp rag doll as he lowered her. How he wanted to instill life into her.

Gargi grabbed Pia and loosened the rope. Eli motioned for the next girl to join them.

"Thank you," she whispered.

"Brave girl," he encouraged and swung her onto the rail in one motion.

His shoulders burned and he knew he had thirteen more girls waiting behind the canvas. He could feel the wind on his face and he wondered at the increased pressure building behind each gust. Pulling the rope back up over the side, he hesitated and listened. Footsteps sounded coming in his direction.

Crouching low, Eli pulled the gun from his belt and slunk toward the small remaining group of girls.

"Stay still," he ordered. "I think we're about to have company."

Holding the gun close to his chest, he squinted into the night.

Two men came and leaned on the rail and one lit a cigarette. The other leaned over and gazed down at the launch.

"What are the captain's plans?"

Eli hoped Gargi and Matthew had taken cover. He inched closer to hear better.

"Who knows? You know his temper, he's boiling. My guess is that he will kill the prince's men, and send them back in pieces."

"He's a fool if he thinks he can get away with this. The prince has people everywhere. Even aboard here, I'm sure."

"Ha, the sooner this trip is over the better."

Flicking his smoke out to sea, the seaman leaned over to watch it sail to the water. "I think there's someone on the launch."

"The captain stationed a guard there," Eli heard the other man say.

"No, more than one man."

Both men took hold of the rail and leaned over to check out the launch.

Eli stood and walked up behind them. "What's it to be, gentlemen?" He pushed the gun into the neck of the seaman closest to him. "Want to swap sides and win the approval of the prince or take your chances with the sharks?"

Turning, both men held up their hands. "I'm with you, man. The captain is no friend of ours. Already lost three buddies tonight."

Eli knew he had two choices. Kill them or trust them to help him.

Lord?

He couldn't kill them, but if he trusted them and they put the children in danger?

"Come on, man. We have to scurry if we wanta get out of here." The seaman ignored Eli's gun and swung his leg over the side of the rail. "I'm going with you."

"Wait," Eli commanded.

The man lowered himself down a rung on the ladder and looked up.

"Girls, come."

The girls scrambled to the railing and Eli lowered one down to the seaman. "Hold on to his neck, sweetheart. Don't look down."

"Are you kidding me?" the seaman spluttered as the girl took a stranglehold on his neck.

"Drop her and it's the last thing you will do," Eli threatened.

The seaman next to Eli grabbed two small girls and pushed them toward the rail. "Ladies, once I'm over, one on either side." He grinned and slipped through the railing.

Eli swung the rope around the smallest child and passed her over.

"The other one?" the man demanded.

"No, get going."

"I'm okay on my own," a small voice stated strongly.

"Good for you," Eli said. "But we need to secure you with rope."

Nodding, she held up her arms.

"What the hell!" someone yelled from behind.

Pushing the girl over the rail, Eli grabbed the arms of the two remaining girls and lifted them up and over the rail. "You will have to go without rope. Hold on tight, be careful."

The sound of feet pounding toward them sent a rush of adrenaline through Eli. He sped along the rail and untied the rope securing the launch to the ship and threw it overboard.

Matthew appeared on deck. Eli could imagine his new friend's question as he looked toward Eli.

"Go," Eli hollered, madly waving his arms.

Matthew saluted then turned his back on the vessel and disappeared out of sight.

A child's scream and the sound of the splash as her small body hit the water sent a chill down Eli's spine.

Climbing over the rail, Eli searched for her in the water.

The sound of Gargi screaming for Neha twisted his heart.

A bullet whizzed past his ear.

Focusing on the spot he'd last seen her; Eli threw himself over the side and dived into the choppy ocean.

He kicked his legs to swim deeper. Everything slid into slow motion as he searched the inky darkness for the child.

Swiveling his arms and bicycling his legs, Eli stayed in one place as he scouted around.

He couldn't see her.

The saltwater irritated his eyes and he came up for air.

Spiraling around, he searched the swirling water, desperate for a sight of her.

Could she swim? Had she ever been in the ocean before?

He felt helpless.

Lord Jesus, help me! Sucking air deep into his lungs, he dived under the waves. He kicked off his shoes then thrust his arms through the water.

Gargi had called her Neha.

Sadness clawed at his lungs, begging him to give up.

Lashing out at the water, he went deeper, pumping his legs furiously at thought of not finding her.

His lips opened and he took a small breath. Water filled his mouth. Spluttering, he headed for the surface.

A buoy landed beside him and he swung his arm through the hole.

Gargi hung over the side of the launch and pulled at the rope. "Can you see her?" she screamed.

Turning from the pleading in Gargi's eyes, Eli yelled into the pounding waves.

"Where are you?" His heart slammed his chest. He swirled

around looking for the girl. The shadows, darkening the waves, mocked him.

The water churned up around him and the sound of the launch's motor starting sent vibrations through him.

The buoy yanked forward, and he felt the water rush past him. Grabbing hold of the buoy with his other arm, he pushed his head into the hard plastic surface and closed his eyes.

Shouts came from the *Jag Tan*. Eli ignored them.

The buoy skimmed through the water. Eli forced himself to hold on. His eyes burned with the saltwater and he blinked as his salty tears disappeared on his face.

Chapter 42

"Phillip, I want to set a date," Charlotte exclaimed. Her life seemed to be skipping from one drama to the next and she was sick of feeling as though she had no control.

Resting her hands on her hips, she was determined to grab every moment of happiness she could.

Leaning back in his chair, Phillip raised one eyebrow and folded his hands behind his head.

"Don't look at me like that," Charlotte growled. "I'm serious."

"Sit down, Charlie." He reached over and pulled out a chair.

"I don't want to sit down. I'm sick of sitting down."

"What's the matter?" The corner of his mouth lifted in a slight smile.

Her insides churned. All she wanted to do was focus on something nice.

What was wrong with that? Why couldn't he just leave her be?

Chuckling, Phillip sat up. "If you could see the expressions flying across your face, you'd understand why I'm interested to know what's going on in that beautiful head of yours."

Charlotte rested her head in her hands. How could she explain how she felt when she didn't know herself?

Phillip touched her chin.

As she looked into the deep softness of his eyes, she saw understanding.

"I'm sorry," she whispered. She touched the bandage on her shoulder. "I don't even know where Eli is, or if Gargi is alive. But I have this—this desperate sense that I can't keep putting my life on hold while I wait to hear if the people I love are okay."

"Charlie—"

Charlotte held up her hand. "I don't want a big wedding, but I do want a wedding. I need to be able to hold you at night, not say good-bye to you when I—when I need—you the most." Her breath caught in her chest and she swallowed.

"Okay, let's set a date. How about this afternoon?" Phillip murmured. "I have the license."

"You do?"

"Yep. I like to be prepared. I could phone Tanvir, see if he has a spare hour. I'm sure your mother will understand."

Charlotte's face flamed. She didn't want to deprive her mother of being present at her wedding, and she knew she was being emotional and overreacting.

Phillip cupped the back of her head and kissed her gently. Pushing his chair back, he stood and pulled her to his chest and deepened the kiss.

She relaxed into him and sighed. Her arms snuck around his waist and her heart rate went crazy.

He picked her up, swung her in a circle then nuzzled her neck.

Giggling, she threw her head back.

"What's it to be?" Phillip asked. "Do I sneak you away to elope or do we phone your mother and tell her we want to set a date for a month away?"

"Put me down, Superman," Charlotte laughed.

Setting her on her feet, Phillip stepped back and folded his arms.

Excitement bubbled up inside her. "I think I'll phone Mum."

~

Pain stabbed at Gargi's heart as she saw the tears glistening in Eli's eyes. Water dripped from his body and pooled around his feet, but he seemed unaware of his surroundings. His shoulders stooped and he buried his face in his hands.

Moving across the deck, Gargi hesitated. She'd never comforted a man before and was frightened she'd say the wrong thing and make it worse.

A knowing she'd never experienced before cemented firmly in her mind.

She loved him—and he was *her* man.

If not her, then who would comfort him? Who would share the pain and understand what had been lost?

She took his hands and pulled them from his eyes.

"It will be okay," she stated.

Eli's gaze locked on hers. His lips trembled. "I couldn't find her. I didn't rope her."

"You had no choice. I saw the men on the deck coming at you with guns. You gave her the only chance she had."

"I should have made her wait for me and gone with her down the ladder," he said condemning himself.

"Stop it, Eli. You are not to do this. You had to free the launch." Gargi grabbed his face in her hands and tipped his chin up so he had to look at her. "It was not your fault," she said firmly.

"Why?" he sobbed.

"I don't know." She wrapped her arms around his shoulders and covered his face with kisses.

Water seeped into her clothes as she hugged him, but Gargi refused to let go. She sighed when he pulled her closer and rested his chin on her head.

Tears streamed down her face. It was bittersweet, losing Neha but finding Eli.

"Neha told me she liked counting the seconds it took to watch the sun rise. We will do this together, Eli, and know that she is now with Jesus."

Clearing his throat, Matthew held out two towels.

Gargi took one and wiped Eli's face and neck.

Matthew laid a hand on Eli's shoulder. She watched the silent message pass between the two men. Matthew stepped back.

"Call the prince and explain what's happened," Matthew suggested.

"I'm thinking I should phone my friend Isak and the police," Eli countered.

Matthew grabbed Eli's arm and pulled him aside.

Gargi stiffened. She was not going to be left out of any decisions they made. She'd been through too much to be set aside and ignored now. Stepping up to Eli, she took hold of his hand and confronted Matthew. "I'm a part of this."

"Girly, you go look after the children. No disrespect meant, just that you've been through enough. Time someone looked out for you."

"Thank you," Gargi said sweetly, "However, I don't intend—" she yelped as Eli pinched her fingers. Pulling her hand from his, she turned to glare at him. He smiled apologetically.

"Matt, it's okay. I value Gargi's opinion. What's on your mind?"

Shrugging, Matthew folded his arms. "The way I see it, we need to contact the prince while we're still at sea. Give him time to adjust to the fact that your mission was successful at the cost of all his men. He is a powerful man and his influence reaches far."

"The thing I don't understand is why the captain allowed us to board if he knew it was just going to be a bloodbath."

Eli flexed his shoulders then lifted his hand and kneaded his neck.

"What I heard," said Matthew, "was that the captain thought he could persuade the prince's men that there was no one on board and that he knew nothing about any trafficking."

"So what went wrong? Why start shooting if he was fearful of the prince's power?"

"The captain is a fool. And he thinks he can dock and not feel the consequence of his actions. We need to contact the prince immediately," Matthew exclaimed.

"I think Matthew is right," Gargi agreed. "If this prince—sheikh—helped free us, then maybe he can help us find the two girls that were taken off the ship before you arrived."

"What?" Eli took hold of Gargi's hand again.

"Girly, those children are gone. The men who took them were heading for the desert. I'm sorry."

"Eli found me, we can find them" Gargi folded her arms.

"First we have to find a way to get you out of the country," the old sailor insisted. "No passports or papers, and the police could make it difficult."

Eli looked troubled. "As much as I want to do this right, if the prince can help us get back to India with less drama, then I'm all for that. Gargi?"

She agreed. Her stomach growled and suddenly the idea of letting Eli take care of everything felt like a great option. Her head felt woozy and she swayed.

"Gargi, are you all right?" Eli put his arm around her shoulder.

"No, I'm not all right. I'm tired, hungry, and angry. Matthew's right, I need to check on the children."

Leaning down, Eli kissed her cheek. "There's probably food on board. Why don't you and the children eat and settle down for a sleep?"

"How long is the trip to land?" Gargi asked, already moving away.

"About an hour. I'll wake you."

"Thank you." Impulsively she went up to Matthew and kissed him on the cheek. "Thank you for helping us escape. Without you, we'd still be locked away."

Matthew's feet shuffled. He pulled at his collar, trying to hide the redness of his neck. "Always knew God had a reason I was on that ship. Hated being there from the moment I signed up."

~

Eli squatted and helped Matthew secure the ropes around the bollard. It was good to be back on land. He saw movement out of the corner of his eye and looked up to see two men coming toward them. He glanced at Matthew and saw him waggle his eyebrow.

"Seems your welcoming party is here." Matthew swung the final loop over the bollard.

Standing, Eli ignored the two men standing on the dock

waiting. "Matthew, I don't know how to thank you."

"No need."

"I've got your number. I'll keep in touch and next time it'll be a social call." He extended his hand.

Matthew yanked Eli forward and hugged him firmly. "You are a good man and I will pray for you."

Footsteps sounded on the jetty. "When you are ready, Mr Turner," an impatient voice stated stiffly. "We will escort you and your group to the palace. Prince Saeed has arranged for your friend Mr Isak and the police to join you there in due course."

"Thank you." Eli turned to help Gargi and the children. Glancing down at Pia, he smiled. "Want a ride, little one?"

She glanced up at him through her eyelashes but said nothing. Seeing the nod from Gargi, Eli picked Pia up.

He didn't like the way she went limp, her arms and legs dangling like they had no muscles.

Holding her closer to his chest, he swept his arms under her knees and changed the position he held her in. Everything in him wanted to protect her, never let her be hurt again.

His chest ached as he gazed at her. Did she have a family to go back to? Looking over her head, he widened his eyes at Gargi.

Gargi reached over to touch Pia's hair. She caressed the child's face and Eli's throat tightened.

She was a born mother.

The side door of one of the two seven-seater vans swished open and a man stepped out to help get the children strapped in.

As Eli went to place Pia inside the car, her hands snatched his shirt and clung on.

Gargi pried Pia's fingers from Eli's shirt. "I'll sit in the back with you, Pia. Come on."

The connection Eli felt to Pia pulled at his heart. He hadn't wanted to let her go. What would Ashok think of the little girl? Straightening his shoulders, he yearned to hold his son and never be separated from him again.

Taking his seat in the front of the van, he stared straight ahead. The joy he should be feeling at having rescued the children was overshadowed by the questions that raced around his head.

What would happen to the children now? Who would look after them? Would they go back to the families who had sold them in the first place?

Arriving at the palace, the children and Gargi were whisked away to be refreshed. Eli was relieved Gargi had gone quietly and not argued about being present to meet the prince.

It wasn't that he didn't want her with him. She would probably understand this male-dominated culture better than he did. All her life, cruel men had controlled her. If he could whiz her out of the country without any more scenes, he would do it.

The same man who had served him beverages the last time he was here appeared by his side. "Prince Saeed is expecting you. Come this way, please."

He entered the prince's office and hesitated, unsure what was expected of him.

Two men in conversation with the prince nodded at Eli and moved to stand by the door.

Eli stood before the desk and waited.

Prince Saeed sat with his elbows leaning on his desk and his fingers steepled. The silence lengthened and Eli began to feel uncomfortable. Should he speak first?

The prince stood and waved his hand at his companions. "Leave us," he ordered.

As the door shut behind the men, the prince sailed around the desk, his white robe making him seem regal. "Eli, it is good to see you. I am saddened at the loss of Ahmed, but… he will be avenged."

"My condolences, Prince Saeed. If there had been some way I could have returned to the ship to see if any of your men survived, I would have."

"Yes, yes, I believe you. I must inform you that the launch has camera surveillance and we were able to gain some footage of what happened. It is very distressing to hear that the captain of the *Jag Tan* had little respect for me. That he opened fire on my brothers in such a way."

Nodding respectfully, Eli felt the weight of what happened, his responsibility. "I cannot thank you enough for your assistance and the cost of many lives to make this rescue possible."

A shadow crossed the prince's face. He lowered his body into the large sofa and gestured for Eli to join him.

Eli took a seat and was reminded of his state of dress. He had been soaked and needed something dry to wear, but the flowing robe he'd found on the launch felt alien to him and he couldn't wait to change into his own clothes.

"Tell me, Eli, what are your intentions for the young woman who is accompanying the children?"

Sitting forward, Eli frowned. "I love Gargi and wish to make her my wife."

"Has she accepted your offer?"

"She has told me that she loves me. We have yet to discuss marriage."

"Good, this is right. You will marry before you leave here, yes?"

Shaking his head, Eli swallowed. "I think Gargi will need time to recover from her ordeal. We will marry in India."

"I cannot let you accompany the children back to India as an unmarried man with a single woman. The children must stay here."

"I'm sorry you feel this way, Prince Saeed. However, you cannot stop me."

"You are wrong. Please do not take offence. I am thinking of your Gargi's honor and reputation."

"I appreciate that. You need to let her decide for herself. I will not put pressure on her."

"Women need decisions made for them. It is the right way."

"No." Eli felt his patience about to snap. Breathing in deeply, he tried to calm down. The prince had the authority to forbid him from seeing Gargi again.

"My decision has been made, Eli. It would go better for you if you accept this."

"How can you expect me to convince her to marry me in a

strange country without her friends and my family present?"

"If she loves you as you say, then she will embrace the idea. Be masterful."

Eli's lips twitched as he thought of being masterful with Gargi and he knew he would enjoy the argument that would follow.

"Why is this necessary? I understand what you are saying, but there must be more to this than what you are implying." Eli's jaw jutted forward.

"You are right, there is more to this than meets the eye." The prince stood and paced before him. "You would have me arrange travel for you and these children and then wipe them from my mind. I cannot do this."

Standing, Eli scanned the prince's face, not liking the way things were going. "With all due respect, Prince Saeed, these children are not your concern."

"I lost my daughter and it is my deep concern that these little ones are taken care of. Perhaps they would be better off remaining in my country."

"Absolutely not!" Eli exclaimed. "They need to be returned to India. It is their right. My sister has a home where they can go and be cared for. They will be loved and protected there."

"You are a passionate man." The prince nodded. "We will compromise, yes?"

"I'm listening," Eli replied stiltedly.

"Good. I will arrange all the documentation for you and all the children. However, you must agree to this marriage to provide a proper escort."

"How is this a compromise?" Eli demanded.

Prince Saeed ambled back behind the desk. "You get to leave the country alive. And more importantly, you get to secure our ongoing friendship."

Chapter 43

Struggling to open her eyes, Daya panicked. Her lids felt heavy and glued together. The drug they'd forced them to take had made her head feel woozy; now that she was awake, she had a dull throb behind her eyes.

Part of her didn't want to wake up and see where she was. She wanted to pretend Gargi was with her and that everything would be all right.

A movement on the bed startled her. She forced her eyes open and swung her legs over the side of the huge bed. Standing on shaky feet, she stared down at Amita spread across the white sheet, sound asleep.

Sighing in relief, Daya tiptoed across to the window and shifted the heavy silk curtain.

She realized they must be several stories up in a building. The landscape before her was beautiful.

Grass so green that Daya longed to touch it. Water rose

like towers from small objects popping out of the trimmed lawn and spiraled through the air in a dance before dropping to the ground.

She'd never seen anything like it. From her height she could see hedges fashioned into a maze and she wondered what was in the middle of the branching pathways.

Running her hand around the windowsill, she felt for an opening and was surprised to see a latch. Her fingers struggled to open the catch. She took a good look at the handle and realized there was a steel clip securing the lever like a key.

She tried to pull it out, but it wouldn't budge.

"Where are we?" Amita asked in a croaky voice.

Turning, Daya went and sat on the bed and grabbed hold of her hand. "I don't know. Whoever owns this place must be very rich."

"Do you think they bought us?"

"Maybe." She grabbed Amita in a tight hug. "We will be all right. We are together, aren't we?"

"Yes," Amita said.

"We mustn't forget what Gargi said. No matter what happens, we are not alone. Jesus is with us."

"I know." Amita brushed a tear off her cheek. "I'm scared."

Pulling her knees up, Daya lay on the bed next to her friend. "I think we should pray every day that God helps us be strong."

"I can't pray right now, Daya. I feel too frightened to even think. Where is this place? Where is Gargi? Who will come through that door?"

"That is why we must pray. We don't know the answers to any of those questions. I will pray for us." Daya tried to still her racing heart by inhaling a deep breath. Closing her eyes, she tried to claim the peace that Gargi had told her was hers no matter what people did to her.

"Jesus, I love you. Amita and I don't know what's going to happen, but we ask that you help us not give up or be so scared that we die. Thank you that you are with us and that we have each other."

The door to the room opened and a woman entered, carrying a large tray.

Scrambling off the bed, Daya grabbed Amita's hand and they stood close to each other.

The woman placed the tray, laden with food, on the table. She bowed before them and backed out of the room and closed the door.

Glancing at Amita, Daya felt confused. "She didn't speak to us."

"Look at all this food." Amita picked up a plate and popped a date into her mouth.

Daya surveyed the room. There was a bathroom off to one side and she stepped inside to relieve herself. The bath was like a small pool, and the bottles of perfumes and creams made her widen her eyes.

It was like they were princesses in a palace of luxury.

~

The shrilling of the phone echoed through the house and Macy pushed up on her elbows and glanced at the bedside clock.

It said 4:00 a.m.

Bill swung his legs over the side of the bed and headed for the door.

Clutching the sheet to her chest, Macy closed her eyes. Her heart pounded and she knew she couldn't wait for him to return and tell her who'd called.

She charged down the stairs and saw the smile on Bill's face.

The tension eased out of her like a gush of wind. Would she always brace herself against bad news?

Sighing, she rubbed her eyes and waited.

"That's wonderful news." Bill held out his arm for her. "Yes, we can do that."

Macy itched to know what was being said. Moving to lean against him, she mouthed, "Who is it?"

"Eli, your mother's bursting with questions." Bill paused. "Yes, I'll call Charlie and give Mum your love. Bye, son."

"Oh, I wanted to talk to him." Macy snatched the phone from him to hear the dial tone. "Bill!"

"Eli had to go, sweetheart." He took the phone from her to place it back on the cradle. "Let's go wake Ashok, I have good news."

"I'm awake," Ashok said from the top of the stairs, and then he bounced down to meet them at the bottom. "I heard the phone."

"Eli has found Gargi and she's safe!" Bill stated triumphantly.

Ashok burst into tears and flung his arms around Bill.

Macy felt light-headed. She swayed.

"Grandma, I'm so happy." Ashok laughed and spun around to hug her.

"There is more news." Bill raised Macy's hand to his mouth and gently kissed her fingers.

"Bill?"

"Grandpa?"

"Eli and Gargi are getting married before they leave Jeddah."

"What? Why can't they wait until we all can be there?" Macy felt her stomach drop. How could Eli deprive her of this moment?

"Eli didn't have time to tell me much. He sounded tired."

Ashok tugged her arm.

Macy placed her arm around his shoulders.

"Grandma, does that mean—that Gargi will be my mam?" His voice broke and tears welled up in his eyes.

Macy lowered her gaze. Why did she always think of how things affected her first? This poor boy was beside himself with questions, and she needed to share his joy.

"Yes, darling." Pulling him close, she cuddled him. "Gargi will be so excited to be your mother. She loves you so much."

Ashok sobbed.

She rubbed his shoulders and glanced at Bill.

"Are you okay, Ashok?" Bill laid his hand on Ashok's shoulder.

Nodding, Ashok wiped his cheeks. "I—am—so—happy,"

he hiccupped. "I now know tears of happiness, Grandma. Jesus, I am thanking you."

"I am thanking you too, Jesus." Bill laughed.

"Me too," Macy added, giddy with joy. "We can have another celebration with them when they get here."

"Oh, about that." Bill winked at her. "Eli asked us all to meet him in Mumbai in a week."

~

"I don't like being told what to do." Gargi pressed her lips together.

"You don't want to marry me? Is that what you are saying?" Eli widened his eyes.

Stepping back from Eli, Gargi sighed. Of course she wanted to marry him, but not like this. Not in a strange country in front of strangers.

"It's not that I don't want to marry you—I do. I just had a different picture of our wedding."

"I'm sure we could say no." His voice sounded edgy and tense. "We have a choice here, but I feel that it's what God wants us to do."

"How do you know that?" Gargi crossed her arms.

"I feel it here." Eli placed a hand over his heart. "The prince is adamant that we marry to protect your honor. He has other reasons, I am sure, but it doesn't matter."

"How can you say it doesn't matter? This is marriage we are talking about." Gargi turned from him and paced across the room. How could he make light of such a thing?

Marriage was forever and he was prepared to marry her here and now because it was easy.

She felt hurt.

Grabbing her arms, Eli stilled her pacing.

"What are you thinking?" he asked with a grin.

Trying to shrug out of his embrace, she avoided looking at him.

Eli slipped his hands down Gargi's arms until he held her hands. He dropped to one knee.

Pulling at her hands, Gargi tried to free herself.

"Gargi, please, let me speak," he begged.

The serious look on his face startled her. This wasn't a game for him.

Sucking in her lips, she gave a small nod.

"I am sorry we find ourselves in such a predicament." Eli dipped his head and seemed to struggle to get his breath. Standing, he pulled her close. "I love you. I have loved you since the first time I saw you at Phillip's. You looked so fragile and hurt, yet you were so brave and beautiful. You stole my heart."

"Eli—"

"No, please. Let me finish."

Her gaze searched his face and she forced herself to stay still.

A sense of belonging washed over her. Overwhelmed, she momentarily closed her eyes.

She loved him. The joy that bubbled up inside her longed to be released, but she slanted her chin down and refused to look at him.

The woman in her knew that if she spoiled this moment, she would regret it. Never get it again.

A small smile escaped.

The corners of Eli's eyelids crinkled. "Gargi?"

"You were saying? Please continue." She batted her lashes. "If you want to get down on your knees again, that's okay with me."

Throwing back his head, Eli laughed and swung her around before placing her on her feet.

He kneeled. "Gargi, would you please marry me?"

"Yes." This was a dream come true.

Standing, he took her hand. Where the ring came from she didn't know, but it was beautiful and fit perfectly.

Tears streamed from her eyes and she didn't care.

Eli leaned forward and kissed the moisture from her cheeks and held her as if she were his most prized possession.

"I love you, Eli."

"I know you do."

Chapter 44

Gargi felt more nervous about her approaching meeting with the prince than she had about her marriage to Eli. She glanced down at her wedding ring and marveled at the goodness of God.

Her husband, now her lover—and it had been so wonderful. He had been so gentle and made everything seem new, if that were possible.

Being forced to be with men was so different to making love with the man of your heart. As Eli had helped her undress, she had felt as shy as a young girl.

Jesus, you make all things new. Thank you.

A soft knock on the door alerted her to the time.

She needed to keep her head, speak calmly, and request the prince's help. Moving across the room, she opened the door and followed the man to the salon where her meeting was to take place.

"Welcome, Mrs Turner." The prince bowed. He waited while she went to stand beside Eli. "Please take a seat. Eli has mentioned that you want to request my help, yes?"

"You have been so generous to us, Prince Saeed, and I am forever grateful to you," Gargi said softly. She glanced at Eli.

He smiled and gave a slight nod.

"I know you have arranged for the children to travel with Isak back to India, but I have spoken to Eli and we would like to keep Pia with us. She has no family in India, and we wish to adopt her and have her as part of our family."

"You will have many children of your own," the prince stated. "This child will travel with the others and be a gift to a family who has need of a daughter."

"You are wrong," Gargi said urgently. "I cannot have children. I was…"

"What my wife is trying to say is that we already love Pia. We are unable to have children of our own, and to be blessed with such a precious child would bring joy to our hearts." Eli spoke calmly, and the sound of his voice gave Gargi confidence.

"The ability to have children was stolen from me when I was imprisoned in the brothel, so I beg of you—help us keep Pia."

"I see." The prince rubbed his chin. Gargi held her breath waiting for his answer.

"This little girl is much traumatized, yes?"

Gargi felt tears gather in her eyes. "She hasn't spoken a word for days. She needs a lot of love and patience to help her through the pain locked up inside her."

The prince's hard eyes seemed to assess her and Eli, and then they softened. "Very well. She will be yours."

"Thank you," Gargi whispered.

"I have arranged with your Mr Isak for the other children to be looked after until they have passed through your customs and placed in the care of your sister. We value our children, and it saddens me to see the little ones displaced like this."

"I agree." Eli took Gargi's hand and smiled. "Once we are back, we will be able to make sure that they are looked after."

"You have another request, Mrs Turner?" The prince lifted a white porcelain cup to his lips.

"Yes. There were two other girls on the ship. Daya and Amita. I grew to love them and they were taken the night before Eli rescued us."

The prince glanced over his teacup and placed it back on the saucer. "What is your request?"

"I want you to help us find them. I love them and the thought of them being sold and abused breaks my heart."

Standing, the prince stared past her to a painting of wild Arabian horses on the wall.

Gargi's breath caught in her throat at the stern look that flashed across his face.

Prince Saeed waved his hands expressively. "You will not find them. They will be long gone. I am sorry."

Stiffening, Gargi shook her head. "This cannot be true. You were able to rescue us, it is possible."

"No," the prince snapped. "You think I would lie to you?"

Gargi stood to face him.

Eli laid his hand on her shoulder and she shrugged it off.

"I do not think you would lie to me, but how can you say it is impossible?"

"Forgive me, Mrs Turner. Let me explain. My precious daughter was taken from me and I searched and searched until she was found dead." He smacked his palm against the surface of his desk.

Gargi went to speak, but the prince held up his hand. "Had I not made such dangerous enemies, my daughter may still be alive. She was killed to send me a message." His eyes darkened and Gargi glanced down and saw his clenched fists.

"These girls may be alive, but to you they must be dead for them to live."

"I—don't think I can do that," Gargi cried.

"You must. I will not discuss this any further. Prepare to leave."

Eli stood and joined Gargi. "Prince Saeed, I must thank you again for all you have done." He bowed. "Your friendship is deeply valued. If there is ever anything I can do to repay my debt to you, please let me know."

"Our friendship, Eli Turner, is of great value to me. You are most welcome here anytime."

"Thank you." Eli turned and took Gargi's hand. She took a breath.

"Prince Saeed, words cannot express my gratitude to you." Her hand cupped her throat. "I am saddened that your men lost their lives to save us. I will pray for their families and ask God's blessing upon you all."

"As I will for you." Prince Saeed smiled and there was

something touching about the softness that flashed across his face.

Just before the door closed, Gargi looked over her shoulder at the prince. The transformation on his face startled her.

His face seemed harder, like he was angry.

"Eli," she whispered. "Do you trust him?"

"Only as far as I could kick him," Eli answered.

~

Amita was annoying Daya. She couldn't seem to sit still and was roaming around the room touching everything.

"Why don't you go take a bath, Amita? Soak in the perfume and relax."

"I don't want to. We have all we could want in this room. Food, clothes, books—but we are prisoners! I want out."

"So do I, but moaning about it isn't going to change the situation."

Running over to the door, Amita rattled the handle to see if miraculously it would open.

Daya ambled over to the window. It was her favorite place. She imagined herself free to wander the gardens and smell the flowers. She watched the cloud formations sail across the sky in the warm air and she was thankful that no one had come to join them. At least there had been no expectations placed on them.

"How long have we been here?" Amita snapped.

"Maybe a little over a week."

"I'm going to go crazy in this room," Amita declared. She picked up a cushion and tossed it across the room.

"Amita, stop, please," Daya begged. "You must calm down. Have you not noticed the camera in the corner?" she pointed to the ceiling and widened her eyes.

"I don't care. Surely they are playing with our minds, keeping us in this room like this."

The sound of a key in the door startled them both. Amita raced over to stand behind Daya.

"It's okay," Daya whispered.

A tall man in a white robe entered. Behind him stood a small woman completely cloaked apart from her eyes.

The tall, dark man stepped closer to Daya and she dropped her gaze to his hands. There was a large ring on his middle finger and the shape curled around the knuckle. Everything in her wanted to retreat farther away from him, but she clasped her hands together and waited.

The man smiled. "I welcome you to my home. This is my wife. And you"—he touched Daya's arm gently—"will be our eldest daughter."

Daya heard Amita gasp.

"Your friend will be your sister."

"I don't understand," Daya said. She dipped her head in respect. This man had the power to hurt them and she did not want to antagonize him.

"You don't have to understand. It is a great privilege that you have been chosen to take a place in my family."

Amita edged around Daya and stepped forward.

Daya laid her hand on Amita's arm, trying to warn her to be quiet.

Amita shrugged her off. "I can't be your daughter, I want my mam."

The man's mouth thinned. His hand swiped out and he slapped Amita across the face. "Do not speak to me unless you are addressed."

Swallowing past the emotion that flooded her throat, Daya made herself stay still. Amita would be all right. She didn't want to make it worse.

The man's face hardened. He turned to her. "Your name will be Janai. Princess Janai."

"It is a beautiful name." Daya curtsied.

"You are very beautiful. You hold a resemblance to our daughter who has died. Her name was Soraya, and you will take her place. Janai's means *one who replaces*. It also means *God has answered*. You will replace our only child."

"I am honored," Daya whispered. She blinked back the moisture that flooded her eyes.

"I am Prince Saeed and this will be your home. You and your sister will be happy here."

Chapter 45

Sitting on the hard plastic seat, Ashok watched the planes land outside the window. He passed his wooden eagle from hand to hand and tried to stop the nerves racing through his stomach.

They still had twenty minutes before his baap's plane landed. He wanted to run around shouting that his baap and mam were on the way.

Laughter behind him drew his gaze to his family. Aunty Charlie was holding three balloons that bobbed in the air and bounced off Uncle Phillip's face. Ashok grinned at the picture they made.

His grandparents sat calmly as if it were an everyday event that they waited at the airport to greet his parents.

Ashok went back to gazing out the window.

Would Gargi want him with them now, or would they make him go back to Australia so they could go on a honeymoon like his friend Shane had thought?

He didn't want to go back to Australia. As much as he had grown to love his friends and the school, he wanted to live in Mumbai.

This was his home. He wanted to grow up and be a doctor like Uncle Phillip and help make India a great place.

"Ashok, the plane's landed." Aunty Charlie beckoned him over.

Jumping from the chair, Ashok raced to her and took her outstretched hand.

He loved his Aunty Charlie. She often talked to him about Shanti, and it helped.

Beep, beep.

"Oh, that's my phone. I have a text message." Aunty Charlie glanced at her phone and smiled. "Ashok, the message is for you from your baap." She handed him the phone.

Glancing at the small screen, Ashok slowly read the words aloud. "Ashok, we have a surprise for you."

He looked up at her with wide eyes. "They had time to buy me a gift? This is not important to me," he stated solemnly. "I just want them."

Ruffling his hair, Aunty Charlie laughed. "They love you. Of course they want to get their son a gift."

"Come on," Bill called. "Let's go watch for them over there."

Ashok twisted his hands. He was so excited, he felt sick.

God must love him very much.

A father and a mother.

Tears spilled from his eyes, and he quickly wiped them

away, not wanting to worry his family.

People started to pour through the gates. He scanned the faces for his baap.

"There's Eli," Macy screamed and raced toward him.

Ashok held back.

It felt like his legs were too stiff to move. He watched as everyone hugged his baap.

Angling his head, Ashok peered around Baap, trying to see Gargi.

Where was she? Fear tightened his chest and he moved forward.

"Baap." He pushed to stand in front of Baap.

"Hello, Ashok." Baap smiled but did not move to touch him.

Ashok's mouth trembled. He was scared. Why hadn't his baap grabbed him and hugged him like he used to?

Gargi stepped forward and took hold of Baap's hand.

Ashok searched Gargi's face.

She smiled and Ashok could see love for him in the soft, warm look in her eyes. He wanted to swamp her with kisses.

But he waited.

They were not calling for him, or reaching out to love him. His heart pounded his chest in worry.

"Ashok," Baap said softly. He stepped aside to reveal a girl. "This is Pia."

Ashok's gaze dropped to Baap's hands on the girl's shoulders then up to his baap's face.

Ashok saw the tears in Baap's and Gargi's eyes and he started to tremble.

His eyes snapped back to the girl.

She glanced up at him then dropped her gaze to her feet.

Her face was a soft brown and scabby. She looked so skinny and sad.

His heart raced.

He couldn't breathe. It was like all the air had been sucked from his lungs.

Who was she?

Inhaling loudly, Ashok turned to his father. "Baap, have you adopted Pia like you adopted me?"

Baap's gaze locked on Ashok's. "We plan to, if it's okay with you."

Opening his mouth, Ashok tried to speak; but the feelings inside of him stole his words. Could he love her like he loved his Shanti? Tears flooded to his eyes and he sucked air into his lungs.

Pia's shoulders hunched, making her appear smaller.

The little girl needed him. He felt warm inside, as if God had chosen him especially for this important job.

He loved her instantly.

Straightening his shoulders, he stepped forward and took her hand.

Pia's tiny fingers clung to his.

He wanted to make her feel safe and loved, but he didn't know what to say to her.

And then the words came to him.

"I've got you."

Gargi put her hand to her mouth. Her eyes grew wide, and she shared a look with Baap.

Ashok hugged his sister. “Hello, Pia. I’m Ashok. I’m your brother—and—I will love you forever.

Other books by Tracey Hoffmann

You can view all of Tracey's books at
www.traceyhoffmann.com

CPSIA information can be obtained
at www.ICGtesting.com
Printed in the USA
BVHW031947190421
605323BV00016B/192

9 781503 137189